YOUR CORNER DARK

DESMOND HALL

A A Caitlyn Dlouhy Book
atheneum
New York London Toronto Sydney New Delhi

atheneum

An imprint of Simon & Schuster Children's Publishing Division
1230 Avenue of the Americas, New York, New York 10020

Text © 2021 by Desmond Hall
Jacket illustrations © 2021 by Erin Robinson
Jacket and case design by Debra Sfetsios-Conover © 2021 by Simon & Schuster, Inc.

For information about special discounts for bulk purchases, please contact Simon & Schuster Special Sales at 1-866-506-1949 or business@simonandschuster.com.
The Simon & Schuster Speakers Bureau can bring authors to your live event. For more information or to book an event, contact the Simon & Schuster Speakers Bureau at 1-866-248-3049 or visit our website at www.simonspeakers.com.
Interior design by Irene Metaxatos
The text for this book was set in ITC Slimbach Std.
Manufactured in the United States of America
First Edition
10 9 8 7 6 5 4 3 2 1
Library of Congress Cataloging-in-Publication Data
Names: Hall, Desmond, author.
Title: Your corner dark / Desmond Hall.
Description: First edition. | New York : Atheneum, [2020] | Audience: Ages 14 up. | Audience: Grades 10–12. | Summary: Seventeen-year-old Frankie Green yearns to leave Jamaica and study in the United States, but when his father is shot he is forced to give up his scholarship and join his uncle Joe's gang.
Identifiers: LCCN 2020011962 | ISBN 9781534460713 (hardcover) | ISBN 9781534460737 (eBook)
Subjects: CYAC: Fathers and sons—Fiction. | Gangs—Fiction. | Uncles—Fiction. | Jamaica—Fiction.
Classification: LCC PZ7.1.H272 You 2020 | DDC [Fic]—dc23
LC record available at https://lccn.loc.gov/2020011962

In memory of my mom: I'm sorry I didn't do more to help your little brothers, who died under the wheels of a corrupt machine.

One

frankie put down his empty water bucket on the side of the steep mountainside road that was just wide enough for a sedan and two well-fed goats. The sun had only just started to warm, too early for the post office to be open. Still, Frankie gazed at the ramshackle building. His scholarship letter could be inside. It was nearly all he thought about these days. If it came—if it brought good news—he soon might be headed off to study in America. Jamaica was so bankrupt it could hardly afford hope, but hope was Frankie's light, and one he shined often.

In the distance lay miles of lush green forest and fields, and beyond that, the capital city of Kingston. A handful of twenty-story structures sat at the center of the skyline. Near the

Olympic stadium, where he'd once seen the Jamaican sprinters practice relays, stood the University of the West Indies campus. Frankie knew he could get into their engineering program, but all a Jamaican diploma guaranteed was debt. Jobs for young people were just too hard to find.

Gnats circled. Frankie stuck a forefinger in the corner of his eye and removed a dead one. He studied it—his own career might be as short-lived, even if he got the chance to study at the University of Arizona. A classmate's older brother had recently come back from America—he hadn't been able to secure work even though he had a *master's* degree in engineering. No way was Frankie going to let that happen. He flicked the gnat away.

The rev of an engine broke the early morning quiet. A black Toyota barreled down the mountain toward him. A thumping bass and pulsating rhythm rippled through the humid air, Sizzla's raspy voice and reggae lyrics flowing from the car stereo. His uncle Joe's long, sinewy arm emerged from the window of the shotgun seat, in his hand, a Glock revolving in a slow, tight circle like a predator stalking prey.

Frankie smiled, then pulled it back to a smirk. His uncle always kept a round in the chamber. Pulling the slide took time, and time was what you didn't have when things got ugly. Uncle Joe had his finger on the trigger, and the road had a lot of potholes. A step to the left or right to get out of range would have been the smart thing to do—cuz accidents happened. But Frankie held his ground.

The Toyota rolled to a stop in front of Frankie. "Pop, pop, pop, pop!" his uncle shouted, his thick brown dreads making his angular face look even more so. He lowered his gun and extended his fist. Frankie bumped it with his own, catching a whiff of weed so skunky it had to be good. Uncle Joe's red eyes confirmed it. Ice Box was at the wheel, engulfing the driver's side with his massive frame. He was one of Joe's enforcers. His other, Buck-Buck, sat in the backseat talking on his cell phone.

"Wha gwan, Nephew?" Joe asked. "You hear about the scholarship?"

Frankie couldn't go anywhere without being asked that question. "Not yet, Uncle."

Joe pulled back his locks, gazing at him. "If you get it, you going to run away from Jamdown. You going to leave your people." Joe was still smiling, but his words felt like a slap.

"I'm not running away, Uncle."

Joe held up a hand—*wait*—as his phone buzzed. He searched his pockets, pulled out a flip phone and a Blackphone, and answered the Blackphone.

The flip phone was prepaid, Frankie knew, with nothing that tied his uncle's name to it, and the Blackphone had special encryption in case he had to send a message.

Like Joe had just sent a message with his dis: *You going to run away from Jamdown.* Sure, Frankie wanted to leave Jamaica for the job opportunities in America, all his friends did. Jamaica was like a messed-up parent: You loved it, but at the same time you wanted to leave it. You said bad things about it, but you'd get mad if anyone else said anything bad about it.

Frankie wanted to explain that. He paced while his uncle barked at whoever was on the other line.

Finally Joe clicked off the phone. "Yes, Nephew."

"I'm not running away, Uncle," Frankie said again. "Once I set myself up over there, I'm coming back, gonna do some big things for Jamaica."

"Big things, eh?" Joe nodded slowly. "Ambition is important, just no forget is here you born, is here you should spread your roots. And you must watch out for Babylon. It's even bigger in America than Jamdown."

Frankie nodded back knowingly. For his uncle, and all Rastafarians, "Babylon" meant corruption in the government and police forces. Joe loved to rail against Babylon as much as he loved to smoke ganja.

"All the wickedness and oppression them perpetrate is a sin me tell you," Joe went on. "Them allow rich man in suit and tie to steal money them don't even need. Poor people steal to eat and them go jail." He sucked hard at his teeth.

Frankie looked away toward the post office, then back to Joe. "But Uncle, you do jobs for the PNP."

Joe wore an *oh, please* look on his face. "Me work with the devil that pays me. But that doesn't mean me won't call them a devil. P-N-P"—he slowly drew out the letters—"that's supposed to be the People's National Party. Now, you going to stand there and tell me they really do anything for the *people* except feed them bogus theories on how people fi live?" He tapped his gun against the side of the car. "And the other joke. JLP. Jamaica *Labour* Party—they don't create any decent jobs for normal people."

Frankie folded his arms. He'd been doing a lot of reading

up on America lately—he might spend four years there! They had two main parties too. As far as he could tell, the JLP was conservative like the Republican Party, and looked out for businesses. The PNP was liberal, and pushed for the rights of workers. But it couldn't be that simple. Some kids in school were really political, but Frankie thought they just sounded like they were repeating things their parents had said. Would he become more political if he went to America? He wasn't now, here in Jamdown.

Joe shook his head. "JLP, PNP, whatever, every fucking political party is the same thing." He frowned. "Yeh, mon, like me say, I have to work with them but me don't have to agree with their bullshit." He looked toward Kingston in the distance. "Them protect me from police, and me get them votes. And you know how important that is, right? Whoever wins the Kingston vote, wins Jamaica. I tell you, it's just one big shitstem."

Joe's Rastafarian accent was thick, sometimes even difficult for Frankie to understand. But there was no doubt he was down for the people. It was probably the reason everyone in his posse loved him so much.

Ice Box tapped Joe's shoulder. "We going to be late, mon."

Joe turned to Frankie. "Me would give you a ride but me have business in town. Later, Nephew." He slapped the dash. The Toyota pulled away.

Frankie watched until the wave of the dust kicked up from the tires settled. Things were always exciting when Joe was around, even if nothing really happened. Frankie liked that thrill. He knew he shouldn't. Posse life wasn't for him. But still.

It was time to get back to work. He headed over to the old standpipe on the other side of the road. Setting the bucket beneath it, he twisted the iron handle. Water rushed out, water he and his father would use to drink, cook, and flush their toilet. Bucket filled, he gripped the handle and began his mind game: in order to keep his daily task from becoming life-sucking boredom, he would challenge himself to spill not a single drop. He straightened up, but too fast; water sloshed toward the metal rim. Frankie froze. Losing before he even started would make his journey up the mountain feel endless. The water calmed, then settled. He exhaled, took a slow step. Next step, next. As he strode up the road, he moved faster and faster, putting more skin in the game, determined not to spill anything.

A mile into the two miles to home, his arm muscles burned. He paused to shift the bucket to his other hand.

Just past a row of flowering breadfruit trees, Frankie looked out over the gully at the explosion of green—coffee plantations that had been there for decades. The Blue Mountains wore mist like fine jewelry. This could be a scenic overlook, he thought, something to bring in tourism, and money. It wouldn't even take much construction. A small loader tractor and a few volunteers could do the trick. The problem was the town across the way to the right. Stony Mountain housed a concrete juvenile detention center so massive, so overcrowded, it was practically its own city. The sun glistened off the stream that rippled down to the bottom, and Frankie looked at it longingly. There were underground streams higher up the mountain, and he knew there had to be a way to pipe the water down—like Roman aqueducts—to his own town. People were used to the hour-long journey for water each day—but they shouldn't have to be! It was something he could do for his town, for others like his—once he came back from America with a degree. If only he could get there. He set off again.

Once the road flattened, the strain on his legs easing Frankie entered the town of Troy. The butcher's shack, the small elementary school, the rum bar, and Mr. Brown's general store, where Frankie worked, weren't open yet. He passed several one-bedroom houses nearly identical to his own, then glanced down at his bucket; small swells lapped the sides, but not a drop spilled. Yeah!

Then a scream, followed by a yelp, pierced the silence. Frankie scanned the area. Damn. In the clearing just past his house, Garnett, Afro funkier than ever, was gesturing angrily at someone sprawled in the dirt.

What the hell was Garnett doing here? He had moved away from Troy last year, to everyone's relief, especially Frankie's best friend, Winston. Garnett was always after Winston. Now Frankie noticed the fine clothes—the distressed denim shirt and pants. Huh? Garnett wasn't smart enough for a paycheck job.

He had to have signed on with a Kingston posse. A whole heap of guys were doing it.

And now Frankie knew exactly why Garnett was here. And who was on the ground. He set down the water bucket just as Garnett sprang toward Winston and kicked him in the stomach. "You haffi' learn respect!" he barked.

Frankie assessed the situation: Garnett's shirt clung to his body—no weapon bulged in the front or back. So he sprinted forward.

Winston rolled away, clutching his stomach. "Me didn't mean anything."

Frankie launched himself at Garnett as he was readying to unleash another kick, driving his shoulder into Garnett's back.

They slid onto the dirt. Garnett swung, clipping Frankie's nose. Eyes watering, Frankie hit back, pounded his knuckles into Garnett's ribs—once, twice. Garnett curled in a ball like a spider about to die as Frankie hopped up, poised to keep swinging. Backing away slowly, eyes on Garnett, he said, "Winston, man, you okay?"

Garnett slowly unfurled, slowly stood, dirt on his fancy shirt, jeans, his cheek. "Me see your uncle drive past," he scoffed. "You a big man only because him protect you."

It was true. The thought of Joe was the only thing that kept Garnett at bay right now.

"Just go," Frankie said in as calm a voice as he could manage. But he knew this wasn't the end of it.

Winston braved his way over to them. "You lucky Frankie stopped, or you would get a proper beating," he jeered.

Frankie smacked Winston's arm; goading Garnett would only make things worse. But Winston always had to save face.

Garnett smacked his lips as if his mouth was full of bitter fruit. "Me not done," he said, spreading his fingers menacingly before he turned and stalked away.

"What's he doing up here anyway? I thought he left." Frankie said as soon as Garnett was out of earshot.

"Don't know. Visiting his ma?"

"Maybe. You all right?"

Winston slapped his ample belly. "Well padded, mon." He stood there, chest out, as if *he* had just fought Garnett and won.

"So, what'd you do to piss him off this time?"

Winston smirked. "Me just point at his fancy clothes and ask if him win a gift certificate at the Dollar Store." Winston's eyes darted from side to side. Then, in a low voice, he said, "Wait till him find out me in a gang too."

Frankie gaped at him. "Gang? What gang?"

Winston's eyes went wide. "Shhhh."

Frankie spun around: Was Garnett back? No—but nearly as bad, here came Samson. Frankie's father was a sinewy man, a half foot shorter than Frankie, but his fury always made him seem a half foot taller.

"Frankie!" he bellowed now. "What the hell is this? Me can't believe it, you out here fighting on the street!"

"Yes now, Spanish Town, you daddy gonna beat you with the doo doo stick!" Winston hooted as if they were still in grade school.

Samson's quick, chopping steps brought back memories of past beatings, each one accompanied by some version of *My daddy did beat my behind till I reached twenty-one!* Frankie was nearly eighteen, too old for this. Still, he shrank back, braced himself.

His father's hand hovered by his belt buckle. "Me don't want you on the street fighting! How much times me have to tell you?"

Frankie wanted to say this wasn't like the last time, this was Winston, he couldn't turn his back on his best friend. It was just how things were. "Garnett started this," he blurted out instead. Those words were easier because he knew how his father felt about Garnett.

"What?" Spittle flew from Samson's mouth. "Don't blame nobody for this."

"You don't even want to know what happened!"

Embarrassment flickered across his father's eyes. He wasn't used to this kind of pushback, Frankie knew, not in public. Frankie usually tried to make things work, walk the tightrope when he had to. But he'd just done a really good thing—stood up for his friend—and it was like his father didn't want to know about it—

"Me going beat you." Samson took his belt off and whipped it through the air so fast Frankie didn't have time to dodge, and it hit Frankie's hip bone like an electric shock. The next pass cut across Frankie's back. Spinning away, Frankie grabbed at the recoiling end. He missed, but it was enough to shock Samson. His father stood there for a moment, heave-panting, then stormed back toward their house.

Frankie glared after his father, then glanced at Winston, who gave Frankie a see-you-later chin up. But then he came over for their special handshake—fist bumps, snaps, and crossed elbows—and said he'd stop by the store where Frankie worked after school. He walked gingerly, hunched at the waist, chest no longer peacocked out. Garnett got him good after all.

Frankie watched until Winston made it home; he didn't trust

Garnett not to sneak back and jump him. As he turned back around, he nearly knocked over the water bucket. That would have sucked! He bent to pick it up, finish his daily game of delivering the water without spilling any. A sharp zing of pain made him flinch, and fury at his father flared, the sense of injustice like a mad dog that couldn't be reasoned with. He cupped a handful of water, a taste as sweet and refreshing as any he'd ever had. Then, glaring at his father's house, he tilted the bucket, released a slow stream, and angled it until it was empty.

Two

frankie snapped an aloe stalk from the spiky plant by the front door—his mother had planted one on either side years ago. He went into his house, and he eyed the twelve feet from the living room to the kitchen. Good, Samson wasn't there. Crossing the floorboards—some maple, some walnut—to the kitchen, he found a knife and split the stalk. Then, lifting his shirt, he ever so gently spread the sticky, cool juice on his back, the puffy lash mark searing like hot grease. As he swallowed down a gasp, he made a vow to himself: this would be the end of it. If he got the scholarship, there was no way he was coming back home to visit if there was another beating. He had to make that clear to his father.

At least he'd put up resistance this time. Hadn't made a

sound. Hadn't given Samson that satisfaction. Not to mention hadn't let Winston hear a single howl, grunt, or groan slip from his mouth. That would have been even worse than the physical pain.

The door opened, and Samson glided in, anger gone, an almost meek look on his face. He set his finger on a tiny crack in the wall, blocking the light from outside. "Me don't love to beat you, you know? Me get beating until I was a grown man, you know?"

But Frankie remembered his father's face when he'd drawn his belt. A forehead didn't crinkle up for duty. Eyes didn't narrow for duty. Duty was calm. Samson's face had been pure fury.

So Frankie stuck out his chin defiantly. "It wasn't my fault."

"Fault, Frankie? Fault isn't important. Things happen fast out on the street. Damage comes quick and it doesn't care about fault."

"He was beating up Winston!"

Samson waved his hand as if shooing a fly. "Winston. That boy don't know when his tongue becomes his enemy."

"He isn't stupid—"

"Plenty smart people don't know how to conduct themselves. Keep your mind on the scholarship, you hear? Your mother— she dreamed—"

"It *is* on the scholarship!" Samson didn't need to remind him about that, or about his mother. The scholarship wasn't icing on some damn cake—it was the whole cake.

Samson pointed to the aloe branch. "You put the sinkle Bible on your back?"

Frankie nodded, and his father came toward him, raising his hand. Frankie flinched.

Samson paused, blinked, and then pointed at Frankie's head. "You need haircut, you know?"

"I'm okay," Frankie said, shrugging, shifting away.

Samson frowned. "You think since me unemployed, me don't know how to cut hair anymore?"

"I didn't say that."

"So come, mon, bring the chair. Me will give you a proper cut."

Frankie brushed a hand over his tight curls. Haircuts—his father's way of making peace. "It's okay. I'll get one when I go town."

Samson folded one hand over the other. "Why you want to spend your money when you don't have to?"

"It can wait. Besides, you cut the sides too short last time," Frankie said, thinking this was the moment to draw the line on the beatings. A voice, maybe his mother's, had always held him back before, counseling him to have patience with his father.

He's having a rough time at work, Frankie. This too shall pass.

Thing was, things hadn't worked out for Samson as a short-order cook, a handyman, a barber, or even his brief stint as a boxer. So he never stopped beating Frankie.

When he was little, Frankie had looked at his father's formidable jaw and imagined that no professional boxer would ever take a shot at it for fear of breaking a hand. But of course one did and had shattered that jaw. Now it looked outsize, not befitting a man of Samson's height. He was five inches too short for that jaw. And Frankie was too tall for the beatings.

"I think it's time for the beatings to stop," Frankie said, all the while wondering how the hell his father would respond.

"Oh?" Samson raised that chin. "You know why me beat you?" He unfolded his hands.

"It's got to stop," Frankie repeated, holding his father's gaze.

"My father beat me till I was—"

"I know. I know. But I'm not you. And I'm not going to take it anymore." The last sentence took all his courage, he felt almost faint.

"As long as you live under my roof, is me in charge of you." Samson cracked his neck, left, right. "Frankie, me no love to do it. But until you learn to keep away from trouble—"

Frankie gaped at him. "You don't think I know that?" Samson was clueless! "I work hard at school. I come in first in all my classes. First! I work hard at my job."

"And one mistake could take all that away!" Samson roared.

Even though it was only the two of them—had been for three years now—his father didn't notice *anything*. It was useless. Frankie turned to walk away and tripped over the molding that ran across the middle of the floor, one of Samson's makeshift attempts to keep the house together.

In the backyard, humidity was thick, hard to breathe. Frankie pulled his bike away from the pimento tree where it leaned. He'd found the abandoned frame of the ten-speed near his school in Kingston, slowly added parts. After some tinkering, he'd gotten one gear to work. One was enough—he didn't want to spend the money to fix the other nine. One was enough to get back and forth to where he needed to go.

He straddled the bike, thinking that it was about time to head to school—damn, it was going to hurt sitting in a chair. He stared back at his house, a green-and-yellow box with one back window, a colorful cage that shut out the world. His mother had painted it with so much attention, so careful not to get any of the paint on the window.

He glanced at the neighbor's house, red and brown, set just past a sprinkling of arching lignum vitae trees and tall beech. Same planking as his. Most of Troy's houses were made from the wooden storage-room walls of the now defunct sugar factory. At least they weren't corrugated.

Frankie's grandfather—a bushman who had harvested what he found in the forests for money—had left Samson the land, but it was Samson himself who had managed to build a house and get actual furniture.

Frankie remembered when, just after his nineth birthday, Samson had brought home an old ham radio that needed fixing. His mother, cancer free back then, had wiped her fingers on her apron, threads dangling from the embroidered roses, and sauntered over to his father. "Our junkyard is looking good. All we need now is a mattress and an old car out front," she'd said, her voice teasing.

"When me done with this, we'll be able pick up stations from all over the world," Samson had replied, spinning a screwdriver into the back plate of the radio.

"I don't doubt you, but does all the junk in Jamaica need to end up in my house?" She rubbed the tips of her fingers together as if working loose cake batter.

Samson had laughed and dropped the screwdriver, his eyes full of affection.

Frankie dashed over to pick up the screwdriver. He held it to the web of circuits and wires and blew air out of his mouth, emulating the whir of a drill.

"No, mon!" Samson snatched the screwdriver out of Frankie's hand, pushing him away. "You not learning this line of work. *You* will do something better."

His mother had added, "You're going to college. You will be the first one in the family." She patted down a fraying rose.

His mother . . . Frankie blinked away the memory. Blinked at their house—it was a shack, really. He wanted a better place, with more space for his father to live in, a building they could take pride in. *You're going to college. You will be the first one in the family.* His mother had outlined the path for a better life, but she hadn't told him how that path would change *other* things. He thought of all the hours he had spent hitting the books while his friends ran around in the woods and went on adventures. She also hadn't told him that he would begin to see the world differently from them. The more he had learned, the more he had drifted, like his genes had transformed. His education had given him some sort of strength, but it was also a weight, a pressure he had to carry that the others didn't. Things were expected of him now.

Frankie had just placed a foot on the pedal as Samson walked into the yard, shoulders swaying, chin up, carrying the clippers and a white towel.

"Me won't cut the sides too short this time." Samson clicked on the clippers. "We got ten minutes before you need to go to school."

That was as much of an apology as Frankie would get and he wanted it, he did, but he could feel the push, his pride a dam against the words. Still, he hesitated, lowered his foot. The right thing, the practical thing, spun through his gut, fighting the anger he still felt in his head, in his back. An ant was making its way toward his shoe. Frankie watched it for a moment and thought about stomping it . . . then simply dug his shoe into the dirt and scared it away. He sat up tall on the bike seat. "Okay, you can cut it."

Samson stretched out the frayed towel, draping it over Frankie's shoulders.

He rubbed Frankie's head; his fingers, warmer than the air, hardened by a life of physical labor, dug into Frankie's temple. Then he leaned in close and began running the clippers away from Frankie's forehead toward the back of his skull.

"Remember, always cut your hair backward. You want the grain growing out this way."

How many times had his father said that?

Samson stepped back and squinted at the side of Frankie's head. He moved forward. The cold steel of the clippers whizzed at the edges of Frankie's ears.

Straining his neck, but not quite pulling away, Frankie hoped the clippers wouldn't cut too close.

Three

frankie swung onto Constant Spring Road, passing a Bank of Jamaica and a bus. A dark charcoal stench seeped from the muffler. Frankie caught his reflection in the window of a sneaker store. His school-issue khaki pants looked okay, but his khaki shirt could have used a bit of ironing. Whenever he took his five-mile bike ride to school, which was always, he felt like there was a sticker on his head that said COUNTRY BOY. And the front wheel of his bike was wobbling again. Damn.

Still, every time he passed under the gold crest on the West Kent school gates, he thought of his mother. She'd flat-out beamed when he'd been selected to go to such a prestigious institution. *Our kind of people don't get many chances like this, boy. Don't mess it up.* He didn't, but without the scholarship, his mission was incomplete. And at the moment he was feeling down about his chances. Maybe it was the fight with Garnett, or the problems with his father. And what the hell was up with Winston? A *gang*? He had to talk to him, smack that thought right out of his dumb head.

The guard at the gate nodded as Frankie rode past. Two girls in school-issue white dresses with green belts and loosely fitted neckties also nodded. He didn't know them, but he waved anyway, not to be a jerk; being a senior had privileges and responsibilities. Still feeling down about the scholarship, he chained his bike at the end of the bike rack. Then he looked up at the two-story admin building. His guidance counselor's office was in there. She was always so positive—seeing her was like going to a pep rally. He had twenty minutes before his first class, so he decided to go visit.

Scholarship or not, he had to admit he was going to miss this school. He'd worked his butt off and was proud of all he'd achieved. He had to admit that, too. Glancing around quickly to make sure no one was looking, he took hold of the school crest hanging in the foyer and carefully tilted it—it had been carved from thick mahogany several years ago by a group of students who'd also come from less privileged communities. Pulling back, he eyed it, making sure it was straight.

"Hey, Frankie!" It was a guy in his engineering class. "Want to work on the final project this weekend?"

"No, mon, I handed that in like a week ago."

"But dude, it's not due for three weeks."

"Why wait till the last minute?" Frankie grinned. "Likkle

later." As he walked toward Mrs. Gordon's office, he remembered the crazy number of hours she'd spent with him throughout the entire application process for the scholarship—and she *always* had something positive to say.

Finally to the end of the corridor, he walked through the large open meeting room and stood outside Mrs. Gordon's office. She looked up, a big smile spreading across her face as if she was expecting good news. Frankie felt like crap. He couldn't tell her he was feeling depressed, not now. She was counting on him. He couldn't let her down by being down. "Not yet, but fingers crossed," he told her.

She nodded, put down her pen, and crossed fingers on both hands.

Feeling like a total fake, Frankie forced a smile, turned away, and headed toward class.

Sitting behind the register in Mr. Brown's store after school, Frankie tried to read the notes he'd taken in statistics class, but his handwriting looked like a fuzz of long straight lines and loopy letters. He gave up and grabbed the issue of *Popular Mechanics* he'd borrowed from the library the other day. "Tech Wars" was the cover story. He'd read it twice already.

He tossed the magazine on the counter. Man, was he bored. He stood up and stretched, forgetting his back until he felt the sear. Gahhh! He pressed his palms against his eyes until the pain quelled, not wanting to think of that beating. He was forever getting caught up in Winston's craziness. Then Frankie looked up at the clock—Winston was late. Typical. He said he'd stop by the store to talk. Frankie needed to straighten him out. The thought of Winston in a gang, Winston with a gun, made his gut clench.

And when the heck had Winston even done that? Frankie had pretty much been looking out for him since kindergarten. Two big third-grade girls had been pulling on Winston's lunch bag, trying to take it from him. If Frankie hadn't gone over to help, they would have gotten it too. And for a week the girls kept coming back to torment Winston, so Frankie kept coming over to help. It must have been something about the way Winston looked. He was just the type of kid bullies gravitated to.

And if Frankie got the scholarship, he'd be off to America in a matter of months. Who'd keep an eye on Winston, then? Keep Garnett away from him? Garnett. Dude's face had looked like a hyena's when he'd pounded on Winston, his lips twisted all nasty. Frankie knew Garnett wouldn't let it go. Yeah, he had to talk to Winston.

Just beyond the pyramid of yams, dirt still clinging to the roots, Frankie snuck a peek through a partially opened door made of reinforced steel into the storeroom. His boss was hunched over two of the dozens of orange ten-gallon poly bags Frankie had stuffed with marijuana earlier in the week. This was the part of his job he didn't tell Samson about—the part that made his paycheck more significant than it should have been.

Frankie decided to have some fun. "Need anything, Mr. Brown?"

Mr. Brown flinched, his nostrils flaring. "You interrupted my count, Frankie." He turned back to his work, this time mouthing the numbers.

Shrugging, Frankie passed the walls of wooden shelves—noticed that the Nescafé and cans of butter beans needed replacing—to the front door. Where the heck was Winston? Just outside, perched on milk crates at a rickety folding table, two old men silently studied snaking lines of dotted ivory.

"Yes now!" one shouted, and slammed down his domino.

"You gimme di game!" The other old-timer wound up like he was going to chop the table in half with the domino in his hand, but at the last minute landed the double four softly as you please. That set off a twister of insults and sharp comments.

Frankie laughed. He hadn't played dominoes in eons. He remembered a rare late-night domino party in his own back-yard. Remembered the pungent flavor of curry goat his mother had made. She had barged her way into the game he was playing with Samson and some of their grown-up friends. "I only know how to match," his mother had said, as if she were meek and helpless, her doe-like expression all innocent. Frankie couldn't forget the way Samson's eyes held her.

The game had become intense, both sides close to reaching the total number of points they needed to win. Frankie's mother was surveying the tiles, probably counting the matches. Frankie remembered looking at the line of dominoes on the table: the four and two domino matched with the two and the six. He had figured that if his mother had a six in her hand she could play, but if she had a double six, or some other way to block the game so no one else could make a move, she might be able to win, because she had the highest point total. But double six . . . no way.

Just as he was thinking that, his mother smacked her fist down on the table and slowly opened her hand like a magician. Double six. "I suppose this means I win," she said, and the tipsy guests exploded with laughter, some shouting loud complaints of clever deception.

The remission was what was truly deceiving. Frankie had thought that remission meant the cancer had been stopped. But little by little it snuck back, ate away at her until it took her life. Watching the old-timers now, Frankie realized that his father hadn't played dominoes since his mother had died. Damn.

Just then Winston strolled up, looking sheepish.

"You're late," Frankie called out. "You said you were coming by forty minutes ago."

"Me here now, mon," Winston said, shrugging past him into the store.

Frankie shook his head and followed him in, returning to his spot behind the cash register. Winston began thumbing through Frankie's statistics book. "Me don't understand one word in this thing."

"Maybe you should go back to school—"

"School? That's for you. Me have to scuffle. Me name 'Sufferer.'"

"What's *my* name, then? You see where I work." Frankie pressed a key on the ancient cash register. He knew it wouldn't even open.

"You package the ganja for Mr. Brown, though," Winston

countered. "Him pay you extra for that, no true?"

Frankie gave him a cold, blank stare; he'd never told Winston about the side-hustle part of his main hustle. Winston clearly had his ways. But there was one thing Winston didn't know about. "He let me drive the other day, his van, you know?"

This gave Winston pause. "Brown did? Where?"

"All the way into Kingston."

"Him was in the van with you?"

"Yeah, but I drove, mon."

Winston twitched a shoulder, playing it off. "So, what about the foreign t'ing? The scholarship?"

Frankie was as weary of that question as he was of working in the store. "Don't know yet." He was so lucky to have gotten into the fancy school. Winston and his other friends had, one by one, dropped out of their dinky high school on the mountain. None of them were graduating. Fact was, Frankie couldn't stop feeling kinda guilty about it, like he was an imposter or something. Like, why him? How was *he* worthy of all he'd gotten, and might still get if he actually got the scholarship? Yeah, he'd worked hard, but still. Why him? There were others all over the island, just as deserving, maybe more. Like, why not Winston?

Winston picked at his teeth with his thumbnail, a habit he'd had for forever. Their mothers had become friends when Winston was in second grade, after his father took off. Mamma helped take care of Winston while his mother worked. Winston always piled his plate with more than he could handle, stuffing himself *as if the future had no more*, his ma used to say. Frankie considered this. Winston always got caught up in saying and doing things that came across as desperate; guy was always trying too hard. He always needed more. . . . Frankie knew how his psych teacher would describe it—needing to be more than his father was, and at the same time, not worthy, because of his father. And Frankie's spin on it was, it all made Winston sometimes act like an idiot. Frankie had felt that way about his *own* father, still did from time to time.

Still, there was no doubting Winston's friendship. Back in fifth grade, Frankie had been crazy sick with a high fever, the whole town saying prayers for him. Winston had been so freaked out that he had tried to steal a toy car as a gift for Frankie. Of course, Winston being Winston, he got caught. But still. His mamma always said Winston's heart was in the right place. That had to count for something.

Winston closed Frankie's textbook. "So, you know you better watch out for Garnett now." He tapped the counter for emphasis. "You know that, right?"

Frankie half nodded like it didn't matter, but felt his heart quickening. "Which posse he's in?"

"Taqwan's. He—"

Frankie drew in a breath. He had read the newspapers, followed the killings. Taqwan's name was attached to a lot of shit, all over Kingston. "Yeah, I heard about Taqwan." If Garnett was part of Taqwan's posse, then he had even more to prove than Frankie had guessed. Pride was everything. There were killing reprisals between posses all the time. Not good. Not good at all. And now Winston was getting caught up in all this mess? "Winston, how 'bout you? Tell me 'bout the—"

"Hello, Franklyn!" a voice called out. Aunt Jenny, Samson's sister, swept into the store, breezing right past Winston, who was totally checking her out.

Frankie flicked the back of Winston's ear, motioning for him to keep his damn eyes in check.

Over Aunt Jenny's shoulder were two large handbags, one stuffed full, the other empty. She placed the full one on the counter. Frankie suspected it was stuffed with cash, payment from one of Mr. Brown's distributors. His aunt used many covers to avoid police while acting as a courier for Mr. Brown and for Uncle Joe. No one would suspect that at her waist was a Glock 41, a weapon made to remove chunks of flesh with a single round, a gun so appropriate for her, the weapon's logo could be a picture of her face. Ice Box and Buck-Buck were his uncle Joe's muscle in the posse, but Aunt Jenny was just as dangerous and way smarter.

Always full of airs, she sauntered over to the discount vegetables, chose two St. Vincent yams, and deposited them into her empty handbag as if taking perfume samples in a mall. She continued shoplifting: two star apples, a tin of Ovaltine, and a can of butter beans. Frankie watched without watching—how much could fit in that bag, anyway?

Mr. Brown poked his head out of the back room. Now Frankie watch-watched. Considering Mr. Brown's high blood pressure, Aunt Jenny's appearance could be a life-threatening situation. Mr. Brown was hiking his belt up so high he looked like Black Santa. Then he lowered it until it slipped under the shade of a significant overhang of fat. Then, like an eager teenage boy, he beelined straight to Frankie's aunt.

"Lawd God, you batty well round, Jenny." He craned his neck to check her out.

Aunt Jenny let a slow smile cross her face, and Frankie knew she was computing fast.

"You think so?" Aunt Jenny brushed back her shoulder-length dreads.

"Every man knows it, I swear."

"I'm just happy you do." Aunt Jenny shifted the grocery-packed handbag to rest on the curve of her hip. Mr. Brown pressed up against her for a hug, overlong. Nauseating hip grinds. This was his aunt's front, the deception she used to give her an edge over the men who saw women as hip grinds, which by Frankie's count, was just about all of them. He'd seen it again and again—she let them think they were in charge, that she sought their attention. But she was in charge the whole while.

Mr. Brown finally released Jenny, only then noticing Winston, who was back to ogling Aunt Jenny. His face went blood-pressure red. "What you doing here, boy? You steal anything from me? Get out my store!"

"Don't talk to me like that!" Winston fronted, all outraged.

At that, Mr. Brown lifted his shirt a mere inch—enough, however, to display a gun handle.

Frankie had witnessed this transformation before in Mr. Brown. Time to leave. He laid a hand on Winston's shoulder. "Mr. Brown, is this a good time for me to take my break?"

Mr. Brown, giving Winston the stink-eye, said, "Sure, go ahead."

Over his boss's shoulder, Frankie could see Aunt Jenny take the opportunity to lift a box of water crackers and slide it into her bag. She winked at him. The wink felt less conspiratorial, more like she was bragging. He waved goodbye.

Through the woods, Frankie and Winston reached a concave clearing in the mountain slope—their private meeting spot. Just past a Jamaican doctorbird sticking its long beak deep into a hibiscus plant's business, they sat. Frankie dug into his brown lunch bag, unwrapped the tinfoil around his sandwich—a thick spread of bully beef between two hunks of buttered hard-dough bread—and chomped. A mongoose and a skinny field rat trashed through the dried leaves.

Frankie held out the sandwich. "You want half?"

Winston shook his head, patted his belly. "Watching my figure." He laughed.

Frankie laughed too but got straight to the point. "You think gang business is right for you, Winston?"

"How you mean?" There was an instant defensive edge in his friend's voice.

Frankie stared at his sandwich. Winston's skin was as thin as kite paper, and he had used the wrong words, sounded like a parent.

Winston thrust his chin out. "You're not smarter than me. You're book smart, and you talk better than me, but me know the street. And me know gang runnings better than you too." With that, he oh so casually pulled out a pocket Beretta and oh so casually aimed it at a tree.

Frankie tried to hide his surprise. And *did* Winston know the street? Really? Frankie remembered a blazing-hot day, back when they were twelve or something, and Winston had talked him into playing hooky, going down to Kingston. On a dare from Winston, they'd checked out a bad neighborhood in West Kingston. On this one street, a man grabbed a woman in a black leather skirt and knee-high boots, probably his prostitute, and shook her hard. Winston had yelled, "Hey!" The pimp immediately let go of the woman and came stalking, digging in his pocket for something. Frankie had quick-scanned the area. There weren't many people on the street, at least no accomplices. He broke into a run. After a few strides he looked back. Winston was still standing there on the corner, the pimp, a switchblade now in his hand, closing in. "Winston!" Frankie had yelled. Winston turned, eyes so wide. Frankie shouted, "Run, mon!" And only then had Winston finally taken off. The pimp, thank God, turned like an airplane doubling back on its direction. When Winston caught up to Frankie, he'd said, disappointment in his voice, "Me think me was going to see you use your fast hands, and punch him up." Winston was thinking that Frankie had been a coward, but actually, Winston hadn't understood what to do in moments like that one. Big difference.

A click brought Frankie back to the moment. Winston had removed the clip from his gun. Shit. The only other people in Troy who owned guns were Aunt Jenny and Mr. Brown. His uncle's crew had plenty, sure, but they lived at the encampment at the top of the mountain. Joe. Wait—was Winston in *Joe's* gang? No way. Noooo—

"How much is Joe paying you?" Frankie asked, and pretended to wipe his brow just to cover his shock. Joe had to have given Winston the gun. This wasn't good. What the hell was Joe thinking? No telling what kind of trouble Winston could get into with a gun.

Winston refused to look Frankie's way. "Don't know yet, but Joe says it's going to be good money."

"So you're going to sell ganja?" Frankie took a bite of his sandwich, like the question was no biggie. Just conversation. He could have shoved it all in his mouth and chewed forever.

Winston shook his gun like a pointer. "No, mon. He wants us to do some jobs for the PNP. If we do okay, we will get better pay, even get to go live up at his camp."

Winston suddenly raised his gun, braced his shooting hand with the other, and fired a shot. It didn't look like he hit what he was aiming at. Still, he nodded, clearly pleased with himself. "We been getting some practice with Buck-Buck."

Frankie's ears were ringing. "Well, practice a little farther away from *me* next time." He pointed at the gun. "You have that thing on you the other day when you were fighting Garnett?"

"No, mon. Him lucky, too." Winston offered it to Frankie. "Want to try?"

Frankie shook his head. He'd fired a gun before; Joe had taken him for target practice once. Frankie had emptied half the magazine, but only hit the tree he'd been aiming at a couple of times. Joe had joked that he must be a tree lover. Irritated, Frankie aimed again. As Joe leaned close and whispered that he missed because he was aiming at the target instead of using the sights,

Frankie adjusted, used the sights, and blasted chunks of bark off the tree. Then he felt stupid. What was he doing out there anyway? He'd let himself be pranked into feeling he had to be Joe's kind of tough guy—out there shooting when he didn't want to.

Winston was admiring his gun like it was a new girlfriend. "Who else joined?" Frankie asked now, even more casually.

Winston looked through the sight. "Marshal, Baxter, Greg, Big Pelton, and some others."

Whoa. Frankie had been hitting the books crazy hard the last few weeks, but how had he not known all this? "Why didn't anybody tell me?"

Winston shrugged. "Joe said we shouldn't talk about it."

"I get that, but I'm not exactly a stranger, Winston."

Winston looked away again. "We in a posse now, mon. You're not."

Frankie threw the rest of his sandwich into a bush. Folded the tinfoil into smaller and smaller triangles.

"Joe probably didn't want to distract you from your studies, you know?" Winston said at last.

Winston's words were genuine enough, but there was a layer of condescension there. The idea that Frankie couldn't handle the news, that he couldn't rise above it. "He asks me to join the posse all the time," Frankie felt compelled to say.

Winston leaned forward, his shoulder almost touching Frankie's. "Hey, you want me to talk to Joe about it? Maybe get you inna the posse?"

"What did I just tell you? If I wanted to be in the posse, I would be. He's *my* uncle, Winston." What the hell. It was like Winston was saying he was closer to Frankie's family than Frankie was.

Winston threw his hands up. "Okay, you go talk to him, then."

"I don't want to talk to him—it's not the right thing for me," Frankie said, thinking, *How can Winston not get that?* And then he realized: he had the perfect segue to say what he most wanted to say. "It's not right for you, either."

Winston sucked his teeth. "Me all right."

Frankie rolled up his bag, stuck it in his back pocket to use again tomorrow. "I don't mean it in a bad way, Winston. It's just—"

Winston waved him off. "Listen, Frankie. You join, and you get a gun. You going to need one if Garnett is looking for you."

And who the hell's fault was that, *Winston?* It was useless talking to him. Frankie got up. "Later, mon." Slapping leaves away from his face, he descended the slope toward the street. Not thirty seconds later, he heard a twig crack, then something like leaves rustling. He turned to see Garnett atop the slope, a long kitchen knife in his hand. Shit.

"Me tell you me no done with you," Garnett called out.

Frankie's stomach fell and kept falling. Part of him knew that to run would be smart, but the other part wanted to get this over with now. Maybe there was a soul somewhere inside Garnett.

"Winston didn't mean what he said to you the other day."

Garnett swayed back and forth like a tree in pre-storm wind. "Bullshit." He took a few steps closer.

Frankie reached behind his back, pretending he was going for a gun. "You want this smoke?"

Garnett paused, uncertain, but he didn't look *scared*. He probably wanted to make a name for himself in *his* new posse.

A gun slide clicked. "Me *know* you don't want this." Garnett whipped around. Winston appeared on the slope above Garnett, Beretta aimed directly at him.

Smirking, Garnett turned back to Frankie. "Me with Taqwan. You hear me? And me going to tell him 'bout this." And with that, Garnett slipped back into the bush.

Frankie stared after him, his hand still on his back pocket, maintaining his bluff. But his mind was spinning: Had he just provoked a gang war?

Winston skid-stepped down the decline to Frankie's side. "Still think you don't need a gun?"

Four

he full moon sliced through charcoal-dark clouds, and
Frankie was glad for the beaming light—he could actually
see where he was going as he hiked up the deserted mountain road to Joe's camp. Passing two of Joe's men—lookouts—
he continued another ten minutes up to the top, to where
the road emptied into a wide circular driveway. Fifteen one-
bedroom wooden houses and a handful of shacks lined up in
a curving row along the edge of the mountain, thick brush
and trees everywhere. The silhouetted peaks of the rest of the
Blue Mountains behind them seemed to go on forever. A fast
synth rhythm, matched up with Sizzla's voice, and coursed
out of a portable system, haunting the night with raspy medi-
tations. There was no electricity this high up the mountain, so

kerosene lamps dangled all over, providing the only light the camp had.

Like always, Frankie got a warm welcome from Joe's posse members, their wives and girlfriends, too. In an odd way, the camp always felt enchanted to Frankie; it was as if he'd stepped back into a simpler time, where rebels lived off the land, free from all rules but their own.

They were just sitting down for dinner, and beckoned Frankie to join them. Large singed pots sitting on the rock fire pit were simmering with a Rastafarian stew of okra, pumpkin, and coconut milk, much better than his half a sandwich. Frankie filled a huge bowlful.

After he ate, he leaned into the flickering light to watch the Ludi game his uncle, Ice Box, and Buck-Buck were playing at the far end of the table. Though practically everybody had a Ludi board, Frankie had never seen one like this—painted in the red, black, and green Rasta colors. His uncle noticed and invited him to a game. That was cool, given that he wasn't part of the posse. Still, he shook his head. He needed to stay on task . . . get a quiet moment to talk to Joe about Garnett. But Joe had already handed the dice to Buck-Buck and nodded to Ice Box, and soon they were well into their game.

Nearly as soon, Buck-Buck was ahead. He scooped the dice. A lucky roll would hand him victory; Frankie hoped he would win fast and end the game.

Aunt Jenny strolled up, in baggy jeans and a denim shirt—a different look for a different occasion. She took a seat beside Joe, staring down at her cell phone.

"You think Buck-Buck is going to win?" Joe asked her.

"You know I don't play games," she said. Her voice was flat, the flirt packed away as tightly as the bag she'd stuffed with groceries earlier.

Ice Box, the furthest from victory, tapped his red game piece. "Buck-Buck, you nah go win this time."

"No, mon. Me going to win this game now," Buck-Buck said.

"Want to bet?" Ice Box challenged.

Ice Box always reminded Frankie of one of those kids at school who never opened his books, but was super insightful when it came to people.

Aunt Jenny looked up from her phone. "A fool and his money don't know each other for a long time."

"Who you calling fool, Jenny?" Ice Box folded his arms, his muscles rippling.

"You, fool," Buck-Buck said, laughing.

Joe lit a spliff, took a long draw. "Roll, mon, and please roll a six and finish di game. Me can't listen to you two all night." He exhaled.

In Troy, people only bonded together when a river flooded or a fire raged; it took mass destruction to pull people together. But here, there was a genuine spirit of camaraderie. Joe had told Frankie on one of their many walks that the posse had to be a real family, with Rasta values. Not like the Kingston posses, where everyone sat around lazy, or went robbing and marauding to get some petty revenge on another posse. When Joe told him that he sometimes had them all go over Bible study topics, Frankie had been floored. The light was always burning here at camp, Frankie thought wryly. At his father's house, the light went out with his mother. That was when Frankie started coming up to the camp more often. Hanging with Joe and Aunt Jenny made him feel less . . . alone. Yeah. They were always glad to see him, have him around, a stark contrast to his father's silence. Not that Samson and Frankie had ever really gotten along when his mother *was* alive, but they'd been, at least, more cordial, less distant than they were now.

Buck-Buck rolled. The dice tapped across the board. "Six, me win it!" Buck-Buck turned to Ice Box. "See, you should never bet against me."

Frankie smiled—they could have been him and Winston. He smiled also because his uncle looked to be in a good mood. "So," he said low. "Uncle, can I talk to you a minute?"

"Come, Nephew."

Frankie followed Joe along a path that led away from the shacks and into the bush, legs brushing against waist-high ferns. Joe always liked to talk and walk. Even at night. Frankie wondered, not for the first time, what his life would have been like if Joe had been his father and not Samson. The thing was, while Joe could be fierce, Frankie could *talk* to him about things— learn things—that Samson would never know. Joe was also powerful, and though he didn't flaunt his money, he had to be pretty wealthy. Frankie wouldn't even need the scholarship to do the things he wanted to do—

"So, what's on your mind, Nephew?" But Joe was already smiling knowingly. "Garnett?"

Frankie froze. Had Winston already spilled about the fight?

"Don't worry, Nephew." Joe stretched his arms, turning them in small circles. "My eyes is long."

Frankie nodded. "I think . . . I'm pretty sure he might be looking for revenge." He stopped short of asking for help. He wasn't about to get himself in a situation where he was indebted to his uncle. Asking for advice was as far as he could go.

Joe dismissed Frankie's concern with a *pffft*. "Garnett works for Taqwan, but Taqwan isn't going to cross me over some little fight. Other things, maybe."

Frankie remembered the scowl on Garnett's face, the eyes that didn't seem to have any life to them. "But Uncle—"

"Is no problem, Nephew."

Frankie wasn't going to push; Joe knew his business. "Okay."

"So, how is you father?" He didn't ask about his brother very often. "Him find a job yet?"

Frankie felt a fleck of embarrassment for his dad. "He's looking, Uncle." His father had been out of work for half a year now—but he refused to take Frankie's money for groceries or anything. Samson's freakin' pride was a roadblock. He was going into the bushes to get their food every day, digging yams, picking bananas and grapefruits. No way was Frankie going to tell his uncle *that*.

Joe spat, leaned closer and closer to a guava tree, inspecting it. Then he began to prune the dry limbs with an intensity that reminded Frankie . . . of Samson. Joe paused. "Your father can give help but him can't take help." He started back at the branches.

It was true. Samson would help out other people even before

family. Not a month ago, Frankie had found a basket full of yams, breadfruit, and mangoes on the doorstep as he was heading to school. A note was taped to the basket. Childlike handwriting said that the family down the road had sent it. Samson had built them a new roof and hadn't charged, because, "They got it hard, Frankie. Not like us."

Frankie had brought the package inside, already anticipating feasting on the mangoes after school; he was completely sick of the bananas. But Samson read the note, folded it back up, then gestured for Frankie to take the basket and follow him.

Twenty minutes later, along a dirt trail, the sun already hot, his school uniform soaked with sweat, Frankie wished he'd just left that freaking basket on the doorstep.

Finally his father pointed at a ramshackle house almost swallowed up by vegetation. An elderly couple lived there—so frail they rarely came into town.

Frankie got the gist immediately. He set down the basket, pulled out paper and pencil from his backpack to write a new note.

"Put that away," his father whispered, taking the fruit and heading toward the shack. He left the basket by the door, then hurried back to Frankie.

When they were out of earshot, Frankie asked why they hadn't left a note.

"You hold open a door fi somebody to say thank you or you do it because you feel it is the right thing?"

Frankie could almost taste those juicy mangoes—even now. It wasn't like they couldn't have used the extra food. But that was his father. It wasn't that he was too proud to take charity—though that had to be part of it—it was more that Samson didn't need to tell the old couple about the gift he left on their doorstep in order to feel good about what he'd done. Frankie's friends at school always sported big grins and bright eyes when they reported a new like on their Instagram. Frankie'd want likes too, if he was on Instagram, which required a phone, which he didn't have either. But his father, not so much. He was an old Jamaican man, from another time.

"You like my vineyard?" Joe was asking, standing back up, apparently satisfied with the weed-to-tree ratio in front of him. He swung his arm in a wide arc toward skinny, three-foot-tall marijuana plants, row after row after row of them, every other one set in small tires with its own soil, a trick to get more minerals from the rockier areas. His own Rastafarian Eden. The last time Frankie had been up here, the plants were barely seedlings.

What a complicated pride ran in his family, Frankie thought.

"Business must be good, Uncle."

"Can be better. Me always looking for more good people." Joe let the hint sink in.

"If I run into any, I'll send them your way, Uncle."

Joe gazed up at the moon for an uncomfortably long time, but Frankie stayed quiet. A firefly blinked by. Finally Joe said, "Come, Frankie, it's late. Ice Box can give you a ride home. Don't worry about Garnett. Soap and water isn't afraid of dirty clothes." He bunched his dreads in his hand. "Me going to send

Blow Up down to talk with Garnett's mother. She's a reasonable woman. We will work it out."

As they returned to the clearing, the clench in Frankie's back muscles eased. He hadn't started a gang war.

"Coming to my party Sunday evening? Me going to have it down in Troy. Get the people excited for the election."

That Frankie could say yes to! "Can't wait, Uncle." A Joe party was a good party, always. He caught the waft of fragrance—a flowering jasmine bush must be in bloom.

Joe suddenly reached into the air and closed his fist. When he opened it, three fireflies floated away, blinking their lights against the nighttime sky. It looked like magic.

Five

frankie's father had once told him that the old breadfruit tree—trunk broad as the door of their house and stretching five times as high—had been there longer than the town had. Frankie couldn't imagine how it could have been there for almost a hundred years. He'd heard that in America there were Sequoia trees that were over three thousand years old. If he got his scholarship, he would go see them.

At the standpipe yet again, he filled his water bucket, carried it to the post office, and sat against that breadfruit tree. And waited. People were making their way to the bus stop en route to work. How many people had passed that tree day after day? Some rarely had never been outside Kingston. Few had ever left Jamaica. If he didn't get the scholarship, Frankie would become one of them.

Finally he heard the telltale footsteps and the click of locks behind him. The postmaster had arrived. The man rolled up the grating. Frankie took a deep breath and followed him in.

And there was the letter!

He would be doomed if it was bad. Had he misspelled something in his essay? He should have had his school counselor read it over one last time before submitting it! If it were a rejection, the agony would be all over his face. No way was anyone going to see him that way. Frankie slid the letter, carefully, carefully, into his back pocket. He would open it at home.

All the way up the mountain, the crimson and blue University of Arizona logo burned at his brain. The first thing he wanted to do, if he got to America, was to go to the Hoover Dam, to set his eyes on the 60-story-high, 660-foot-thick wall of concrete. It was an engineering coup, for sure. But what if the letter wasn't . . . no! He wasn't going down that road. Compared with the burden of the unopened letter in his back pocket, his bucket of water was light. The stakes in his game doubled. The water sloshed, but not a drop spilled over. He was starting to feel dizzy, cold, as if he hadn't eaten in days. Each step racked his nerves, even after he reached his yard. He had to open that damn letter.

Behind the house, he slid aside the sheet of zinc covering the water drum and spilled the full bucket in. He yanked the zinc back into place, careful not to slice himself against the curved rusted edges.

In the kitchen, his father was pouring exactly a quarter tin's worth of condensed milk into a steel pot simmering with cornmeal porridge. The heat from the stove made the small kitchen sizzle.

"Wait till it cool," his father warned, taking the dish towel off his shoulder and wiping the counter.

But it was the letter in Frankie's pocket that felt on fire. Frankie pressed his elbows into the kitchen table, rocking it side to side. Should he look? Should he wait? The letter was so thin. But how much room did a yes or no take up? How much room did his *future* take up? He edged a fingernail under the seal, but the adhesive was too strong, his finger too shaky. So he carefully pinched the side of the envelope and ripped the edge off sliver by sliver. Gulping, he pulled out a single folded sheet, a creamy textured parchment. He read the first paragraph, then read it again: *On behalf of the University of Arizona and the Presidential Regional Collaboration program, I am pleased to inform you that you have been selected by the Department of Engineering to receive an undergraduate scholarship, inclusive of room and board, starting in the fall semester later this year.*

Frankie couldn't read any further, a sort of tunnel vision setting in. He could only decipher that first paragraph. He looked up at his father. "I got the scholarship."

Samson paused, blinked. He threw the dishcloth back over his shoulder, then went to the side table and picked up a black-and-white framed photo of Frankie's mother. Staring down at her image, he said, "Me almost forget, today would be your mother's birthday. Me going to lay flowers down by her grave. Why don't you stop down there after you're done with school? Pay your respects."

"Yeah, okay." Frankie read that first paragraph a second time. A third. One sheet. That was all his future needed.

"Me tell you you would get it." Samson set the photo back down and started drying some bowls.

Now Frankie stared after him. That was it? It wasn't that he resented his father choosing *this second* to remember his mother's birthday—the way he had looked at her said everything—it was just, well . . . he'd just gotten a scholarship—a full ride—to the United States! And Samson barely seemed to register the news. A sensation like billowing smoke seared at Frankie's nose, down his throat, and filled his stomach with toxic, burning acid. His ma—she would have been hooting and hollering, hugging him and reminding him to be as respectful of his American professors as he had been of his Jamaican teachers. And when she finished hugging him, she'd start hugging him all over again. She'd have gone on for days!

He ran his hand over the short, bristling hair of his new cut. Strange, he thought again, how instead of his ma's death bringing him and Samson closer, it left them more isolated. Sometimes . . . sometimes he couldn't help wondering if Samson would have preferred it if his mother had lived and Frankie had died. The only time his father ever noticed *him* was when he was doing something Samson didn't like, even if—thinking about the last beating—it wasn't his fault. His grades were already top of the class. He'd never skipped a day of high school, not once! Maybe he should have just become a bushman—seemed like that was when his father was happiest. Frankie swallowed hard and looked back at the letter.

This was no letter.

It was a portal, the transport to his future.

Six

frankie strode down Troy's main street after school like an emperor with a new groove, a legit one. His teachers, his classmates, they were all full of props at the scholarship news. Mrs. Gordon went ballistic, in the best way. Dragged him by the hand to tell the principal, even! Today hope wasn't a one-word prayer to a God who laughed at well-thought-out plans. Frankie nodded happily at everyone he passed.

He fished out his bandless rotary watch from his pocket. Under the scarred glass, the dial read four thirty. He was a little late, but his father would be right on time; he always was. Frankie picked up his pace. Past the rum bar, he took the snaking dirt path toward the cemetery. He wondered if he should find some flowers, then figured he would see some once he got closer.

Though he'd done so eighty-seven times already, at least, Frankie had to read the letter again to prove to himself it was real. This time, he focused on the last paragraph: *I am delighted that the University of Arizona Board of Engineers has recommended you for a full scholarship. If this offer is acceptable to you, please let me know in writing two weeks from the date of this letter.*

Acceptable? Were they kidding? How could the offer not be acceptable? Who would turn down a winning lottery ticket? Frankie looked around, and satisfied no one was there, he broke into his own little happy dance. Immediately, a thought nagged, warning him not to feel too good, trust fortune, but he ignored it and full-on danced, hands in the air, twisting and spinning, laughing.

At last he folded the letter, eased it back into the envelope. He might read it out loud when he reached his mother's grave. She'd like that. He wished he could tell her the news in person. He broke into a trot.

A hundred meters ahead, Frankie spied his father in the small cemetery. He was kneeling, head bowed, staring at the poured concrete that was his wife's grave, hands clasped. Frankie froze. A pang gripped his throat.

The tip of Samson's machete pierced the earth, the machete tilting sideways as if it hadn't the strength to stay upright, like his father right at that moment. What might happen if Frankie went up to him, put his arm around his father's shoulder, tried to share the grief they had never talked about?

Samson was all he had, Frankie told himself, so why not

go to him now? He felt like he was teetering on the edge of a cliff. And then Samson groaned. Frankie shrank back, wishing he could become invisible, let his father's moment be his alone. For Samson, pain was private, not to be shared, not even with his son. At his mother's funeral, Samson had demanded that Frankie not cry. So now he backed away, each step soft and silent. His father was wrapped tight, sealed like a package. Maybe Frankie might open that package one day. But not today.

"Frankie." His father's voice sounded like a beacon, an announcement, like dinner was ready.

Hesitantly, nervously, Frankie walked toward the grave, toward his father, reaching past him to run his finger along the stone. Dirt had gotten wedged into Ma's surname. Frankie edged his fingertip into the date of his mother's death and followed it, digging out the remnants of a leaf. He traced the rest of the letters, felt the rough texture of the crevices. The stonecutter could have done a better job.

"Come, mon," Samson said, a paper bag crunching in his grip as he moved to sit on the slope.

He opened the bag and pulled out something wrapped in reused tinfoil. "You must be hungry." *Is he proving to his wife that he is feeding her boy?* Frankie thought wryly as he joined his father.

He wasn't particularly hungry, no. But they had eaten at his mother's grave before—in fact, Samson always brought food. It was a kind of ritual.

The package crinkled as Samson unfolded it, and Frankie smelled the spice bun immediately, saw the orange Gouda center. His favorite sandwich. His father had remembered. The few times Frankie's mother had been too ill to make lunch, his father had stepped in and always made a spice bun sandwich, winking, saying they didn't have to tell Ma. So Frankie took the bun, raised it in a sort of salute to his ma, and bit into it, sinking his teeth deeper, bursting a raisin before reaching the sharp cheese.

His father unwrapped a bun and bit into it. This was what they had left—mealtimes together. Frankie tore off a chunk of bread and popped it into his mouth. Lots of raisins, and the dough was soft. Samson must have timed it perfectly to get a bun this fresh; the bakery was in the farthest part of town. For a moment, it felt like old times.

"One night we went to this restaurant," his dad started up out of the blue. "It was on a boat at a dock near Mobay. Your mother never drink but she had a white wine. Mon, after all the customers gone, we danced right next to the table on that boat."

Samson seemed to be gazing at her right at that very moment. Maybe he could see her dancing.

Seven

ate Sunday morning, shadows creeping across the backyard, Frankie's father pounded the final nail in the back window for a makeshift security device—a broad machete without a handle, attached to two strong springs.

"Okay." Samson nodded to Frankie, ready to test his latest invention. He lowered the window to set the position, leaving it partially open, just enough for someone to slip their hands under the frame and lift. Then he eased a two-by-four under the window frame to pry it open, as a burglar might. He raised it another five inches and . . . the springs uncoiled, sending the machete slicing into the wood with a loud thwack.

Frankie came close, poked at a spring. His father really belonged in the last century. Still, he said, "Works great, Dad."

Then Samson surprised Frankie by saying, "Frankie, me really proud of you and what you accomplish by getting the scholarship. Me pray you would get it, and me will miss you while you gone, but me glad all the same."

Frankie tried to stay chill. He couldn't remember the last time Samson had said he was proud of him. Maybe never.

"I'll miss you, too," he said back, all awkward, but still.

And for the first time since getting the scholarship letter, the reality of leaving, leaving Jamaica, leaving his dad, hit. He'd never been away from his family. *Pffft.* Up until now, it was family leaving him. Now he was about to be on his own. And he wanted it. Wanted it so bad. But yeah, he'd be leaving. And leaving his father all alone.

Samson was yanking, yanking the machete blade until it came loose. He reset his contraption. "We have to celebrate when we finished here," he went on. "Me will make some cow foot and kidney beans."

Cow foot and kidney beans! Frankie loved that even more than spice buns. He imagined sinking his teeth into the tender meat, heaping his plate twice; his father always made double. Then with a jolt he remembered: tonight was Joe's party. Shit.

"Samos, you back here making mousetrap?" It was Joe, of *course* it was Joe, and right behind him, Ice Box and Buck-Buck.

Samson wiped his hands against his pants. "You never know what kind of common thief might come into your backyard." Of all the tightropes Frankie walked, this was the thinnest. His father loathed Joe. Joe loathed his father.

Seeing the frown that flitted across his uncle's face, Frankie called out quickly, "Hello, Uncle."

"Nephew, blessings, and big up on di scholarship."

What? Frankie hadn't mentioned the scholarship to Joe yet.

"Yeh, mon. Like I say, my eyes is long."

"Why are you here?" Samson asked.

"That no sound like no welcome. You no long fi see your brother?"

"Is what you want, Joe?"

"Me haffi' want something?"

Samson gave the spring a small adjustment. "You always do."

"Like me say, me come fi greet up me nephew. Him going foreign fi go turn big man. Me want fi see him first. Celebrate."

If Uncle Joe brought up the party, Samson's head would explode. "Thanks, Uncle!" Frankie said, loud, shifting the conversaion. "I was worried about it for a long time. But the University of Arizona is really good for engineering." Keep talking. "I'm even going to see the Hoover Dam—it's close by!"

"Mr. Engineer." Joe stroked his chin. "Samson, you ever wonder how Frankie would do inna *my* business?"

Samson eyed his brother. "Why don't you ask him?"

His father had not just said that!

"Well, Frankie? Wha' you say?"

Think fast. "What kind of pension plan you have, Uncle?"

Ice Box and Buck-Buck laughed. Joe flashed them a grin and turned back to Frankie. "We don't have no 401K or no IRA, mon."

"Sorry, then, Uncle. I have to think about my retirement."

"Yeh, mon. And like the Bible say, honor thy father." Joe

grinned. "But remember, Nephew, come back here to spread your roots." To Samson he added, "Good luck with the mousetrap, Samos."

"You're the one who needs the luck, not me."

Joe's eyes narrowed. Damn it. He'd been about to leave! "Uncle—"

"Hold on, Nephew." He jutted his chin, a chin not as prominent as Samson's. "So, you think *me* need luck?"

"That's right, you need luck on top of those bodyguards." Samson pointed his hammer.

"Them? Them not bodyguards."

"What are they, then? They're not choirboys."

"You don't know that. Maybe them can sing." Joe smirked and sauntered out of the backyard, Ice Box and Buck-Buck trailing. They were always like this—Samson would do anything to piss off Joe and vice versa. It had all started—their fight, the one that would have come to blows if his mother hadn't begged them to be civil—over how to treat her cancer. Joe had said he had the means to send her to Cuba for a new treatment he'd heard about. Samson had dismissed the idea as simple Rasta foolishness. Joe had shot back that the God *Samson* believed in clearly wasn't going to save her. And now that Frankie's mother was gone, there was no way to fix it.

His father was back to hammering at the windowsill, making a slight adjustment. No way could Frankie tell him he wanted to go to his uncle's party. Samson would shut that down faster than the machete hit the sill. But Frankie was aching to go; Joe only had parties a couple times a year. He could celebrate the scholarship with his father tomorrow. So he took a gamble. "It's late to start the beans—how about we celebrate tomorrow instead?"

"Good point, *college* boy. Okay, no problem."

"I can start the beans first thing in the morning," he added, walking away before his father could ask any questions. No such luck.

"What you doing tonight, then?"

Dang. "Oh, there's a party in town. I promised I'd go."

His father paused. "Whose party?"

"It's—an election party."

"Whose election party?"

Damn. "Joe's . . ."

Samson fumbled his hammer. "When you talk to him about it?" He'd go as hot as the day's temperature, but Frankie wasn't going to lie.

"The other day."

"Why?" His father gripped the hammer again.

"I had to ask him about something," Frankie said evasively— not quite a lie.

"What?" his father pushed.

Frankie's teeth felt too big for his gums. "The kid I had a fight with the other day. Garnett."

"Lawd God. What good you think could come of that?" He waved the hammer, orchestrating the sermon that was coming. "Your uncle is a criminal, you know?"

"He's my uncle."

"Me don't want you going to any party him throwing."

"It's for all of Troy, though. And it's just going to be at the end of the street. At the clearing," Frankie implored. "Even people from Stony Hill are coming."

His father's face grew dead serious. "Frankie, it's a rally for the PNP. Me tell you already the PNP and JLP, they are the ones who brought guns to Jamaica. You forget, mon? There's no gun factory in Jamaica. It's the politicians that imported them. You don't see it? You think this is a party—it's what they want you to think, but it's really serious business."

"It's a *party*," Frankie insisted, knowing his tone was harsh.

"No, mon, it's politics. Joe's only throwing a party to get everybody to follow him, vote for who he says. The JLP and PNP build tenements, give out jobs, Lord, they even give out cheese to anyone who help them get elected."

"What's wrong with that? People need places to live. Food." Frankie balled his hands. He could already hear Winston telling him about how great the party was, how he missed this and that.

Samson took a step toward Frankie. "You think you're smarter than me?"

"Yes." It shot out of Frankie's mouth, no taking it back. He took a step backward. But Samson, having gone ramrod straight, simply said, "Hmm. You still live under my roof. When you gone foreign, you can do as you please. Only then."

There it was again, the because-I-said-so. "I promised I'd go."

His father's face stayed rigid as a mask. "Okayyyy." He drew out the word, then turned back to his work, striking the hammer against the sill, again, and again.

Okay? What did *okay* mean? It probably meant his father was hurt, furious, but holding it in. And that stung. At the same time, Frankie deserved some fun. He sighed, watched Samson toil at his stupid *mousetrap*, a man from the country. He was backward. Frankie knew that when he moved forward with his life, got educated in America, there would be no making peace with his father, no way of really relating, again. Maybe that package would never get opened after all.

That was when he decided that *okay* meant he was going to the party.

Eight

having changed into his good shirt—the blue one with the collar—Frankie passed his father sitting at the table without a word and went out the door. He walked past Mr. Brown's store, toward the party. A small hill, eroding for decades, had formed a natural amphitheater with a dirt-and-pebble floor. Homebuilt six-foot speakers on either side stood like two giant bookends, the reggae music so loud that it got distorted, ricocheting in Frankie's ears. Both electric and kerosene lamps bobbed on ropes suspended from trees and telephone wires. Villagers from all over the mountain milled about, heading in the same direction.

As Frankie approached, he thought about what his dad had said, how the party was only to influence people. But the fact was—and it was a fact his father refused to admit—Joe already took care of many things that the government didn't. A year back, gullies were littered with trash. Garbage trucks had stopped coming up the mountain because of the financial crisis. But now Joe paid someone downtown, and the trucks rolled up and down the narrow roads twice a week. Even the standpipe was being upgraded. Public works probably hadn't even known where Troy was on the map until Joe got involved. Maybe one day Troy would even have running water.

"Frankie!" It was Blow Up. His hair—short dreads that stuck straight up in the air—suited his temper. Frankie had always thought enforcers should be cooler, calm like Aunt Jenny or Ice Box and Buck-Buck. But Blow Up's name was his name for a reason. The handle of a Glock stuck out of his waistband—a clear Don't Mess with Me. "Hear you get di scholarship! Up, up!" he hooted now.

Frankie gave a chin nod, cool, no big deal. Blow Up nodded in turn. "Got to get some ice, mon. Likkle later."

As Blow Up left, Frankie eyed his gun. Several rubber bands encircled the handle, probably to keep it from falling down his pants leg. Probably all of his uncle's men had brought weapons—they never took chances. Probably never relaxed, not really.

A mass of people were gathered just ahead, the party already spilling beyond the main area, people already dancing. He waved to an ex who was looking really good in her track shorts and tube top. She waved back, then dug into a line dance with her friends, winding low in a corkscrewing motion, nearly to the ground. She'd cut her hair, he noted, curls falling to her shoulders. So much like, well, another girl he'd dated last year. Leah. He hadn't seen her around lately—just as well, as it ended really weird: she kind of ghosted him. Didn't matter, he was leaving Jamaica anyway.

He made his way past several older women in fitted dresses working their more conservative gyrations. Behind them, three teenage boys from the bottom of the mountain, still in khaki school pants, were twisting their knees like windshield wipers; then they jumped up and slammed their feet on the ground, kicking up dust, shooting forward, pumping like pistons. Frankie chuckled: the Excuse Me Please was always gonna be a thing. Everyone was getting their own dance on, it seemed. Maybe he'd get out there—after he ate, because, man, the aromas were making him salivate. Someone was making bammy—deep-fried cassava cakes—the line was insane. An old bald guy, Gummer, was turning jerk chicken and jerk pork on a barbecue, the meat slathered in what looked like spicy pimento like the one Aunt Jenny used. Just the sound of the sizzle made Frankie's stomach growl.

He had just gotten in line when a murmur spread through the crowd. Frankie turned. Joe, the provider, had arrived, making his grand entrance, striding through the crowd as several people stepped forward to offer their respects. Joe bowed his head to each, like a seasoned politician, then pressed on. Several children ran up to him. He chose one to pick up and toss high in the air, catching him on the way down. Joe knew the game, for sure.

Frankie scanned the rest of the grounds. Aunt Jenny, sitting at a table in an impossibly tight sequined denim shirt and pants, waved. She was playing *her* game again, the Aunt Jenny version of how businesspeople wore a suit and tie. Mr. Brown approached her carrying two plates overflowing with curry goat, plump dumplings, rice and peas, and fried okra. Jenny turned her head away, picked up a half-folded newspaper, and began to fan herself. Pretending, Frankie could tell, to be all casual, pretending not to see him. When Mr. Brown arrived, she turned to him and delivered an impressive display of surprise, stretching her eyes wide, throwing her hands up: *for me?!?*

Over by the DJ station, Winston and the rest of his friends huddled, heads nodding, beats dropping. Frankie went to join them, then stopped short. No freakin' way. His father? Frankie gave his head a shake, but dang sure enough. It was Samson jogging, weaving through the crowd, heading his way. Frankie's cheeks went hot. Samson was going to press him to come home, or just as bad, stay there to look out for him. Samson so didn't get it. Then—

POP! POP! POP! POP! Shots rang out. There was a screech of tires. *TEK, TEK, TEK, TEK!* Frankie lunged to the ground. Where was it coming from? People all around were flinging themselves down. Where was his father? Frankie lifted his head an inch.

A white BMW, its headlights off, was closing in quickly. Two men leaned out of the windows, machine guns in hand, and they just started blasting. Bullets tore into tree trunks, into the dirt. Half the crowd was now running, the other half seemed frozen in disbelief. Frankie saw one, then two, then three people fall to the ground. *Where was his father?* He saw Joe dive to the ground as a second round pelted several people who were just standing there in terror. Flesh ripped. Screams shrilled from so many directions, Frankie couldn't even think.

He couldn't move.

He couldn't stop looking.

Holy shit, holy shit—two bullets hit Mr. Brown in the belly, blood spurting, his curry goat spilling to the ground. Aunt Jenny came into view, eyes wide, reaching into her waistband for her gun. More shouts. *Where was his father?*

To the left, Ice Box and Buck-Buck were on the ground, crawling commando-style, guns in hand. A mother with three children stood like a deer in headlights. Two of her children broke away from her, running, crying. A guy in his twenties scooped one of them up and sprinted away, his arms and legs pumping. Bullets caught up to him; the child tumbled from his arms as the guy fell, and scrambled away. More bullets ripped apart the speakers, a high-pitched screech ringing out.

Frankie kept looking for his father. He caught a flash of Joe rolling over, drawing a gun, and starting to shoot. Ice Box and Buck-Buck were standing now, shooting at the BMW with assassin-like calm. Jenny was doing the same thing from the other direction. Tires screeched again as the BMW made a sharp U-turn and fishtailed back up the road—then there was a loud crash. Joe and his men ran toward it. Frankie got up on one knee: five hundred yards away, the front end of the car was crumpled around the trunk of a lignum vitae tree.

Frankie could hardly breathe. Palming his face, squeezing hard, he tried to calm himself, to gain hold of his fury, his fear.

The speakers screeched on, but their sound wasn't enough to muffle the cries of those hit, and the wails from villagers, turning back, gunfire now over, finding their loved ones wounded or worse. People ran through the landscape of twisted bodies, the sea of agony. Frankie'd seen this before, the same kind of nightmare, but never in Troy! Both those times he'd been in Kingston riding back from school, feeling for strangers—and it had felt so unreal.

This was real.

His father! Now Frankie was running forward, his legs leaden, as if they were pushing through a viscous liquid instead of air. He wove past a splayed body, then another, and another, until he saw ahead, a man, his father. Not moving. As if floating, Frankie was suddenly there—he had no idea how. He dropped to his knees. "Daddy—"

Nine

dust particles twisted in the midday light in his house; Frankie stared past them at the machete in the windowsill. *Pff.* Samson thought he was protecting them—nothing had protected him last night. Frankie'd been lying on the couch so long the small of his back was aching, but the energy to move wasn't there. The screeching sound from the shot-up speakers still rang in his ears; the sight of his father lying there on the ground at the party refused to go away.

The front door creaked open. "Frankie?"

He sat up, a hand on the floor, ready to charge. It was Winston. Frankie grunted, lowered his head back down.

"Wha gwan, mon?"

"Me all right."

"Respect." Winston came farther into the house. "How you feeling?"

"Okay." That was what his father had said, *okay*, when Frankie'd said he was going to Joe's party. Frankie went mute, feeling the echo of that word "okay." Winston walked to the back window and stood silently.

"It was my fucking fault," Frankie said at last.

"Wha' you say?" Winston was inspecting Samson's "burglar alarm."

"Right before the party, he told me—my father did—about the JLP and PNP, how they were."

Winston looked up in surprise. "Your father knew they were coming?"

"No. But he told me not to go."

"Come on, mon. That's not your fault. It's election time; posses make hits all the time."

Winston didn't get it—didn't get that Frankie should have stayed home, celebrated his scholarship with his father.

"Listen, me come to give you some good news."

Frankie lifted his head. About his father? Joe had gotten ambulances up the mountain in seconds, it had seemed. Samson was put in the very first one. Ice Box had raced Frankie and Jenny down the mountain to the hospital, but they hadn't been allowed to see Samson. "Ice Box, Buck-Buck, and Blow Up hit the posse that was responsible." Winston waited, practically beaming. Was he expecting a freakin' happy dance? "They got three of them, plus the ones in the BMW—that makes six. Supposed to be just a couple more. It was only some small posse trying to come up."

"They were with the JLP?"

"Yes." A half smile lifted the side of Winston's mouth. "But not no more."

That wouldn't help his father, but "Good," Frankie said weakly. At least it wasn't Taqwan. At least that.

Winston poked at the machete. "Hear anything about Samson?"

"Still can't see him. They made me come home cuz they had to operate."

"Don't worry, mon, Samson's tough. Maybe tomorrow."

"Yeah."

Winston nodded at the booby-trapped window. "Smart," he murmured, then said, "You can't just stay here all day."

Frankie pushed himself to his feet. "I'm not." He reached for his backpack.

"Where you going?"

"School."

"What? Why?"

"To tell them I'm not coming." Frankie held the backpack by a strap.

"That no make no sense . . . school started hours ago." Winston pulled a phone out of his back pocket. "Use my phone and just call them."

"No, I'm not going back to school *for a while*. I need to talk to my counselor."

"Your dad—he's going to be all right, mon –"

Frankie slammed the backpack on the floor—*splat*. "Give it up, okay? Just give it up! Stop trying to cheer me up and shit.

He's lying in the hospital and he might not get out of there, mon."

"Okay, okay." Winston paused at the door before leaving. "Me not your enemy, mon."

Frankie wanted to say something, let his friend know he wasn't hating on him. But the words weren't there. He looked back at the makeshift security device. If only it could have guarded Samson.

Gripping the arms of the chair like he was on a roller coaster with no safety belt, Frankie waited for Mrs. Gordon to get off the phone. He had explained what had happened to his father. He'd asked for time away from school. Now his counselor was talking to the principal on his behalf. Fury was building, building. He should not have come to school; he should have just used Winston's phone. He needed to be at the hospital, the surgery had to be over by now. It was his duty to be there, especially since it was his bumboclot fault that his father was there in the first place.

The counselor placed the phone back in the cradle. "Okay."

There was that word again. It plagued him—*you should have listened, you should have listened.*

"The principal will make a concession this one time, given your excellent record and that you've turned in your final engineering assignment."

Frankie loosened his grip on the chair. His fingers felt as cramped as if he were still holding on. "Thank you."

"But you need to keep up with your regular classwork," she

went on. "And check in once or twice a week with your teachers until—" She patted the table.

Frankie shifted uneasily. Checking in once or twice a week was no big deal, but he couldn't see coming full-time until his father was back on his feet. How long would that take? They wouldn't even let him *see* his father yet. "Thanks, miss. For everything."

"Now, have you told anyone?"

"Ah, the people back in Troy know."

"Anyone here?"

"No. I came to see you first thing."

"Frankie, it might be best . . . if no one at school knows that your father was shot."

He wondered where she was going. "Okayyyyyy."

"Confidentiality might serve you better." She cleared her throat. "If anyone asks why you're not in school regularly, maybe just tell them you have an illness in the family. Does that work for you?"

Actually, it made sense. If somebody, some idiot classmate, made some bad joke about his father getting shot, he might go off, he was so pissed. "Yes, that works."

She intertwined her fingers. "Good. I wish your father Godspeed."

So caught up in his thoughts, Frankie nearly walked right into another student as he left the office. He moved left—she moved in the same direction and they nearly crashed again. Frankie looked up just as the girl did. She. Her. Leah. The same girl he was thinking about before Joe's party went sideways. She laughed, then said, "Frankie. Hey, stranger." He was an instant mess—part happy to see her, part nervous to see his dad.

Leah was a senior too. Her groove was art. She wore her green school tie lower than any other student he'd seen—the knot halfway to her belt. With one quick move, she could shake it loose—defiance of school policy that she wore real well. Teachers must have said something, but knowing Leah, she probably talked her way out of it. Last year he thought he and she were about to start something. Then all of a sudden she got all spooked, started to avoid him.

"How're you doing?" Her smile—perfect—two dimples.

Talk about a loaded question! He quickly sidestepped it, saying, "All right. You?"

She eyed him up and down. "Excuse me for saying this, but you don't really look all right."

He half shrugged, suddenly having the urge to unload—part of why he'd been so surprised when she up and disappeared on him was that they'd seemed to be able to talk to each other so easily. But, Dad. He had to go. "Yeah, well, I can't really talk right now." That came out totally wrong. Moron!

"Okayyyyy." She smiled strangely, like she was smiling reassurance. "I get it . . . I wasn't very cool about things the last time we . . . I was shitty, right?"

This was an apology he'd never heard before. *I was shitty.* It was so in-your-face. "Yeah, I guess." He *wanted* to just say it was cool, and *be* cool, but damn, he needed to go.

"Just yeah?" Her smile widened, even as she said, "You have every right to be mad."

"I don't need your permission to be mad." Permission. He hated that word. *Permission to go to the party. Permission not to go to school with a sick father. Permission to be mad.* Enough! "We had something going. And you just stopped. So yeah, it was shitty."

"Like I said." She was still smiling.

"What *is* this? I mean, why are you here stepping to me now, anyway?"

"I thought we could talk . . . but you don't seem like you're in the mood."

"No . . . now's not good—" He was an idiot.

She lifted her head high. "Later, then." Then she was gone.

The school crest on the wall—the words YET HIGHER—seemed to mock him, like how much lower could he go.

Two excruciating days later, Frankie sat in the outdoor waiting area of the hospital. He'd been back and forth a half dozen times now, sitting in almost the same spot, hearing the same news, that his father was still in intensive care and couldn't be seen. He tapped his feet against the ground, feeling mad with worry. At least Samson was alive, right? At least that. And at least this time, Uncle Joe and Aunt Jenny came with him. They knew how to get answers. They knew the game.

Flanked by a frail older man's bony shoulder on one side, and the hefty, sweaty arm of a young woman on the other, Frankie peered up at the five-story building, a big off-white concrete slab that he couldn't stop thinking of as an unfinished headstone. The sun pounded down; convective heat bore into his skin. Whoever had built the hospital hadn't considered the sun's path, but they could have, should have. There was plenty of room to orient the area to diminish the effects of the heat. He started making mental calculations, envisioning ways to correct the problem, to keep himself from thoughts of Samson, as oppressive as the heat.

Uncle Joe never seemed to break a sweat—what was up with *that*? He was pacing back and forth, growling into his cell phone, his free hand swinging like a hammer.

"Listen to me, Buck-Buck, me don't care about that. Me want everybody who did come to my party to get a bag of grocery, with *meat*, not only the people that got shot. Everybody."

Joe's smooth Rastafarian delivery had been replaced by a militaristic staccato, a captain on the battlefield.

"Flowers? No, mon, I tell you, me want them to get food and things they can use." He clutched his forehead like he had a headache. "The people need to know me is there for them. Is two innocents dead, a dozen hurt, you know, mon?"

Frankie rubbed away the ash that clung to his knuckles. He'd forgotten to wash up this morning and now couldn't remember if he had done so the day before, either. Mr. Brown had commented on his dirty hands once—said Frankie had to think like a businessman, consider how the customers would feel buying food from someone with dirty hands. Mr. Brown had been all buttoned up, even about selling yams, when he was making a hundred times more selling ganja. He was old-school, and Frankie missed him. And then there were the other people: Mrs. Jenkins's grown boy who'd also killed, Winston's friend who'd taken a bullet to the calf, and the guy who grabbed that little kid—he just got released from the hospital today.

Frankie suddenly wanted to slam his fist into the faces of the men who had shot up Joe's party. But they were dead. He smacked his thigh instead, nearly dropping the bag he was holding.

Joe tucked away his cell phone. "Jenny still talking to the nurse?"

Frankie shrugged. All he knew was that Jenny was inside, dealing with paperwork that had to be cleared before they'd be allowed to visit his father. Every night he replayed the moments before the shooting, the moment of. He couldn't stop picturing his father lying in the dirt—lying on his back—so clearly coming *toward* Frankie when he'd been gunned down. Not running away. Running *toward*. These thoughts pinched Frankie's chest, and he fought to push them away. Also pinching his chest was the possibility that a fight could well occur between his father and uncle once they were let up to see him. Joe was simply here to pay his respects. But his father—Frankie knew—he'd blame Joe, blame him for what happened. . . . It was so stupid. Family was family!

At last the hospital doors slid open, and Jenny emerged, beaming, alongside a nurse who carried herself with precision, her all-white uniform pristine. Success!

The cool air felt like the first splash in a river. Air-conditioning! At least Samson had air-conditioning. Frankie wondered for a split second what hospitals in the US were like. Were you allowed in without being asked a thousand questions, or having to fill out a half-dozen forms? Up ahead, a man in a wheelchair sat facing the wall. From behind he looked like Samson, Frankie thought, then crashed right into a garbage can. Down fell his bag. Bandages—three different sizes—and three cans of ginger beer hit the tile. Frankie squatted just as the nurse did, his head barely missing hers.

"You okay?" Her voice was soft, calming.

"Sorry. I just thought that man over there was my father."

She nodded, noting a set of white sheets that hadn't quite fallen out of the bag, the ones Aunt Jenny had told Frankie to bring. "It's good that you brought all this. The hospital is really in a crunch right now." The nurse smiled as she stood. "It's a nice thing that you're doing," she added. Jenny had been right—sheets earned nurse points!

But Joe stepped forward, forhead furrowed with impatience. "We need to talk about my brother."

A flicker of fear crossed the nurse's face. Then it was gone, and she once again was in control. "Yes, well, as I told your sister, the surgeon removed the bullet from his chest, but there were some complications. At first we thought he'd contracted a gram negative infection, but it seems to be a staph infection called MRSA—"

"Come now, nurse, chat English," Joe interrupted.

"Well . . . the bullet wound is infected, badly. And the anti-biotics we have aren't strong enough to treat it—"

Joe slapped the wall. "With so much gunshot in Jamaica, how you no have proper medicine?"

His uncle was just upset. Frankie knew how third-world

Jamaica was in so many technological ways. There just wasn't enough money to get things done. Farmers couldn't even irrigate crops on slopes until Israel gave them the right products.

Aunt Jenny laid a hand on Joe's shoulder as if gentling a big cat. "Nurse, how bad is this infection you're talking about?" she asked soothingly.

The nurse's eyes grew softer. "Well, to keep it simple, we give patients like your brother antibiotics right after surgery, but unfortunately, staph infectionsare a whole different story, and are on the rise here. We need a stronger course of treatment."

Frankie frowned, wondered why the infections were on the rise *here*. There were too many stories about mistakes made in Jamaican hospitals, like nurses injecting patients with the wrong medicine and killing them. Though they might be exaggerations, there was a reason for the saying, "If it doesn't go so, it go close to so." And then the thought occurred to him.

"Is the treatment expensive?" he asked warily.

"Yes, that's what I wanted to talk to you all about." The nurse tugged the hem of her uniform, straightening it out. "I do have to warn you this is going to be quite costly."

"Here it comes." Joe folded his arms, the sleeves of his T-shirt tight with muscle. "The big rip-off. Everything in Jamaica is costly."

Frankie's heart felt like it was ballooning against his breastbone. The nurse had said costly. What did *costly* mean? He repeated his aunt's question. "How bad is the infection?"

The nurse's eyes went soft again. "Let's just say he needs the treatment to survive."

Frankie's chest grew tighter. His father didn't have a job, never mind savings. "How much is the treatment?" he asked flat out.

"I don't have an exact amount—there would be some savings if a generic version is available, but we need a drug called Linezolid, and since it's relatively new, it's very costly."

"Can you give an estimate, though?" Frankie urged.

The nurse gripped her left forearm. "First, let me say the Linezolid *should* work, but I have to be honest—he may need other medicines. Antimicrobial resistance has become a real problem."

"Anti—what?" Joe flipped his wrist as if shaking dice in a can.

Frankie turned to his uncle but kept an eye on the nurse to make sure he was saying the right thing. "Means antibiotics aren't working like they used to."

The nurse nodded, looking impressed. "Exactly. And given the severity of the infection, your father should get a twenty-seven-day course."

"How much are we talking about, money-wise?" Joe demanded.

The nurse looked uneasily at Joe. "Figure it will be in the fifteen-thousand-dollar range before it's all said and done. We don't have the meds here, so we'll have to send for it from the US."

Fifteen thousand? That was pretty cheap. Then Frankie blanched. Oh no! If it was coming from the US, she might have meant the US dollar, not the Jamaican dollar, which was worth a *lot* less. Frankie could feel the blood pumping in the veins of his neck. Shit, shit, shit, shit. "That JA or US, miss?" he forced himself to ask. *Oh please, oh please, say JA.*

Another glance at Joe, and then she told him, "Oh, that's US. Like I said, we don't have those antibiotics here at the moment."

Frankie had stopped listening after she said *US*, feeling limp as a willow branch. He could have been blown over by a breeze.

"Lawd God, that's a whole heap of money!" Jenny exclaimed, turning to Joe. "That's . . . that's . . . more than two million JA!"

Joe gathered his dreads, pulled them back. "Don't look at me."

But Frankie did—he looked from his uncle to his aunt to his uncle again. Jenny was glaring at Joe. Joe had the cash, but Frankie already knew he wasn't going to part with it—not for Samson. "Why so much?" Frankie asked the nurse.

"It's not just the Linezolid, it's ongoing daily blood tests, IVs, the cost of being in the hospital, fees, and so much more, to be quite honest." The nurse bit at her lower lip. "I want to be clear about this: we don't have much time here."

Frankie fought to keep his voice steady. "How long do we have?"

"The next twenty-four hours—"

"Yes, yes," Joe interrupted. "It's done. Order the medicine."

His uncle was actually offering to pay? Frankie fought the urge to shout for joy. But he didn't. That would piss off Joe big-time.

The nurse clasped her hands. Frankie couldn't help wonder

what it felt like, having to give that kind of news, especially to people who *couldn't* pay. "Okay then, I'll let the doctor know. And you may go up to the third floor and see him for a few minutes. Come with me."

Inside the double-wide elevator, his aunt and uncle stared forward at the doors, neither saying a word. But Frankie felt all kinds of jittery. He pressed the button about eleven times. He longed to see his father—he was scared to see his father.

The elevator abruptly jerked twice, as if it was about to fall back to the bottom; Frankie planted a hand against the wall for balance. It jerked one more time, and then the doors parted. The smell of stale urine mixed with a pungent ammonia that slapped Frankie square. He needed to hack and spit, but where? The nurse led them through a large open room, navigating the checkerboard of beds until she stopped at one, several feet from the others. Frankie gulped. His father. He was so pale. Beneath the threadbare white sheet that cloaked him, a tube emptied into a bag the size of a water bottle clipped to the side of the bed rail, the fluid inside dark amber. Samson's veined hands were folded over his stomach.

"Daddy."

Samson jerked his head in Frankie's direction, then extended his hand. "Frankie."

Frankie took it eagerly, blinking hard as he felt the lack of heft, the infirmity of the grip. When he let go, Jenny brushed by him and ran her hand along the side of Samson's cheek. "Me never been so happy to see your big old ugly face," she said, pulling her hand away at last.

Samson gave a half smile.

Joe kept his distance but called out, "What you saying, Samson?"

His father nodded at Joe, but there was an instant of coldness in his eyes. The same look that'd been on his face when he had come toward Frankie at the party. He'd felt shame when his father showed up at the party—*now he really felt ashamed.* And he still needed to spit. He cleared his throat and remembered what he'd brought—seeing his favorite drink would make Samson smile! He dug inside the bag, found a can of ginger beer, and held it up. Excited now, Frankie grabbed a bag of water crackers and a star apple and held those up too.

Samson let out a short grunt. "That must cost a whole heap of money. Me must be in bad shape?"

Jenny flicked a hand as if the comment were a fly to shoo away. "You going to come back strong." She was shifting from leg to leg, as if a slow song were playing and only she heard it.

"How you feeling, Dad?" Frankie asked.

"Not the worst I ever felt," he answered. Frankie knew exactly what he meant: nothing compared to losing Ma.

Joe stepped forward at last. "Them tell you about your condition?"

They stared each other down as if they were in elementary school, waiting to see who would blink first.

"Them say a whole lot of t'ing," Samson said at last. "Is morning, noon, and night them come around and chat this and that. Draw blood, pills, all kind of t'ings."

Frankie leaned against the bed rail—it was cold. Was his dad cold? "The nurse told us you have an infection, and you need a special treatment. Antibiotics."

Joe raised an eyebrow. "Expensive, antibiotics. How you going to pay for them?"

What?! But—but Joe had just . . . Joe had said . . . what the hell? Frankie looked to Jenny. She rolled her eyes. Then he got it—Joe was messing with older brother.

Samson shook his head. "Me don't need no treatment."

Jenny took Samson's hand, rubbed it. "How you going to get better, then?"

"Me will be fine." Samson pulled his hand away. "Me don't need them medicine."

Frankie glanced at his aunt worriedly. "But the nurse says . . . she says it's critical."

"Yes, she did, Samson." Jenny's voice went young, maybe from when they were little.

"You wouldn't need it if you was quicker on your feet," Joe said, shifting his shoulders like a boxer. "You coulda dodged them shots."

"Oh, it's my fault?" Samson struggled to lift his head. "Yes, thank you for the bullet. It was a nice party prize me get."

Jenny cocked her head. "Samson—come on—Joe didn't—" Joe slapped his hand flat against his own chest, interrupting. "You're blaming *me*?"

Straining, Samson at last raised his head off the pillow. "Is you them come for, not me."

Joe nodded quick quick, but not in agreement, his dreads

vibrating like strings on an instrument. Frankie turned to his father. "Dad, Uncle Joe never wanted this for you!"

"Me no care." Samson slowly sounded out each word that came next. "Me not taking *his money.*"

Joe stepped forward. "Dirty money! Me work hard fi my money, you hear me?"

Jenny laid one hand on Samson's forearm, held the other out to stop Joe. "Wait, wait. You saying you *will* take the treatment, but *you don't want your brother to pay fi it*?"

"Exactly that."

"So, you prefer you dead, then?" Joe asked.

"Mi no 'fraid fi dead."

Joe threw his arms in the air in frustration. "Forget it, then! Me wouldn't pay a single penny fi help you. You can die for all I care. And that is final."

"Okay by me."

Frankie's head was about to explode. "Daddy, you don't mean that!"

"Mean it?" Samson's voice was growing weak. "Me mean it from my heart." He lay back down, folded his hands on his stomach, fronting calm before yawning. "Me well tired. Thanks for coming." He motioned slightly toward the bag. "And thanks for all the t'ings."

Joe spun on his heel and stalked out of the ward.

Jenny leaned over, kissed Samson's forehead. "We talk soon." She shot a look at Frankie, then followed Joe.

But Frankie wasn't going anywhere. He had to talk sense into his father. "Dad—"

Samson pursed his lips. "No."

The shape of the man on the bed barely resembled anything of Samson, except for one thing, the billy-goat-stubborn mentality. Samson would *never* let his brother pay for his treatment. Frankie also knew too well that his father, a man who thought the moon landing was faked, who watched as medicines—treatments—failed to cure his wife, might actually try to go without antibiotics. He could fully imagine him seeking a cure in a mixture of bush tea and willpower. Especially if he found out how costly the medicine was. Frankie was going to make sure he never found out. He could see that Aunt Jenny was waiting for him by the open elevator doors. "You coming?" she called.

"No, you go ahead. I'll catch the bus back home," he said. "I have to do something at school." When Frankie turned back around, his father was asleep. He watched him for a long time. His father seemed like he wasn't moving! Frankie leaned in close, put a finger under Samson's nose, and felt the faint exhale. *Thank you, God! Thank you.* He vowed to do everything he could to keep that breath coming.

Ten

frankie was pumped. He had an idea, a long-shot idea, but if it worked, he might be able to pay for his father's treatment. He made a beeline for the school. After he updated Mrs. Gordon on his father's condition, she expressed her sympathy, but then every other sentence out of her mouth was about the scholarship. That and more warnings about what to look out for, as campus life in America would be different from high school in Jamaica—it was all on him to advocate for himself. She'd popped over to her bookcase to pull out books on stress so many times that Frankie was sure she was going to wear out her shoes. She was lit!

"Thank you. This is all really helpful," he said, then paused, getting ready to address the real reason for his visit. "Can I use your phone? I want to call the university and check on my scholarship." He swallowed his nerves, hoping she wouldn't ask why. There was no way he could tell her what he really wanted to do—she'd never let him make the call.

Sure enough, she looked instantly concerned. "Oh, is there a problem?"

"I just need to verify a few things about the money, bank stuff." Winston always told him the toughest lies to see through were the ones mixed with truth. He surprised Frankie like that, saying wise stuff that made Frankie wish he would get his act together, go back to school, get a leg up, but—Winston.

Mrs. Gordon nodded, convinced. "Yes, of course. Be sure to dial a one first." She smiled that proud smile at him and left the room.

Frankie cracked his neck side to side, then locked the door. He toggled the mouse on her computer. There was a page open to gunshot injuries. Huh. She really *was* concerned. And, yeah, proud of his scholarship. It truly sucked that he was going to have to let her down. Clicking to a new page, he looked up the phone number. Then, before he chickened out, he picked up the phone and dialed. When the man who answered said, "University of Arizona," Frankie had to admit an excited chill raced through him, but no—he had to do this.

"Hello. I just found out that I have received a scholarship to the university, and I'd like to ask a few questions."

The man put him on hold. The woman who answered next sounded all chirpy, like she didn't have a care in the world. Like he might have a chance to figure things out with her.

"Hi—I've just found out I've received an engineering scholarship, and I'd, uh, like to ask some questions about the financial part of it."

"Oh, congratulations!" the woman cooed. "Those scholarships are hard to come by, I know." She paused. It sounded like she was typing on a keyboard. "What's your name?"

"Frankie Green."

"Yes, I see you're on the list to potentially receive one." More keys clicked. "Oh, you're from Jamaica. We went on a cruise there a few years ago. What a beautiful place. Oh, where were we exactly? There was a big waterfall there—was it Ochos Rios?"

"Ocho Rios." Tourists always added an *s*. "I've never been, but I hear it's nice."

"Oh, you have to go. And the people are just so nice."

Of course they were nice; the people she'd met at the resort and waterfalls *had* to be nice. It was their job. But he wasn't going to say that. He needed to keep her in a good mood, loving Jamaica. He needed to get money. His father needed that treatment.

She gave a tinkly laugh. "I'm going on and on, and you have a question about your scholarship, don't you?"

"Yes, thank you. I'd like to know if I could take some money out of the account yet." He wasn't sure if he was asking the right question, but at least the lady was nice.

Except now her tone shifted. "Oh no, dear, we can't do that. The money is in escrow until you arrive."

"Can you make an exception?" He thought wildly for an excuse, a reason for the money. "I'd like to buy my plane ticket," he came up with. "I can get a good price on it right now. I was online, checking."

"Bless your heart. Aren't you sweet? But don't you worry, we'll take care of all that for you."

"Ah, there are a few other things I need to get before coming over there, though. Can I get money for that?"

"All the early expenses, registration and dorm fees, and such will be taken care of once you get here, sweetheart. Honestly, you don't have to worry about a thing."

Dorm? He jumped on that. "Oh, suppose I want to live off-campus? Can I get money for that, rent and things?"

"You can—"

His heart jumped while she paused. A pause didn't mean no!

She continued, "—but you'd have to fill out a few forms and get us a copy of the lease."

He could make that work. He wasn't any forger, but his uncle might know people. This was his father's life—

Then she clucked her tongue. "Ah, but I see here that that doesn't apply to international students. You have to live in the dorms for the first semester before you can apply to live off-campus. I'm so sorry. But our dorms are lovely—"

Frankie tuned her out. He had no more words, no more lies. Just a weight like a truck on his chest. In Jamaica, forms were busywork, not always policy. You could bargain for things in Jamaica. His world was so simple, he realized. He felt his chance slipping away. The only thing left was to be honest. His grip on the phone felt slick as he pressed the receiver hard to his ear. "Miss, my father is sick. He's in the hospital. I need to use some of the money to help him. I don't know what else to do."

"Oh, so you didn't need any plane ticket or anything?" Now her tone was sharp, the warmth gone.

Frankie swallowed and shook his head. It was all going the wrong way. "I . . . I do need a plane ticket! I didn't know you get that for me! But my dad, miss, he's in trouble. He needs medicine. I need to help him."

"Look, Mr. Green, I'm very sorry about your father, but there's nothing I can do. That scholarship is for your education. We can't authorize using it for any other purpose."

Frankie slapped his palm on the table. "But he needs help!"

"Again, I'm sorry about your father, but there's nothing we can do. Is there anything else I can assist you with?"

"No. Thank you."

"Well, good luck. You have a good day." She hung up.

Frankie sat for a long time listening to the dial tone, the dial tone that seemed to be saying, *No help, no help, no help.* It was stupid to have even tried. Who could understand a problem like this?

Out the window, busy students strolled across the mall, passing the flagpole where the flag of his country hung limp, no wind to lift it.

He finally hung up and grabbed a handful of mints from the candy dish, dinner for the long bus ride home.

Home. Without his father. Damn it. DAMN IT.

He had to go see his uncle.

Eleven

the late afternoon sky had turned a hellish shade of amber by the time Frankie got off the bus at the foot of the mountain. The heat bore down as he trudged up the road, and by the time he reached Joe's camp, dusk had turned the trees into silhouettes. Unseen stones clicked beneath his soles. He remembered how his sandals used to slide on stones like these when he was a young boy. The buses didn't go all the way to the mountain back then, so he and his parents had to do a lot of walking. Once, returning from a party in Kingston where the old folks had told duppy stories, Frankie imagined the dark wood they walked by filled with them—red-eyed creatures roaming the earth, hungry for fresh human meat. He remembered leaves rattling, leaning into his father, needing to know he was there. Samson had reached down and taken his hand. With his father's hand clasped around his own, the duppy stories seemed less real.

The sound of cracking tree branches brought Frankie back to the reality of this night, without his father. He balled his fists as a figure stepped out of the dark.

"Wha gwan, Frankie?" It was Cricket, his nine-millimeter handgun pointed at the ground.

Frankie should have expected a lookout. "Me want fi see my uncle," he said, the patois slipping out like it always did when he was angry or scared.

"Him in him cabin."

Frankie felt exactly like he did before taking an exam—no matter how well prepared he was, his stomach teemed with butterflies, and he would wish for focus and luck. He would need both when dealing with his uncle. Frankie pulled the last of the mints from his pocket, handed one to Cricket, and walked on, chewing, thinking, thinking on how best to approach his uncle with the proposal.

At the bend, Blow Up and his Rasta girlfriend were in an intense conversation at the table. Frankie waved and crossed the circular driveway up to Joe's house, yellow and green, in the middle of the camp. He knocked and waited.

Joe, in only jeans, no shirt, edged the door ajar, and seeing it was Frankie, turned to someone in the room and said, "Wait fi me in the bedroom."

"For how long?" a woman answered.

"Soon come." He gestured to whoever it was, his dreads swaying. "No, don't take the herb with you."

Frankie didn't recognize the voice, but figured she must be a Rastafarian. Joe always said he only dated women from the tribe, and many women from the tribe. Frankie shifted uncomfortably until he heard the click of an interior door shutting. Then Joe opened the front door the rest of the way and waved Frankie in.

The musky scent of ganja was everywhere. Joe took a seat at a wooden bench in the corner, pointed to a stool topped with a puffy blue pillow for Frankie.

"Sorry to bother you, Uncle," Frankie started.

"No worry yourself." A fat spliff burned on an ashtray. Joe's eyes widened as if just remembering it was there. "You want a lift?" He gestured to the spliff.

"No, thank you, Uncle." Frankie wondered if he should talk about family business while a stranger sat in the other room; the walls weren't very thick.

"No problem." Joe took a hit off the joint. "So, wha gwan, Nephew?"

Frankie pressed his hands against his legs to keep them from shaking. "Uncle, I need your help with Daddy."

"Oh." Joe put the spliff back down.

"He's so ill with fever—he didn't mean what he said . . . about the bullet." Frankie waited for some sort of sign, but his uncle didn't offer any. "I know it's a lot of money." Frankie paused again, expecting Joe to say . . . anything. This was his brother's *life* at stake. "Well, so I was wondering, I was hoping you'd reconsider. At least . . . at least . . . let us borrow it? I'll pay you back, you know I would, after I get a job and everything.

Every penny!" Damn. He sounded desperate. His uncle *hated* desperate. But he *was* desperate.

Joe pressed at the planks with his bare feet, his dreads spilling over his face. After a moment, he nodded, then clapped once, making some sort of decision. Then, to Frankie's surprise, he abruptly left the room.

Frankie's mind churned in the silence. Except for sounding a little, yeah, desperate, all in all, he hoped that his uncle had been persuaded. He didn't want to have to make an emotional appeal; Joe had no use for sentimentality. Frankie didn't either, but for his father, he would have begged on the floor, *cried*, if he thought it would have worked. And he still would, as a last resort. He was *not* going to lose his father, not after Ma—not if something could be done. Now he could hear his uncle and the woman talking low, but he couldn't make out what they were saying.

The bedroom door swung back open. Joe had put on a yellow mesh marina tank top. He closed the door with one hand. In the other he held a thick stack of money—green US currency.

Frankie fought back a smile while trying not to gape. He fought back a whoop! Despite what his father said, Joe cared. He knew it!

Joe laid the money on the table in front of Frankie.

"Uncle, I don't know what to say." US dollars, two inches thick. Frankie was almost scared to touch it. Yet he just wanted to grab it and run all the hell the way to the hospital before Joe changed his mind.

Joe ran his hand under the bench. He found what he was

looking for and pulled out a handgun. Laid it on top of the cash.

Frankie stared. A Glock compact. There were scratches on the barrel and brown duct tape on the handle. A feeling of utter dread crept up his chest.

This was the price of the money.

This was meant to be his.

Frankie looked up at Joe. No . . . no—

"Me not a bank. Me don't give loans." Joe swung a lock out of his face. "You want to get him the treatment, you come work for me."

What? Was he crazy? Frankie opened his mouth, then shut it, weighed his words, decided labeling his uncle's actions as insane would not be a good move. "But Uncle, I can't do that" was what he said instead.

"You want the money or not?"

Frankie stared at the cash. How much was there? He had no idea. It was more than he'd ever seen in real life, for sure. He met Joe's eyes.

Joe's lips tightened. "It's the only way."

Frankie's jaw began to tremble. He knew that tone. It was clear that there was no bargaining. But—but—this . . . He pictured his scholarship letter. He could see every word, the crimson insignia. Frankie reached for the gun, his fingers feeling so cold. His father complained of cold hands sometimes, claimed he must be getting old. Frankie wanted his father to grow old.

Frankie put the gun on the table, then picked up the cash. The bundle was heavier than he'd expected; the bills felt like the paper the scholarship letter was written on. Both were worth a lot, but—now Frankie lifted his chin, defiant. His father's life was worth more. Samson would kill him for doing this. But at least he'd be alive to do it.

"Take the gun." His first order from his new boss.

Frankie hesitated. Joe's eyes were icy. So Frankie reached out his right hand, fingered the cold steel. He shoved the Glock into his pocket, then wedged the cash into the other. He was nearly out the door when his uncle called after him. "The job is forever, Frankie. People don't leave my posse, not alive."

Frankie turned the door handle and paused. The irony of walking through the door wasn't lost on him. He was walking into a new life. Just not one he'd ever imagined for himself.

"You understand me?"

Frankie kept hold of the handle. He nodded, a final signature for his life.

Twelve

the night had worn on and on—sleepless torture as Frankie thought about giving up the scholarship, thought about Joe's deal and what that meant, fought against visions of Samson in that hospital bed, his skin yellow, his face gaunt—a season of suffering upon him. Frankie couldn't remember his father ever being sick a day in his life. Every time he felt a cold coming on, he'd just boil cerasee tea, gulp it down, and the cold would disappear. If he *was* sick, he never showed it; he never stayed in bed, and never complained.

Giving up, Frankie rose from the couch. He'd considered sleeping in Samson's room. The bed was more comfortable, no springs sticking out. But that felt like bad luck, some sort of signal that his father was going to die. So he had slept on the ragged couch like always; tried to sleep, at least. But he had borrowed his father's better pillow.

Now, putting it back, plumping it up the way he used to see his mother do, he gazed at the empty bed. He ached to see Samson rise from it again fully healed. He closed the door and went to make some ginger tea. He glanced at the water bucket. Turned out that with his father not there, the water lasted twice as long. Frankie would make the journey twice a day, if only . . . Then he squatted over the tin pail and yanked the dirty dish towel off of it, hoping the gun and his worries might have disappeared. But they hadn't. The Glock was right where he'd hidden it last night, and he was still in Joe's posse.

He lifted the gun from the bucket.

He never thought he'd own one, a gun. He pulled away the towel and lifted the gun out from the bucket. Removing the magazine next, he slid back the slide to peer in the chamber, angling it so the sunlight would illuminate the interior. There were scratches inside, and residue. He wondered who had used it before him, and what—or who—it had been fired at. He didn't want the damn gun, or the responsibility of it. The idea of shooting someone terrified him—it was the worst thing about joining a posse.

He heard voices from outside, then a single sharp knock on the door. He practically threw the gun back into the bucket, replacing the towel before opening the door. Aunt Jenny stormed in, followed by Joe, who was chewing on an ice-cream stick.

"Franklyn, tell me your uncle is lying!"

At first Frankie thought she was talking about his father, but judging by the fury on her face, she was talking about him joining the posse.

"Lawd Jesus, you don't want your scholarship no more?"

Frankie ran his hand over his hair, front to back, buying time to make sure he didn't say the wrong thing. "Daddy has to have the treatment."

Jenny swung around, glared at Joe. "You is a wicked man."

Joe bit down on the stick. "Wicked?" He removed the stick. "I am the angel on Frankie's shoulder. I am the one saving his father. You think that man would lift a finger to save *me*?" He grunted. "Him is embarrassed to even look at me."

Jenny crossed her arms. "Samson is your *brother*."

"Enough chatting. Is me run this posse. Not you."

Aunt Jenny coughed the way some kids at school did when they thought someone was talking bullshit.

Joe pointed the ice-cream stick at Frankie, his face fierce. "You took the money and joined the posse. If you don't want the money, you can give it back and back out now."

The days and nights he had given to his studies. The parties missed, the friends he'd avoided in order to achieve the highest grades he could. Then he'd allowed himself one party . . . *one* . . . and . . . Of course he wanted that scholarship. But there was no other option. "I want it. The money."

Jenny threw her hands in the air. "What a fuckery! Joe, you can't do this thing."

"It's done."

She spat at her brother. "A curse on your head, Joe." And she stormed out of the house, the door slamming behind her.

She was so fearless. Frankie felt instant shame for not standing up for himself more. But how brave could he afford to be right now?

"We will jump you in this weekend, eh?" Joe's words were like a finger jabbing at Frankie's chest. He was going to be initiated into the posse—this weekend? His jaw began to quiver.

Joe went to the door, beckoned for someone to come forward, then repeated, "This weekend." He went out as Winston walked in, smile crooked, chest out. He looked totally psyched . . . most likely for Frankie. Then he sized Frankie up. "You look like shit, mon."

It was like what Leah had said. "Yeah, I keep getting that." Man, he'd really screwed up with her.

Winston chewed on his lower lip. "Joe wants me to give you the lowdown on the jump-in this weekend."

Frankie thought back to a few weeks ago—Winston's black eye, busted lip, and pronounced limp, how he had muttered something about getting into a fight. Frankie had let it go, but it must have been when *he'd* been jumped in to the posse.

"You ready?" Winston asked. Frankie laughed to himself. Samson's beatings had prepared him for the very last thing he would want for Frankie.

"I think I know how it goes."

Winston fidgeted. "Yeh, mon, but there's some things you should know."

He *should know* that Frankie wanted nothing to do with this. "I'm good."

"Frankie—"

"I *don't* want to talk about it, okay?"

"Fine. We talk about it in a couple of days." Winston brushed the back of his hand across his nose. "Me pick you up Saturday morning."

Winston's persistence was a pain in the ass, but Frankie had to give it to him for trying. Winston always tried.

Pointing his chin at a photo of Samson, Winston asked, "Hey, mon, why your father never joined the posse?"

Frankie didn't have a good answer—he didn't actually know. And he felt stupid for it.

"Whatever. See you Saturday." Winston left.

Frankie pulled open a drawer, lifted up the thin plastic tray of utensils. Joe's money lay underneath it. He couldn't give it back. Damn it. He slammed the drawer shut and went into the yard, pacing. His skin felt on fire, his throat burned as well from forcing down the bile that kept threatening to rise up all night. He had to calm down. He had to calm down. A branch creaked, a dog barked, a mockingbird sang—how appropriate. Still, he focused on the bird. His mother loved birds—would leave the door wide open just to better hear their songs. Then, as if she was standing next to him, he heard it—her voice. But its clear timbre, though as sweet as her rum cakes, carried a note of dread. It was like she was calling him from the grave. So he decided to go.

On the street, Frankie passed a middle-aged man who nodded, saluting him with a machete that had been sharpened so often that the hook at the end was almost completely worn away. In faded rubber boots, and khakis worn by a whole freakin' life working in the woods, the man veered off the road, disappearing into the bush.

Like the old guy in the wheelchair at the hospital, from behind this one could have been Samson.

At the far end of the street, one of the garbage trucks Joe had commissioned turned a corner, its air brakes pumping in preparation for its long descent down the mountain. Frankie passed Mr. Brown's store. Mr. Brown. He had simply gone to a party, and now he was dead. Frankie had liked working there, liked Mr. Brown, but now the boarded-up store looked small, simple and in some way less important, not only because Mr. Brown was dead but because even if he weren't, posse members didn't work as store clerks. He wondered what rules the posse had that he didn't even know about yet. What kinds of things he'd have to do.

Just past the rum bar, a woman he'd seen countless times walked by, posture as fine as a ballerina's, her wicker basket as always perfectly balanced on her head, today chock-full of breadfruit and green bananas. Frankie always waved politely every time he saw her, and every time she waltzed right by as if he didn't exist. Frankie waved regardless. The woman just continued on. He shook his head, wondering why he bothered.

The street was quiet, everyone still uneasy since the shootings. A concrete revetment to his left was smeared with political graffiti. The green markings were pro-JLP: *POVERTY TO PROSPERITY. A PARTY TO TRUS'. JAMROCK NEED LABOUR.* There were also old scribbles in red, the color of the PNP: *PEOPLE POWER. PORTIA IS DI WOMAN WE NEED.*

At last he reached the graveyard. He bowed his head, slouched down against the headstone.

He so clearly remembered the day he'd carried the bucket of freshly mixed concrete there, to make this very grave top. He had tried not to spill the mixture, using the same focus he used when carrying water from the standpipe. His father had said, "Don't cry now. It's time to be a man," every time Frankie had so much as blinked. He'd poured the concrete while Samson stood, ready with the shovel, to create the most perfect slab in all of Jamaica for her.

What would Ma say to him now about joining Joe's posse?

Closing his eyes, he imagined her duppy form, sitting right there next to him.

Franklyn, you look like you could eat. Have you been eating? I know you feel like you have to give up your scholarship and work in the posse. But it's not worth it, baby. I don't want to see you so soon. Though I miss you terribly.

He would have told her that he missed her also. He would have asked her the question that had been eating at him for the last three years. *Why did you and Daddy wait so long to tell me you had cancer? And how could I not have seen that you were sick? I wish I'd spent more time with you before you died. I could have, if you'd only told me.*

It was yet another thing he couldn't fix, another blade piercing his soul. He glanced to where he and his father had eaten lunch the other day. Samson should have told him Ma was sick. He had left Frankie no extra time to spend with his mother before she was gone. How do you forgive that?

He leaned forward and kissed the headstone. He knew what Ma would say. But she was a mother, not a son.

Thirteen

an hour later, Frankie boarded a bus to the hospital. He didn't want to ride his bike into Kingston with all that cash in his pocket. Instead, he decied to "small up" himself and squeeze into a seat next to an old woman who had a box of chicks in her lap. As the bus rolled off, it filled with the stifling smell of gasoline. Frankie nodded at the woman, leaned across, and cracked open the window. He sat back and sucked in the fresh air.

The bus passed a woman in a ratty apron waving a bunch of yams, her tiny roadside shack made of broad tree branches and a few sheets of rusted corrugated steel. Mesh bags filled with more yams hung from the roof behind her. Farther along, a bowlegged man balanced a bundle of sugarcane on his head, the mountain rising up behind him, its slope thick with bottle-brush trees. A scrawny dog ran alongside, barking when the bus's gears ground as it edged around a blind corner on the narrow road. Two shirtless boys in torn khakis stared as if seeing a bus for the first time. Behind them a concrete house sat unfinished, metal rods sticking out of its walls. Several others just like it followed, dotting the landscape. It was the very opposite of how he imagined America.

America? Shit. He'd never get there. He slumped back, wished for the millionth time that his father hadn't come to the party. Why had he even come? To confront Joe was why. To tell him to stay away from *him*, Frankie. That was why.

He knew something else. No way would Samson take Joe's money. Frankie pressed his palms against his eyes. Everything he'd done would be for nothing if Samson didn't accept the money. The only way out of *that* would be to lie about where the money came from, because Samson being Samson, he would ask. The thought of lying left a foul taste in Frankie's mouth. But the medicine might be sitting at the hospital right this very minute, just waiting for Frankie to pay. The gas fumes were not helping him think. In America, probably the buses were—oh. The scholarship! He could tell Samson that the money was from the scholarship! His father wouldn't find out until he was better, and that was all that mattered. Plus, there wasn't any other believable way for Frankie to get that kind of capital.

As they neared Kingston, the road widened; they were getting close to the rich part of the city now. The bus barreled past groves of fat banana trees, over railroad tracks overgrown with crabgrass, onto streets sporting sidewalks and stoplights. SUVs lined the streets here. Pastel-painted steel fences guarded three-room peach-colored concrete houses, all stacked close to each other.

Next stop was the hospital. As Frankie walked from the bus stop, he kept one hand over the pocket fat with Joe's bills. He couldn't stop glancing over his shoulder; he felt like all of Jamaica had suddenly gained X-ray vision and could see through the cloth of his pants to the wad of cash. He wanted to count it again. No. He'd done it twice last night. Sixteen thousand US dollars—more than two million Jamaican dollars! He pressed his hand more tightly.

A crowd of people stood outside the front doors. Apparently no one was being let in; no one knew why. It could be a gas leak, was the gossip, or staffing problem, or maybe a dangerous felon had to be moved in secret. Mr. Brown had once said that Jamaican people told so many conspiracy theories they should work for the CIA.

Frankie sat between two women fanning themselves with folded newspapers, hoping he looked as inconspicuous as possible. He did math in his head, imagining all the things he could do with two million Jamaican dollars . . . trying not to think of every minute going by when his father was not getting the medication.

When the sliding electric doors finally parted two hours later, the crowd closed in. The same nurse Frankie had met the first time came out, to his immense relief. He hopped up, praying it wasn't too late. Imagine if it was too late?

"Good afternoon, everyone," she said in her slightly British tone. Jamaicans who chatted like that always had good jobs, Frankie had noticed. "First, I must apologize for the long wait. And I do wish I had better news for you." A chorus of groans sounded out. "The elevators are broken. Unfortunately, we have not been able to repair them. I am truly sorry. The repairman has sent for a part in Montego Bay; it should be here tomorrow."

"Make we take di stairs, then!" a man yelled, both hands flailing in frustration.

"Unfortunately, there's an insurance issue with admitting so many visitors through the stairs. And we need to keep them clear for the doctors and nurses. But we are confident the problem will be rectified tomorrow."

"Only in Jamaica!"

"Is the JLP's fault!"

"No talk about JLP! It's PNP that mash up Jamaica."

"Rahtid! Is all day me wait, you know!"

"Lawd God, what a trial."

"Me don't want to hear no fuckery about no elevator!" another man yelled. The woman beside him slapped his arm.

The money in Frankie's pocket was searing through his leg. That was what it felt like, at any rate. He *had* to get it to the nurse; his father *had* to get that medicine. Twenty-four hours, she'd said!

The nurse had raised her hands, palms flat, a call for patience. "I'm very sorry, but we have to do what's safest for our patients. There will be no visiting hours today."

While the grumbling increased, many turned to leave. But

Frankie needed to see his dad today, to talk to him about the treatment, so he sidled over to the nurse. He knew from his uncle that most of the time, no matter how buttoned up someone was, money talked. "Miss, can I talk to you?"

She looked on the verge of repeating that there would be no visiting hours today. But before she could, Frankie, his back to the crowd, eased out an American ten-dollar bill of his own money, scared to deal with the thicker stack of notes. Too many people around. Raising one eyebrow, he gave her a clear offer of a bribe. "I need to see my father today," he whispered.

Her eyes went from the bill to the crowd. "Please come back tomorrow. Again, I am sorry. The elevators should be fixed by then." Then she pivoted to Frankie. "You, come back in ten minutes."

Frankie swore he was levitating; gravity didn't have as strong a hold of him at the moment. He fought the urge to look around to see if anyone had noticed the power he had just wielded. Ten minutes later, he strode up to the nurse, who was indeed waiting for him, to pay for his father's life, to be the adult, large and in charge. He slipped her the American ten. "So, I can pay for the treatment now?" he asked.

She nodded yes, adding, "It's crucial that we order the antibiotics now."

"Order?" A puke-like sensation shot through his stomach.

"Yes. I told you yesterday, we don't have those kinds of antibiotics on hand."

"But . . . you said twenty-four hours—" He gaped. "He had to have them, you said!"

"We had to *order* them in twenty-four hours." The nurse tilted her head. "Sorry if that wasn't clear. But no worries, we are ordering them in time."

No worries? She had no idea what the hell he'd had to do to get this money. What the fuck? He could have used the time to try and figure some other way to get cash. No worries? Shit. It was all worries with this hospital: no sheets, suspect surgeons, broken elevators, and nurses who weren't fucking specific. He had to be more on guard when it came to treating his father.

"When will it come? The treatment?"

"A couple days with a rush order. Our supplier in the US is pretty reliable."

Pretty reliable. He forced himself to stay calm by thinking about what might have happened to his father if he hadn't gotten the money from his uncle. "How is he?"

She exhaled. "He's a strong man, your father. We have a lot of hope. Linezolid has been proven to work on highly resistant infections."

A biology teacher had told Frankie's class about the outbreak of antibiotic-resistant diseases. She had said it was a double whammy. Too many antibiotics were being used all over the world, *and* they weren't being used properly—in a lot of cases, patients weren't taking the full dosages: they stopped when they felt better, leaving themselves vulnerable, allowing the bugs to mutate, get stronger. "But how is he *now*?" Frankie pressed.

"His temperature is still fluctuating, but he's stable."

That didn't sound as promising as he'd like.

o o o

Inside the lobby, skin dotted with goose bumps, Frankie looked for the sign for the administrative office, as the nurse had instructed. His hand instinctively went to his fat pocket. His scholarship dream had to die so his father could live. He went into the office, ready to pay, ready as he'd ever be.

Fourteen

this time, the fluid flowing through the tube was brown. It was the first thing Frankie noticed as he entered his father's room. Brown couldn't be good. Samson's hands didn't even flitter as Frankie came in.

He took a seat, the cheap plastic chair creaking beneath him. Pressing against his leg was the remainder of the cash: a thousand US. Bumboclot, so much money, how do most people get by when shit happens? Samson's eyes fluttered open, and he smiled at seeing Frankie.

As he and his father made chitchat, Samson sounded weaker, raspier. He looked thinner, too—his once muscular neck scrawny. Frankie scratched at his own neck, suddenly so itchy it felt like lice had latched onto his entire body. He itched and scratched, shifted some more. They were running out of small talk. Yes, he had watered Ma's aloe and croton plants, eaten some food, checked the security device. Now it was time for the big talk—to tell Samson about the money.

So, "I have something to tell you," Frankie said at last.

His father turned toward him and the hospital gown moved, revealing a rash on his chest, red like a cherry. "Tell me."

Frankie scraped the toe of his shoe against the off-white tile but looked directly at his father. Lies worked better when you looked the person in the eye, but the trick was not to stare for too long. More Winston wisdom. "I talked to the people in America about my scholarship—I told them what happened to you. They were really nice, really understanding. They said they'll give me the money for your treatment as a loan against the scholarship."

Samson's eyes went wide, panicked almost. "You give it up?"

"No! They said I can use the scholarship next year. But when I graduate, I have to work for them in order to pay back the money." For some crazy reason, the Hoover Dam came to mind. He'd never get to see it.

"Work for them?"

"Yes." Frankie didn't want to give too many details; they'd be hard to remember.

Samson frowned, worry lines etching in his forehead. "How long you have to work for them?"

Frankie nearly glanced away, then remembered Winston's words. He forced himself to look back. "Till I pay it back." Lying to his father sat on his tongue like nausea.

"Yes, but how long is that?"

Frankie hadn't expected this level of interest. "They didn't say, but it can't be more than a year."

Samson took slow, deep breaths, his skin more ashen now than when Frankie had first walked in. "A year? How you going to live with no money? You stay on the campus?"

His father's imagination was his gift, and Frankie's curse. He responded so quickly, he slurred. "Yes, that's what they said. I get room and board till I pay them back. Plus, salaries are much higher in America. Some graduates *start* jobs at forty thousand or fifty thousand US dollars! So even if they didn't, I'd be okay."

Samson muttered to himself, and Frankie willed himself to sit still, stay calm.

Finally Samson asked, "You sure about this? Your mother— she would be crushed, mon."

"But Dad, I *am* going. Just a year later. Just a year." Still, an image of his mother bubbled up—how the skin around her shoulder had become hard, dried out like tree bark. How long had the cancer been doing that to her? If he'd only known earlier. Samson should have told him. He *should* have!

Samson sighed. "Well, me will pay it all back to you."

Frankie exhaled and looked over at a wall, a wall so oddly shaped. It split the large room in half, obstructing the view from the nurse's station by the elevator. The nurse at that desk should probably be able to see the entire room at a glance. The wall couldn't be load-bearing. Ripping it out would be easy, and realigning the beds into orderly rows wouldn't be difficult either. Then nurses would have a clear sight line of all the patients. A simple fix, but one he suspected would never be made.

And the fix *he* could now make would never be simple. He couldn't bear it—his father—in his eyes, was that pride? Pride in Frankie finding a solution? If he only fucking knew. "I have to go now. I have class," he told his dad. The lies were coming easier and easier.

"Okay, take care of yourself."

Frankie pulled Samson's sheet to his chin and left. What would he have done if his father wasn't on board, go downstairs and ask for the money back? What a fucking trip; so many hoops to jump through just to do what was necessary. He wished he *were* going to class; schoolwork was so much easier.

He jabbed the elevator button, heard a patient groan in pain. There was much more pain awaiting him. The initiation. It was . . . only days away.

Fifteen

he Saturday morning sun played hide-and-seek among the thick knots of branches, cloaking Frankie and Winston by turns in darkness and light. They'd traveled this path many times before, hunting for treasures of naseberries, pomegranates, pears, and mangoes. Soon they'd be hanging out more often, like when they were kids. That was at least something. But the thought of the major beatdown loomed heavy. Frankie tried to summon the grit he'd felt the last time Samson had laid into him. But the feeling wasn't there. This was going to hurt like hell. And Winston had told him that he wasn't allowed to fight back!

He skirted a fallen trunk, on the other side of which a stench rose up. It was a dead bird, maggots working away at its neck.

His father's neck . . . had been so skinny, his skin yellowed. Was the fever eating him from inside?

Winston sidestepped the bird. "What your father say 'bout this? Him no love posse business."

For a moment Frankie wondered if the dead bird had made Winston think of his father too, but it was too weird to ask. "I didn't tell him."

Winston's eyes went wide. "Him going to be well angry!"

Frankie shrugged. "No joke. But what choice do I have?" He thought of Winston's question from the other day about why his father didn't join the posse. "Crazy—the one thing my father most wanted was for me to stay away from Joe."

"Well, that didn't work."

"True. I overheard my mother and him arguing once. She told him to stop going on and on about it—said telling me to stay away from Joe would make me want to hang out with him even more."

"Your ma was a smart woman."

Frankie agreed. "Respect."

He held out his fist, which morphed into their special hand-shake: fist bumps, snaps, and crossed elbows.

"This won't be easy, you know?" Winston said, voice now low, worried.

"Guess I won't be entering any beauty contests for a while."

"You ugly already, mon." Winston frowned.

"Not like you."

Winston grinned. "I'll be right there, mon. It's a good posse. Even two Stony Mountain boys are in it now."

"Really? Why?"

"Joe wanted more people over there. The prison is so full up, him afraid that some of the prisoners might come back to Stony Mountain after they're released, set up their own posse. Try to move in on his turf."

Made sense. "How many men does Joe have over there?"

"Four there now, but he has six down in Kingston and five more in Spanish Town." By the pride in his voice, you'd think Winston himself had recruited all those people. "Yeh, mon. The posse is growing."

Frankie wondered who they were. He only knew Joe's posse people on this mountain—good people at heart—well, compared to others, at any rate. At least he'd be a part of something that wasn't anywhere near as bad as the others in Kingston: robbing and fighting over turf all day. That was what Joe had said.

"Ready?" Winston asked. The clearing was just ahead. Frankie squatted, spying something. A leaf of life? It was growing in the shade of a banana tree. He hadn't thought that possible. He picked a small branch to bring to his father; Samson liked to make bush tea out of it. "Yeh, mon. Let's go."

Winston nudged Frankie back a few feet. "Follow me up there. You're not a brother yet."

Frankie swallowed down his irritation. Winston didn't need to do that, he just needed to feel superior. Huh. Maybe the posse was Winston's special place, his special opportunity to grow, like the school in Kingston had been for Frankie? So maybe *that* was why Winston hadn't told Frankie about being in the posse.

As if reading his mind, Winston said, "You'll be okay, you always are." He smacked Frankie's chest with the back of his hand. "It'll be good to have you in the posse, mon. Come."

Frankie had thought they were headed for the camp, but Winston led him higher—three kilometers above Troy, to a plateau covered with rocks that seemed to have exploded from hell.

At the far end was the posse, everyone wearing their game faces. Frankie spotted Aunt Jenny sitting cross-legged on the hood of the black Toyota, a sawed-off shotgun in her lap, and Joe in the passenger seat on his phone. Buck-Buck sat on a boulder, his Glock next to him for company. Blow Up was drying his forehead with a bandanna, careful not to mess up his spiked hair. As Frankie neared, he could make out the nine-millimeter handgun Ramgoat had dangling from his other hand as casually as a shopping bag. Ice Box didn't carry anything—his body was his weapon: foreboding arms, huge round shoulders, and a chest that seemed inflated with air.

Sweat began to trickle down Frankie's forehead, but despite the salty burn dripping into his eye, he didn't move to wipe it. All he wanted was to make it through this without embarrassing himself.

But he couldn't stop himself from glancing back at the path—the way back to Troy. Winston smacked Frankie's upper arm. "Can't go back now. Come, mon. Joe want you to stand by us."

At first Frankie hadn't wanted any special treatment just because he was Joe's nephew . . . but *any* consideration was welcome now that this was real.

"Come, mon," Winston said again. "First meet some of the guys." He sauntered up to the new recruits.

Marshal, really tall and skinny, a dropout from the local high school, an acquaintance, stepped forward and gave Frankie dap.

The next boy—stout, probably a little younger than Frankie, with a low mini-Afro cut—nodded. "Wha gwan? I'm Baxter."

"Frankie," he said, giving him some dap: gripping hands, bumping shoulders.

Greg, he knew a bit better. Teeth jagged, quick-tempered, good fighter. Greg chin-nodded and said, "Respect," with a fist bump and thumb taps. Greg's knuckles were covered with scars.

The next kid Frankie knew well, his girth making Winston look like a model.

"Frankie, wha gwan!" Big Pelton's voice was always at boom level.

Letting go of Big Pelton's paw, Frankie turned to two short, skinny boys, matching white T-shirts hanging off them like sails: must be the Stony Mountain boys.

The first had deep sunken eyes, and the second had ears so pointy that they reminded Frankie of a bat's. Their fist bumps were more like taps, something tentative about them, reminding Frankie of the first-year students at his high school, who didn't know their way around yet. Now *he* was the freshman. But dang, if these little dudes could make it through initiation, so could he.

He was surprised by how glad they all seemed to see him. Still, this was no time to relax.

A car engine whirred nearby, and Buck-Buck and Ice Box

hopped up just as Joe stepped out of the Toyota. All eyes were on the road.

"Must be Bradford coming," Winston announced knowingly.

"Who?" Frankie side-whispered.

Winston squinted. "You don't know anything, mon? Bradford. He's our contact with the PNP. Police sergeant. Him is no joke, mon."

Sure enough, a tricked-out police jeep with oversize tires zipped into the clearing and skidded to a stop in front of Joe, a trail of dust rising.

A burly officer with a big head, bushy eyebrows, and a reddish face burst out of the jeep. Frankie counted three stripes on his shirt. In one motion, the officer leaped up onto a jagged boulder and planted his hands on his hips.

"All you little youths ova' deh!"

"Who him calling a youth?" Winston muttered.

Frankie hated that word too. Condescending as hell. He already disliked this Bradford dude.

"You listening, you damn stupid youths? Take out your cell phones and turn them off. No pictures, no videos, nothing! And don't make me say it again!"

All the newer recruits wrangled flip phones out of their pockets—all identical; must have come from Joe. The older posse members didn't move.

Satisfied, Bradford hopped back down and joined Joe, the two keeping several feet between each other, not even shaking hands. Bradford took up a wide stance. Joe seemed even more chill than usual—maybe for show?

As the two talked in low voices, Frankie suspected he wasn't the only one trying to read their lips. Then Joe pointed toward the new recruits—was he marking him? Bradford nodded. Then, like a stalking beast, he made his way toward Frankie. If he was he trying to intimidate, he was doing it well. As he closed in, Frankie stepped left, Winston jumped to the right, and Bradford passed right between them.

What the heck? Frankie searched faces for a clue. Aunt Jenny could have been the hood ornament. Buck-Buck and Ice Box exchanged a few words and a snicker. Joe's face—expressionless.

Bradford roamed among the recruits, closing in, moving on, closing in again, clearly enjoying the game—a bully, Frankie realized, like Garnett. Frankie felt his shoulders tensing. Guys like that pissed him off, but he knew better than to show it. "Your boss asked me to talk to you." Bradford snorted. "I took one look at you all and told him times must be hard, because every one of you looks like you still wet your bed." He started pumping his fist into the air. "Now, who loves Jamaica?"

What? But Frankie echoed the other new recruits with a timid, "Me."

"I said, who loves Jamaica?" Bradford pumped his fist again.

This time Frankie stayed silent while the others shouted. Sure, he should at least move his lips and fake it, but something felt so wrong about it all—Jamaica—gangs—the police.

"You are about to play a big-time role in supporting the PNP!" Bradford looked over to Joe. Buck-Buck raised his Glock, held it there like his own raised fist, showing his solidarity with Bradford's words.

Wow—a social studies teacher had once told Frankie's class about how Jamaica's political parties had always used gangs to force voters to vote for them. But now it was just on the low. How crazy was it that Frankie was about to be part of this? What the hell was he going to have to do?

Bradford was yammering on. "The JLP will not hesitate to use force. And they want to take control of Jamaica. Of *you*." He brushed past Frankie. "I understand some of their gunmen paid a nasty little visit to this district last week. Well, it's time to show them you won't be intimidated. Elections will be here in three weeks. Until then, you must do what's necessary." Bradford struck a freaking superhero pose. "Sometimes . . . you have to kill to stop the killing."

Frankie dug his teeth into his lips. His dad. Mr. Brown. Everyone else who had been hurt or killed at Joe's party. Frankie didn't like Bradford, but some of what he said made sense. He also knew too well that a policeman in bed with the JLP would be making the same kind of speech to another gang. His brain was in overdrive. It was clear to him now that the People's National Party and the Jamaica Labour Party were the same, both responsible for a lot of deaths. *Their* battle was responsible for putting his father in the hospital, the tubes, needing a treatment—shit, that bag of brown piss. Two political parties, but what numbers in damage? In school, kids had talked about people they'd known who'd gotten shot, even killed, because of election-time politics. Frankie eyeballed Bradford, fury rising. Bradford embodied the pain, embodied the problem, might as well have pulled the trigger that sent the bullet flying into his father.

Now Bradford was telling them that they'd get their assignments from Joe. "Carry them out or you'll hear from me." He turned on his heel, then paused and looked directly at Frankie, somehow sensing Frankie's glare.

With that one look, Frankie felt unmasked. The sergeant's nostrils flared, as if he could smell Frankie's hate for him. But then he kept walking, releasing Frankie like some hypnotist snapping his fingers. He got into the jeep, revved the engine. But instead of heading back down the mountain, the jeep spun around—directly toward Frankie! Holy shit! Greg and Baxter jumped back, out of the way, as did Frankie.

At the last second, Bradford hit the brakes. He narrowed his eyes at Frankie. What was the dude's issue? Frankie's eyes went wide. Mounted on the dash between the driver's seat and the shotgun seat were a laptop and other equipment. Surveillance equipment. Did Joe know about this? Was Bradford using it on the posse? The jeep engine revved once more, and then Bradford drove away. Thank God.

But Frankie's relief was short-lived, because from across the clearing, Aunt Jenny was nodding at him, then started to clap her hands like she was trying to get this party started.

Joe spat out the ice-cream stick he'd been gnawing and beckoned Ice Box and Buck-Buck over as Winston sidled up to Frankie. "You ready?" Frankie was so spooked by Bradford that he'd almost forgotten why he was actually here. "Wake up, mon! Your time is coming." Winston almost sounded . . . eager? "Listen. You can cover up, but remember, don't throw no punch. If you do, you'll get double."

Marshal leaned in. "Buck-Buck is fierce. Speed and Cricket not so bad. You will be lucky if is them you get." He shrugged. "But it might even be Joe."

"No, mon. The big man don't business with initiation," Winston threw out, cocky now. "Is Ice Box you have to look out for. His punch is like a donkey kick. He's well strong."

Frankie could barely nod.

Winston's eyes were all lit up. He *was* enjoying this, the bastard. "Listen, no matter what, you have to stand brave, hear me?"

What the hell did that mean? How brave can you be when you know you're going to get a beatdown and not be able to do anything about it? It was like Frankie's father saying no crying at his mother's funeral.

"You'll get maybe three minutes tops—punched, kicked, slapped, you know. Just hold on."

Winston already savored this world, Frankie could tell. Frankie couldn't remember his friend ever seeming so genuinely confident before. He looked anxiously across the clearing.

Joe gestured for Frankie to come forward, tilting his head as if seeing his nephew for the first time. "It take heart to do this for your father's sake. Respect due. All the same, me can't be nice about this. You overstand?"

Yeah, he understood all right. He understood that Joe totally didn't get that this wasn't what Frankie was about. His uncle *knew* that. Should care about *that*. But he didn't *get* it, and now the deed was done. The money paid. Time to pay the piper. So, "Yes, Uncle," was how he dutifully answered. "I'm ready."

Joe raised an eyebrow. Then, with a nod, he motioned for Ice Box to join them. Joe punched Ice Box's huge arm, leaned in and murmured something to him, like the manager leading the heavyweight into the ring. Ice Box's punch was like a donkey kick, wasn't that what Winston had just told him? Damn.

It wasn't like Frankie hadn't been in a fight before. But they'd all been short affairs, one or two swings, a quick unpolished wrestling move, nothing that remotely approached three minutes of just having to "take it." Sure, Samson had abundantly applied the belt, a telephone wire, and an occasional punch for old-school's sake, but this was going to be a whole other level. Ice Box, at twenty-five, had several inches over Frankie, and fifty more pounds. Frankie glanced uneasily at Winston—the jerk was practically panting, as if gripped by some kind of primeval urge. Asshole. *Okay, let's get this over with.*

Ice Box took two quick steps and a hop toward Frankie and swung his huge right fist. Frankie stood completely still, arms at his sides, and Ice Box slammed Frankie's cheek. The thud reverberated through Frankie's skull and he staggered backward, a laser show of lights playing out behind his eyes.

"Not the head, mon!" Joe bellowed.

Frankie fought his ability to duck and slip punches. He had to stay and take it. A second punch crashed into his chest. Then another. He lost wind for a second; his face was on fire, his legs going toothpick weak. Putting a hand on the ground for balance, Frankie struggled to keep from falling. Lasting one minute already seemed a stretch.

"You a pussy?" Joe shouted at Frankie. "Ice Box, you love the boy or what? Hit him!"

Frankie knew exactly what Joe's intentions were behind the words. He was putting on an act, not showing any favoritism. But did Ice Box know that?

Frankie stepped back, stumbled over a rock, and fell. The new recruits averted their eyes. They knew what was about to happen. It was on their grim faces, their eyes looking everywhere but at him, no one saying a word. Sure enough, Ice Box scooped Frankie up high off the ground like he was weightless, then spun and flung him, like he really *was* nothing. All of Frankie's weight landed on his back. One of the scars his father had made not even a week ago split open, he could feel it. Pain like lightning shot down his left leg—now he couldn't breathe at all.

"Yes, Ice Box!" Buck-Buck was shouting.

"Mash him up, mon!" Blow Up followed up, his fist pumping.

"Get up!" Joe ordered.

Gasping, Frankie staggered back to his feet. Ice Box threw three fast punches. Frankie doubled up. A hook hammered his rib cage and he fell back to the ground, no longer hearing anything, blood pounding in his head. Yet he slowly, dizzily, worked his way up to a standing position. How much longer? Twenty seconds? Two minutes? He would die if it was two more minutes of this. Wobbling, he saw Winston's and Marshal's mouths moving but couldn't hear their words. He turned and saw the blur of a boot speeding toward his gut.

How could something move at the speed of light yet in slow motion, he wondered vaguely, just before the world went dark.

It took a while for Frankie to realize he wasn't standing anymore. Stones dug into his back. Faces gazed down at him. At first he thought he was in Troy, because, well . . . there were Winston and Marshal. Then it came back to him. His lips felt bloated, as if injected with a quart of blood. His cheekbone throbbed. The sharp pain in his ribs cut all the way through to his back.

What was the point of this? If they killed him, or hurt him badly enough, he wouldn't be in the posse anyway! Plus, it wasn't hard to beat the crap out of someone if they couldn't defend themselves. What did that prove? What was the point?

Was it over? *Please, please be over.* Should he ask? He parted his lips—swollen rubber—stretching them as wide as he could, trying to get words out.

Joe pointed at Frankie. He and the rest of the posse were laughing.

Why? Was he dreaming? He hoped so. Maybe he was dead?

"Frankie laughing at you, Ice Box," Joe joked.

"The boy is strong," Buck-Buck said.

"Good job, Franklyn," Aunt Jenny added.

Joe grasped Frankie under the armpits and heaved him to his feet. Gaaah! He wanted to check himself over, but he didn't dare for fear of the pain. He was one large wound.

Joe must have understood, because he let him go gently. "This man here is now part of the posse. Him is a brother, now and forever," he announced. To Frankie he said, "You must walk with us through fire. You understand? You must take the burn if it's a burn that you have to take. You understand?"

Frankie heard the words, but the front of his head felt like something had cleaved into it. The words felt sludgy, plus he couldn't imagine more pain. Only one thought mattered. It was over.

Buck-Buck and Blow Up fired a few celebratory rounds into the air. Frankie thought his head was going to shatter.

Clearly pumped, Joe ushered Frankie over to the Toyota. "You made it through the lion's den, Nephew." He took out a plastic bag and held up what was about to become Frankie's first cell phone: a burner, but still. He could text, but there was no data, which made them hard to track. "Don't talk about posse business on it," Joe told him. "Only use it to set up meetings. You can talk about whatever else you want, but if me or Jenny or anybody in the posse is calling, you take the call. I don't care if you have Miss Jamaica on the line, you understand?"

Frankie nodded dizzily.

"And listen good: you only set up meetings for the same day. Not tomorrow, not the next day, not next week, only the same day." Joe shook the phone to emphasize his words. "Babylon can't react so fast, but them can if you give them time. So don't give them time." Joe extended his arm, opened his hand.

Frankie took the phone. At least he was finally getting a phone out of the deal.

Sixteen

tWO days later. The first had been spent entirely on the couch, where even rolling over was agony. But now, Frankie was back to lugging water up to the house. He had filled it to the very brim to make up for the days he'd missed. He regretted doing that now. His ribs still ached something fierce.

Coming his way down the middle of the road was the woman, the one who always ignored him. A basket was perched, as always, on her head. Her posture, as always, was perfect. And as always, Frankie waved. This time, however, the woman smiled, putting her hand on her chest in a sign of respect. Had he seen that right? Frankie offered a confused nod. Then he understood. She knew he was in a posse.

Funny, she'd respected his getting jumped in to the posse,

but not his scholarship, which everyone in Troy knew about. Then he realized something else—now she was afraid of him. She'd have to know he had a gun. Deep in thought, he didn't see the pothole and stepped right in. The bucket jostled, and water splashed on his sneaker. Game over. Well, at least the cool felt good.

Once home, he couldn't empty the bucket into the drum fast enough. He burst into the kitchen, expecting the savory smokiness of corn pork or the sweet scent of porridge. But damn, the table was empty. Aunt Jenny had promised to come by and make him a delicious morning meal, like she had the last two mornings, before she went to visit his father to make excuses for why Frankie couldn't come. Guilt meals, he knew. She felt bad for his beatdown. Not bad enough, apparently: the table was empty.

Frankie took his gun out of his waistband and put it in the bucket, covering it with the dish towel. Yep, it was a perfect hiding place—out of sight but with easy access. Then he gingerly lowered himself into a chair. Sure, he could have cooked breakfast himself. Samson had shown him how to make all kinds of breakfast specialties—from ackee and saltfish to callaloo with ripe plaintain, and hardo bread. But that wasn't the point—Frankie hated broken promises. From anyone. Even though the cancer had given his mother no choice, he even felt in a way that she had broken her own promise by leaving him. She had sworn she would get well. It wasn't fair for him to think this, he knew that, but he did anyway. He glanced over at her photo. The smile everyone said his looked exactly like.

Maybe . . . maybe he had no right to be hard on Aunt Jenny *or* his ma. Wouldn't he like to break *his* promise to Joe—to get out of the posse and take the scholarship? Hell yeah. He suddenly sat up straight—he needed to mail his letter to the scholarship board at the university, had to let them know that he wasn't able to accept their offer! He'd almost forgotten.

He'd actually started writing it after paying for this father's treatment. It had taken several drafts and a lot of tamped-down anger to make his story about wanting to stay in Jamaica to pursue his studies believable. But he'd carried the letter to the post office *without* mailing it too many times already. He just couldn't get himself to put it in the mail slot, as if, in setting that information free, he was putting himself in a straitjacket.

He looked out the window, hoping Jenny was simply late. Telling himself not to worry, he spun his burner around in his palm before sliding it back into his pocket. He had to admit he felt pretty cool, having a phone to call with. But now he was eager to see his father in person.

A car stopped on the street; its door opened and closed. A few moments later Aunt Jenny hustled in with a grocery bag filled to the brim. Frankie immediately felt bad for doubting her—also *glad* she had kept her promise.

"Your cheek looks good. You heal fast." She put the bag on the kitchen counter. "How you feeling?"

He didn't want to talk about his injuries. They would heal. "Me deh yah, Aunt Jenny," he said, choosing the greeting to let her know he was okay, but not particularly great.

"Yes, I'm here too." She exhaled. "I'm late because I was already in town and decided to drop in on your father, see how he was doing."

Now Frankie felt like such an ass for being upset with her. Aunt Jenny was always on point. He should have known. "I called the nurse earlier. She said the treatment hadn't come yet," he told her, hearing the worry in his own voice.

"Yes, but she said she expected it to arrive soon. No fret 'bout it, mon."

Aunt Jenny was probably right. But still. "Yeah, I'll go see him later."

"Maybe wait until tomorrow. The nurse wants him to get all the rest he can." She reached under her shirt and took out her Glock, laying it on the counter before starting to empty the bag. She noticed the dish towel on the bucket and lifted it. "Oh, that's where you keep your gun? Not bad."

"Where do you keep yours when you're home?"

"On my hip." She pulled a pack of bacon out of the bag.

Frankie shook his head; her commitment always impressed him. He eyed *her* gun. It was police grade. A piece piece. Told people to back off without her even having to open her mouth. Was it because she was a little sister, or because she was a woman working around a bunch of men? He wasn't sure. But there *was* one thing he was sure of, and that was Aunt Jenny's strength. She was tough like mahogany. Frankie hadn't seen one speck of sentimentality from her over Mr. Brown's death. Yet he didn't believe her relationship with him had only been about business.

She put the frying pan on the stove, spun open the knob on the propane tank. "Remember now, baby . . . don't think. Just follow Joe and Buck-Buck and them. Learn first." She started peeling away bacon strips. "You send that letter yet?"

She must have been reading his mind. But no, the letter sat on top of two overdue copies of *Popular Mechanics* at the end of the counter; she must have seen it and was urging him on in her Aunty Jenny way. "Haven't had time, Aunt Jenny." He pictured a dozen other students lined up, waiting to take his place, ready to kill for *his* scholarship. He pictured himself walking past the line, away from his best and probably only chance to become an engineer.

Aunt Jenny speared several strips of bacon with the tip of her knife. "You got a raw deal from your uncle." Really, the woman was clairvoyant. She eased the strips off the knife into the pan.

Aunt Jenny got it, but while she had stood up to Joe, she always backed down. Most did, when Joe wanted to have his way. Frankie was glad at least that she was on his side. But he couldn't stop thinking about the fact that Joe could have advanced Frankie the money. He *knew* Frankie was good for it. So . . . maybe it wasn't time to give up. When his father got better, maybe they could all have a talk, a civilized talk, and Joe could reconsider letting Frankie out of the posse. The pop of bacon sizzling brought Frankie back to reality. Yeah, right. A couple of years ago, a posse member, Leonard Fenton, had tried to leave, but Buck-Buck and Ice Box had tracked him down. When he tried a second time . . . they killed him. A chill ran down the back of Frankie's neck. Still . . . "Aunt Jenny?"

"Hmm?" She was moving the slices away from each other in the pan.

"How did you and Uncle Joe start the posse?"

"Oh, you feel you can know secrets now, eh?"

Frankie flushed. "No, I—"

"Don't worry, Franklyn, just messing with you." She smiled. "Like everything else, it started with sex."

Whoaaa? But then his aunt grinned, almost playful.

"I dated a dealer, a Rasta, who turned me on to the life. I turned on your uncle and the dealer turned him on to Rastafarian ways. After a while we started our own thing up here. That's it, no big secret."

"What happened to the dealer?"

"Dumped him."

"Why?"

"Why?" She looked back at the bacon, then to Frankie. "He left the toilet seat up."

"For real?"

"No, and I'm not going to tell you either." She winked, then asked, "Any other questions?"

He thought about what Winston had asked the other day. "I know Daddy isn't the type, but did he ever think about joining you and Uncle?"

"Samson?" Her laugh shot spittle into the air. "If your uncle or me said the sky was blue, your father would get a ladder and paint it red for spite. Join the posse?" She wiped her hands on her jeans. "Let me tell you something. Since we were kids, your father was always vexed, especially with Joe."

"Why?"

"Why?" She rocked her head, poked at the bacon. "Joe wasn't born first. Our father always told Samson how important he was because he was the firstborn son. It was firstborn son this, firstborn son that. Everything was 'firstborn.' Joe hated that more than anything."

Frankie bit his lip, thinking that Joe was exactly the type to hold a grudge. "So . . . ?"

"So?" The bacon popped. "Don't let the dreadlocks fool you. Joe can be as evil as anybody, especially when it comes to his brother. Joe would always, always do stupid things to get Samson in trouble."

"Like what?"

"Well . . . make me tell you. Our father, he was a hard man, and he was always after Samson to look out fi Joe." She looked out the window. "One day, after school, Samson lost Joe. Couldn't find him for nothing. Everybody in a panic."

She flipped a slice of bacon.

"So finally, Joe found his way home when it was well dark. Daddy beat Samson till him nearly dead. And I remember till this day how Joe kept this sneaky little grin on his face the whole time."

It was the first time Frankie heard about Samson being beaten by *his* father from someone *other* than Samson. "He beat him a lot?"

"A lot? Lord have mercy, my father beat Samson like a rug, I tell you." She moved a few strips around. "But no matter what, Samson always felt this big responsibility for Joe." She sighed.

"But when Joe joined the posse, I think Samson thought it was game over. He had failed Joe. Failed our father. Himself too, probably."

No wonder they were so mad at each other. If Frankie had a brother, he didn't know if he would feel any different than Samson did. "But you're in the posse. Daddy's not mad at you."

"Well, in your father's little mind, I'm just a girl." She flipped the strips of bacon, shot Frankie a look of disgust. "Damn fool, as if *I'm* not looking out fi dem."

Frankie didn't doubt it for a second. Looking out for him, too.

She lowered the heat. "Okay, enough questions."

He thought about how *he* was now looking out for Samson too. The letter—it was time to mail it. And since Aunt Jenny said it would be best to see his father tomorrow, he should swing by school, check in. He'd promised Mrs. Gordon. And why not? He hadn't gotten any posse duties yet. "Aunt Jenny, I want to finish up at the high school."

Jenny was pulling the bacon out of the pan, letting the grease drip off. "I see no problem there. Stupid people don't last long in this business." She was proud of what he had done in school, he could tell. And man, what a relief, that she wanted him to keep going, wanted him to at least get his diploma. He wanted that too. He couldn't imagine telling people he hadn't graduated from high school. He hadn't even *considered* that as a possibility!

Then she looked at the letter. "Me know it grieve you bad. Me even argue with Joe again last night, but he's not changing his mind." She slid a couple slices of bacon on a plate and brought it over. "You can start with this."

The smell of bacon can make a lot of troubles go away, at least for a little while, Ma used to say.

"Franklyn." Jenny had put her game face on. "Joe told me to tell you that your first mission with the posse is this Sunday."

He picked up the bacon and crunched into it—salty, and greasy like Christmas ham—but it didn't make him feel as good as it usually did.

Seventeen

Outside Mrs. Gordon's office, he heard a murmur of voices. A dozen students had gathered around a large screen set up in the corner. His counselor was busy plugging her laptop into a projector. He decided to tell her about not accepting the scholarship before sending the letter. It was almost a relief to see that she was busy; he could delay telling her. Delay didn't make it 100 percent real.

"Hey." It was Leah, walking toward him.

"Hey." Whoa, she smelled good—cedar and citrus.

"This a better time?" she asked, leaning one hip out.

His eyes linked up with hers. All the stuff he hadn't said last time seemed like it was being said just by looking at her, some sort of weird transmission. At last, he laughed. She did too—a dimple popped on each cheek.

"I had a lot on my mind the other day," Frankie said.

"I know." She looked instantly concerned. "I heard you have some serious illness in the family. Sorry."

"Yeah, thanks." If she *knew* what it was . . . "It's my dad."

"Must be rough. He okay?"

"Yeah. Hope so. He's in the hospital." *That treatment better come soon.* "Gonna see him tomorrow."

"No wonder you were all—"

"Hey, last time I . . . ," he interrupted. They both laughed.

"It's okay. I get it," Leah finally said.

He looked down, gathering a little brave—then back to her. "Well, ah, thanks, you know, for giving *me* a chance to give *you* another chance," he said.

She nodded. "That *was* what I was doing, wasn't it?"

"Sounded like it." Cedar and citrus. "So, look, I gotta ask—why *did* you ghost me out like that?"

"I suppose like last time for you, *I* had a lot going on with *my* family."

"Yeah, *that* I get. It all cool now?"

"No." She shifted her weight. "My mom and dad separated."

"Whoa. That's not easy." Definitely a bummer. But he couldn't help thinking: at least she hadn't broken it off because of him. "How you dealing?"

"Dealing?" She looked at the kids in Mrs. Gordon's office. "Probably half the kids here are dealing."

"Yeah." She was right—a lot of his friends' parents were divorced. Winston didn't have a dad. Most of the guys in Troy didn't either. He didn't have a mom. *Come on, Frankie. Leah and you are talking the same stuff. Ask her out, already!*

"Sooo—heard you got a big scholarship?"

Shit.

"Frankie." Mrs. Gordon was waving. "Can you come here a minute?"

Shit. Shit. He held up a finger. "Can you hold on?" Leah nodded, and he forced himself over to Mrs. Gordon. Now *she* was going to ask about the scholarship. Shit was falling out of the sprinklers.

But Mrs. Gordon merely said, "Can you take a look at this? I was going to call AV, but they take forever. I haven't used this projector before, and I can't make it work."

What was it with adults and plugs? They couldn't figure shit out. He looked at her PC and took hold of the cable leading from the laptop to the projector. It was plugged into the wrong place. "You need an HDMI to VGA adapter."

She looked at him like he was speaking Latin, then pointed to the table, where a bunch of cables were tangled together. He picked up the right one and switched out the wrong one, pressed the key, and the projector started to work.

"I'm going to miss having you around," Mrs. Gordon said admiringly.

"Uh . . . thank you?" he muttered uncomfortably, and ducked out before she could ask about the scholarship.

Citrus and cedar. "You're pretty handy to have around. I was having a little trouble with my AirPods the other day and—"

"You flexing?"

"AirPods aren't flexing."

Frankie tilted his head. They were more fashion statement than user-friendly tech. He stood by that.

"Okay, sorta flexing." No smile. Two dimples. "You *do* keep it real." She liked that. Good.

He *did* keep it real. *Pfft.* Not lately, though. But he liked that even when Leah flexed, she could walk it back and be real herself.

"Hey, I gotta go. I have to get ready for an art review tonight. Why don't you come?"

She was asking him out. She did the first time too. His ma had asked Samson out the first time also. She had loved teasing his dad about that. "Sounds good," he replied, all casual, fronting.

"Cool. It's in the gym. Seven. I'll be a little stressed beforehand with all the crits there, but let's hang out after."

"Cool."

"Later." She walked away. She looked back. Dimples.

What the heck were crits? Guess he'd find out.

Eighteen

eight hours later, after having raced home to put on his good blue shirt, Frankie was staring at seven paintings Leah was arranging on the easels in the gym, while several other artists did the same. When he first got there, he couldn't stop casing the place, checking the stands to see if anyone waved to her—a parent, friend, or another guy she might have invited. Someone ahead of him, waiting in line. But no one else seemed focused on Leah, at least not like he was.

Taking in her work now, he decided *everyone* should have been staring at her. The painting she was putting up was an in-your-face political statement, an almost kid-like drawing of a long line of wooden caskets leading from the ghettos of Trench Town to Vale Royal, the garden-perfect mansion home of Jamaica's prime minister. The one next to it was also really political: a yellow steamroller driven by a man in a suit had just flattened a bunch of shirtless teenage boys. *Strange roadkill.* Frankie's favorite, though, was at the end of the row. It looked like Leah had used charcoal to draw a shanty house patched together with corrugated zinc for walls—walls covered with images of dead bodies and graffiti, pointed statements about the JLP and PNP. The art made Frankie uncomfortable, which meant it was powerful. Yeah, people should be staring at Leah.

It was a full twenty minutes of artists shifting what canvas sat on what easel, and where—was it for better lighting? At last they stopped rearranging and stood solemnly by their canvases. Two young-looking female teachers, one with crazy long extensions, the other with close-cropped hair, entered the gym. A gray-bearded male teacher followed them. Carrying notepads, the trio made their way around the gym floor, taking notes, evaluating the work of all fifteen artists. These must be the "crits" Leah had spoken about. He liked how proudly she stood beside her art, not show-offy, like some of the others, but not all fidgety, nervous, which *he* would have been.

After making their rounds, the crits sat behind a long folding table and took turns summoning artists one by one to the table for their reviews. The way the crits did their evaluations reminded Frankie of presenting engineering projects—he had to set up his work, then listen to the teachers' review, and everyone there could hear the critiques. That was always tough for Frankie, and for every engineering friend he had ever spoken to about it. It must be just as painful for the artists here. Difference was, with engineering there was a right and wrong, the concepts either worked within the laws of physics or they didn't. The crits here said a bunch of stuff that seemed like it was just opinions, as far as Frankie could tell. He wouldn't have a clue about how to react.

When they reached a young, dark-skinned woman all in white, even her boots and hat, Frankie realized his palms were all sweaty. Leah was next. Frankie looked over at the girl in white's canvases. They seemed to be a series of painted-over drone shots of Jamaica's cockpit country—the middle of the island, filled with thick vegetation, hills, and gullies. It was called "cockpit" because the area looked like places where people had cockfights. The colors were cool, every kind of green imaginable, but the art didn't make him nervous like Leah's did. It felt like art that rich people would have all over their houses.

All-white-clothed girl was saying, "The classical approach to landscapes, as manifestations of the sublime, presses together pain and terror. But this definition comes from the human gaze. The individual sees the pain and danger, and it's only when seen from a distance and particular angles that the landscapes show hope. In my paintings, I've eliminated the human viewpoint. I show the environment acting on the environment: in other words, nature's gaze upon nature."

The crit with the short hair nodded crisply. "In all your work, the clouds seem ambiguous, always morphing into new shapes, sometimes two shapes at once. The wind affecting the clouds," she said intently.

"I might add that in a few pieces we can see heat rising from the ground, warping the air, if you will. It's a sort of atmospheric perspective. The detail gives a real, and provocative, sense of a tropical climate, without human intervention. It's quite fantastic." This was from the bearded crit, who seemed to use his glasses for emphasis.

"I agree also. Bravo," the third crit said. As the girl in white walked away from the table, she blew a kiss to a woman sitting in the stands.

Frankie rubbed his nose against his knuckles, smelling his own sweat. How many times had he heard Jamaicans go on about Jamaica's problems, but then proudly claim that nowhere was more beautiful? The land was one thing and the people another. Still, this gave Frankie a lot of hope for Leah. He imagined similar praise for her work.

Leah stood motionless, almost regal. The whole time she was setting up, she hadn't looked at Frankie, not even once. He wished she would now, so he could show her some support. It was what he would have wanted for himself.

"Leah Bradford." Leah squared her shoulders, raised her chin. Her stride was strong, her Air Jordans squeaking on the floor.

Frankie leaned forward, surprised at how nervous he was, like he was walking to the table himself.

Leah opened her mouth and paused.

Oh no, she was freezing. He wanted to shout something encouraging.

Then she put on a smile, seeming again fully in charge. "My showing is inspired by the works of the Jamaican artist Kapo.

As you know, he was the leader of the Intuitives, the self-taught Jamaican artists. My project is to reinterpret Kapo's spiritual and church-based work into an indictment of colonialism that depicts the crimes against African Jamaicans."

It was just a string of words to Frankie, their meaning escaping him. He wished he could see Kapo's art, see what Leah was talking about. Her emotion was pulsing, wave after wave.

But the extensions crit seemed to have a different look on her face. She leaned back. "I appreciate your intentions, Ms. Bradford, but exactly as you said, Kapo was self-taught, and you are classically trained. So I don't see how your work can truly connect to his."

Leah waved her hands in disagreement. "I've imitated the—"

Gray Beard cleared his throat. "Ms. Bradford, may I remind you that there is no rebuttal allowed during reviews, only opening statements."

The short-haired crit added, "I have to agree with my colleague, Ms. Bradford. By definition you cannot be an Intuitive. And beyond that, your work does not feel primitive, as Kapo's indeed was. It comes across as intellectual instead of authentically painted. It's just pure politics."

Now all three professors stared, grim-faced. But Leah stepped forward anyway. "Excuse me, but I don't agree with what you just said about my work, and I think I have a right to be heard."

The crits were clearly speechless. The silence that followed was excruciating.

Leah broke it by saying, "You all are so conservative. You don't want anything that talks about our political problems as a country. You just want things that have some . . . tourism value." She looked back at the artist who had presented the landscapes. "I'm not disrespecting it." She looked again at the crits. "But . . . it's like more of the same. It's like . . . tourist advertising. I just think there's a lot more to say."

Frankie covered his mouth with his fist. Could this be worse?

The short-haired crit raised her chin haughtily. "Are you quite finished, Ms. Bradford?"

Leah's nostrils flared, yet she managed to say, "Thank you for your time," before turning on her heel and returning to her paintings.

Frankie was as stunned as he was awed. Leah knew her stuff, what was going down in Jamaica. She must read a lot. He read a lot too—that was his only way to really get a full understanding of things. He yearned to make eye contact with her. But she stood there by her paintings like a statue of resistance and never looked once at Frankie, the crits, or anyone else.

When it was over, another excruciating twenty minutes later, Leah quickly but carefully packed her paintings and headed for the gym's exit.

"Leah!"

She looked up, surprised, as if she'd forgotten he'd be there. Her portfolio banged against her thigh. "Not such a hot ticket, after all," she said, her voice high and pained.

Frankie shook his head, disagreeing. "I don't know anything about art, but I think your work says a lot. It said something to me." When she didn't dismiss him, he added, "Most people I know don't understand where we come from or what we went through. But you were trying to deal with all that. We need to know it." He wanted to reach out, reassure her, in the worst way, at least hold her hand, but that wouldn't be right.

Leah rocked side to side, a ship on rough waters. She was a competitor; she wouldn't have argued with the crits otherwise. He could tell she wouldn't let them knock her down.

"How about a movie Saturday?" Frankie offered.

She nodded at last. "Sounds good."

His first posse mission was Sunday. At least he'd get one final day of good before his life turned on its side.

Nineteen

Sitting by the hospital bed, the air thick as always with the smell of urine and ammonia, Frankie studied his father's jaw. It looked even larger than usual. Had he lost weight and had that somehow made his jaw seem bigger? The nurse had said he was fatigued—his body was fighting the infection. *Keep fighting, Dad.* Where the heck was that treatment? The nurse said delivery had been delayed because of some mixup, but this was getting critical.

Frankie didn't want to talk too much about the treatment for frear of goading his father on. Knowing Samson, he'd start up the jabbering about cerise tea again. Speaking of bush medicine . . . the leaf of life! Frankie pulled it out of his pocket. "Daddy, look."

Samson's eyes lit up. "Leaf of life! Where you get it?"

"Up the mountain." The day he was jumped in . . . Frankie shook that thought off, in case his father was clairvoyant like his sister. "Guess what, though? I found it under a patch of banana trees. It *can* grow in the shade."

Samson looked well pleased. "Will you look at that?" He took it, rubbed a leaf with his fingers. He almost sounded like his old self.

"When you get back on your feet, we can plant some in the yard."

"A good idea, that," Samson said, shifting his shoulders, as if uncomfortable against the pillow. How much did a gunshot wound hurt? Frankie wondered. Now that he was in the posse, was he going to find out?

Samson turned the leaf of life around between his fingertips thoughtfully. "Me should just take my cerise tea and boil up some roots instead of waiting for this damn medication."

"And carry a four-leaf clover, too?" It slipped out of Frankie's mouth. But the damn cerise tea—

His father gave Frankie a pitying look. "It's not no superstition. Don't fool yourself. Most of the cures in this world come from the bush."

"Not from laboratories?"

"You're the technical man, and that's all you see. But wait till them cut down all the forests. That big one in Brazil, too." He smoothed out his sheet. "Mon, you going to see lots of trouble, plenty diseases won't have any cure."

"Science has done pretty good so far. Man-made cures are everywhere."

Silence. It wasn't so uncomfortable this time. They had been talking, really talking.

"Hmm." Samson's eyes darted, seemingly evaluating Frankie. "So, how you doing? And where did that bruise come from?"

Frankie's hand moved to his cheek. "Tripped bringing up water."

"Looks like it hurt," Samson said, his tone surprisingly warm.

And Frankie relaxed a little, decided to share something with his father, something else that would make him happy. "So . . . I met this girl."

Now his father grinned. "Hmm, me could tell it was something like that."

"Get out of here. You didn't know that."

"I was young once too, you know."

"Ever catch a dinosaur?" Frankie teased. His father's chuckle was everything.

"She at your school?" Samson stretched his neck.

"Yeah, she's an artist."

"Her family have money, then?"

Frankie thought about Leah's AirPods. She probably had money, but most kids at his school did, except for him and the few others who tested in from "lesser" neighborhoods. But Leah never carried that air. "Why do you think that?"

"If she's an artist, she isn't worrying about having a real job. Her parents must have money to support that." He dragged out the last words, coated with remorse. "We, your ma and me, always wanted to give you more." Now he was blinking hard.

"Sorry me couldn't give you more, but at least you get that scholarship."

Frankie squeezed the strap of his backpack, squeezed down the guilt. "You gave me a lot, Daddy." He wanted to grab his father's hand, but that wasn't what they did.

His father suddenly looked pensive. "All that reading done you good. Look how far you come."

And there it was, the pride in his father's voice. Damn. No way could Frankie ever tell him about the posse, about the scholarship, no way. He hopped up. "Better be getting home—more reading!" He lifted his backpack, his ribs giving a pang. "Okay, it was good seeing you."

"You too, Frankie. Be careful."

"I will. I'll be back in a day or so."

Just before he left, his father called out, "What's the name of the girl?" His voice was almost tender.

Frankie pivoted. "Leah."

"Nice name."

"I'll tell her you said that."

"No, mon. Don't tell her that. If you lay out an easy road for her, she might prefer the harder one."

It was cautious, old-school advice, but Frankie smiled. Because it was his dad, being his dad.

Twenty

frankie and Leah edged their way to the end of the aisle of the dimly lit theater as the credits played, and into the lobby. Leah started for the bathroom. She was all excited about taking him to eat sushi. *You'll love it,* she'd enthused. He wasn't so sure. He watched her every motion, thinking that for the last two hours, he hadn't thought of his dad, the posse, or his scholarship. Yeah, he'd watched the movie, but mostly he thought, *I'm only six inches away from Leah.* But now the other thoughts crowded forward. He had to tell her about the scholarship. He wasn't going to have that between them. It'd turn into a mountain of lies, reaching to the sky. But at the same time, he couldn't see how she could understand.

Halfway to the bathroom, Leah turned back. "The line is

three times longer than the one for men! More women should go into architecture," she huffed.

Frankie looked at both lines. He'd never thought about this before, wondered why he hadn't. "Can you, uh, hold it?"

"I'm a female, Frankie." She shot him a grin and waltzed off toward the exit.

Outside, Frankie grasped the saddle of his bike with his right hand, even though he was left-handed. He didn't want the bike to be between him and Leah. She'd accidentally brushed her hand across his forearm on the way to her seat at the movie, or maybe it hadn't been accidental, he thought hopefully. All the more reason to start *clean*, to tell her about the scholarship.

They kept walking, passing busy Hope Road before turning down a small side street. Leah stopped at a restaurant he'd never even noticed before. He still wasn't sure he was up for raw fish.

"You ready fi try it?" She raised her eyebrows.

Patois? Not that he'd thought she was one of those Jamaicans who looked down on using patois, but it was good to know he was right. It meant she didn't look down on people from the country. "So, you chat patwah?" He tried not to sound too eager.

"Yeh, mon. Now come try di sushi." She grinned. Oh, those dimples.

Truth was, he had never been in a restaurant. At least not a sit-down place. He'd heard about how some waiters snubbed people with skin like his—assumed they'd be difficult to deal with. He eyed the building warily. He so didn't want to be dissed in front of Leah. And another thing: he had no idea how much the sushi cost. Well, he could leave extra cash, make a statement, and let them know he was somebody.

He locked up his bike and followed Leah inside. The waiter took them to a table, no attitude at all, and Leah finally got to go to the bathroom. Sitting there, Frankie sniffed. No fishy odor. Was this good or bad? He could ask Leah when she came back, but the question, was it a stupid one? The waiter came back with a pitcher of water and two menus. Phew—prices were listed. Not so bad. One less worry. The waiter filled their glasses, said his name was Fitzroy. Frankie had hung out with Chinese Jamaicans before; there were several at school. But this was the first Japanese Jamaican he had ever met, and the first time he'd heard Japanese spoken. For whatever reason, it made him think of Jamaica's slogan, "Out of Many, One People."

Back at the table, Leah scraped at small splashes of paint near her knuckles. No nail polish. He liked that—she was serious about her work.

He ordered a beer by pointing to it, unsure of its pronunciation. Leah ordered something called sake, then took two chopsticks out of a paper wrapper. Chopsticks? He had to use chopsticks? To cover, he said, "Didn't know you had mad chopstick skills."

"There's a lot you still don't know about me." She tugged on the sticks, snapping them apart.

"Well, let me find out something now." He picked up his chopsticks and removed the paper wrapper exactly like she had. "You seeing anybody?"

"You think I'd be here with you if I were?"

"Maybe he messed up and I'm the revenge." He slowly pulled the two sticks apart.

She rubbed her chopsticks against each other like she was sanding them. "You see me as the cheating type?"

He rubbed the chopsticks together too. "Just asking."

"Well, ask me something else." She laid her chopsticks against a tiny little dish that seemed only there for that express reason.

"Like what?" He began tapping his two sticks together in a down-tempo beat. They were kind of cool, these chopsticks.

"Use your imagination. Engineering students have them too, don't they?"

He had a boatload of things he wanted to know about her. But since they were starting from scratch, he'd go to the one he was most curious about. He cleared his throat. "Why do you like me?"

Two dimples. "Who says I do?"

His face went hot. Man, she wasn't making this easy. Her eyebrow arched as she waited for a response. "Well, you don't seem like the type who would be wasting her time."

"Okay, well . . . you're kind of a nerd—not in a bad way! But still . . . nobody messes with you at school. It makes you interesting." Then she pointed a chopstick at his cheek. "What happened there?"

"Things happen out in the country," he said with a shrug, hoping she'd let it go, changing the subject just to be safe. "So . . . how are things with your family? I—"

"Mind if we talk about something else?" For the first time,

Leah looked uncomfortable. The waiter brought the beer and sake to the table.

Frankie gestured at her shot glass. "So, what's that?"

"Sake? It's rice wine." She offered him the glass.

"Where I come from, people think it's disgusting to drink out of the same glass." But he took the glass anyway.

"Troy, right?" She tilted her head. "Country people."

Frankie raised the glass. "Country people." He took a sip. The sake had a sweet metallic taste, reminding him of the type of spring water that tasted of minerals mixed with salt. "Sake, huh? It no bad."

"But you prefer Sapporo?"

"I know beer. But I didn't always like beer. I don't know if anybody likes beer the first time. Do you?"

"I don't drink it." She took her glass back, took a sip, eyes on him. She appeared comfortable staring, never seemed in any hurry to look away. "Your scholarship is like a legend at our school—no one's ever gotten a full ride like that before! You must be totally proud. I wanted to go away for school too, but it didn't work out."

"Ah, where were you thinking of going?"

"University of Miami. I applied—they have an off-campus gallery that's just bananas, but I only got wait-listed."

"So, there's a chance . . ."

"My counselor says I shouldn't count on it." She flipped her hand as if flinging the school away and hit the chopsticks to the floor. She reached down to get them.

Counselor. He still needed to talk to Mrs. Gordon! Frankie

blinked hard. This was the moment to tell Leah about the scholarship. *Tell her.* But he couldn't, he just couldn't get the words out. He cleared his throat, trying to organize his thoughts. *My father got shot and I had to join a posse to save him.* Damn. No way could he tell her this and ever expect a second date.

She popped back up, chopsticks in hand. "I'm so clumsy."

"No . . . you're not." He stared. She stared. It was that kind of moment.

"So like . . . you live pretty far away."

Why'd she say that? Was she pulling back? "It's no big deal. I ride to school every day. I can ride anywhere." He pumped his arms, making a cycling motion, fully invested in the flirt.

"You must have strong legs," she said.

"My legs are okay. I like yours better."

"We're not making out tonight."

"I didn't want to make out, anyway."

"No?" She was clearly calling his bluff.

"No." He leaned back, put the beer on the table. "I want you to respect me in the morning."

Twenty-One

frankie sat with the other new recruits, replaying his date. Had it been a date? If it was, it couldn't have gone better. Even the raw fish was good. He was still hungry afterward, but whatever. Picking up a stick, he drew a large rectangle in the dirt—it looked like a blank canvas, he realized. This made him wonder what Leah was doing. Was she putting something on a new canvas? Then he wondered what he might be doing today, what he might put on *his* canvas. He looked over at Winston and Marshal, the light of the new sun a glow on their sleepy faces. But it didn't feel like a sleepy Sunday morning. It was probably the anxiety, waiting for Joe to find out what their first mission would be. Two lizards rustled through the surrounding brush; Frankie startled. Goats cried out, their barks like machine guns. Crickets chirped as if it was still nighttime. All of it only heightened the tension. Frankie dropped the stick, rubbed his hands together, trying to warm them up.

Marshal was studying his M1911 as if it had a bad smell. "This kind of forty-five jam sometimes," he said apropos of nothing.

Frankie thought about his own gun. Really, truly, the last thing he wanted to do was shoot somebody.

"That a why me glad me get a Glock," one of the Stony Mountain boys piped up.

"Yeh, mon, Glock is much betta," Marshal said. His skinny neck made him look like a puppet.

"Glock is more accurate, too," Greg said.

Big Pelton nodded, both chins shaking. "Is true, you know?"

The other Stony Mountain boy, the one with the sunken eyes, held up his own gun, a Springfield. "Me don't trust my gun neither. Me might buy a new one when me get my paycheck."

Big Pelton farted.

"Damn it, Pelton, something alive in your belly," Winston said, grimacing.

Then Greg blew air between his palms, making a farting noise. The others joined in, creating a symphony of mock flatulence. Frankie felt like he was back in grammar school, and yeah, call him ten, but it was still funny. He put his hands to his face and started blowing, joining in the farting chorus. After a few bars, he and the others couldn't stop laughing, Winston wiping tears from his eyes. But their laughter drew to an abrupt halt when Joe, Jenny, Ice Box, and Buck-Buck strolled over, *really?* looks on their faces.

Joe sauntered closer, pulled one of his ice-cream-stick tooth-picks out of his mouth. "Hear me now! Today you might become men. But right now you're still likkle youths. You all in training, but you going to have the best of the best with you. Buck-Buck, Ice Box, Jenny, and me will be with you on this one and all through the PNP jobs. You must listen, learn, and take orders!"

Frankie looked at the others. They all nodded their heads like they were at church. Every single one of them wanted to be a man. But what were they going to have to do to become one? Worse yet, what if Frankie couldn't do what was required?

As if mind-reading, Joe told them, "We're going to deliver a message to some JLP people in Toms River." Then his voice became edged with malice. "And listen, me hear say one of the gunmen who shoot up the party comes from this town. This is payback."

The other boys nodded, some trading fist bumps, their over-the-top excitement making Frankie wonder if they actually got what might happen. Underneath it all, were they scared? Like he was?

"What's the plan?" Winston asked, all big.

Aunt Jenny wagged her finger. "To shut up and follow orders. Think you can follow that plan?" Then she pointed toward the truck, indicated they should get in.

After they piled into the bed of the F-150, Buck-Buck drove them west, following Joe, Jenny, and Apache in the Toyota, tak-ing small winding roads, rattling over potholes, avoiding traffic on the A-3. Forty minutes later, they sped by a sleepy village down in the valley, then endless sugarcane fields on either side of the road. As the fields changed to trees and the road grew wider, they entered Toms River.

There was no getting off this roller coaster.

The vehicles pulled onto a big patch of reddish dirt by a thick wood. Joe raised his finger to his lips and waved them off the truck.

About four hundred feet away, a young teenage boy wearing sunglasses, carrying a bucket, stopped in the middle of the street.

The boy suddenly started walking quickly, taking out his cell phone as he turned the corner. Frankie pivoted to Joe, pointing. "Uncle, I saw—"

"Yes, me know," Joe said, all eerie calmly. "Come!" He beckoned everyone to move faster.

Shouldn't they leave? Frankie wondered. Clearly they'd been made. But Joe didn't seem concerned. He broke for the forest, then dropped to one knee, surveying the area.

Heart pounding, Frankie knelt in the brush with the others. He couldn't stop looking over his shoulder, wondering if the kid with the sunglasses had connections with a gang, or local police. Joe *had* to be thinking the same.

"Frankie!" Joe hissed. ·

Frankie whipped around, meeting Joe's icy gaze.

"Focus!" Joe then turned to the others, waving for them to follow.

The only sound was of boots snapping twigs, crushing leaves. The air was humid. The trees' shade shut out the sun. Frankie had never been afraid of the woods in the daytime before. He was now. Out of the corner of his eye, he was sure he saw an arm. He raised his gun, taking aim. It was a dry branch on a dying tree. Winston looked at him, eyes wide, inquiring. Swallowing vomity saliva, Frankie shook his head and lowered his gun.

Joe knelt again. The others followed his lead.

Pointing ahead, Joe told them that the forest twisted around to the front of a church. "We're going to split up, surround the church."

"Is church we going?" Winston blurted out.

"Shut up!" Ice Box groaned. "Just follow orders."

Joe pointed his finger. "Now, Jenny and Ice Box, take the Stony Mountain boys and go through this side. Buck-Buck, you take Winston, Frankie, and the big boy, and go over there. The rest of you come with me."

Aunt Jenny and Ice Box's team took off down the dirt path. Joe wove his own team past a tangle of sundew ferns onto another trail.

"Come," Buck-Buck said. He turned and ran to the left. Frankie, Winston, and Big Pelton followed. Something sharp jabbed Frankie's shoulder—a tree limb, ripping his shirt, exposing a thin, bloody gash underneath. Bumboclot. He was better than this. He'd been running through woods all his life, and he was at least as smart as anyone in the posse, except for maybe Aunt Jenny. And yet here he was, running into bushes like a scared dummy.

Just then Buck-Buck's cell phone dinged, loud and clear. He held up a hand for them to stop.

Was it Joe? Was it bad news?

Buck-Buck flipped open his phone with a frown. "Yeh, mon."

Frankie glanced at the others. Winston shrugged, clearly just as confused.

"Me want my money, mon!" Buck-Buck snarled into the phone.

So it wasn't Joe. Was it other urgent posse business—or was Buck-Buck working a side hustle? Frankie scanned the area, trying to catch sight of anyone who might be waiting for them. Winston crept over and whispered, "Them must be at the church by now."

Damn. Buck-Buck was going to screw it up for all of them. Frankie took a breath, then tapped him on the shoulder.

Covering the speaker, Buck-Buck waved them on. "Go, go! Follow the path! Wait at the clearing. Me will catch up."

"This way!" Winston said, sprinting through the brush like a deer. Frankie and Big Pelton raced after him.

Then Frankie heard singing. It didn't make sense at first. But then he realized, duh, it was a church, with people inside, worshipping.

"Be holy, be holy, just like me . . ."

There were fewer and fewer trees and more sunlight, and then Frankie could see the simple stone building. The windows were open—people were singing from hymnals.

Joe's team was already approaching the front. Aunt Jenny and Ice Box crept low, leading their team to the right.

Winston slowed at the edge of the clearing.

Opposite, Frankie saw three teenagers sprint out of the forest.

He recognized one—the same kid he'd seen on the road, the one with the Ray-Bans. Then Frankie's eyes bugged—the kid in the lead, a red bandanna around his neck, was raising a handgun, aiming it at Joe's team. The two others were right behind him, pulling their weapons as well.

The posse had been completely outmaneuvered.

"Move and bumboclot dead!" the red bandanna kid yelled. "What the bumboclot you doing here?"

Joe slowly turned, raising his hands to his shoulders, nodding to his posse to stay calm.

Frankie hugged the line of trees just behind Winston. Red Bandanna and the other two hadn't seen them, they were so focused on Joe.

Winston had a clear shot at any one of them. The cold, tense moment was his. He pulled his gun. Frankie held his breath, braced for the shot. But Winston didn't pull the trigger. And he didn't pull the trigger. And he didn't pull the trigger. He stood there, shaking, arm out, unable to do what he had bragged so much about. Unable to shoot.

Everyone seemed transfixed. Everyone except Frankie. Joe was going to die if Winston didn't shoot! Frankie had to do something. Now. Right now. Frankie stepped around Winston, aimed his gun, and squeezed the trigger twice. The bullets exploded from the chamber, the recoil easier to handle than he expected, almost nothing. And—nothing happened! It made no sense—it was like he was in a freeze-frame in a film. Was he imagining things? He heard nothing. No singing from inside the church. No kids shouting. No reaction from Red Bandanna or his crew.

Nothing. And then—like a tear in time, the opposite occurred. A church lady in a brown dress screamed in the doorway, and a man in a sweat-soaked shirt ran out of the building. A boy's face peeked out a window and a minister tugged him back down. Buck-Buck rushed past Frankie, arm extended, finger on the trigger. *POP! POP! POP! POP!* Shots blasted Frankie's ears, and a spray of bullets cut into the rival gang. Red Bandanna crumpled. The second boy fell. Ray-Ban Boy dropped his gun as a burst of red splattered from his chest.

"Back to the cars! Now! Go!" Joe bellowed. He kept his gun aimed at the church door, backing away. Ice Box, Aunt Jenny, and everybody tore past Joe, rushing for the safety of the forest.

But something drew Frankie across the grass. Though he hadn't hit anyone, he felt as guilty as if he had. He found his legs moving of their own accord, as if they weren't his, stepping forward, air thick as mud, not moving away but toward Ray-Ban Boy. He found himself standing over him. Maybe the boy's spirit had led him, carried him, forced him to view what he—they—had done?

The wound blossoming red on the clean white tee, the black Ray-Bans by the kid's side.

Ray-Ban Boy was JLP.

JLP shot Samson.

But revenge didn't feel anything like he'd thought it would. Where was the relief?

"Go!"

The word brought Frankie back to this world. Joe nodded at him like a father, like Samson.

Frankie knew he should run, but now his legs were doing the opposite—at last, he backed away slowly.

Joe eyed the church, silent except for the wailing that was coming from inside.

"No one here shall vote JLP! No JLP! You hear me!" Joe yelled out. "Don't come to no poll on Election Day!"

It was only then that Frankie noticed the handwritten signs that hung on the side of the church: *JLP: Labour. Prosperity. A Better Way Forward.*

Then—*pop, pop, pop.* Joe put a bullet dead center in every *O*, his bullets stamping their mark—Joe's initials.

Shit. He'd never seen anyone shoot like Joe. Shit. Despite the mess up with the other gang, Joe still remembered the political message he came to deliver. Frankie couldn't even think straight. And, at last, Frankie turned and fled. He stumbled over a lignum vitae tree root—had to windmill his arms to keep his balance. Something seemed to shift behind the large ficus. Spooked, Frankie ducked. It was just a bird. That was Joe behind him, right?

Time disappeared again, and, out of breath, unable to remember how he had gotten there, Frankie found himself sitting in the back of the truck next to the other recruits.

Boots thrashed along the forest floor. Ice Box swung around with his gun, but it was Joe. Ice Box lowered his weapon. Engines started. But instead of his own ride, Joe went straight for the F-150, eyes blazing. Frankie thought he was coming for him—angry that Frankie had missed. But Joe stopped in front of Winston and thrust out his hand. Winston had no reaction—

it was as if he couldn't see Joe or the fury in his eyes. While Frankie felt a flood of relief that it wasn't him, he instantly felt guilty, because Winston was in for a shitload of trouble.

"Joe," Frankie started.

"Shut the fuck up!" Joe barked, then swung back to Winston. "Give me your gun. Now!" Drawing closer, he raised his hand as if to slap Winston.

Finally Winston fished the gun out of his pocket and gave it to Joe, hand shaking, just like at the church. Was that really only moments ago? When Winston couldn't shoot Ray-Ban Boy?

Winston had lost his nerve.

Frankie's stomach began to ache.

"You're out of the posse." Joe glared at Winston. "You lucky me no make you walk."

Twenty-Two

Rastas never drank alcohol. Joe didn't even allow the posse to have booze at the camp, so when Buck-Buck and Ice Box insisted that he accompany them to the Urban-Might-Ee Lounge for drinks to blow off steam, he made a significant concession, saying he understood the need to let off steam after a day when blood was spilled. Aunt Jenny added that it was good for the boss to spend time with employees. Frankie had no desire to join them. The image of Winston getting off the F-150, head lowered, walking out of camp, all alone, haunted him.

So while everyone paraded into the lounge, Frankie slipped away. He headed straight to Winston's house, but no one answered his knocks. He couldn't tell if Winston was avoiding him or if he wasn't home. After a time, Frankie gave up. The whole walk back, his brain kept pulsing: *You killed someone. You killed someone.* The fact that he'd missed didn't matter. He hadn't intended to miss. So it was the same thing.

Outside the lounge, dance-hall reggae thrummed the ground, seeming to match the pulse in his head—like even the earth knew what he had done. There was no way to take it all back, no rewind. Bile rose into his throat. The door cracked open.

"Frankie." Buck-Buck came out and tapped Frankie's chest with a bottle of Red Stripe Bold. "Been looking for you. You turn a man today. Joe not telling you that, but him say that to me."

There was no relief in Buck-Buck's compliment, either. Frankie felt only more nauseous; Buck-Buck was a killer. Frankie tried to step back, but Buck-Buck elbowed his arm, a conspiratorial knock. "And don't say nothing 'bout my little phone call, right?"

Until then, Frankie hadn't even remembered the phone call. Hadn't remembered that Buck-Buck had put the mission on hold, how they stood in the woods before the shoot-out.

"Nothing wrong with making a little money on the side, right?" Buck-Buck went on, slapping Frankie's chest with the back of his hand. When Frankie didn't answer, he added, "We cool 'bout it?"

Frankie snapped back into focus. "Yeh, mon. No problem."

"Good. Come."

Inside, the gangly lounge owner lugged a packed tray of Red Stripe and Dragon Stout beers. He landed the drinks at the corner booth, where the rest of the new recruits were squished together like a team that had just won a game they thought they were going to lose. Ice Box held court with the rest of the posse at the bar. Cricket put money into the old jukebox and blatantly chose "Murderer," Buju Banton's classic. Buck-Buck scooped up a Red Stripe, handed it to Frankie, and raised his own.

"Respect due to Frankie Green, killing machine!" he shouted.

Joe raised his Ting soda. "Yes, yes! Once him learn how to aim, he will be unstoppable."

Everyone broke out in laughter. Frankie forced a smile, tried to laugh, but the humor didn't grow on him—it was a seed sown in the wrong field.

"Frankie Green, killing machine," Big Pelton repeated, nodding at his own cleverness.

The other boys' heads bounced as if to the same beat.

Marshal leaned forward and said, "Frankie, mon, you're like Keanu Reeves."

"Jim Wick to back side!" the Stony Mountain boy with pointy ears said.

"Jim Wick?" Marshal yelped, and everyone busted out laughing.

"What?" the Stony Mountain boy asked.

"It's John Wick, mon." Marshal put his beer down. "Keanu Reeves plays John Wick. Jim Wick is some other kind a' Wick."

"Jim, John, whatever. Me no see di movie yet." The Stony Mountain boy folded his arms defensively. "But me have it 'pon DVD."

"DVD!" Greg said. "You no have Wi-Fi at your house?"

The Stony Mountain boy looked down at the table. "No, mon."

Frankie took a quick swig of his beer. "Me neither."

All the boys, one by one, admitted that they didn't have Wi-Fi either, until finally Greg admitted the same. The laughter rippled. Frankie began to relax. He smiled—one of the boys, just having a beer—and it felt . . . okay. He wasn't alone, at least that.

"Me don't love Keanu Reeves movies too much, though," Big Pelton offered.

"Memes of him are fire, though," Marshal said.

Big Pelton said, "Yeh, mon."

Heads nodded again like they were in church, making Frankie think of the stone one—and Ray-Ban Boy. He chugged his beer, pushing the thought away.

Then sunlight sliced into the dark room as the door swung open. Ice Box and Buck-Buck spun around, whipping out their guns. Even the lounge owner snatched one from behind the bar.

But it was only Winston, the desperate look on his face growing as he walked toward Joe.

Joe folded his arms, and Frankie tightened his grip on the bottle neck. It was so hard to understand Winston sometimes. He'd probably gone out of his way to ask around about the posse, just so he could come here and put himself in the middle of Joe's crosshairs.

"Winston, I tell you already, you are no longer welcome!" Joe said, his voice flat, as expressionless as his face. "And me hope is not trouble you looking for, because you will find it in here."

Ice Box and Buck-Buck shifted, ready to pounce.

Now, Joe made his way toward Winston, who looked like a lost child.

Frankie set down his beer and in three steps was at Winston's side, throwing a hand on his friend's shoulder. Winston smacked it away, so Frankie rammed Winston with two hands, shoving him away from Joe, back toward the door.

Winston's nostrils flared. "Fuck off."

"We have to go, mon," Frankie hissed, mustering all the intensity he had.

Winston looked past Frankie's shoulder to Joe and pressed back.

"Easy, buddy. I have an idea. Just give me some time." Frankie planted his palm on Winston's back, urging him toward the threshold.

And to Frankie's immense relief, Winston turned.

Frankie walked side by side with Winston, wary of talking about posse business on the street. His mother had said often, *God gave you two ears but one mouth—listen more, talk less.* Once they reached their private meeting spot, Winston threw himself on the ground. "I'm a dead man."

"There might be a way—"

Winston banged his forehead into the dirt. "There's no way, mon! I'm a fucking dead man. When Garnett hears about this, *pfff.*"

"Look, I can talk to Joe. No way will he let Garnett—"

"Stop that shit!" Winston pushed himself up. "Just because you shot, you feel all good, right?"

All good? All good? *Nothing* was good. Winston had no clue. But, "No, I don't feel all good, Winston" was all he said.

"Bullshit. 'Frankie Green, killing machine.' Bullshit." Winston smirked, cold. "Yeh, me overhear what them was calling you." He stomped at a line of black ants.

Winston. He could flatten a line of ants, but he couldn't pull the trigger. Then, like a wave at the beach, one he didn't see coming, it hit Frankie that *he* could. Then Frankie's brain went into overdrive. But did that mean Winston was really a coward? Or just that Winston wasn't a killer? And what did it mean that *he*, Frankie, could pull the trigger? Did that mean Winston cared more about people, about life? Frankie'd learned about double-edged swords in school. And dang, on one hand he'd been able to shoot, which saved lives, but on the other hand he'd helped to kill three kids. He sat down heavily beside Winston.

Winston leaned back. "Fucking Joe."

Frankie eyed Winston. "What? What did you say?"

"Me say Joe not even a real Rasta."

Winston was just bitter, Frankie knew. But he felt compelled to say, "Watch it, mon, he is my uncle, you know."

"Real Rastas don't use guns, Frankie." He spat. "They don't go shoot up churches for politics. Shit."

He wasn't wrong . . . and yet at the same time, how else could Joe look out for the community? Make sure *worse* didn't take over?

Winston's exhale was long. "What's your big idea, anyway? You said you could do something."

The weight on Frankie's chest was considerable. He was about to promise something, and he suddenly didn't know if it was right.

"What?" Winston pressed.

"I'll talk to Joe. Next week. We have another mission. He might have cooled down by then. I'll talk to him when we meet up."

Winston picked up a handful of gravel, weighed it. "Hmm." Then he let the grains slip slowly through his fingers.

Twenty-Three

When Frankie next went to the hospital, he was psyched about the nurse's news. The treatment had finally arrived. Samson had had the first doses. Frankie was eager to see his father, but he was sleeping. His color looked the same. The circles under his eyes were darker, though. At least Samson was getting what he needed. Hopefully he'd be feeling better soon. All Frankie had done had not been for naught.

Not wanting to wake his father, Frankie headed for school to check in with his teachers. They were pleased to see him, not demanding much, because of his situation. If they only knew. Frankie trudged down the hallway of the admin building. The letter—the G-damned letter—was in his backpack. He had to mail it. It was ridiculous!

Ahead, the school logo gleamed on the wall, YET HIGHER catching his eye as always. He slowed. It was time to tell Mrs. Gordon. Maybe about the whole thing? Yeah, that'd go over well: "Oh. And by the way, I joined a posse and gave up my scholarship and tried to kill a kid—" He shook his head hard, exhaled just as hard, and knocked on Mrs. Gordon's half-opened door.

"Frankie," she said, glancing up. "Come in!" He wiped his hand across his brow and onto his khaki pants before sitting. She looked at him, happy on her face. "Now, what's on your mind?"

The only way out is through, Samson would say when Frankie messed up as a kid, scared to tell what he'd done. So Frankie went right there: "Miss, I think I have to give up the scholarship." His surrender was also his reality.

She adjusted her glasses and folded her hands carefully on the desk. He could tell she was struggling to keep her composure. "Is this about your father?"

Yes, keep it about his father. It *was*, after all, about his father—the whole damn mess. "Yes. He's got a long . . . recovery. And with my mother gone . . . I think I need to stay close to home." His temple started to throb. "I was wondering if . . . there was something, some way I could rework the scholarship, maybe use it another time, next year?" Why did he even say that? There would be no next year. He might be killing people next year, or be killed himself.

"Frankie—" She stopped, again composing herself. "I seriously doubt that the university can do that. I don't even know if they'll be offering the scholarship next year." But, ever hopeful, she turned to her computer and clicked at her keyboard.

He realized he was rocking back and forth, a horse at a starting gate. He put his hands on his knees to still himself, praying for a lifeline.

Mrs. Gordon looked up from her computer a few moments later, frowning. "The deadline to accept the scholarship has passed. It was last Monday."

"What does that mean?" His shoulders were pinching tighter and tighter. He'd been right—the joy was crushed from her eyes.

"It means there's nothing I can do. Frankie, are you *sure* you want to turn it down? I might be able to speak to the university on your behalf."

As if his desire had anything to do with it. His shoulders went tighter still, as if caving in on his chest. "Yes, I think I have to."

"I'm sorry to hear that, Frankie." Her voice had gone flat, just like the admissions officer he'd spoken to in America. He had to get out of there.

He'd blown his chance. His mother had warned him. She had! He was almost glad that she would never know this.

The art building was at the other end of the campus mall, where Leah had said she'd be all day. Frankie debated heading over there.

What was the use of seeing her now? He now, officially, *wasn't* a single thing that she thought he was. Not a scholarship winner—just a boy in a posse. But—but—they had something, a spark, he could feel it. And maybe—maybe, why not see if she'd understand that he truly had no choice? Because that *was* the truth of it.

In the cool, dark corridor, a girl with yellow highlights in her hair pointed out the art studio. Frankie pressed his face to the window in the door. A guy was working clay at a table in one corner. In another was Leah, hovering over a canvas. Her face was a frozen moment. His breath quickened.

He pushed open the door to the sickly sweet smell of paint and turpentine. The sculpting student glanced over, then back to his clay. Leah didn't even glance.

Frankie came behind her and waited. "You never looked at me like that," he said at last.

She looked up, startled. "You're not a blank canvas."

He looked down. The canvas was blank.

"Then again . . ." She paused. "Maybe we're all blank canvases."

He searched her face. "What do you mean?"

"I don't know. Maybe we kind of go around each day sort of lost, just kind of feeling our way through it."

"That's deep." Did she always feel that way, or was it just because she was trying to come up with an idea? So he asked her exactly that.

"Close to it." She smiled in a way he'd never seen before. "I always feel that way."

"That's pretty dark, Leah."

"Don't you think things are dark?" She was sizing him up, fully engaged now.

"Well . . ."

Leah stepped back and gave him an appraising look. "Well, everything's sunny in your world. You're going off to the land of milk and honey. Baseball, hot dogs, apple pies, Disney World, and Drake, Mr. Scholarship. You must be doing cartwheels."

More like belly flops, from thousand-foot diving boards. Covering, he joked, "Drake's Canadian."

"Close enough," Leah said.

Bitterness soured his mouth. It was time to tell her about it. He looked at the kid in the corner. He was out of earshot, so . . . "There's—uh—something you need to know."

"Oh yeah?" She planted one hand on her hip.

"I'm not taking the scholarship. I'm staying," he said in a rush. As her mouth made a perfect O, he added, "My father . . . see, the reason he's in the hospital . . . he got shot."

Leah grasped his arm, her voice suddenly full of concern. "Shot?"

He thought carefully before answering, "A drive-by thing." Okay, so an *almost* truth. "A stray bullet."

"So, what's going on? Is he going to be all right?"

Frankie tried to sound sure. "He's getting a special treatment."

"That's good, at least." Then she crossed her arms. "Don't get me wrong. I think it's pretty cool that you support your father like that. But once he recovers . . ." Her eyes were full of sad. "Will you be able to go to America then?"

Frankie looked over at the guy, bending, twisting his clay. "I should just stay home, you know? He might need me. He doesn't have anyone else." He shrugged. "It'll be okay."

She hugged herself. "Well, I'm really sorry, Frankie. You must be crushed."

"Dealing with it," came out of his mouth as he reminded himself of what he *could* hope for. And he did have things too: his father's recovery, a high school diploma. Lots of kids didn't even have that. And . . . given Leah's concern, the way she was taking the news—maybe her, too?

"Isn't there anything you can do about it? Can you apply next year?"

When he shrugged, as noncommittal as he could be, she reached for his hand. "I know you must be feeling bad, but . . . truth. It'll be good to see you around."

That sliver of hope swelled. "How about we go out again, have some chicken this time?"

"You liked the sushi that much?"

"I think I like . . . you."

And he'd done it—for good or for bad. He had declared himself. He knew the first one to admit it in this game always lost, but he felt that if he didn't, he'd lose anyway.

"Cool. Maybe next week, then?"

She hadn't said she liked him back, but her eyes were soft, her head sweetly tilted, and she'd agreed to go out again. That had to mean something. He could work with that.

She looked back at her blank canvas. "Not to kick you out, but I've got to get back to this. Seems I need to fill it up with something."

Twenty-Four

Sunday morning, Frankie sat beside Aunt Jenny in the back of the Toyota, a knapsack fat with weed between them, the musky scent so strong it would seep into his clothes. The car crept through downtown Kingston. Ice Box, driving, leaned back, hand resting on the wheel. Cricket, in the front passenger seat, picked at a loose knot in his cornrows. Frankie gazed out the window, *Frankie Green, killing machine* drumming through his head.

"Frankie, this a no shopping trip, you know, mon. We driving close to Taqwan's turf," Ice Box said, face stern in the rearview. "You're a lookout, so look out."

"Yes, mon." Frankie squared his shoulders. He started watching the streets, which he knew were watching them. He edged his elbow against the handle of his gun, making sure it was still there, in case things got twisted.

The buildings they were passing reminded him of the architecture in New Orleans he'd seen in a magazine once, ornate columns, off-white, light pink, and beige. Three men in short-sleeved shirts and straight-leg pants stood next to one of the pink office buildings. One stared back at Frankie, pulling something out of his pocket.

"There!" Frankie shouted.

"What?" Cricket asked.

It was just a cell phone. The man looked down at it, answered a call.

"Nothing," Frankie said quickly. Stupid! He resumed scanning the street. Focus! Women with crinkled shopping bags dangling from their shoulders stood in front of a dollar store. A few feet away, a homeless man held his pants up with one hand and begged with the other.

A clutch of schoolgirls in blue-and-tan uniforms walked by a grilled-window moneylending store. One had the same honey complexion as Leah. The time he'd first seen Leah, some invisible vibe forced him to focus on her and only her. It was as if he'd suddenly discovered a new way of looking at people. One of the girls turned his way. She was wearing Ray Bans—and then he was seeing Ray-Ban Boy, lying in the dirt, dust still circling from his fall, the spreading red. Focus!

Ice Box pulled to the curb across from the crafts market. Aunt Jenny turned. "Frankie, you and Cricket come with me."

Ice Box looked at her in the rearview. "You sure me shouldn't come? What if Taqwan knows about this deal? Him must want Brown's connection too."

Taqwan? Hell yeah, Ice Box should come! "Yes, Aunt Jenny. Let Ice Box go instead of me!" Frankie urged. He thought he was only coming along as lookout. That was what Joe had told him.

"I have my gun too, big man. We'll be okay," Jenny assured them both. "We're simply going to a meeting. It's a very important one and I don't want to scare off the distributor, not that she scares easily, mind you."

"Distributor?" Frankie asked.

"I've been negotiating to get Brown's contact down here at the market and a few other places."

This Frankie understood. It was about turf, and growing the posse. Winston had said the posse was growing. It would grow even more now.

Winston! Frankie wondered how he was doing. He had to talk to Joe about him. After this. "So why do you need me?" he asked his aunt.

"You'll find out. The contact is skittish about something, and I don't know what." Then she added under her breath, "Hell if I'm going to let her back out of this deal." She patted Frankie's knee. "So don't overreact to anything, but you have to look ready and be ready, you understand?"

Ready for what? But he knew enough not to ask, nodded as if he *did* know.

"Good. Put on the backpack." Jenny swung open the car door and got out.

Frankie and Cricket followed as she strutted onto the

sidewalk in front of a fit dark-skinned man in a crisp white shirt. Her bag slipped and fell to the ground. The man reached down and picked it up.

Jenny elbowed Frankie. "You see how Cricket is alert?" Frankie turned. Cricket had drawn his handgun, his finger on the trigger.

"When you come on this type of job, you must always be ready." She took the bag from the stunned man and headed for the outdoor market. Frankie gaped—the place was huge! Rows of vinyl tents were spread out over the entire block. Drums filled with shirts, bins of blue jeans everywhere. Water coolers housed cool drinks for sale. Cheap plastic toys and imitation Nikes and Adidas sat on cinder blocks next to boxes of plastic-wrapped candy. A woman in a worn apron sat on a milk carton. She lifted her hand in a half wave, and Jenny nodded back. She must be a lookout.

Jenny turned down a row thrumming with light-haired tourists, all speaking a throaty language Frankie didn't recognize. Their number and the way they moved as a pack suggested they were fresh off a cruise ship. Jenny skirted the crowd until she reached a powerfully built woman with a wooden cross around her neck. The woman picked up a pile of black shirts and disappeared through the slit of the tent flap to her stall.

Jenny told Cricket to wait as she beckoned Frankie to follow her.

Inside the stall were stacks and stacks of garbage bags, all full. A teenage girl perched on a stool, a nine-millimeter handgun on her lap, her finger on the trigger. Frankie tried not to look shocked. And now he wondered if he should have his hand on his own gun. But that might provoke an incident. He could put his hands behind his back and look tough, but that was just stupid. So he let them fall by his side.

"This must be your nephew," the woman with the cross said. Tall and dark-skinned, as dark as Frankie, she had propped herself up on one of the garbage bags, stuffed tight. "Yes, I see what you've been saying. A very smart young man. I see him figuring out what to do already."

Frankie blinked hard. Was she an Obeah woman? Could she read minds? Could she cast spells, too? Frankie glanced at his aunt. And why would she tell this woman about him?

"So, explain to me, Denetria. I thought the deal was done." Jenny's gold bracelets jangled as she gesticulated. "Me know is not Taqwan you worrying about."

Denetria took a tee from the stack, one that read JAMAICA, NO PROBLEM, and started folding it slowly.

His aunt shifted from one high heel to the other. She was nervous! "If you go with Taqwan, you have to get more muscle, you know? Teenager on a stool isn't going to cut it. Taqwan will try to pull you under his influence." Denetria's eyes narrowed, but Jenny powered on. "You won't be independent no more. You know him have party connection with the JLP. I know you don't like dealing with them. You're a PNP like Joe, like me, like Brown was."

Though Frankie kept his eyes fixed on Aunt Jenny and Denetria, he was fully aware that the girl with the nine-millimeter was staring at him, had been the whole time. If things went sideways, like with Ray-Ban Boy, he would be dead. Like Ray-Ban Boy. Still, he resisted the urge to pull out his gun.

Denetria finished folding the tee and set it down. "Yes, okay, Taqwan wants me to distribute here and at the seaports. But I like you. Plus, Brown trusted you and I trust Brown, God keep his soul."

"So, what's the problem, girl? You will get the same product, it's just coming directly from Joe, instead of Brown. Farm to market, girl."

Denetria picked up another T-shirt. JAMAICA, NO PROBLEM. "Problem is, Joe is doing enforcing for the PNP."

The girl on the stool shifted the gun to her left hand, cracked her knuckles, then returned the weapon to her right.

"He's intimidating voters," Denetria went on. "I know it has to happen. Election is a few weeks away, but me don't want no bloodbath like inna Seaga and Manley times."

Seaga. Manley. Frankie knew those names. His tenth-grade teacher had talked a lot about them. They were political candidates way back in the 1980s election, when more than five hundred people were murdered because of political affiliations. He'd actually lived through all that madness when so many people got killed during elections.

"Joe can't take it too far, not on Taqwan's turf." Denetria put the T-shirt away neatly on top of the other one she'd folded.

"War is bad for business," Aunt Jenny agreed, picking up a T-shirt and starting to fold herself. The tent flaps rustled. Frankie slid his hand to his gun as sunlight spilled into the room.

Three teenagers stalked into the tent, two with handguns at

their waists, the third clutching some sort of sawed-off shotgun, the barrel pointing down.

"Time fi go, boss," one said.

Denetria held up her hand—*wait*—then turned to Jenny. "It's a deal—as long as you understand that I can't have a war in my backyard. Taqwan controls turf two streets from here."

Aunt Jenny nodded. "Me understand, Denetria."

Denetria raised an eyebrow. "Does *Joe* understand?"

Another nod. "Yes, girl. He's been understanding."

"Okay. I assume the backpack is the first delivery to make things official?"

Aunt Jenny nodded, extending her hand. "So, we have a deal, girl?"

"We have a deal." Denetria shook Aunt Jenny's hand. "And as you can see, me have much more than teenager on a stool."

Aunt Jenny then nodded at Frankie.

Sliding the knapsack off his shoulders, he put it on the folding table. He somehow understood that when you made illicit transactions, you never handed the merchandise or money to the customer, no matter how safe the environment seemed. Then he wondered how he knew.

Denetria looked at Aunt Jenny. "Yes, very smart boy. He knows how it's done."

"Yeh, mon. No flies on him."

No flies? Then he chuckled—Aunt Jenny meant he wasn't a dumb shit.

As well as the transaction had gone, he was happy to get out of that tent, see Cricket and sunshine again. He noticed two other grim-looking boys standing nearby, clearly more of Denetria's people. Denetria knew what was up—that was for sure.

As he and Aunt Jenny and Cricket made their way out of the market, Frankie kept looking back over his shoulder. The two teenagers were still fiercely watching. As dedicated and focused as, well, he'd been about engineering. Like he'd better become, if he wanted to stay alive.

Twenty-Five

the nurse clutched Frankie's father's medical chart to her chest as if it were a sick child. "The doctor feels the treatment hasn't had enough time to take effect yet," she was telling Frankie. "The delay in getting the Linezolid didn't help, and your father's blood pressure is lower than we'd like, but we still have hope."

"Hope. *Pfff.*" His father looked up at the ceiling, clenched his jaw.

Frankie's mouth went dry. When the treatment had come, he'd expected a quick recovery. But his father's face was still tinged with an unhealthy yellow, and now his eyes were sunk deep, as if etched in with some sort of tool. His arms were covered in goose bumps despite the fever. Frankie wondered if the nurse was just being hopeful. Maybe the treatment wasn't going to work after all? Still, he had to be hopeful also.

Frankie bobbed in the cheap plastic chair, his nerves electric. His father could easily decide to say to hell with the treatment and walk out of the hospital, banking on cerise tea. Bumboclot! "So, how long do you think it will take for him to get better?" Frankie asked.

She pulled harder on the chart. "I can only say that the doctor remains hopeful."

Samson slapped at the rail. "Lawd God, you people even know what you're doing?"

The nurse sighed. She was pretty, in a tired way. "Mr. Green. I sincerely wish you were feeling better. We're doing what we can," she said.

Frankie didn't wait for his father to start in about using bush tea or any other country cure. "It's okay. We're grateful for all you're doing." He nodded firmly at his father.

His father turned his head away in disgust.

The nurse hooked Samson's chart to the bed rail. "All right then. If there's nothing else, I'll leave you two alone." Odd— she wasn't looking Frankie in the eye anymore. And her words seemed more clipped than usual, like she was nervous. She was scared, he realized. Was it something about Samson's prognosis—or had she somehow gleaned that Frankie was in a posse? No, he was just being paranoid.

"Thank you," Frankie called after her.

Soon as she was gone, Frankie's father slammed his hand against the mattress. "This is bullshit. Me have a good mind to just leave this damn place." He was breathing heavily.

"You can't do that, Daddy!"

"All that money," he muttered. "You know what? Get me clothes, mon."

"No, Daddy." Frankie tried not to sound desperate as he grasped his father's forearm. The skin felt hot, the muscles soft. "You need to do this. I've got it taken care of. Just lay back down."

"In all this time me not getting any better. It's bullshit, mon!" He stabbed a finger in the air. "All them want is money."

Frankie kept his hand on Samson's arm. "We just have to wait for the treatment to work."

His father pulled his arm loose and struggled into a sitting position. Frankie knew the effort this took him, the cost of the show.

"Frankie, look, thank you. But next thing you know, them going to want more money. And me don't want you spending no more. Me don't want nothing to interfere with your scholarship. That is your future. God knows you worked hard for it." Beads of sweat pooled on Samson's forehead.

A gnawing ache started up in Frankie's stomach. It was as if the lie was something he'd swallowed, something rotten, now eating away at his insides.

"Come boy, go get me clothes. We're leaving." Samson started pushing the sheets down, pushing trays away, yanking at the bed's safety bar. He clearly had some reserve of strength.

"Dad! You have to lie down! You have to give the medicine a chance!"

But his father was swinging his legs—stick thin in only two weeks—over the side of the bed, his breath raspy. His father would die to secure Frankie's future. Commit medical suicide. Frankie couldn't let him.

"Dad!" Frankie felt pure panic. Samson was trying to stand, his arms shaking the bed rails so hard the entire bed was rattling. Where was that nurse? For once, of course, no one was around. Frankie couldn't think of anything else to do except what he dreaded most. It was the only thing that might stop Samson from leaving.

He said it fast, certain he would vomit. "Dad—I got the money from Uncle Joe. It's not from the scholarship."

Samson went deathly quiet. Bizarrely, a phrase his mother used to say popped into Frankie's memory. *He was a man who'd spent a long time growing a seed into a plant only to find it chewed away by a squirrel in the night.*

Samson's face seemed to contract: his eyes were suddenly closer together, mouth inched up to his nose, the furrows on his brow had taken over his forehead—a shrunken head of despair. "Damn you, Frankie!"

"I made a deal for the money. I'm doing some work in the posse." There, he'd said it. He wouldn't elaborate.

His father slumped back onto the bed. "That son of a bitch," he said first. Then, in a voice gone shaky, as if pleading with God himself, "You can't do this."

"I did it already. I had to. Daddy, look, you have to stay and let this treatment work. You *have* to."

"Don't tell me what *I* have to do. I'm your father and *I* tell you." His father glared at him. "Boy, you don't know what you've done."

"I do." But Frankie fought the urge to break down in sobs. "And it's done already. So please, tell me you're going to stay and keep taking the treatment. Or I've done this for nothing. I can't lose Ma *and* you—"

Samson started twisting like he was tied up with a rope and was trying to escape. "Lord, see my trial! Frankie, you're a damn fool. This will not abide." The anger got him going again. He started to sit up, but he was weakening, "You let Joe, Joe of all people take you!"

Frankie summoned all the calm he could muster. "Look, Dad. I think you have to consider how much you hate Uncle Joe, and how much you love me. And which is more important to you."

Samson stopped. With the look on his face, he could have been a duppy. "What is this you're saying?"

"Dad, if you love me more, you will stay here and keep taking the treatment." Frankie was spent. He had nothing more. "I can't say it any clearer."

Down the hall, a bedpan hit the floor. The elevator bell rang. His father sat nodding as if he'd never stop. They sat there a long time, could have been minutes, or maybe hours, both of their heads down. The silence was torture.

"Okay," Samson said at last. "You throw away everything, Frankie. Lawd help you." He shook his head as if ridding it of mosquitoes. "When me get out of here, me going to talk to Joe and straighten this out. Owing money to that man is like owing it to the devil himself."

Frankie felt faint. "Okay, you're staying?" He had to hear the actual words.

"I just said so."

Frankie had to believe him. There was nothing else.

Twenty-Six

foolishly, Frankie had let Leah choose where to go on their next date on Saturday, so long as it wasn't for sushi. But now she was so psyched up about her choice: an art museum—the National Gallery by the busy harbor, yet another place he'd never been before. To show him her world, why it was so important to her, she said. But how could he argue against all her enthusiasm? The girl had soul.

As Leah bounded ahead, pointing at this painting and that painting, Frankie began to feel woozy. He couldn't focus on the damn paintings. Now that he'd told Samson about Joe and the posse, he had to tell Leah. And all the rest of it, everything that had fallen on him like an ambush on a moonless night. He ran his hand over his face. He needed water. The room felt eerie. The paintings seemed to float off the walls like spirits from another realm. The sculptures seemed to jail shrunken Africans, reminding him of the duppy stories he'd heard as a boy. His grandmother, deformed by age, had told him about the rolling calf, about humans who walked with curses, and about the tortured bodies of dead slaves reanimated, stalking the night, chains rattling as they sought a flesh offering. Wo!

He lurched out of the room into the hallway. There—a water fountain. He turned the knob, cupped the cold water, and splashed his face. He had to do it twice more before his thoughts would settle. What the hell! He had seriously freaked in there. Was that what an anxiety attack was? He took another minute to compose himself—glad Leah hadn't come out—then headed back to the room.

Leah was circling a massive sculpture of a man, probably a great man, looking straight upward. Was he praying for help from above? Would he get it? Frankie could surely use some.

Leah looked so happy, so peaceful. He couldn't bear to break that spell.

He joined her at last. She turned and smiled.

"Who is he?" he asked.

"It's called *Negro Aroused*."

"Impressive."

"Isn't it? What does it make you think?"

"He seems to be a great man, and—"

"And . . . ?"

"I don't know. It's stupid. What do I know?"

"You can't be wrong. It's your interpretation, so just say it."

She smiled in a way that made him get that she really wanted to know what he thought. Okay then.

"Well, it's like—to me, anyway—he's looking up to the past. You know how most people feel messed up about the past because of slavery? But he's looking back to a different past, a way back past . . . to . . . a time without slaves, when Black people were free. From the time before shackles . . . to a *better* past." He blushed. Where had that come from?

"You're a poet, Frankie," Leah said.

"Oh yeah, that's me," he scoffed, embarrassed. He thought about her at her art review. There were so many questions he wanted to ask about it but had been afraid to. Yet she'd defended herself in front of *crits*, so he asked, "The night of your art review . . . How did you find the, whatever it was, to talk back to those crits like you did?" He couldn't have done that—and yet he'd talked back to his father in the hospital yesterday, something, huh, he'd hardly ever been able to do before.

She began inspecting the statue again. "That's ancient history, Frankie."

"Well . . . this is an ancient history kind of spot, isn't it? I mean, what better place to talk about it, right?"

Dimples. "You have to speak from your heart. That's my thing." She came full circle, was back at his side.

Was he more *head* than *heart*?

"My canvases have intellectual truth, but they lack emotion," she said, imitating an official voice. "My teacher told me I needed to be strategic in how I put out my canvases, especially since they were so political." She shrugged. "She knew they'd hate that work; she wanted me to—advised me to—start with simple portraits and save my abstract work for last. But I didn't listen. I had to present my line of caskets all the way to the prime minister's house, first, right in the crits' faces." There was fire in her eyes.

She had marched so defiantly to the crit table, then come away slump-shouldered, the fire in her step out. But it was back, that fire. "So, why did you do it?"

"So here's the thing. I knew my teacher was right. The crits are way conservative. But I just felt like doing it my way." She picked at a smudge of paint on her fingernail. "I get like that when I'm close to things I want. A bit self-destructive, maybe."

Man, she knew herself so well. How could she be so aware, and still do something self-destructive? And so he had to ask, "When you get close to guys you want, do you act that same way? Self-destructive?"

She laughed, then gave him a piercing look. "We'll see, won't we? I've never gone with a guy before. Seriously, I mean."

He wasn't head now—all heart.

She strode toward a big bright painting and pointed. "Look at this one. Watson's *Conversation*."

Three Jamaican women in head scarves, plain blouses, and skirts stood having a conversation. Frankie didn't notice anything particularly unusual about the image. He'd seen women like this all his life.

"See their hips, the way they're pushed forward? Pride, right?" Leah gestured with her own hips. "Those hips are saying we're going forward, and nothing's going to hold us back. Damn right . . ." Her voice trailed off like vapor.

Jeez. She got all that looking at one painting? He watched her move to the next painting, his brain in overdrive. For the past four years, he had been studying math and science, his whole goal to get away. Sure, he wanted to come back to Jamaica someday and make changes. But he could tell Leah loved Jamaica, her people. She loved this life. She was trying to make a difference *now*.

And here he was, in a freakin' posse. Frankie sighed, bumped his shoulder into Leah's. "You all right?"

"It's just—this one is fucking perfect."

Frankie liked it, but "perfect" wasn't the word he would choose. "Truth? I'd rather see more of your work." And he wasn't joking.

"Shut up." Her smile was crooked and beautiful. "You sure this isn't boring the hell out of you?"

Frankie touched her shoulder and suddenly, without even thinking about it, he soft, soft, kissed her.

And for a moment she leaned in, soft, soft. Then, abruptly, she pulled back. What? She was rummaging through her bag. What? And then she pulled something out.

"What, did I win something?" Frankie tried to joke.

She opened her fist to show him a prescription bottle. Watching him warily, like a deer about to startle, she pressed the bottle into his palm, then reached back into the bag and removed another.

Zoloft. Lexapro. He had heard of the first one. It treated

depression, so he assumed the other was similar. Those were big-time meds. Whoa—what was she dealing with? He moved to pull her to him, but that would come off like pity. So he held back. "You *are* dealing with drama . . . ," he started, remembering what she'd told him early on. Family drama . . .

"Don't worry. I don't take them at the same time. I used to use this one, and I just sort of keep it on me—" She took one from his hand. "Does it weird you out?"

Frankie shook his head firmly. "Nah, everyone's dealing with something." Now it was his turn to open up! But he couldn't. For some ridiculous reason, he thought of Winston unable to shoot and felt a wave of empathy. "Anything else in the bag?" He smiled.

"Gum. Want some?"

"My breath that bad?"

In answer, she leaned forward and kissed him . . . longer this time. "No," she said at last, pulling away. "Your breath's all right."

His entire body was throbbing. "You want to talk about it—the meds?"

She shrugged. "My mom is a freak and my father's an asshole." She took back the other bottle and popped both in her bag. "You need to know more?"

"No. You don't have to tell me anything."

"Let's have dinner."

"You have money to just go to restaurants all the time, huh?" he teased.

"At my house, dummy."

Frankie froze—that meant meeting Leah's family. But there was no way he could refuse, so, "Sure, why not?" was what he said.

"You don't sound very enthusiastic."

"Meeting your girl's parents isn't exactly like going to a Vybz Kartel concert."

"He's in jail. And don't be like that."

Okay, so that wasn't the best thing to say.

"Besides, you'll only be meeting my grandmother, maybe my dad." She took out her phone, typed out a text, and hit send. "Let's go. They know you're coming."

Twenty-Seven

eah's house wasn't a mansion up in Cherry Gardens or Norwood, but it was one of the nicer houses in Vineyard Town, a fancy Kingston area only five miles from the National Stadium and two miles from the American embassy.

Frankie kept close to Leah on the litter-free sidewalk, wondering if people came and cleaned it. He knew he'd better make a good impression at dinner, but he also knew he wasn't sure how. "So, what's your grandmother like?"

Leah gave a short laugh. "Be ready—she's not easy. She's retired but used to be in real estate. Sold a lot of expensive houses, but she thinks *she* bought them, if you know what I mean."

"So she's stush?" Frankie joked in patois.

"One of the most stuck-up women you'll ever meet."

"Your mom and dad—are they divorced? You mentioned that they were separated."

"They should get it over with, but no . . . not yet. My mom doesn't live with us, though. Haven't seen her in a year, actually. She has a lot of problems, emotionally, I mean." She looked away. "Dad—he's a control freak . . ." Her voice trailed off as if she didn't want to say more about her family. Huh. So *her* mom wasn't around either. Did Leah miss her as much as he did his own ma? His thoughts were interrupted by Leah elbowing him. "That's my house."

Frankie gaped. How many thousands of millions did *that* cost? It was a sprawling white ranch-style house, completely gated in. The metal grilling protecting the windows was expensive enough, but there was also a large cooling unit—central air—at the side of the house. The copper pipes alone must have cost a fortune. "Guess you're not starving." Gah! What an idiot thing to say!

And she called him on it, stopped at the gates. "What's that supposed to mean? Yes, my family has money. Can you deal with it?"

"Yeah, I can deal," he assured her.

She pushed open the gate. "Now, don't get freaked out by what my grandmother might say."

"She doesn't mean it?"

"Oh, she does." Leah gave a wry smile, led him past an East Indian mango tree and a carport. "Just don't get freaked out."

She paused in front of an open window. "Damn, left it open again."

He thought of Samson's security device. "You get burglars in *this* neighborhood?"

"Not really. My dad just gets on me when I let the AC out." She continued walking. "But I like fresh air, don't you?"

"I get that. I live on a mountain. Best air there is."

The front door, all carved in walnut, was so heavy it whined on its hinges. The foyer was paved with maroon-patterned tile—his mother would have loved it. She'd made a border around their small garden in the backyard with cast-off pieces of tile she'd found here and there. She'd have flipped over this. Off to the right, the living room looked massive, twice the size of Frankie's whole house, at least. The bowed legs of the table in the dining room—mahogany—made him think of the one Samson once made for Mr. Brown. The paintings on the wall looked real, in ornate gold frames. He felt like he was at the museum. But oddly, none of Leah's paintings were on the walls.

He spied a framed poster in the entryway to the dining room. The poem on it was one of his mother's favorites: "Footprints in the Sand." Back in Troy, church ladies—his mother among them—had often quoted the words to him: "My precious child, I love you. . . . During your times of trial and suffering, when you saw only one set of footprints, it was then that I carried you."

A woman, a shade or two lighter than Leah, with the same high cheekbones, wearing tight pants and a white shirt that clung to her rail-thin frame, swept into the room. She looked at Frankie the way salespeople in Kingston stores always did—the type who watched his every move; made him feel guilty, even though he hadn't done anything.

Leah tapped his arm. "Frankie, this is my grandmother, Penelope Bradford."

Frankie walked forward and extended his hand.

Her grip was soft. She let go too fast. "So, you gave up your scholarship?"

Frankie nearly choked in surprise. A hardness settled into the sides of Leah's mouth, but before she could say anything, Frankie responded with, "Things happen." He should explain, but if he explained the problem, he might have to explain the solution. Plus, his father being shot was proof enough that he didn't belong here—they wouldn't have the bad taste to let such a thing happen in this neighborhood.

Penelope huffed. "Nothing more useless than a man who gives up. I'm going to microwave the dinner. It's gone cold—you young people have no concept of time. Frankie, have a seat." She watched him until he sat at the dining table, then left the room.

"I warned you!" Leah said with a grimace. "I should help her. Just wait here."

"Sitting on the hot seat," he added, trying to laugh it off. He watched her leave, feeling like a kid in detention at school. A chair sat at the head of the table but not at the other end. That seemed kind of weird. He moved to that chair, taking up the posture of a king. He would show Leah's grandmother that he wasn't afraid of her. Then he heard a voice behind him.

"Who's this sitting in my chair? Can't be Goldilocks. He's too black."

Frankie couldn't even react to the insult because—that

voice! He knew it! He whipped around. No. It couldn't be. Shit. SHIT.

There in the doorway stood Sergeant Bradford. The very same Sergeant Bradford who'd come to Joe's camp before Frankie's initiation.

"Frankie, right?" Bradford went on. Dude was still in uniform, still armed. "Wondering how I know your name, right? Eavesdropping. Part of the job. Don't worry, I'm not tracking you . . . yet." He walked over and stuck out his hand. Frankie's brain was sending off sparks. Leah's father . . . was . . . a cop? *This* cop? Oh my God. Had Bradford told Leah about Frankie being in the posse? No, probably—not yet. No way would Leah not mention *that*.

Bradford's hand hung in the air.

Frankie's arms felt frozen.

The sergeant's strange, light brown eyes went icy. Finally Frankie reached up to shake the man's hand.

"I like a man who can take charge," Bradford said, crushing Frankie's hand in his grip. "But not too much charge, right?"

Frankie pressed back, trying to hold his own. He stood up, their hands still gripped. The man towered a good six inches over Frankie, taller than he remembered, and creepier. He recognized Frankie, no doubt. He knew who he was. Bumboclot!

"You been out in the sun?" Bradford asked.

Huh? "Why do you say that?" Frankie said in surprise.

Bradford released Frankie's hand. "You look well black, mon. You should use sunscreen. SPF 400 might do you." He wasn't joking; he was trying to cut Frankie down, just like some light-skinned kids at school had tried to do once. No way Frankie could snap back, though—he had to be cool about it.

"This is as dark as I get, and as light as I get." And not for nothing, Bradford's own daughter was way darker than Bradford was. Leah's mom must have been dark-skinned, like Frankie. Where the hell was Leah, anyway?

Bradford sucked air through his teeth as if trying to dislodge a piece of whatever poor sucker he'd just chewed up. Then he surprised Frankie by saying, "Good, you shouldn't take shit, not even from your girlfriend's father."

When Frankie'd thought about making a good impression, this wasn't what he'd had in mind. Then Bradford's words struck him—Leah had told him he was her boyfriend?

Bradford pulled him back to reality by telling him to sit back down.

Frankie eyed Bradford's gun in his holster.

"No, sit where you were sitting. I want you to." Bradford smiled. No warmth there.

"It's okay, I can—"

"No, I insist." He rubbed his holster with his palm, as if scratching an itch.

Frankie sat back down when Leah came in with a tray piled high with chicken.

"Dad! You're home early," she said, looking worriedly at Frankie.

Bradford swiped a chicken leg off her tray and bit into it, not taking his eyes off Frankie for an instant.

"We have a guest," Leah said smoothly, setting the tray on

the table, "but it looks like you two have already met."

"Not formally," Bradford said, his mouth full of chicken, "but your guest seems to have made himself right at home."

Frankie was ready to bolt out the door.

Leah put on her full-wattage smile. "Dad, this is Frankie Green. Frankie, this is my father. I guess you can call him Lloyd."

Leah's father just stood there, gnawing his chicken. Finally he smacked his lips and corrected her. "You can call me Sergeant Bradford."

Penelope walked in bearing a gleaming teak salad bowl. "What's everybody standing for? Sit down, please."

"I need to take a shower first," Bradford told her.

"Can't you do that later?" Leah sat to Frankie's right. "I mean, you were so hungry you couldn't wait for the rest of us."

"I need to wash off, Leah. Criminals stink, you know." He added, "Isn't that right, Frankie?"

"How would he know?" Penelope said. "Take a seat, Lloyd."

"Guess I'm in demand." Bradford forced a laugh, picked up the chair next to Leah, and walked it to the empty end of the table and sat.

"Really?" Leah rolled her eyes.

Leah's grandmother placed her cloth napkin on her lap. "Lloyd, you're being bellicose."

Frankie told himself to stay calm and stay quiet—don't slip. But his mind was racing. What kind of game was Bradford playing here?

"I didn't go to college, so I don't know what 'bellicose' means,"

Bradford was saying to his mother. He took another chicken leg. "Why don't you tell me what college *you're* going to?"

"He *was* going to the University of Arizona in America, but he had to give up his scholarship," Penelope said, passing the salad.

"That so?" The muscles in Bradford's jaw shifted. "Why's that?"

Frankie held his gaze. "My father got shot, so I'm going to stay here until he's better."

Penelope's eyes went wide. But Bradford merely nodded. "So many people getting shot these days. Seems it can happen to *anybody*."

"Why would you say that?" Leah was mad.

"I'm just sympathizing. The boy must be upset." Bradford tapped the table, as if to get Frankie's attention. "You upset, Frankie?"

Frankie hated the way Bradford said his name—he was mocking him. *But stay cool, stay cool.* "Yes, I am."

"You don't look it, though." Bradford waved the leg. "You must be the hold-it-all-in type."

Leah cleared her throat. "Give him a break, huh, Dad? This isn't an interrogation."

"Frankie doesn't think it is. Do you, Frankie?" He bit into the leg. "A father has a right to know who his daughter is *dating*."

"Nobody said we were dating," Leah fired back. But she turned her gaze on Frankie and grinned.

Bradford's phone rang. He took it out and looked at it, then at Penelope. "Things jumping off downtown." His toying with

Frankie morphed into grim focus. "I have to go." To Leah he said, "Want to see your new works later." Then he turned to Frankie. "Guess you'll be gone when I get back. Maybe I'll see you again. Maybe not."

"Just go." Leah flicked her hand at him, but playfully.

Bradford got up, ran his hand over her hair. "Oh, you know you'll miss me."

She brushed his hand away. "Bye, Dad."

Dad.

Frankie played it cool for the rest of dinner: polite, not giving much away when he responded to Penelope's barrage of questions. Afterward, walking him to the gate, Leah asked why he'd been so quiet, and he explained he was worried about his dad. A half truth? He was going back to the hospital very early in the morning to check on Samson.

As he biked home, pedaling like a bat out of hell, he felt spooked. All he could think was, out of all the fathers in the universe, Bradford had to be Leah's. And never mind what *her* reaction to him being in the posse would be—being with the daughter of any cop wouldn't go over well with Joe *at all*. Being with the daughter of Bradford? No dice.

Twenty-Eight

the next morning, Frankie sat beside Winston at the edge of the circular driveway at Joe's encampment. He watched his uncle, Aunt Jenny, Buck-Buck, and Ice Box as they deliberated while standing around the big wooden table about a hundred feet away. Frankie had just pled Winston's case, urging them to give Winston another chance, but now he felt queasy and second-guessed himself, wondering if he had said the right things, pushed the right buttons. They'd been so stone-faced, even when he'd told them how the posse meant everything to Winston. Frankie's stomach rumbled. He rubbed it, but that didn't help. Looking up, he saw a bottlebrush tree just starting to bloom. His ma always had a tea ready that she made from bottlebrush leaves for belly issues. Frankie sure could use some now.

Winston, head down, was splitting a leaf apart by its stem. How ironic that Winston was now out of the posse and Frankie was firmly in: *Frankie Green, killing machine.*

Winston leaned back, still fiddling with the leaf. Frankie focused on the scar under Winston's eye. "What if they let you back in and you have to get beat up again? You know, jumped back in?"

"Me no 'fraid." Winston let one section of the leaf flutter down. "Beating is the *least* of my problems. Me need di money."

Frankie wasn't so sure that it was the *least* of Winston's troubles. He wished the others would hurry up and decide. He looked back again. Buck-Buck wouldn't stop talking, his every word accompanied by wild hand gestures. This might take forever. But maybe Buck-Buck was on Frankie's side? He *did* owe Frankie a favor—Frankie had never brought up that phone call Buck-Buck made during the church mission. Aunt Jenny didn't even seem to be listening—more interested in her phone, maybe waiting for some message from Denetria? But seriously, what could be taking so long? Either Winston would be allowed back in the posse or he wouldn't. Truth was, while Frankie hoped for a yes, he fully expected a no. He snatched up a stone and chucked it into the bush. Some small creature scrambled away. There was another thing—he should tell Joe about Bradford before Bradford told Joe. But he could deal with only one thing at a time.

Frankie glanced at the Toyota parked nearby. Sunlight flared off the side mirror, like off sunglasses. Ray-Bans. No—he wasn't going there. But the image pushed its way through anyway. The growing pool of red, that permanent look of wide-eyed surprise, plumed in his mind.

He felt like lately, everything set off some type of memory. Carrying water from the pipe to his house, tying his shoelace, even the freakin' bottlebrush tree. He couldn't get away from them, like being stuck in Anansi's web. He ran his hand down his face as if wiping the web off. Boots crunched the gravel— and Frankie looked to the encampment. Joe.

"Nephew." Joe beckoned.

Frankie eyed Winston. Winston gave a short nod and Frankie went over, trying to read Joe's face.

But there was no need—Joe got right to it. Folding his long, sinewy arms, he said, "Me can't let him back inna the posse."

Despite expecting this answer, hearing it said out loud gave Frankie a desperate sensation of free-falling. "Uncle, I'll vouch for him."

Joe's expression remained unchanged, as did his answer. "No, mon."

But Frankie knew how Joe worked with his men. He took them at their word. So he tried again. "I mean it. I'll vouch for Winston."

"Vouch?" Joe snorted. "You can't just give out your word, you know. It has to mean something, Frankie. You haffi' believe in it before the next man can believe inna it."

"I believe in him, Uncle. I've known him all my life." Frankie held Joe's eyes, wanting him to believe, urging him to believe. Without the posse, Winston was a marked man. Dead man walking. Garnett would be looking for him. He kept holding Joe's gaze, trying to project unwavering resolve.

"Believe in what, Frankie?" Joe asked at last. Frankie saw that he couldn't win the argument with words.

"Uncle, Winston wants to pay."

"Is what you saying?"

"The police pay Winston's salary, don't they?"

Joe laughed without making any sound.

So he was right. With that for confidence, Frankie continued. "They aren't going to keep paying as much when they find out you don't have as many men as when you started. Why don't you just take a cut of Winston's salary and give him one more chance?"

"Nice try, schoolboy," Joe said, but he didn't leave. He began walking in a circle around Frankie, his head bobbing. At least Frankie'd piqued his uncle's interest, or greed. Joe finally stopped. "But what make you think me can't find somebody else to do Winston's job?"

"Give him a chance, one last chance, Uncle." Frankie thought about what Winston had said, that he needed the money. Hell, he'd probably *pay* a lot to be in the posse. "Uncle, how much of his salary would it take?" He could hear his own heart beating, the thump seemingly coming from his neck. He willed himself calm.

Joe stood nodding. Finally he pushed his dreads from his forehead. "Hmm? It can happen if me get two hundred US out of his salary."

"Two hundred?"

"Problem?" Joe's eyebrows arched up so high they looked cartoonish.

"No problem," Frankie said quickly. He pumped his fist, both for relief and to further affirm that he was okay with the deal.

Joe pointed a finger at Frankie. "You can answer for him?"

"Yes." Frankie couldn't shake the feeling that he was making another bad move. But what else could he do? Without the posse's protection . . .

"Is this your idea or his?"

"His." It was clear Joe didn't believe him; Winston just wasn't that smart. Shit.

But Joe merely said, "Me haffi' chat with the crew first." Frankie was nearly shaking with relief, but then Joe said, "Buck-Buck was on your side. Him acted like him owe you one."

Relief gone. "Ahh—"

"Don't bother lie. Now, *you* owe me one." He started walking away.

"Thank you, Uncle."

Joe remembered something and walked back. "How Samson doing?"

"I only got to see him for a little bit this morning," Frankie explained. "But not so good, mon. But the doctor is hopeful." *Hopeful.*

Joe scratched through his dreads, shrugged, and turned once more.

Favor on top of favor. Frankie's argument had been flimsy. Joe would never have considered taking Winston back if someone else were asking. Frankie squatted where he was. He drew in the dirt to contain his nerves—an outline of a circuit board.

He was lying left and right lately. He had to remember why he was doing this. It was odd how he kept having to do that, remember the reason behind it all. His father.

A whistle cut through his thoughts. Joe waved. "Bring Winston."

Frankie motioned to Winston, who popped up and jogged right over. "Thanks, mon," he said.

"Hold on," Frankie whispered. "He only went for it because I said you'd give him two hundred US out of your pay."

Winston's eyes bugged. "What the hell, Frankie?"

Frankie tipped his head back in frustration. Winston just didn't get it—didn't get the bigger picture. As in the *dead* picture. Who would take care of his mother and sister *then*? "You want in or not?" It really wasn't easy being Winston's friend.

Winston wagged his head side to side like he was having a conversation with himself. "Whatever."

"Not whatever, mon. You either want in or you don't."

Winston looked sheepish. "In. And—thanks, man."

The rest of the posse had gathered by Joe, their game faces on. Frankie's stomach dropped. Winston was paying two prices. Oh, Winston.

"Stand over here," Joe commanded Winston.

Frankie opened his mouth to protest, but the look on his uncle's face held him back.

Winston, however, raised his head high and faced them all, legs wide, already taking a stance that might allow him to stay on his feet. Not that that would help. But there was no cowardice *there*.

"Yes now, Winston. Everybody in di posse is going to get a taste of the money you paid to get back in."

Frankie blinked in surprise. He'd thought Joe would keep the money for himself. But he should have known—posse first.

Joe continued. "And now, everybody is going to take a piece out of your hide." He licked his lips. "You first, Frankie. One good shot."

Frankie's eye twitched. There were so many times he'd wanted to punch out his friend, for being an idiot—but no way did he want to do it like this. No—

"We have a mission tonight, you know," Joe barked. "Now."

Frankie exhaled, balled his fist, and slammed it into Winston's chest. As his friend grunted, all Frankie could think was *Damn you, Joe.*

"No, mon," Joe said. "In the face."

What?

"In the *face*," Joe repeated.

Frankie smelled his own sweat. *I'm sorry, Winston. I'm sorry.* Balling his fist again, he stepped forward and smashed Winston's fleshy cheek. The contact sounded like a slap, one that echoed in Frankie's head.

With Winston doubled over, heads on his knees, Joe barked, "Go." The whole of the posse moved, an avenging force.

It was over quickly. Big Pelton and Greg were hauling Winston to his feet. Joe handed Winston back his gun. Frankie nearly puked with relief.

"People! Hear me now. I don't want no dead people on this next mission! Take no chances. We're not getting out of the vehicles. Is a drive-by t'ing. No killing. We're going to shoot up a corner, but not the people. Let me repeat. This isn't no killing t'ing! We want to scare the voters in that district! That is all! Shoot over heads."

Frankie rubbed at his aching wrist. Buck-Buck noticed, came over. "Okay, we even now." He smacked Frankie's shoulder and walked off.

Frankie rolled his wrist, making sense of what Joe had said. He thought back to being in Denetria's tent with Jenny. Denetria had pretty much agreed to distribute for Joe as long as there was no shooting, no violence that could erupt into a war with Taqwan. So this mission had to be in Kingston, somewhere near Taqwan's turf. That was the reason for Joe's lecture. Thing was—Joe had sounded odd. His voice was somehow lower, heavier than normal, not Joe's comfortable-in-his-own-skin voice. Like he was nervous and trying to hide it. His face bore the same look as when they'd spotted Ray-Ban Boy dropping his water bucket and whipping out his phone. Joe had seen him do it. The danger was obvious, but he bullheadedly went ahead with that mission anyway. Joe should have called it all off right then and there. He should have, but he didn't. And so people—kids—died. Joe was in over his head.

Damn.

Frankie glanced over at Aunt Jenny. *She* would have read the situation correctly. She wouldn't have misread the situation and just charged ahead with the mission after being made by

Ray-Ban Boy. She handled Mr. Brown, Denetria, everyone in the posse, even Joe to some extent, and she wasn't afraid to do what was necessary.

Damn.

Ice Box was laying out the route they were going to take and went over the gangs they might come across. Joe cracked his knuckles, over and over. Frankie felt increasingly nervous—because no denying it, Joe was nervous.

What Leah had said the other day came into his head: *Maybe we kind of go around each day sort of lost, just kind of feeling our way through it.* Was that Joe? And how was Leah so aware? How the hell was he in such a bumboclot mess? How?

In the back of the F-150, Frankie's nerves turned to worries. What part of Kingston did Bradford patrol? And Winston—he was clearly in pain, subdued, yet still fidgety, his lip busted and crusted with dried blood. A knot was rising on his forehead. *Stay alert, buddy. Don't screw this up,* Frankie mind-meld messaged him.

Joe was sitting shotgun in the front of the truck instead of his usual position in the lead Toyota, and he kept glancing back, his eyes on Winston too.

They drove through an area of West Kingston between Tivoli and Trench Town, a network of rival garrison communities ruled by various factions whose income, Frankie knew, was based on drug dealing. A dry concrete riverbed of aqueducts snaked its way through the garrisons. Shanty homes were hunched so close together they could have shared one long corrugated zinc roof—maybe that had been the inspiration for one of Leah's paintings. Frankie hoped she was doing something nice right now, like painting. He hoped like hell he could see her soon.

The six new recruits kept their arms folded on the handles of the shovels each had in front of them. They were posing as laborers, as Joe had advised. It was so hot out that the metal burned to the touch. As the traffic grew heavier, the vehicles slowed. Near a busy street corner, a pair of ten- or twelve-year-old boys in dingy mesh marinas were playing that game where one person held out his hand while another tried to slap it before the first person could move it out of the way. Frankie and Winston glanced at each other—they'd played the same game when they'd been in elementary school.

On the opposite corner, Frankie spotted two teenage gang members, matching crescent-shaped burns on the side of their faces, in crisp legit-looking American sports jerseys down to their knees. One of them narrowed his eyes as Joe lifted his megaphone.

Frankie took a deep breath and let it out slow, searching for calm. He was going to have to use his gun again, and hopefully he wouldn't hit anyone this time either.

"No one here shall vote JLP!" Joe shouted through the megaphone. "A vote for JLP means death!" He knocked on the back window, the signal. Frankie dropped his shovel, and the clanks of the other metal shovels hitting the flatbed followed. He raised his Glock and started firing into the sky. The other recruits joined in. Gunshots thundered, the collection of sound building and threatening as if it could shatter Frankie's skull.

"JESUS CHRIST!" *"LORD JESUS!"* *"BUMBOCLOT!"* people shouted in terror. The two boys were scrambling away in different directions. A woman dropped her bags and ran; some bright red ackee and fat jackfruit rolled on the ground. The teen in a Miami Dolphins jersey fled. The one in a Chicago Bears jersey dropped to the ground, cringing.

Shots blasted into the upper wall of a grocery store, chunks of concrete breaking away. Parts of the sidewalk splintered as if it were glass.

Frankie's jaw ached, he was clenching his teeth so tightly. This was insane! Even if they weren't aiming at anyone, a ricochet could kill someone standing in the wrong place. Shit! Had Samson been hit by a ricochet?

Frankie looked at Winston. What the hell? His gun was in his hand but aimed down. He hadn't even raised it, much less fired a shot! He seemed to be staring a thousand yards away. Like he was back at the church, frozen. Oh shit, oh shit, oh shit!

Frankie had vouched for Winston. He'd given his word, promised Winston would be a good soldier. And he did *this*? He didn't even have to aim at anyone! Out of the corner of his eye, he saw Joe turning toward them. Holy shit. He was going to get kicked out of the posse for sure. Winston couldn't get himself up and do a little bit of nothing? What was his huge problem? Thinking fast, Frankie made as if he were pushing down Winston's gun, raving, "Shit, Winston! Save some bullets, mon! Stop firing, mon!"

Joe seemed to buy it—he turned his attention to the road ahead as they drove toward their next target. He was fist-bumping Ice

Box, so they had to be pleased with the chaos they'd all caused. Word of the drive-by would spread, and potential JLP voters would be too scared to even walk past polls on Election Day for fear of getting caught in a cross fire.

Frankie clapped Winston's back. "Up, mon. Up, up." But Winston just stared sullenly at his feet. "Winston, what the hell, mon?"

Winston shrugged. "Me no know."

"You better figure it out. Quick too."

It was as if Winston had the yips, like how athletes sometimes lost confidence and couldn't do even the simplest things. There was a cricket bowler once—he was the best on the national team, but after a bad game he completely lost his way. He couldn't even throw the ball to a teammate in warm-ups. Pretty soon he was let go, off the team. Frankie couldn't let that happen to Winston.

Twenty-Nine

Joe did, in fact, deem the terror mission a success—they'd hit a half-dozen other JLP neighborhoods in the next half hour. It was a freaking relief that Winston had gotten over his yips, at least a little, in the next towns, and managed to get off a few shots, at least enough so that Joe didn't notice. But Frankie was still concerned. Suppose Winston had to defend himself? Would he get the yips again?

With only ten days left before the election, the posse's main work was done for the time being. They all turned their attention to their "day jobs": tending to the ganja fields, making drops, and collecting. Frankie only had to go up to Joe's camp for a few days at a time and help prep and bag the ganja for delivery—much like the work he'd done for Mr. Brown. And now he had time for Leah.

He sat in the art studio, feet up on a chair, a *Popular Mechanics* in his hands. He'd gone to visit his father earlier, but he couldn't see him, since they were running some tests. The nurse assured him that they still had a lot of hope. He *hoped* they were right. He'd also just checked in quickly with his teachers—all was good with school. At least there was that.

A few minutes later, Frankie laid the magazine on his lap. He'd read the same paragraph about megapixel capacity three times. But the only information sinking in was that he *had* to tell Leah about the posse.

She snuck him a sweet smile, then tucked a tendril of hair behind her ear as she leaned over her latest project—she wouldn't let him see it yet. She seemed so focused, so happy to see him. And he was back playing yo-yo in his brain. Why screw that up? But why lead her on? He liked her so much. He liked her too much to keep that shit from her. *A lie of omission is still a lie,* his mother would say when he had trouble fessing up to something when he was little. He had to stop lying to Leah.

"Please don't tell me this is what you read for fun." Leah had somehow snuck up on him, peeking at the page open in front of him. "'Hardworking Software'? 'A Brave New World of Surveillance'? Riveting." But he could tell she was teasing.

"Don't you read art blogs? 'How to Clean Your Paintbrush Weekly' or something like that?" he teased back.

She stuck her tongue out at him, then reached into his backpack and lifted out the letter he'd never sent to the University of Arizona admissions department.

"It's my letter turning down the scholarship." Frankie lowered his head, tapped the cover of the magazine, and looked up at Leah. "Just never got around to mailing it. I'm sure they get the message, though."

Leah bit her lip, then put the envelope back into the bag.

"It's cool," he said quickly, trying to brush it off.

"Serves me right for looking at other people's stuff."

The light, bright energy of a moment ago vanished as the loss of the scholarship rained down.

She laid her hand on his shoulder. "Okay?"

He nodded a lie.

She leaned closer and kissed him, her soft lips hard against his, then pushed away with a smack.

At the table behind them, a student cleared her throat, breaking the spell. Frankie took Leah's hand and pointed to her new work. "Can I see now?" And to his surprise, she nodded.

Leah had painted black angels hovering over a blood-splattered child who lay splayed on the ground, seemingly life-less, next to a wall covered with lots of JLP and PNP signage. Shaking, Frankie stepped away. "I think . . . I think you cross a line with this one, Leah."

"Good. That means it's working." She grinned, proud. "Or at least getting there."

Scared as he was, he couldn't hide his admiration. She wasn't going to back down. She was painting what she wanted. It was a canvas of hopelessness, and yeah, a thorough indictment of the government, the *shitstem*. His phone buzzed. It was a text from Aunt Jenny:

Come to hospital. Your father.

o o o

He and Leah hopped off the bus while it was still slowing to a stop and ran-walked the block to the hospital. Frankie checked his phone for the hundredth time. He'd texted his aunt over and over, but still no response.

Frankie scanned the scores of visitors around the outdoor waiting area. No Jenny.

"Come on!" He grabbed Leah's hand, his stride fast and choppy. His chest grew tighter with each step as they rushed inside to the front desk.

"My aunt texted me," he blurted out, breathless, at the attendant's confused face.

"Is your aunt a patient here?"

Leah pushed past Frankie and leaned on the desk. "His father is Samson Green. He's the patient."

The woman sifted through several documents on her clipboard, taking her time, thumbing through page after page. *Hurry the hell up*, Frankie screamed in his head. If he'd said it out loud, it would only make her slow the hell down.

At last she glanced up. "What did you say his name was again?"

"Samson *Green*," Frankie said in frustration.

The woman glared at him, then adjusted her glasses and looked back at the lists.

Leah edged close, ran her hand up and down Frankie's back.

He felt a sudden chill. "Stop, Leah." He pushed her hand away. "Miss, where's the bathroom?"

She pointed toward the elevators. Frankie jogged across the

lobby and straight-armed the bathroom door. When he was done, he caught sight of himself in the mirror at the sink for the first time in who knew how long. His jaw seemed wider, or longer, he wasn't sure which, his eyes more intense. He looked like . . . Samson. Odd. He'd always thought he took after his mother. He splashed water on his face and dried it with his sleeve.

Back at the front desk, the woman was gone. Leah was pale, her eyes glassy. He grasped her arm. "What's wrong? Where's that lady?"

She opened her mouth, then closed it.

"Leah, where is she? What's the—"

She put her fingers to his lips to stop him. "Frankie, I'm sorry, I'm so sorry, but your father died."

He couldn't be hearing her correctly. He closed his eyes, trying to conjure his father's face. But he couldn't. He opened them to the shock of fluorescent lights. He didn't understand. There had to be a mistake.

"What are you saying? Where's the woman?" Frankie spun around, looking for the attendant, then spotted her clipboard. He snatched it up, unclipped the papers, rifled through them with shaking hands. There, handwritten at the bottom of a list of typewritten names . . . No. No, no, no. His father's name: *Samson Josiah Oswald Green, deceased.* The pages spilled out of his hands onto the floor.

"What's going on here?" a security guard demanded, barreling over. "That's hospital property right there!"

Frankie ducked past the guard as if he didn't exist, as if no one, not even Leah, existed. Leah caught up to him just outside the sliding doors and put an arm around him. The people in the outdoor waiting area, faces going grim, turned away quickly.

"He's gone? My dad—he's gone?" The words felt so completely foreign he had to squeeze them out of his mouth.

A single tear slid, almost in slow motion, down her cheek. He pulled her close, pressed his cheek into hers. What happened? How could this happen? Samson was just getting tests this morning. Frankie'd seen him just the other day. Then a wave of guilt crested. He should have stayed—waited until his father was back from the tests! Why hadn't he been there? Why hadn't he stayed? They should have talked. He should have done so much more. And now? And now?

Frankie released Leah and stormed back into the hospital lobby.

"Where is he?" he barked at the attendant, who was back behind the desk.

"Don't raise your voice in here, young man," she said.

The elevator doors opened, and there was Aunt Jenny, his father's nurse beside her.

Jenny rushed toward Frankie, her lips pressed tight, and pulled him to her. Her cheek felt wet, her skin hot. Frankie moved away and broke for the elevator doors.

"You, wait there!" the security guard commanded.

Frankie slipped inside anyway and jabbed the button. Leah slid in just as the doors were shutting. The elevator jerked and creaked as it went up. Leah was full-on crying now, but Frankie could only manage to focus on the closed doors, willing them to open.

A myriad of thoughts pummeled at him. Drug-resistant or not, why hadn't the fucking treatment worked? Why hadn't it come sooner? He hadn't been the son he needed to be! And the worst—he hadn't been there! Frankie stormed through the ward, gagging at the foul urine and peroxide smell, eyes darting, searching for his father's bed.

"May I help you?" a nurse asked, rushing toward him, another nurse by her side.

Frankie turned down a row of patients and broke into a jog. He could see his father's bed ahead, empty, a few ghosted stains on the sheet near where it tucked under. He grabbed the rails. They were cold.

"Oh, I see it. It must be di son," the second nurse said to the first.

The first nurse shook her head. "Yes, me see di resemblance."

Frankie strained to sense something of Samson, but there was nothing. His father was gone. Frankie yanked the sheet up off the bed, holding the cool fabric to his face. Then, tightening his grip, he tried to rip the cloth to shreds. Leah reached for his arm. He shrugged it away. He strained, and tugged, and finally threw the sheet on the floor. He couldn't breathe. The next thing he knew, the room was spinning and he was on the floor. Why couldn't he breathe? Maybe he was going to choke to death, right there. Die on the dirty floor. He should have been there. He should have been there. It was too much, the guilt too heavy, pressing, pressing. Then, he became aware of someone standing over him. Leah or a nurse? No, he was in the shadow of a wrinkled old woman.

"My dear," she said. It was as if her words performed some kind of obeah on him, for a calm fell on him. She extended her wretched-looking arms. Frankie pulled himself up and hugged the woman and started crying into her bony shoulders.

"It's so good of you to come and see me, Johnny."

The woman didn't know who he was. Frankie didn't care. He just held on, tight, his eyes burning with tears.

Thirty

TWO days later, still in a fog, Frankie slogged into his back-yard with a spade and a bucket. The bucket held a small coconut tree he'd dug up by the bushes near the clearing, a few kilometers up the mountain. Carrying the little tree was a lot easier than carrying water from the standpipe, but still, his shoulders felt tight. The burden of his thoughts? In the corner of the backyard, he stopped near another dwarf coconut, the one his father had planted for his mother after she had died.

"You're not going to plant that now, are you?" Aunt Jenny. He hadn't even heard her come into the backyard. "It's for Samson, right?"

Frankie nodded. "Thought this was probably the best spot." Lots of sun.

Aunt Jenny squinted into the sky. "Is a crescent moon tonight, you know?"

Frankie shrugged. "What's wrong with that?"

She studied the heavens as if there were instructions there. "A full moon is the best time."

"I don't think so, Aunt Jenny." Frankie pointed to a twenty-foot coconut tree at the other side of the backyard. "My father and Uncle Joe planted that during a crescent moon. I think it was seven years ago."

"No, Frankie, it was a full moon. And it was ten years ago." She smiled sadly and looked at the house. "It was for your grandmother. She's been gone for ten years."

The memory rushed back. His father and uncle had let him carry the then-tiny tree, in a bucket, just like now. "You're right." He'd been so sure about the moon and the number of years. He shook his head, trying to clear it. "It's just that it's . . . not fair."

Aunt Jenny rocked back and forth. "It isn't. He fought so hard. Maybe if the treatment had gotten here sooner, but how can anyone predict all dem complications, him going into shock? His body just couldn't keep fighting." She looked intently at Frankie. "I hope you're not blaming yourself. You did everything you could to help him. You gave it your *all*."

Was she for real? Of fucking course he was blaming himself. If he hadn't gone to that party, his father wouldn't have come after him. He'd sacrificed his scholarship, and his father died anyway. Could a head explode? If so, his was about to, into a million tiny pieces. If Frankie had done nothing at all, the result would have been the same.

Jenny rubbed her cheeks with her palms. "I have a delivery," she said, pulling her gun from her waistband, checking the slide. "There's some food for you on the stove." Aunt Jenny's way of saying goodbye.

And leaving him alone. Because that was what he was now, alone. In his father's house. Now his house. He wanted to hit something. He looked at the tree, still in the bucket, its fronds so green, so alive. It would die if he didn't replant it. He picked up the spade, grabbed the bucket, and left for the clearing where he'd dug it up in the first place.

Thirty-One

time had become erratic. Seconds were unreliable, minutes slurred together, and hours were moody, too fast or too slow. All he knew was that the funeral was tomorrow, whenever that was, and the only task he could manage was pressing his good shirt and black pants.

The heat rising from the steel iron on the stovetop warmed his chin. If he lingered, it would singe him, and if he waited long enough, it might burn, but then maybe he could feel something.

He heard Aunt Jenny. He looked out the window over the sink, and there she was, in the front yard, talking into her cell phone, one hand gesturing incessantly.

Frankie figured it was posse business because that's what

always seemed to be at the forefront of her mind. He envied her intense focus, especially now that he felt so scattered.

He closed the knob to the propane tank and wrapped the old rag, the one his father had used so many times, around the handle of the iron. Age and use had thinned it. The heat seeped through to his hand almost immediately and started to burn. There were worse kinds of pain. He carried the iron to the table beside the couch, where his sole white button-down shirt lay atop an old towel. Pressing the iron down on the collar, he worked his way from one side to the other, wearing away the wrinkles; his father had done the very same thing with his own shirt for his mother's funeral. Three years. Three years ago, he had parents.

Frankie was on the last sleeve with the iron when Aunt Jenny walked in, Joe so close behind they could have been playing tag. Wow. Frankie hadn't even heard a car drive up. Man, he was out of it.

"Nephew, me want to talk to you and your aunt," Joe said, pulling a chair from the table and taking a seat.

Aunt Jenny leaned against the kitchen counter. A long stalk of sugarcane had been sitting there since before Samson had been shot. Jenny snatched it up and, with the long kitchen knife, chopped the stalk in half.

Frankie brought the iron back to the burner, which he hoped was still hot. His pants still needed ironing. He hoped his aunt and uncle wouldn't stay long.

Joe slammed his hand on the table. "Hear me now. Me don't want to give Samson no funeral."

Frankie nearly singed his skin testing the burner. He jerked his head away.

Joe went on. "This is not a money thing, so don't jump to no conclusions. Me even pay the workers for the tomb already." He began to shake his head, slow, slow. "Rasta don't believe in death. Samson is reincarnating right now, if he hasn't already."

Aunt Jenny wedged the knife into the center of the stalk. "Samson wasn't a Rasta."

"The concrete tomb will hold no connection to my brother." Joe turned to Frankie. "Or your father. It's only a place to keep his bones."

Jenny pushed so hard that the knife sliced right through the cane bark and thwacked into the wooden countertop. "It's what he would have wanted."

Frankie didn't know how to begin to respond. This was too unbelievable! Joe and Samson had battled over everything, including Frankie. But this went beyond that. His uncle wasn't content with defeating his brother—he wanted control of him even dead!

Joe kept on preaching. "Both of you must see that there is no such thing as beginnings and endings. Jah intends for all the things on earth to continue. Energy just transfers, it does not disappear."

Aunt Jenny cut away the last piece of bark. "Joe, I respect your beliefs, but you have to respect Samson's, too."

Joe's smile was not a happy one. "I am respecting the man's *soul*. His spirit doesn't need no ceremony, no send-off. His spirit is still here."

Aunt Jenny chopped the cane into pieces. "I don't know. A whole heap of people are coming to the funeral tomorrow." She tossed a piece to Joe and handed one to Frankie.

Was she weakening or just playing an angle, about to give up something to Joe that would ultimately give her more power? And—now Frankie felt a slow burn—were they using his father's funeral for a power play?

Frankie touched his finger against the iron and pulled it away quickly. He was ready. "I think," he began, "my father would be happy to be buried next to my mother. I would be happy to see it."

Jenny dropped the knife on the counter. Joe gathered up his dreads and let them fall again, his expression sphinxlike.

For the second time, Frankie picked up the old rag and wrapped it around the iron's handle. Knelt in front of the couch. Pressed the iron against his pants. He felt his aunt and uncle watching him. He didn't care. He didn't hurry. He was pressing his pants for his father's funeral.

Chair legs ground against the wood floor. "Likkle later," Joe said at last. The door slammed behind him.

Aunt Jenny sighed, picked up her phone, and made a call. "Yes, it's me again. Let's talk about the thing." On to posse business again, no doubt. And she walked out.

Frankie knelt on the floor worn smooth from years of footsteps, his mother's, his father's. He clutched the handle of the iron, welcoming the heat, smoothing away the wrinkles.

Thirty-Two

With dozens of mourners gathered twenty feet away around his father's grave, Frankie stood on the slope of the hill, the exact spot where he'd seen his father last commemorate his mother's birthday. He'd decided to let Samson grieve in private, that day. Sure, Samson had eventually called him over to the grave, but if Frankie had just walked over and stood next to Samson while he was grieving, things might have been different. He and his father could have shared something, something more than a couple sandwiches, something important that they'd both take to their graves. But Frankie hadn't done any of that. Now, as he stood here, he wished like anything for that moment back. The irony of him in the same spot, also alone, was rich in a twisted way.

The humidity was cloying. Frankie's arms were lathered with sweat; his scalp itched. Mosquitoes made strafing runs at his neck. He ignored them, suffered their bites with unrelenting composure. In the clearing, beside his mother's grave, a crowd of people gathered around his father's, a slab of concrete that resembled a coffin. The local handyman and his son had poured the cement throughout the ceremony, creating the boxlike tomb. Now they were scraping away the excess concrete with spades, perfecting their work.

From the shadows, Frankie counted eleven members of the church choir. They must have been sweltering in their black robes, though they didn't show it. In her black dress and hat, Aunt Jenny stood beside the minister, who was orchestrating with his hands, counting out the beats. They started swaying side to side. And somehow everyone at once started to sing "Back to the Dust." The sound of all those voices lifted up in praise was powerful, even beautiful, Frankie thought. Heavenly thunder, his mother called it. It always had the power to pull him away from his cares. But this time, Frankie felt nothing.

"Respect due, mon." It was Winston, his black polo shirt wrinkled, but his black pants new. He might have bought them for the funeral. They gave each other dap. "You all right?" he whispered.

Frankie shrugged. "Don't know." Honest.

Winston glanced around. "Your father was all right, mon." He rubbed his nose. "Too strict on you sometimes, though. Him always reminded me of a police. But him was all right."

Police. Frankie looked left and right. "Yeh, mon," he said,

his voice cracking. No Bradford. No to Leah, either. He hadn't invited her, fearing that she'd mention it her father, and who knew what *that* would set off. And Frankie still hadn't told her about the posse. In spite of all that, he still wished she were here.

Winston play-punched his arm. "You going to be all right, mon. Me will look out."

Frankie nearly laughed. Winston would look out. *Right.*

Two villagers suddenly glanced Frankie's way, their eyes going wide. Had they spotted him lurking on the fringes, dismayed that he hadn't joined the mourners, that he wasn't singing? But they seemed to see something beyond him. Bradford? Frankie turned and saw his uncle at the top of the path, and behind him, Buck-Buck, his head slowly panning left to right, vigilant. Joe was expressionless. Frankie looked over to Aunt Jenny. She had stopped singing. Her expression had gone as blank as her brother's. Was this what life in the posse did to you, made you immune to emotion?

Frankie heard a whir and slapped his neck. He pulled his hand away; two mosquitoes were squashed to his palm. He stared at the blood, then could hardly wipe it away quickly enough. He couldn't stand there for one more second. Without a word, he left Winston and strode past the choir to his father's grave, the smell of wet concrete strong and familiar. The man troweling away the loose bits looked up. Frankie stuck out his hand. "Can I?"

The man took the cigarette out of his mouth and handed Frankie the trowel. Frankie knelt, pushed away a curl of concrete, smoothing out the area closest to where his father's head lay, easing the old mason's tool back to front, repeating his leveling. All that mattered was that everything should be kept even, the sides not daubed too short.

Frankie nearly had two sides exactly right when he heard a gasp, then urgent whispering. Joe and Buck-Buck were walking away in a hurry, heading toward the road, guns drawn. Aunt Jenny scrambled after them, her high heels digging into the dirt. Winston, his gun drawn, was not far behind. What the hell? Frankie dropped the trowel and jumped up after them.

Joe was in the middle of the street, squatting, elbows on knees. Buck-Buck and Speed stood like sentinels behind him.

Joe eyed them. "Taqwan coming up the hill."

Aunt Jenny unclicked her black purse and eased out her own handgun. She thumbed the safety.

Nothing was sacred, not even a funeral, Frankie thought bitterly. He smacked his fist to his forehead—he should have had his strapping too. Even Winston was prepared, but—the funeral—he just wasn't. Idiot.

Joe—how did he know? He nodded to Buck-Buck, who pulled a second gun, a Beretta like Winston's, from the back of his pants. "It don't have as many rounds as your Glock," he said apologetically to Frankie, handing it over.

Not as many rounds? Frankie turned the gun over in his hands; it was heavier than his. Were they in for a serious shoot-out?

Frankie heard the roar of the Toyota and seconds later, Ice Box and Blow Up jumped out, guns in hand, leaving the doors wide open.

A branch cracked and Frankie looked to the trees—it was only some young villagers at the edge of the woods, eyes wide with excitement. They shouldn't be here. It wasn't safe, but there was no time.

Three SUVs crept around the bend, their engines growling. No one spoke. A Benz, a GMC with tinted windows, and a Denali stopped just fifty feet from where Joe stayed squatting. A man the size of Ice Box, and a light-skinned man with dark glasses, stepped out of the Denali, followed by five scowling teenagers, bedecked in bling and denim. No sign of Garnett. At least.

Now the Benz doors eased open, and Taqwan, ropes of gold chains glittering, emerged. Frankie was mesmerized. They all were. Taqwan was a sight. Frankie'd wondered what he looked like, but this . . . His black shirt had red roses stitched in at the shoulders, and he had rings on almost every finger. If he weren't dripping charisma, they might have laughed. But there he stood, tight gabardine pants, patent-leather long-toed shoes, and the slightest hint of mascara. And his skin, the wildest thing yet—his skin was bleached. His neck was darker—way darker than his face. He must have been using products to make his face look whiter, striving for the "chrome" complexion that some of the guys at school wanted. "Me look too black."

"Girls like it when you light skin." Damn. Taqwan was a trip; a Kingston don but not even comfortable in his own skin.

Two teenage girls, blouses cut low, erupted from the Benz next, big leather bags slung over their shoulders.

"The man has no shame," Aunt Jenny muttered under her breath.

Frankie shook the Beretta uneasily, testing the weight, hoping he didn't have to see how it fired, wondering what the hell Taqwan was doing up here, on a day like this.

Taqwan leaned on one hip as if posing for some rude-boy magazine. "Joe. Me come fi pay respects." He rubbed his chin. "Yes now, your brother must be in a better place."

Joe spoke slowly. "Just another place. Him no really dead."

"Oh right. Jah Rastafari." Taqwan tapped his chest with his fist three times.

Was Taqwan mocking Joe? Frankie grew certain when he saw a small smile grow at the corners of Taqwan's lips.

"Yes, Jah is my God. And what's yours, Taqwan, the almighty bling?" Joe said, calm, so calm.

Taqwan's tiny smile became a grin. He snapped his fingers at the girls, who reached into their large bags.

Frankie started to raise his weapon. Aunt Jenny smacked his shoulder with the back of her hand. "Easy, Franklyn," she whispered.

The girls took out four fancy-looking bottles filled with brown liquid. Faces blank, demeanor like models on a catwalk, they walked right up to Joe and set the bottles—Hennessy cognac—on the ground in front of him.

"Dem bottles is XO, next level up from VSOP!" Taqwan folded his hands over his groin. "The Japanese love that shit! Pay big money for it."

The muscles in his uncle's jaw tensed. This insult came without a veil. Taqwan had to know Rastas didn't drink alcohol. This was part of Taqwan's show, a presentation of dominance.

"I hear you make a deal with Denetria." Taqwan's smile grew wider still, the gold grille over his teeth flashing. "You getting a bigger influence in Kingston."

"Trees grow, Taqwan. That's the way it is."

"Tree? No mon, weeds." Taqwan wagged his finger. "And weeds get cut, Joe."

Frankie swallowed. He figured this was it. The moment was coming. He tightened his grip on the gun.

Taqwan's teenagers backed up and shifted their stance, their hands at their sides.

Taqwan unclicked his gold grille from his teeth, looked at it all casual. "Don't grow any further, Joe. Me dislike gardening work."

Joe nodded to a bush to his left. Winston, Marshal, Baxter, and Big Pelton stepped out from their cover. "Me growing all the time, Taqwan."

Taqwan clicked his grille back in. "Listen now, Kingston ain't the fucking mountains. Shit no live so easy down there." Then Taqwan turned away, but on second thought he swung back around. "Another thing, me hear your nephew had beef with one of my people. I told my man to squash it, but shit does happen, Joe. I can't always control my men, you understand?"

Garnett! Frankie had to stifle his cough. Shit!

Joe reached out and scooped up the bottles, two in each hand. He popped upright, nodded at Taqwan, then with one synchronized swing smashed the bottles. Shards of glass sprinkled like diamonds on the road. He spread his fingers wide and let the bottle necks fall. "The road up here is dangerous,

Taqwan. Me wouldn't recommend you come any further."

"No worries—I'll see you in Kingston, Joe." Taqwan took his time strolling back to the Benz, one hand held high like a ring-master's. The rest of his posse got into their vehicles. Engines revved and the caravan turned around and drove off.

Aunt Jenny already had her phone out. "Denetria. Yes, girl. Can we talk?"

Joe huddled with his men, and Frankie wondered apprehensively what they were saying.

But his showing up here, today, at Samson's funeral, doing what he just did, had all but ensured a war.

Frankie thumbed the safety of the Beretta. He had to get back to his father. And as he thought about the graves of his parents, he pictured his own, right beside them.

Thirty-Three

the abbreviated ceremony—a simple, songless sealing of his
father's grave after Taqwan's little "visit" this morning—
left Frankie feeling restless, wanting something more. Even the
Nine-Night celebration of his father's death, raging in his backyard, wasn't enough. A half hour earlier, he had left the party
to get some air. As he walked back toward home through downtown Troy, the heat oppressive and his father's too-tight square-
toed shoes pinching, it dawned on him that Samson could have
been dead for weeks, months, maybe even since his mother had
been gone. The entire week had become formless, an undefined
jumble of actions.

So many people had spoken of his father's life. So many that
Frankie couldn't match the faces with the voices. "He was a

very brave man." "You could always count on him." "What a good man." How long was the service and what passage had he himself read? He couldn't recall. But then Taqwan came to mind, like one of Leah's hellscape paintings. And everything snapped into focus again. Back to reality.

The pain he felt wasn't going to go away or get better. He could wander alone for days or years and still not leave it behind. He knew this because the breath-stealing gut punch of his mother's death was still present. So why would this new emptiness ever leave?

He neared his house, the vibration of a familiar beat under his feet, the mega bass from the DJ's distort of a Jimmy Cliff remix, "Many Rivers to Cross." His father's Nine-Night was going strong, and should have lasted many days, as was tradition, except Joe had put the kibosh on that—one day was all he'd allow. He'd already made a concession to have the funeral, was his argument.

It seemed the entire village was spilling out of his front yard, filling the street ahead like a roadblock. Aunt Jenny broke through the crowd and handed him a bottle of Red Stripe, already warm. He gratefully raised the bottle to his lips.

He'd forgotten that he had to act like some sort of host. All he really wanted was to sit and be alone for a while, a day, maybe a week. There were many things to deal with.

He made his way to a rickety wooden chair next to the pimento tree, and sat and watched, letting people pass him and clap him on the back. He tried to remember to smile and nod in appreciation for the kind words. He glimpsed Aunt Jenny escorting a short woman with a large church hat through the front door. The woman held a handkerchief over her mouth, sobbing. Her tears reminded Frankie of how stoic his father had been at his mother's funeral, ordering Frankie not to cry, not crying himself. In that moment of his worst grief, Samson had stood rigid like a statue, a barricade against self-pity. Frankie raised the Red Stripe, making a quiet toast to his father, vowing not to cry today. He'd honor his father by withholding the tears, even though he knew his father was wrong. A boy crying at his mother's death wasn't any sign of weakness. It was a tribute to how much she had meant. His father had to have known that. Just like he had to have known that he should have let Frankie know how sick his mother was. Even if *she* didn't want him to know. Because it cost them so much time when they could have been together. And Frankie never really had a chance to tell Samson how pissed he was about that. And now he never would. *Never* seemed enormous.

The sweet scent of coconut milk and thyme wafting through the air had him thinking about his mother's favorite way to make rice. She made it when Frankie wasn't feeling well. He looked up. "Blessings, Frankie," an old friend of his mother's said, the gorgeous smell rising from the plate of rice and peas in her hand. He stood as she grasped Frankie's hand, as so many had throughout the day, shaking it slightly. "May di good Lord look out for you." She handed him the plate, explaining she'd made the rice in honor of Samson—it was one of his favorites that Frankie's mother had cooked. It was? He'd had no idea.

"Thank you." He gave a slight bow, and as she left, he glanced at the house's back window—at least he'd remembered to disarm Samson's natty security device, removing the machete. He made a mental note to reset the machete after the party. It struck Frankie that his father would have thought the very same thing.

He wandered his own yard, spooning the coconut rice into his mouth. A throng of villagers were dancing in the back. They spun, dipped, fell back, bobbed, and wound their hips like waves in an angry storm. He found himself at the trunk of the pimento tree, his boyhood place, his vestigial escape, and gave a wry grin. He was always drawn to this spot. Even today. It was one of the few empty, quiet spaces in the backyard.

If Samson could part the clouds and peek down, what would *he* think about the party in his honor? He might not like all the fuss and might even wish for the people to leave for their own yards. He'd worry about the coconut trees being damaged. When was the next full moon, anyway?

Winston was pushing his way through the tangle of dancers, swaggering as he led Big Pelton, Marshal, and Greg, each gripping bottles.

"Him look too sober to me!" Winston slurred as he reached the pimento tree. He must have been at the rum bar or out on the street smoking ganja.

"The man needs a strong drink for true!" Marshal added happily.

Big Pelton held out a half-finished bottle of Johnnie Walker Black. "Yeh, mon."

Frankie had to admit he was glad to see them. Glad that they'd come. So he smiled and thought, *Why not?* He raised the bottle and took a big sip, his lips making a popping sound when he took the bottle away. An instant burn flared in his chest. That was some strong shit.

"Remember when your father give us drinks, when di hurricane hit?" Winston asked.

Marshal and Big Pelton nodded. "Yeh, mon," Greg said.

"Pass the bottle. We all fi take one next drink," Winston called out, his eyes glassy, his patois thick with drink. He took another swig, then howled like a dog in the night.

They'd been in grade school—fifth? sixth?—and it was during the tail-end of a hurricane's assault. They'd been desperately looking everywhere for Marshal's dog. And though the wind had died down, rain crashed like waves from the sky. Samson had led them down the mountain. When they'd reached the road near the bottom, they were shocked to see that it had become a small river. A torrent of water dragged along uprooted trees, bushes, two-by-fours, and random pieces of clothing.

Suddenly Samson pointed. Marshal's dog. But it was wedged against a branch, bobbing in the current. Samson wasted no time. He bellowed out orders, raising his voice above the driving rain and the river roar. Frankie marveled at how sure, how positive, how in charge his father had been that day. No way was that dog—what was his name? Yes, Pele—going to drown on Samson's watch. He got Frankie and the others to lock arms and brace against the river's rush, creating a human chain so he could wade out in the water without being washed away like all the branches speeding along the relentless current.

Samson had sloshed into the water, repeatedly losing his

footing as the thrust of the water pushed against him. He stumbled, his arms jutting out to the side, a counterbalance that somehow kept him from falling, being swept away.

"Daddy! Don't give up!" Frankie remembered yelling. Whether his father had heard him over the rushing water or not, Samson fought on. Pele whimpered as Samson extended his arm and scooped the dog out. He cradled it under his arm and slowly made his way back to land.

Once home, Samson offered each of the boys one shot of Johnnie Walker Black. Frankie smiled, remembering. And was touched, actually, that Winston had, right down to the exact brand of liquor.

Frankie had always wondered if his father had heard his shout. Or if he had known how proud Frankie had been of him. His father had been a hero.

He took another sip of whiskey. He had forgotten that story, but Winston hadn't. Frankie looked at the circle of friends. Come to think of it, not one of them even had a father they lived with, or who even visited. Damn. But Samson—had been there for them that day.

The bottle circled back around. Frankie inhaled the smoky smell but took only one last small sip. He couldn't get drunk now, not on the day when he had buried his father, not when he had promised himself, and his dead father, that he wouldn't cry.

"We going over to di lounge," Winston said. "Come no, Frankie?"

His friends had had enough. Even in the few minutes they were there, he could tell. The service at the grave, and bearing witness to older people's dancing and revelry—ugh. Frankie wanted to leave with them, escape the sudden responsibility, the carousel of people who came around to him demanding his attention, demanding it like he was suddenly different, older. . . . But for Frankie, there was no leaving, no matter how much of a relief it would be to go drink himself numb with his friends. He represented the family—dead and alive.

"Likkle later," Frankie said.

The posse offered various salutes and respects, their gestures like shadows that stayed with him as they slipped away, single file, fading into the crowd. Frankie was surprised at how alone he felt without them. He felt pain in his palms, realized he was digging his nails into them. Truth was, crying would have been such a relief.

Thirty-Four

frankie turned off the water at the kitchen sink, stopping the trickle. Out the window, the yard was empty, finally. No more guests. He noticed a limb of the breadfruit tree was heavy with fruit, hanging over his house. *His* house. He'd never get used to that.

He dried the last dish—the one his ma's friend had brought the coconut rice in—careful to stack it in the right pile. Several neighbors had loaned what they could for the Nine-Night. Thankful as he was, he had thought they'd never leave. Tomorrow morning he'd return everything and thank everyone for being so considerate, for coming. They would probably tell him all over again how sorry they felt, and that he could count on them for anything. He didn't look forward to all the pity. All he wanted was to be alone for a while, to take time to understand what all this meant, life without his father. Things had changed, but the differences weren't clear.

Aunt Jenny idly straightened the stack of plates and let out a long sigh. "I wish you'd let me help you clean up. You've been at it for hours, Franklyn."

He looked down at his hands, his wrinkly fingertips.

"I know you're grieving. We all are. But don't be so fast to be all alone." She rubbed the back of her neck. "Your uncle and I were talking. We feel it's safer for you and the others to move up to the camp." She pinched her nose to stop a sneeze. "All the other boys are moving up in the morning."

Frankie didn't have to ask—he could feel the reason. Still, to confirm, he asked, "Taqwan?"

"Just in case," she said, then held up a finger for him to wait, as her phone buzzed. She frowned and started quickly typing.

Sure, Taqwan must be plenty pissed about losing the Denetria deal, but it hadn't been his in the first place. But that was logical thinking, Frankie knew. And logic didn't always come into it. Like leaving. Logically, he knew he should. It'd be easier in some ways—leave behind the memories, leave behind the loneliness—but at the same time, this house was all he had now of his parents. How could he leave that? Logic didn't come into play here. He looked to the floor where Samson—so many years ago—had built a bridge between the two styles of wood in the floor. He'd done such a good job that the maple and walnut actually blended. Frankie almost laughed out loud: it was like a goddamned metaphor. He and his father were the two different woods, except there was no chance of that bridge now, was there? He looked at his aunt. Did she feel the same way, about his dad? "Thanks for all you've done, Aunt Jenny. Looking in on me and all," he blurted out as she put away her Blackphone.

Her face turned concerned. "Frankie, you don't get it. You're going to move up to the camp first thing in the morning."

He shook his head. "I want to stay here for a while. Maybe in a couple days I'll come."

She sat back, searched his eyes. "Franklyn, this is no time to be sentimental. This is Taqwan we're talking about. He doesn't joke."

He thought of all the chores. The plants needed watering. Water! "I do get it, Aunt Jenny. I just need to do some things first." His father would have taken care of business first. "You know, I wanted to get away from this house so bad." He laughed, a resigned sound, no joy there at all. He looked at the caulking between the sheets of wood that made up the wall. Some was crumbling—he'd have to dig it out, add new caulking. He'd watched how Samson had done it before. "But now I need to stay." He gazed imploringly at his aunt. "Just for a day. I just need a day."

"Lord, Jesus." Her phone buzzed again. She looked at it, then put it back down. "Listen, Franklyn, your father didn't want you in the posse. But you're in it now, and you have to forget what you regret."

"Forget?" Behind Jenny was the black-and-white picture of his mother, the one his father was holding when Frankie told him he'd gotten the scholarship. Forget?

Jenny's eyes went soft, for a moment only, but he saw it as she said, "Tonight only. Me and Joe are your family now, Franklyn."

And the posse—Winston, Marshal, Greg, and Big Pelton, especially the way they'd shown up at the party—were there for him.

Aunt Jenny swung open the door. "You need any help, you call. But remember, we only talk about where to meet, no posse business on the phone."

"I understand, Aunt Jenny."

"Come ya, mon." She opened her arms and hugged him, swaying into it the way his mother used to do. Reassuring him that no, he wasn't alone.

Later, Frankie twisted the opener along the tin lip of the bully beef can. The corned beef smelled like hard-boiled eggs. He daubed the purple mash over the buttered hardo bread, then chopped a slice of onion and landscaped the pieces over that. The chair creaked under him as he sank his teeth into the salty, pungent blend.

He couldn't remember if he'd eaten anything at the party. His head ached from the whiskey, that was certain. His father loved bully beef, but as Frankie went to dollop more out, strangely, there wasn't much left in the can. Yet the sandwiches Samson made for Frankie were always thick, thick. Frankie paused, knife in the air. Because Samson gave most of it to *him*. He turned from the sandwich.

His father's silver hair clippers lay next to the dog-eared King

James Bible on the small table by the couch. Sighing, Frankie plunked himself down. The clippers were heavier than he remembered. He lay back and pressed the button. The battery still had juice, the sound was—his father. His father and the first Saturday of every month. He would trim his own hair, then he'd trim Frankie's. The buzz was oddly comforting, like rain outside the window on sleepless nights. Frankie's shoulders melted into the thin, lumpy cushions.

Thwomp! Frankie woke up from his sleep and sprang off the couch. Light from the kerosene lamp shimmied across the wall. A scream. It sounded like a man in pain. Frankie scanned the room, settled on the back window. It was just dawn, a muted pink and gold outside. His father's machete was cleaved into the sill! The trap had been sprung—there was blood on the blade. *Damn Dad—the thing worked!* Hazy, unbalanced, he rushed to the bucket, smacking his shin on the counter leg, and grabbed his gun. He peered outside to see someone running away in the distance, clutching his hand. It was Garnett—it had to be. Frankie left the house and bolted across the yard onto the street. He raised his gun and took aim, but before he could fire, Garnett sprinted into the dark bush, out of sight.

"Fuck you!" Garnett's shout echoed through the quiet town. Frankie raced back into the house, adrenaline flowing. He grabbed his khakis, thrashed through the pockets for his phone. There was a knock on the door. Frankie froze. But Garnett wouldn't knock. Still, Frankie raised his gun, checked the rear window to make sure he wasn't being set up. His hand was trembling, his finger ever so close to pulling the trigger.

"Frankie, open up! It's me." Big Pelton. Only Big Pelton. Frankie practically panted with relief. He lowered the gun and ran to the door.

Sweat dotted Big Pelton's forehead. The relief was short-lived. "Come quick, mon. It's Winston. Me think him dying."

Thirty-Five

big Pelton tore down the street, arms pumping. Frankie followed, trying not to picture Winston in any way but his chubby-cheeked grinning self. Not like Ray-Ban Boy. Not like that. But as they stopped in front of Winston's house, Frankie heard sobbing, and his knees went weak. Then, as if in slow motion, he brushed past Big Pelton and up onto the small porch. Creaking open the door, he stepped inside the dimly lit one-room house. Greg was already there, slouched against a wall. His face was a wreck of emotion. "Somebody said it was Garnett. Everybody out searching. We don't know if Taqwan is about," he told them, his voice raw.

And there—there was Winston. He lay on the couch, his head on his mother's lap. He could have been taking a nap. Frankie rushed forward and fell to his knees. Winston's eyes were closed.

There was a stench of urine. His skin already had a bluish tint; the corner of his bottom lip sagged as if he was about to cry. Frankie looked around wildly. Had anyone tried CPR? They'd had a course in high school. But then he noticed Winston's shirt. His white polo was stained dark red, a small neat hole like the eye of a storm in his chest. A fly buzzed, landing on the arm of the couch. Frankie felt fury at this fly. He was not going to let it land on Winston. As he swung at it, he at last took note of Winston's mother, his little sister, Tanya, their faces blank, gazing at him as if unable to comprehend what he was doing. He swatted again at the fly, hitting it. Suddenly the fly was gone.

Winston was gone.

Frankie's stomach turned rotten. The rot rose to his throat.

He rushed out the door, doubled over the porch railing, and vomited. Winston. Winston was dead. He vomited again.

A breath returned, but he didn't trust it. Big Pelton was beside him saying something. Frankie couldn't hear the words. He closed his eyes. Another full breath of air—he had to get a grip. But . . . Samson and now Winston? Winston?

"Franklyn, you all right?" Aunt Jenny was here? How did she get here? How did she know?

He tried to respond. His throat ached.

"It's all right, Franklyn. You understand?"

Was she insane? It *wasn't* all right. Nothing was all right. His best friend had just been murdered. It wasn't all right. But he lowered his head, nodding because he had to. If he didn't nod, he didn't know what he'd do.

Thirty-Six

aS Frankie stood on the porch, hours later, after Big Pelton and Greg had left, the world came back into focus, and along with it the shock of Winston's death. He knew, of course he knew, that he'd never talk to Winston again. Greg had said the same, voice cracking when he had told Frankie what he knew about Winston's death. All packed, excited, probably still drunk, hovering just a few feet from his house with some boys from the area, Winston had been bragging about moving up to camp. Frankie understood. Winston wasn't so much worrying about the coming war with Taqwan as he was pumped about moving to camp. Camp was a big thing. That meant Winston was a big thing. Big until Garnett slipped out of the night and shot him. It was easy to picture Garnett, stalking his prey, a beast in the night, eager to settle the score with Winston.

Frankie had asked Greg if Winston had a chance to use his gun, wondering if he had gotten the yips again. Greg didn't know. No one would ever know.

Blowing out a long stream of air, Frankie longed to talk to his ma. The words he had imagined her saying at her grave echoed. The posse wasn't for him. He had to leave. He had to figure out a way.

Frankie stood on the sloping porch of Winston's house, looking out at a sky too beautiful to be following the ugliness of the night before. Two women walked past, their eyes widening at the sight of him, as if inquiring, wanting news. He looked away.

Aunt Jenny came out to tell him Winston's mother wasn't feeling so well. "We send for a doctor."

"Can I do anything?" Besides screaming for the rest of his life, he thought.

"Nothing." She rubbed his shoulder. "Why don't you go check with the others? See what's going on."

Frankie hopped off the porch, glad for a reason to leave Winston's mother's hiccupping cries, and her daughter's disbelieving face. He walked past the old breadfruit tree, its fallen fruit decaying on the ground. At the end of the street, he paused at Mr. Brown's store. Only a month ago it had been full of life, and now it was empty and boarded up.

Then he heard a shout. A group was gathered down by the gully, just off the main road. What was up with that? A few steps closer and Frankie could practically smell the tension, the danger. Whatever was going on, it wasn't good. He felt for his gun and hustled over. Big Pelton and Marshal and a few of the other new recruits were shielding—who? He got closer. Ice Box and Buck-Buck. Ice Box and Buck-Buck were behind them, holding Garnett! Duct-taped to his right hand was a blood-soaked rag.

Samson's device. Tears pressed at Frankie's eyes. His father . . . his father had literally saved him from the beast in the night—the rolling calf.

Garnett's eyes were wild, pleading.

Beyond Garnett was a precipitous drop-off, a two-hundred-feet plunge into a shrub-laden gully, trunks of trees intertwined like the veins of a grandmother's hands. Frankie struggled to take in the situation—everything seemed to be spinning to the surreal. Garnett? They'd caught Garnett? Yes, they were holding him by his skinny arms. Yet the scene in front of him seemed impossible, and an absurd thought came to him: standing on the precipice, with the capital city of Kingston in the background, Garnett, Ice Box, and Buck-Buck made for a macabre postcard: *Greetings from Troy, wish you were here.*

Joe was just arriving too, dreads swaying, striding past the others toward Garnett. A bit of theater for the crowd's benefit. Frankie felt so strange—there, but a million miles away. He could have been watching a movie.

"You love to take life in cold blood?" Joe was saying.

Garnett opened his mouth to respond, but closed it. His silence was a strategic consideration, Frankie guessed.

Joe wasn't having it. "You can't talk?"

"I sorry," Garnett squealed at last.

"Sorry?" Joe mocked. He smiled big. Teeth so white, despite all the ganja he smoked. "Sorry? Me wasn't born when me mother gone to market. You not sorry at all."

Frankie had such hot hate for Garnett; still, he could feel the horror of his impending doom. Joe was only setting him up with all the fake humor. Garnett would be dead soon.

"No, Joe! Me not calling you stupid—" pleaded Garnett. He cut himself off, mouth falling open. Frankie spun around—it was Cricket and Blow Up. They were carrying a discarded tire. Garnett suddenly started to struggle, twisting his arms away. But Buck-Buck was ready with a fat fist to his stomach. With an *oof,* Garnett doubled over, but Ice Box yanked him upright. Cricket and Blow Up lifted the tire over Garnett, like a straitjacket custom-made by the Goodyear company. Garnett started whimpering as Buck-Buck took out a bottle of kerosene oil and doused the tire and then Garnett. The stage set, Joe approached, holding up a disposable Bic lighter. *Click.*

Frankie stepped back as people—where had they all come from?—rushed past him, bumping into his shoulders, desperate for the spectacle they would retell, even to others who were present. He turned and walked away from the gully. There would be no satisfaction in what was about to happen. Garnett's end would only be a new beginning of the same. Was he the only one who felt shame, and dread, and disgust?

He was passing Mr. Brown's store when a heavy hand

dropped on his shoulder, skunky ganja scent taking the oxygen from the air. Joe leaned in, his spliff burning.

"Frankie, take your things out of di house; you moving up to my camp now. This is war."

Tell me something I didn't know, Uncle Joe.

Thirty-Seven

after racing every last plate, cup, and utensil back to its owner, Frankie performed one last chore, a walk through the house to check for anything he might need at the camp. He opened the door to his parents' room, taking in the tiny single bed, wondering how his parents had ever fit in it. He picked up the ham radio his father had restored and clicked it on, and a radio announcer tagged RJR: Real Jamaican Radio.

After turning off the radio, he packed it with his other stuff, then gently closed the door and scanned the living room. He'd locked all the trinkets, things his mother had collected, inside the small closet, not that they were worth much. Funny, when he'd found out he'd gotten the scholarship, he'd wondered if he'd miss home when he went to America. Now he *knew* what he'd have missed. And it wasn't this house. It wasn't a what, either. It was a who. A whole lot of who's.

Maybe he could loan the house to someone? But no one moved to Troy. Only away from it.

His phone vibrated. Leah. Her text consisted of three words: Hellshire Beach today?

It was like a message from another world. He was in another world. When?

2pm?

Another world. He could hardly answer fast enough.

A car honk nearly made him drop his phone. He'd answer her in a minute. Ice Box was waiting for him, supposedly to help him get his stuff up to camp, but Frankie knew better. Ice Box was on guard duty. Guarding him. He wondered if he could ask Ice Box to drive his stuff up to camp while he went to the beach. All he had was the one crammed crocus bag, a coarse-hair sack frayed all over, and his old Frankenstein of a bike.

But the honk wasn't Ice Box. "Wha gwan, Nephew?" Joe came in, a cigar-size spliff burning between his lips. This couldn't be good. Frankie snapped his phone shut. "Me deh ya, Uncle."

"Moving day." Joe looked around the house like a potential buyer. "Yeh, mon, it will be good for you to leave here."

"Uncle, I have something to do downtown."

"No, mon. We have a meeting this afternoon."

"Can't I skip it this time?"

"Skip it? Frankie, we going to war! Time to grow up."

Frankie went cold at the insult. After all he'd already done for the posse, for his father . . . "Uncle, I am grown up," he said tersely.

"Okay, stop acting like a likkle youth and start acting like a big man, then. We have business fi take care of. Me wait fi you in di car. And don't tek no long time," he said in a thick and annoyed patois. He spun on his heel and out he went.

Eff this was what Frankie wanted to say, but instead he picked up his bag. Then, at the last second unlocked the closet. A kerosene lamp with a faulty switch, two chipped bowls, posters with religious sayings on landscapes, mismatched candleholders, a glued-together ceramic map of Jamaica, and all the other worthless things that were now his inheritance. He had already taken everything he wanted to bring. He relocked the closet, pulled out his phone, and texted Leah that he wasn't coming after all. Another day? Then he stood at the door and took a final look. The house looked so small. How had they all fit in it? And now he didn't fit in it at all.

Thirty-Eight

at the encampment, Joe dispatched Frankie to the smallest shack. It was the one at the far end, next to the trail that led to the ganja field. His uncle was probably making a statement to everyone that he didn't play, even with his nephew.

The room smelled like oak and pimento. He'd just unpacked his bundle: Samson's ham radio, a dented windup clock, two pairs of pants, four tees, the white button-down shirt, underwear, socks, sneakers, boots, and Samson's shoes—pretty much everything he owned. A cardboard box, which he unloaded next, held a framed picture of his mother, Samson's clippers, a couch cushion, several notebooks, and a *Statics & Dynamics* textbook. Why had he brought the book? Some foolish hope? He should check in with his teachers but . . . whatever.

He sighed, propping the couch cushion up against the wall. He would use it for a bed tonight. Joe's crew had given him a warm welcome, but he felt more alone surrounded by them all than he ever had at home. Maybe it was being there when Winston wasn't. He wanted Leah. He opened his phone. Closed it. Opened it. Nada from Leah. She was pissed, he figured. She had no idea how *he* was feeling.

He closed the phone once more and wandered outside. The other recruits would be arriving soon. Moving in. What had they told their families? What did their families think? If he'd told Samson he was moving up here, Samson would have lost his mind. Well, at least he didn't have to worry about that. Yeah . . . they'd all be moving in . . . except for Winston. Winston. DAMN IT!!! Would Winston have gotten the house next to his? Would they have bunked up together? It would have been tight, but fun. He'd never know. Winston and the others had been such good friends to him at the Nine-Night. He could practically smell the wet hay scent of the whiskey they had brought. Then came the smell of wet concrete as he scraped the sides of his father's tomb. He couldn't recall what the choir had sung. He hadn't been able to remember his father's favorite hymn when they'd asked him. And now their faces were a blur. The only face he could see, wanted to see, was Leah's. So he took his phone out once more and called her.

"Change your mind, asshole?" She sounded cheerful and pissed off at the same time.

He had the meeting, yeah, that damn meeting. But he needed her more. He had to tell her what he was doing, especially now that he was living at the camp. Fuck it. The posse could wait. It was just a meeting. Someone could fill him in. "You want to meet up now?"

"The sooner the better."

"Meet me at the entrance," she said.

"Yeh, mon." He found his bike leaning against a guava tree near his shack. Avoiding any eye contact, he walked it to the road. He'd ride to Troy, then catch the bus to the beach. Fully expecting to hear someone shout his name, he tried not to hurry, not to call extra attention to himself. Twenty feet down the road, his stomach fluttering, he hopped on and started pedaling fast, swerving around potholes, breaking into a smile as he fled on a runaway's high.

Thirty-Nine

When he first saw her at the entrance to Hellshire Beach, the sun highlighted the side of her face. She was beaming. As they walked in, she took a fat square of tinfoil out from her backpack and unwrapped banana bread—her self-proclaimed specialty. He had no gifts but ate graciously: enjoyed it, enjoyed the closeness, enjoyed not feeling alone.

The sands glittered as he trailed Leah's footprints, her shoes and his in his hands. Once they were far beyond any lingering beachgoers, he knew it was time.

"Leah, I have to tell you something."

She turned with a smile. It faded as her eyes searched his.

He swallowed. "I didn't lose my scholarship the way I told you." He watched her lips part, her eyes go guarded. "When he got—when my father was shot, he got really sick, you know that. He needed a special treatment, a course of crazy-expensive antibiotics from America, and the cost was a lot more than we had." He looked to the sea; a wave had just crashed and was now receding, just like everything in his life. How could he tell her this? He *had* to tell her this. "I had to get the money somehow—it was my *dad*—so I went to my uncle." He waited a beat, gauging her reaction. Her eyes had narrowed. Shit. But he went on—there was no other way. "My uncle, well, he's a don, back up on the mountain. He'd only give me the money if I joined his posse."

Her eyes were now slits. "You're in a *posse*?" Her voice was ice.

Even now, the words seemed impossible. His cheeks burned. "Yes."

She looked at him incredulously. "So, was there even a scholarship?"

What? Okay, okay. He got it. He'd lied about so much, he could have been lying about that. She didn't know what to believe, and why the hell *should* she? "Yes, there was a scholarship. I was supposed to respond a few weeks ago. You *saw* the letter! They've probably moved on, given it to somebody else by now." He dug one foot in the sand. "But like I said, the only way my uncle would give me the money was if I joined his posse. It was the only way to try and save my dad. That's the truth."

Her chest rose and fell, rose and fell. But she hadn't left. Yet. "That why you didn't ask me to come to your father's funeral?"

He thought about Taqwan and his crew. "Yes."

She let out a careful, meted breath. "What kind of things do you do? In the posse, I mean?"

He knew she was asking, was he also a crazed dog? He dug deeper into the sand, deeper to where the sun's warmth no longer reached, where it was colder, denser. "I had to use a gun one time." He would stick his head underneath the sand as penance if it would make all he'd done go away. "I shot at a kid." He dared to glance at her. Her arms were folded tight now. "I didn't hit him! But I had to do it."

Now she was blinking hard as if holding off tears. He had to make her understand. "He was about to kill some people, my friends. But I didn't kill him." Ray-Ban Boy's body collapsing, falling, T-shirt white to red. He hadn't done that. But he'd *tried* to. Pretty much the same thing—

"Shit. Shit!" she cried. "Damn it, Frankie! Why are you telling me this *now*?"

"Leah, I want out of the posse. I want out so bad. It's a lifetime thing, but I'm going to try to find some way out." There was no way out. He could hear the pleading in his voice. For that way out. For *them*.

Leah pivoted and resumed walking, but not in a way that seemed like she was running away from him like he was evil, corrupted, like it was over between them.

Looking at the trail of footprints she'd left, he prayed he could continue to be honest with her. That she'd let him. Another wave rolled in, leaving behind white foam as it rolled back into the impossibly blue ocean.

Waves rolled on no matter what else was taking place. That kind of strength—did they have it? But she was still walking away.

Until she wasn't. "The boy you shot at, you sure he was going to shoot you?" she called into the wind.

"I didn't kill him!" He felt desperate to make that clear. "I didn't hit him! And yes, I think he would have killed me, all of us, if he'd had the chance."

She nodded, then set her gaze on a trio of children in the distance, diving, running, splashing in the shallow water. "I don't know if I trust you."

He watched the little girl do a cartwheel. He used to be able to do handstands. He used to do a lot of things. Now it was all shit. He wanted to say that he didn't have to tell her everything; he could have left out the shooting. But that could make things worse. "I was wrong for not telling you before," he said at last. "I know that. I do. But I'm telling you now. It wasn't easy to say this to you because . . . I can't even believe it myself. I wake up every morning hoping it all was . . . a nightmare . . ."

She threw her hand out, stopping him. "Hold on." She sat on the sand and wrapped her arms around her knees. And then, to Frankie's surprise, she gave a quick, hard laugh. "What I would give to see the look on my father's face right now."

Did this mean Leah wouldn't tell her father about any of this? And did it mean that . . . did he dare hope? He sat down next to her, dropped the shoes, smoothed the sand around them with the flat of his palms. "So, do I still have my girl, or are you going to turn me in?"

"I gotta say, you're a lot tougher than you look." She rubbed her nose against her knuckles.

There was an insult in there, one that made him want to laugh. How could this be his life?

"Look," she went on. "I don't like it—I hate it, in fact. But I kinda get it. You had some sucky choices to make. I don't know what I would have done if I'd been in your place."

And he knew she wasn't going to break up with him. He felt like he'd escaped, but he still wasn't sure. "Leah, I'm *going* to quit the posse." He looked at her. "My father's gone." He rolled his shoulders. "There's no reason to be in it anymore."

"What is it like being with the posse?"

"Hmm." He watched the little kids running back and forth away from the surf. When he and Winston were ten, they'd gone to the beach once and Frankie had stepped on a sea urchin. "It look bad, mon," Winston had said. "You need a quick cure or else you have fi go hospital. Me have to pee on it, mon." Frankie protested, but the pain was intense, and he'd once heard some adults talk about this very cure. So he gave in. Winston's pee was hot, and since he'd had a couple of grape sodas, there was a lot. When he finished, Frankie asked, "You sure this will work?" Winston said, "Me doubt it, mon. But me sure did have to pee." Frankie hopped after him as he ran away. He'd never have a friend like that again.

Leah was waiting for an answer. "It's hard to say, you know?" he said at last. In the distance, fat-leaved trees grew out of the sand, twenty feet from the water. Under their shade sat several older Jamaican women, like guardians of all the prior generations. In a warped way, that was what Joe thought he was: a guardian of the way he wanted Jamaica to be, and making big money off that at the same time. Joe, Aunt Jenny, Big Pelton, Marshal, the Stony Mountain boys, and the others. He would miss them, but they weren't worth dying over.

"Was it, well, exciting to have a gun, to make big money? Did you—did you want revenge for your father?" An edge of angry fringed her voice.

He squinted into the sunlight until he had to shut his eyes. Two dots drifted behind his eyelids like black tears. "Maybe."

"Did you *get* the revenge? Still want more?"

"What are you doing?" He felt dizzied by her questions. "I'm saying that I'm done with posse business."

"Are you really, though? And—do *you* say you're done, or do *they*?"

He nodded hard and turned to the surf, which was crashing, foam rushing to the shore. "You keep on like this, I'm going to start thinking you want me to stay in it."

"It's not about what I want."

Frustrated, out came, "Don't you want *me*?"

Unnerved by her quietness, he took her hand. She didn't pull away. He looked at it. "You know, I thought it would have been softer."

"You try using paint thinner every day." Then, out of nowhere, she punched him in the arm, punched him again, harder. Then she got up and stomped away.

What? What had he done now?

Then she stopped and glared over her shoulder. "You coming, asshole?"

Something quietly sad dawned on him, something that oddly also made him feel a little better: Samson would have liked Leah. He would have liked her a lot. Frankie hopped up. If she kept going all the way to the end of the island, jumped in the Caribbean, and started for Cuba, he'd be right by her side.

After fifty feet of silence, Leah went toward a collection of dried-out crab shells wedged in the sand. She kicked one free and began dribbling it as if it were a soccer ball.

Frankie ran after it. She turned, shielding him from the shell, sticking her back against his chest, defensive moves. He slid his leg between hers and tapped the shell away. He stepped around her and broke for the shell. She lunged forward, stuck her leg out, and tripped him. As he fell, she jumped on his back, pressing hard. "You're such an asshole! Why didn't you tell me you were in a posse? You can't keep things like that from me." She pressed harder, and harder.

He swung to the side, knocking her off his back. He smiled at her, thinking that she was playing. But her expression was the same kind of stern he'd seen when she'd confronted the crits. She wasn't playing. She might have been trying to forgive him, but she wasn't there yet.

"Leah, I'm really, really sorry."

She brushed the sand off her legs and stood up.

He reached for her.

She stepped back. "I have to go, Frankie. I'll see you around."

The pit in his stomach became a sinkhole. "That's it? Leah, I said I was sorry. I'm really sorry—"

"See you." She walked off. And this time she didn't stop, didn't turn around. And when he was sure she wasn't going to return, he drew back his leg, ready to kick that shell till it crumbled. But something stopped him. The curl to it, the flash of peach in the center—his mother had loved these kinds of shells. He'd been what—seven, eight?—and Samson had brought them to the beach, a rare adventure, and his mother, late in the day, found a crab shell washing up with the surf, as if the ocean was presenting it to her as a gift. She'd been so happy—carrying the shell home, placing it on a shelf by the window. Whatever happened to that shell?

Frankie lowered his foot, then squatted and picked up the shell. Then he tucked it gently into his pocket.

Forty

It was dusk by the time Frankie got back to his shack. He moved his father's old ham radio to the left, to the right; then he lay the shell he'd found at the beach on top. He didn't know much about how his mother and father had met. Had they ever broken up and gotten back together while they were dating? Could he and Leah? He banged the back of his head against the wall, hard.

Almost like an echo, a sharp knock sounded at the door.

"Frankie, open up di fucking door."

Frankie pressed his face against the wall, peering through a crack between a plank and the doorframe. Ice Box and Buck-Buck. Frankie let out a long breath. No one had looked him in the eye when he'd come back from the beach. They all knew this was going to happen. Joe must have told everyone that he would be punished for missing that damn meeting.

"Frankie, no make me bust down this door, mon."

Frankie was enveloped by the same heavy sense of doom he felt when his father was going to beat him. He held the door latch, reminding himself he knew what to do, how to take it. But when he pulled the door open and stepped outside, he gasped. The entire camp was there. To bear witness. He'd never actually seen everyone standing together before: about thirty people, posse and family members, all looking like a soccer team posing for a photo. Joe stood in front, his face hard, whether out of anger or disappointment, Frankie couldn't tell.

Buck-Buck's and Ice Box's expressions were grim. Frankie waited for them to say something, but they seemed to be waiting for him. He remained silent—he had no excuses. None that would matter to them, anyway. Whatever his punishment, he was going to have to take it.

Buck-Buck broke the freeze, rocking side to side, then suddenly lunged, belting his thick fist into Frankie's gut.

As the air rushed out of him, Frankie began to fall, a flash of feeling light as paper, a flash of remembering the hospital floor. But Buck-Buck caught him by the shoulders, shook him hard, kept him standing. He punched Frankie again, so fast Frankie didn't see it coming. He doubled over, then felt his shoulder hitting the dirt. Clutching his stomach, he pulled his knees up tight. Everyone was now walking away, their gaits slow, quiet as if their team had lost a game. No one looked back.

Buck-Buck hunkered down, his breath sour and hot. "Joe

tell us to come talk some sense into you. Him say you can't run away from camp and miss no meetings. You should know who you work for and own up to your responsibilities—"

"Me think him say duties," Ice Box interrupted.

Buck-Buck shrugged. "What difference it make? Duties is the same thing as responsibilities."

"If you say so." Ice Box looked away, annoyed.

Buck-Buck turned back to Frankie. "Duties not the same as responsibilities?"

Frankie, still gasping for air, was not sure he was hearing this conversation correctly.

"You don't know?" Buck-Buck pressed, irritated. "You should know, mon. You no get big scholarship and thing?"

Gray lights floated down in front of Frankie's eyes.

"Now listen, Frankie," Ice Box said. "Because Bradford couldn't make it, di meeting get rescheduled for tomorrow afternoon. Don't miss it or any other one, fi dat matter."

The meeting was canceled and he still got this kind of beating? What would have happened if there actually had been a meeting? The absurdity of it all got to Frankie. And in spite of the pain, he had to grin. "You have a hell of a punch."

"Yeh, mon. Muscles isn't everything. It's about your hand speed." Buck-Buck punched the air.

Ice Box flexed his own arm. Muscles rippled. "My punch finish fights. Yours can only start one."

"Oh, I can finish fights too. But me not going to kill Frankie."

Frankie caught his breath.

"Frankie, between Ice Box's punch and mine, which one hotter?" Buck-Buck asked now, patting Frankie's back, friends.

"You can't ask him that. I punched him weeks ago now. If you really want to test it, we both have to hit him one after the other."

"No thanks." Frankie started hobbling toward his shack. "Let's just call it a tie." He heard them laugh as he shouldered the door, fell to his knees, and sprawled out on the floor.

The next morning Frankie was up crazy early, stomach aching, feeling mad at the world, and mad hungry. Breakfast wasn't on yet, so he decided to go to the packaging shed, hoping to work so hard he would stop thinking about Leah, about Winston, about his dad, at least for a little while. He also needed to make good with the posse for missing the meeting that wasn't.

The windowless packaging shed—a good three times bigger than his shack—reeked of ganja. Thank goodness they'd harvested this batch a little early, or else he might need a mask. About to flick the switch on the vacuum-sealing machine, he remembered that the battery was low. Didn't want to deal with wrinkly bags again and have to remove the ganja, then go and reseal it all over again. He reminded himself to tell Joe they should buy a new one that didn't mess up when the battery got low. Even though his uncle was cheap, he'd understand how the wrinkles could let air in and start molding his holy crop. Then again, maybe he should try to talk Joe into putting up the money for canisters. They'd probably keep the ganja better and there'd be no crushed bud problems. Nah, Joe was too cheap. Besides, he'd said he didn't care about crushed buds. Damn, why should Frankie care? He slammed his hands on the table, lowered his head. This wasn't what he wanted to be doing in his life, freakin' packaging weed in a dark-ass room.

Frankie took a breath. The weed smell was intense. Shit, at least this was better than firing bullets at people. He went about changing the battery, loaded up buds into a plastic bag. Ready, he lined up the open edge in the machine, locked it, pressed the button, and the machine whirred, sucked the air out, automatically sealing the bag at the same time.

After an hour and a half, Frankie's eyes were burning, worse than cutting onions, and he was bored out of his mind. Stretching, he clicked off the machine and went out for some sweet mountain air. The camp was just stirring. Joe's girlfriend, locks sticking out of her cap, was removing yellow ackee fruit from its red shells. She picked out the poisonous stem and dropped the fruit into a big clay pot that sat on three oval stones over a fire. Samson had always cooked ackee with saltfish for breakfast, called it Jamaica's national dish. Frankie didn't know if it was or wasn't, but the sight of it was making him even more hungry.

In the middle of camp, Joe was sitting cross-legged with Blow Up, Cricket, Marshal, and a few others. They all looked totally chill, so Frankie bet Joe was leading one of his Rastafarian discussions. Buck-Buck had mentioned that he held them once a week, that it was a cool experience. So Frankie started walking over there. Might as well check it out since the posse was all he had. At least until he could figure some way to get out of it. Might as well see what it was all about.

Aunt Jenny cut him off halfway there. "Franklyn."

"Hi, Aunt Jenny."

"You should get started on the bagging."

"I'm almost done."

She dropped her jaw in a mock gesture of surprise. "Hard-working man."

Ice Box joined them, scowling big-time. "Jenny, Buck-Buck say me have to go collect today."

Aunt Jenny threw her hands on her hips. "That's right."

"Bumboclot, me hate that job, mon," Ice Box moaned. "Why me always haffi' do it?"

"Anybody ever refuse to pay you?"

He raised his chin in pride. "No, mon."

"Well, that's why. You're as a big as a house. You scare the hell out of them."

He still frowned. Like a petulant little kid, Frankie thought. "Me still no love it, mon. Me haffi' listen to bumboclot stories all di long day. 'Times are hard. Money is scarce.'"

Frankie saw a way to help out and stay out of the packing shed at the same time. "What's the job? Maybe I can do it?"

Ice Box raised an eyebrow. "You? You can't even drive."

"I can!" Frankie said proudly. "Mr. Brown taught me."

"Yeah, how you going fi deal with pocket or pay?"

"What?"

"The police, mon. Dem stop me all di time say me speeding or whatever. Dem jus' want pocket money. Pay them right there and you gone clear, otherwise dem give you a ticket or try fi harass you some other way."

"Franklyn, you think you can collect protection?"

He considered. "Sort of."

She gave him a look, knowing full well he didn't know about protection. "All the shopkeepers in this entire area, and even some down in Spanish Town, pay us to take care of them," she started.

"How uh, exactly do we do that?"

"Well, for one, Joe gets their garbage picked up. The government surely doesn't, plus since we look out for them, they don't get robbed."

Ice Box spat. "And with all dat, dem still have 'nuff stories about how dem can't pay."

"Huh." Frankie couldn't help but think that bullies pretty much did this same kind of thing at school.

"Youth, you never hear of that before?" Ice Box's voice went condescending.

"No, I just didn't think we did that kind of thing."

Aunt Jenny landed her hand, butterfly-light, on Frankie's shoulder, looking Ice Box in the eye. "He's not ready for something like that. We need you." Her voice was soft.

"Me know you samfi me, you know?"

"Me not tricking you, Ice Box." Her voice was softer.

"Is all right." He spun on his heels, leaving a lot less agitated than when he came over.

Man, Aunt Jenny could handle anyone, anytime. She turned to Frankie. "So, what are you doing now?"

He gestured toward Joe. "I was going to go to sit in, hear what it's all about."

Curiously, she took her hand off his shoulder. "Why don't

you wait a while, Franklyn. See if that's really right for you." At that, she walked away, not even waiting for any response.

Frankie stared after her. That was totally strange, totally. Wasn't Jenny a Rasta too? And yet Winston had said how Joe wasn't a real Rasta, because he used violence. He'd thought Winston was just being bitter because he'd gotten kicked out of the posse, but now he wasn't so sure. Now it seemed clear that even Aunt Jenny was hinting that Frankie shouldn't follow Joe.

But back at the shack, seeing the shell sitting on top of the radio, there was something—someone—he just couldn't wait for. Leah. Once and for all, he had to know. He thought for a minute—what day was it anyway? She was probably at school. He grabbed his backpack. Outside, the smell of ackee and salt-fish and Rasta ital stew beckoned. Man, he was hungry, but he had to get to school. He made a beeline for Aunt Jenny, told her he had to pick up some homework assignments.

She studied him as if taking X-rays of his soul. "You no have things to do?"

"Not much. I can finish when I get back."

She held his gaze, taking more X-rays.

"I even started on tomorrow's."

"You know about the meeting this afternoon, I trust?"

Frankie nodded fast. "Yes."

"You must look out for Taqwan's people."

"School is on the other side of town."

"I know that, but every day the bucket goes to the well, one day the bottom will fall out."

"Me not looking for any more trouble, Aunt Jenny."

She turned away, and he took that to mean it was okay for him to leave.

Frankie peeked through the window in the art studio door. She was at her usual spot right in the corner of the room. His mother would say about relationships when they'd gone bad, *It spoil.* Maybe, but theirs was too new to spoil. He put his hand on the door, took a long breath, and pushed. He'd grown to like the chemical smell of paint—Leah's "perfume" besides the citrus and cedar.

She was leaning back, her arms folded. Lined up on the table was a row of pill bottles, including the two she'd shown him at the museum. They couldn't be all hers, could they? Reflexively, Frankie glanced over at the two other students working near the big windows. When he looked back, Leah was staring at him.

"Hey," he said, moving closer. He touched the cap of one of the bottles.

"They bother you?" Challenge in her voice.

"No, just . . . there are other people in here. . . ."

She let her arms drop by her side. "It's an art project, Frankie."

"Yeah, but you're letting people into your business."

"The art I make already says who I am."

He nodded, thinking that was true. *What you do is who you are.* He blinked that thought away—he wasn't going down *that* path right now. "So, you're making an exhibition of your meds?"

"No, somebody already did that. Got a great review for it

too." She rearranged the bottles. "Just opening myself up. I need some inspiration or something, I guess. Kind of blocked right now." She paused, then said, "Why are you here, anyway?"

The words were like a hand on his chest, pushing him away.

"Still mad?" he asked.

"Why wouldn't I be?"

He looked toward the other art students again. "Can we go talk somewhere, please?"

"I'm good."

One hand began to tremble; he made a fist, quick, to hide it. "I'm sorry, Leah. I know it's no excuse, but I—" He stepped closer and lowered his voice. "It was the only way I could see to save my dad. And believe me, I tried. I even tried to trade in my scholarship for money! It was before you and me. I just—didn't figure on you and me. And how much I feel for you. I just knew that . . . if I told you . . . you'd walk."

"Yes, yu' corner dark," she said in patois.

So maybe she did understand? That there had been no good choice to make—not with his father, or with the posse. Every corner was, indeed, dark.

"As a cop, my father does some pretty messed-up stuff."

Frankie watched her carefully, hardly daring to breathe.

"But it's Jamaica, and the way things are, he has to make compromises," she added. "I can see that in you. I always saw that in you." She looked down at the many bottles in front of her. "I appreciate what you have to go through. I do."

His mind was spinning. This was sounding like she was finished with him.

"Thing is, like I said at the beach, I don't know if I can trust you. I don't know what else you might be keeping from me, Frankie."

Why was everything so fucking hard?

"Frankie, stop pacing."

Was he pacing? He stopped.

"But I don't see why—why—you still think that! I mean, I'm *telling* you this. I explained everything, and you—no, no one—no one gets any of it. Shit!"

Water welled behind his eyes. He didn't want her to see. He stormed toward the door, the steel handle smashing back on the concrete wall with a hard clang. He had to get out of there, out of everywhere.

"Frankie!"

Leah was behind him.

"Frankie!"

She ran to catch up. "Frankie, stop. Please!"

He wiped at his face with his forearm. Hesitated.

Leah caught up, and hugged him from behind. He turned and landed his head on her shoulder, shaking. He could have stayed like that for a long time, but one of the students came out of the room to see what was going on. Frankie took Leah's hand and moved farther down the hallway. When the student ducked back into the room, Frankie leaned against the wall. He felt so damn tired. He felt so damn relieved.

She put her hand on his chest. "Don't ever lie to me again."

He took her gaze in, whole, raw. "I won't, girl."

"Don't," she said. Then she closed in against him.

But his throat tightened. There was one more dark corner between them: her father. He had to gamble, keep this one last thing from her, and hope.

Sitting on a bench with Leah in the middle of the campus mall, Frankie looked up at the Jamaican flag that hung limp on this hot, humid, and windless day. Its slackness reminded Frankie of when he had sat in his counselor's office and called the university in America to get an advance on his scholarship. The day he'd made the deal with Joe for the money to save his father. And that worked out so freaking well. He *had* to figure a way out. He had to be at the damn meeting in two hours. Wait, Bradford was supposed to be at that meeting! Frankie jolted straight up on the bench, startling Leah.

"Hey, you all right?" Leah held his upper arm.

"Huh?" He collected himself. "Yeah."

She pulled something out of her backpack—a crisp copy of a *Popular Mechanics* magazine. "It just came out. I noticed you didn't have a subscription. You almost didn't get it."

He almost didn't get *her*. Gripping the magazine with both hands, as he looked at the cover, his eyes blurred. She'd taken the time to think of him, get him something, even when she was totally pissed at him. He didn't trust his voice to say thank you.

"Hey, you can read it later, you know," she joked.

He looked up and kissed her. Hard.

She pulled back, smiling, even her eyes.

But, "I have something to tell *you*," Leah said next. Her tone was heavy—whatever was coming next wasn't going to be good.

"I was going to tell you at the beach, but . . . the whole posse thing came up and—"

His chest went tight. "You're not breaking up with me, are you?"

"No!" She waited for a group of students to walk by, then: "Remember I told you I got wait-listed for University of Miami? Well, someone dropped out of the art program." Her voice went wobbly. "I'm going."

Frankie eased his hand away, strained to digest this. Now? She was telling him this now? A surge of anger swelled; he tamped it down.

Leah put her arms around him and pulled hard, like she was trying to merge them together. "I wanted this so bad, and now . . . now . . . there's *you* . . ."

He pressed his head against hers. He should be happy for her! Yet a streak of jealousy flared—he couldn't help it. And— she was *leaving*? He shouldn't feel jealous, he knew it. But it was there anyway.

She put a hand on his shoulder. "You all right?"

He must have been staring into space. Time to forget about himself and big her up. "Me well happy fi yu', mon." He hugged her hard. "Amazing, Leah! You must be so psyched!"

She was all joy, he could see it in her eyes. It was replaced with a look of intense concentration. "Frankie . . . the posse stuff . . . nothing good is ever going to come of it. I know you know that. You could end up—" She choked up. "Listen, why don't you come with me? Come to America. We can figure it out."

"You—you—you—" It was like he was juggling his words in his mouth, and they were getting stuck somewhere between hopelessness and regret. *You can't leave a posse just like that and live.* She got into her college and now she was leaving. But he had to stay.

"Frankie, you said you'd find a way out of the posse. *This* is a way. You can stay with me." Her eyes were warm and hopeful—a complete opposite juxtaposition of his uncle's when he said joining the posse was a lifetime commitment. Shit. Just—shit. "I don't know. I don't even have a passport. The university was going to take care of everything for me. Hell, I don't even know where my father kept my birth certificate."

She lowered her voice. "What if you . . . run away? There are 'ways' to get out of the country, you know."

"But then I'd just be a criminal all over again." Never mind that he had no idea how to get into America illegally. And—shit—what if she was thinking about asking her father to help? Shit!

"We could find a way." Leah interlaced her fingers with his.

Frankie thought about her father. "Hey, I have to go to a meeting." Leah gazed at him. She seemed to be waiting for him to say more. "I'll look into some things. See what I can do about leaving." He knew she wanted him to say more, but it was all he could offer her now.

Forty-One

frankie sat by the huge guinep tree behind his shack; he'd caught a bus from school immediately, so he was back early for the meeting. The views of the mountains were the kind that tourists would spend lots of money to see so they could post their photos on Instagram. Blanketed with tree ferns, they sloped like proud soldiers, poised side by side, brothers in arms, tidy shoulder-lengths apart from each other and lifetimes away from anything modern. A few doctorbirds called back and forth to each other. No clouds in sight. It all seemed so peaceful. Leah just didn't get how complicated going to America could be. You couldn't just show up in America.

A sudden breeze rattled the guinep leaves like castanets, shaking a few fruits to the ground. Frankie picked one up.

Ma had made jam from these. Seemed she was always boiling something, making jam, bread . . . a home. He sighed. He sure would love to see Hoover Dam. It was only six hours from the University of Arizona—he'd looked it up.

"Frankie." It was Big Pelton.

Frankie chucked the fruit toward the soldier mountains and sprang up. "Time for us to go to the meeting?"

"No, mon."

Hell, he could have stayed with Leah and not left her sitting there. "Canceled?"

"Joe just wants you to come."

Bradford. Shit.

He tried to find some sort of calm. He doubted Bradford would do anything here, but he might say something—might have already. Why wasn't the rest of the posse invited? Why else was Frankie being singled out?

In the middle of camp, sitting at the table in deep conversation, were Buck-Buck and Ice Box, who flanked Joe, who sat next to . . . yep, Bradford. Aunt Jenny was pacing behind them, the setting sun behind her shining light on the mountains.

Frankie walked up to them, swallowing. At least they weren't talking about him.

"It's up to you," Bradford was saying, bobbing his gigantic head, "but me telling you this, you want his stash house too."

Frankie stepped closer, too uncomfortable to sit. They hadn't even looked at him yet. Wha the hell gwan?

"We have plenty supply up here. You no see our vineyard?" Joe said, big-time pride in his voice.

"Look, me no mean no offense, but you have ganja." Bradford held up three fingers. "Him have ganja, heroin, and cocaine."

"Crack?" Aunt Jenny pinched at her chin, pacing, pacing.

"Crack? No, mon, cocaine if you want rich people's money," Bradford corrected with a greedy grin.

Aunt Jenny whistled. "Cocaine's big money."

Joe cracked his knuckles. "I, mon, deal in herb."

"Yes, and here's my main point. Right now possession of up to two ounces of ganja is no longer a criminal offense. We know that."

Ice Box snorted cynically. "Bullshit law. Me smoke more than that in an hour." Only Buck-Buck laughed.

"Maybe so, but now the government is considering further legalization," Bradford said, flat.

Bumboclot. That couldn't be good for Joe's business. Still processing what Bradford had said, Frankie realized the sergeant could only have heard this from politicians. Man, dude was well connected.

"What's that you say? Fully legalize it?" Joe scratched into his dreads.

"I hear things," Bradford boasted, a big man. "And though probably not a full legalization—more medical marijuana and some other that bullshit—but any incremental steps will hurt your business . . . since you only deal in . . . herb."

Frankie grunted and hoped no one heard. This was major

shit. This was Joe's livelihood. But it was Jenny who made the next move.

Standing in front of Bradford, she asked, "What about the election? If JLP wins, they want to do more legalization too?"

"Well, let's hope fi both our sakes that PNP wins, but yes, I hear both parties are considering it."

The way politics and the drug business mixed with the gang world led Frankie to thinking about Leah's painting, the one of the dead child and the wall beside it, filled with political graffiti. Dang. She could really see things.

"If we get Taqwan's drugs, you'll want a bigger cut," Jenny challenged.

"Hell, yeah. And if it was me, I would go take out his stash house the same time I go hit his mansion." Bradford stood and hiked up his pants. "Make me know what you want to do."

Frankie lowered his head, thinking, thinking. This was an all-out attack that Bradford was proposing. The church shoot-out would be nothing compared to what might go down.

"Okay. Suppose we want to hit the stash house"—Joe hopped up as well—"how far is it from his mansion?"

"Don't know."

"You joking?" Joe shot Ice Box and Buck-Buck a look.

Bradford looked ticked off. "He changes up his stash house regularly, moves from one place to the other. I do know how you can find it, though."

How would Bradford do that? That had to be one well-kept secret. Then again, there was that surveillance equipment Frankie'd seen in Bradford's police jeep a few weeks back.

"His shipments from South America come into the airport like clockwork," the sergeant continued.

"Bolivia?" Joe asked.

"Not important. What is, is that Taqwan's people use bulletproof cars to pick up the shipments. Follow that car and you find his stash house. What you need to know is which car."

"Bulletproof car doesn't make any sound when you hit it," Joe said.

How the heck would Joe know that? *Props,* Frankie thought.

Bradford pointed a fat finger at Joe. "Make me know what you want to do." Then he turned to leave.

Frankie, feigning an itch, scratched the back of his head, hiding his face with his arms. Bradford walked past. Thank God, he didn't say anything. As soon as Bradford was out of range, Frankie stopped scratching.

Joe waved away everyone but Jenny, saying, "We need some time to chat."

Buck-Buck and Ice Box left, muttering to each other as they went. Frankie turned on his heel, hoping . . .

But Joe called Frankie back. What now?

"You missed di meeting yesterday, and me punish you for it. It no matter that it got canceled, neither." Joe drove his finger into Frankie's chest. "Miss another one and di punishment will be double, you understand?"

Frankie nodded, and imagined both Buck-Buck and Ice Box pummeling him again while arguing over whose punch was more powerful.

"Hear me now: me kept di meeting small because me want more secrecy about this. So you're not to talk to anyone about what was said."

"Okay, Uncle." Frankie's shoulders slumped, relieved that this talk with Joe wasn't about Leah.

"Another thing . . . me want you think about what we discussed and come up with some ideas."

Frankie blinked hard. Did he hear right?

"You have a problem with that?"

"No, Uncle."

"Good. You have brains, and it's high time you start using them fi di posse."

Aunt Jenny was nodding in the background. It almost looked like she was encouraging Frankie. Had she put Joe up to this?

"Okay, Uncle." Was Joe crazy? Frankie didn't know anything about planning a mission. And what they were thinking about sounded more like a *death mission*.

The posse argued over everything during dinner: Taqwan, the upcoming election, how much Scotch bonnet pepper to add to rice and peas, whatever. Bradford's appearance had a ripple effect; Frankie could practically see the tension thrumming through the air, the frayed nerves.

When Ice Box told Frankie to clear the dishes, he hopped right up, the obedient soldier, doing the necessary. He scraped away the remains of callaloo, rice, yellow yam, and boiled banana into a plastic bag, then stacked the plates, feeling a sense of déjà vu; this was something he'd have done at home, but with a lot fewer leftovers—Samson believed you had to eat every morsel on your plate.

Gripping the bag in one hand, he hoisted the plates in the other, using his chin to balance the top of the pile. As he teetered his way to the far end of the camp, he could hear Buck-Buck, Blow Up, and Ice Box chuckling at his domestic circus act.

Big Pelton and Marshal were already kneeling at the well, washing the pots, hands covered with soapsuds, their guns on the ground beside them.

Frankie smiled. "Don't forget to moisturize afterward."

"Fuck you," Big Pelton groused. "Me didn't join no posse to wash dishes."

"What you complaining about? You know how hard it is to scrub this bumboclot pot?" Marshal countered. "Yellow yam no easy to get off."

The plates were getting really heavy. "Gimme some room. I can't hold these all day, you know."

Big Pelton smirked. "Don't drop them. Buck-Buck and Ice Box might come looking for you again." He and Marshal high-fived, suds splattering. But they scooched over a few inches, letting Frankie in.

"Where did you go, anyway?" Big Pelton asked as Frankie began scrubbing. "When you left camp? You know you woulda got a bigger beating if it didn't get rescheduled."

Rescheduled or not, he had gotten a pretty proper beating.

"Must be a girl," Marshal chimed in, grinding away at the pot.

"Yeah," Big Pelton hooted. "She have a friend?"

"Not for you." Double-dating with Big Pelton—whaaa? Plus, no way was he mentioning Leah, no way, no how.

"Yeah. Me know it was a girl." Big Pelton flicked suds at Frankie. "Me know her?"

Frankie shook the last plate dry, picked up the bag, and headed toward the compost. "Later."

"She so ugly you don't want to tell me?" Big Pelton yelled after him.

"No, Pelton, *you're* so ugly I don't want to scare her."

Big Pelton trotted after him. "Frankie, me hear Winston's funeral is Saturday."

"Yeah, okay," Frankie said, and made a big deal of emptying the bag. He'd already decided not to go to Winston's funeral. There was no sense in it. Being there wouldn't bring him back. He'd be there in a minute if it would—he'd camp out days before, waiting for the minister. Sure, there was something to representing for your friend, but he couldn't handle another funeral; he just couldn't. He'd check in with Winston's ma, give her a little money to help them get by. She'd understand.

On the way back to his shack, the strong scent of ganja met him. Buck-Buck, Ice Box, and Blow Up were lounging on Ice Box's porch.

"Frankie, you figure out which one of us hit harder?" Buck-Buck shouted, sounding like he was on his third spliff.

"My grandmother hit harder than both of you," Frankie joked.

"Bring her and we have a contest," Buck-Buck said. "We see which one of us knock you out first." Blow Up and Ice Box cracked up.

An hour later, the camp was quiet. There were no meetings to be missed. It had been an early dinner. Kingston was only an hour's ride. Leah was only an hour's ride away. He walked over to his bike, reached down to check the front tire, and caught a whiff of himself. Whoo! Being a busboy had left a stench. Shower time.

Bar of soap and old striped towel in hand, he headed up the path to the outdoor showers, hoping the water drums had been refilled. Buck-Buck would probably ask him to do *that* next. He'd been fetching water all his life, so it would be more of the same—and completely different.

Forty-Two

frankie sped past New Kingston's fancy hotels, high-rises, and manicured lawns, the air steamy, but he was fresh and clean, and rode so fast the wet didn't have time to settle. He passed lit-up mansions dug into the mountainside on the left and a billboard promoting an exhibit at the National Gallery on the right. He'd have to tell Leah about it—maybe they could go.

He wove his way to Vineyard Town and finally got to Leah's house. He deliberately didn't think about what he'd do if Bradford were there. Leave, probably. But even trying to see Leah was better than not seeing her at all.

Yeah! The carport was empty; Bradford must have been out shaking someone down, stirring shit up. Frankie had an idea where Leah's room was from the last visit. He eased the gate open. Yes, her room was alight, window open, AC spilling out. He set his bike against the East Indian mango tree. The mangoes looked so ripe he couldn't resist picking one, pulling the skin off, and sinking his teeth into it. Sweet juice ran down his chin.

He glanced around, then worked his way up the tree. It was just a long stretch over to the carport. Its roof felt sturdy, so he crept across it to Leah's windowsill and peeked inside. There she was at her desk, reading.

An offensive smell was rising. He hoped it wasn't him. *Oof.* His underarms were foul from the bike ride. Well, at least he had mango-sweet breath. He whipped off his shirt and was down to his white tank before he remembered the gun at his waist. It seemed such a part of him now, but it would freak Leah out, so he wrapped it up in his shirt, swung back down the tree, and hid it under some leaves by the garbage can.

That was when he spotted them, next to the can: paintings. He nearly fell backward in dismay. Leah's work, all of it, was a row of discarded canvases: the charcoal drawing of the shanty house with JLP and PNP slogans written all over, the painting of a steamroller paving a road with the bodies of teenage boys . . . There was a hole punched through where the steamroller should have been. All her work from the review—thrown out like food wrappers. Frankie scrambled back up the tree, reached through the grille, and tapped Leah's windowpane.

She looked over as if she wasn't even surprised to see him, but simply debating whether to acknowledge his existence. At last she came over hesitantly. "What are you doing here? How was your 'meeting'?"

"I'm sorry I had to take off like that, but I couldn't be late."

"Posse business?"

He nearly looked away but knew that was the wrong move, so he looked her in the eye. "Yeah, just a meeting. My uncle has a thing about people being late."

She glanced back to her bedroom door. "Go around the back."

"Can't I come in?"

"My grandmother's room is next to mine."

He smiled wryly. "She's not a fan, huh?"

She looked down at the sill and back to him. "Nope."

"Well, can she hear through walls?"

"Among her other superpowers." She pointed. "There's a utility room. The key is under the mat."

At the utility room, an add-on made of unpainted cinder blocks, he found the key and ducked inside. The strong smell of paint was everywhere. Leah. An easel in the corner next to two buckets filled with paintbrushes held a half-finished painting depicting an almost cartoonish image of an ocean, and beneath it, dozens of black-and-white images of shirtless African slaves in chains. He touched the top, the blank area above the ocean— what was she going to put there? He spotted several other canvases leaning against the wall and knelt to fan through them. Again, that sense of pride shivered through him. She was so good! Footsteps. Eager to show her how what was important to her was important to him, he couldn't help but smile.

But no one came in. And he had an eerie feeling it was

Bradford at the door. But it was Leah's grandmother, in her nightgown and puffy slippers, backlit in the doorway, holding a machete.

"I thought it was you. So, you're in a posse, Scholarship Boy?" Her voice was a sneer. "That's right, my son told me everything."

Frankie blinked hard. Was Bradford on the way too?

Penelope's nostrils flared. "Now know this. You're not good enough for Leah, and you'll never be good enough for her. Even if you live a hundred lives. You know that, don't you, black boy?"

His eye twitched.

She gave the machete a slice through the air. "Don't think I'm afraid to use this. Now get the hell out of here." She spat on the ground for emphasis, a move *his* mother would never have done. She—his *black* mother—would have considered it low-class. Disgusting.

And *black boy*? To hear it from this woman, this woman whose son was . . . Bradford? Did she know who *he* was? Frankie made for the door. The look of triumph on Penelope's face made *him* want to spit.

Leah was running toward them. "Grandma, what are you doing?"

"He's not for you, Leah," Penelope said dismissively.

Leah grabbed her grandmother's wrist. "That's not your choice."

Penelope's eyes turned steely, but Leah pulled harder.

"Grandma, let go."

Frankie braced himself, ready if the old woman turned on Leah.

But after another tense few seconds, Penelope lowered her arm, and the machete dropped to the ground.

Leah gave a head tilt, for Frankie to leave. "I'll call you tomorrow."

Frankie paused by the mango tree to get his gun and saw an ant crawling on the half-eaten mango. He felt Penelope's eyes on him. *Black boy*, he fumed. Light-skinned Jamaicans like her had so many damn issues with people who looked like him. A young Taqwan had probably heard crap like this too. Frankie cursed Penelope out beneath his breath. No matter what she thought, he was the son of good people. Decent people. Honorable people. Like Leah said, it was just that his corner was dark. He slowly, carefully unwrapped the gun and tucked it into his waistband. Then, at the last minute, he grabbed Leah's discarded steamroller painting, tucked it under his arm, and hopped on his bike. He hoped Leah noticed. Oh, how he hoped.

Forty-Three

frankie'd gotten up early and gone right to work so no one would suspect he'd been out late. But really, he was killing time, waiting for Joe to come outside. It was time to talk.

He heaved two crocus bags filled with yellow yams over his shoulders and brought them over to Joe's girlfriend, who, with Big Pelton, was shelling gungo peas. The three-rock fire always seemed to be burning, and someone always cooking. Blow Up and two others had just left to make a delivery, the back of the white van stuffed with what looked like at least two hundred pounds of weed. Frankie still had more yams to dig up, but almost back to the field, he stopped in front of Joe's house.

He'd been up half the night, thinking, thinking, staring at Leah's painting. What it meant. It was *true* what she had painted. But did it have to mean the future was dark, *always*? Did it?

It was time to ask out of the posse.

Ask Joe to help him get a passport and visa.

Sure, Joe didn't play favorites. But Frankie had to make him understand. They had to be able to make some kind of deal. He'd find a way to pay him back. And pay him back double, even if it took ten years, twenty. But he had to get out. Frankie was his only nephew. His uncle had to take that into consideration.

To Frankie's surprise, Joe was already in the backyard, with Jenny, Buck-Buck, and Ice Box. He was smoking from a clay pipe, a plume of ganja clouding them all. Whoa. That pipe was reserved for serious sessions: this must be about Taqwan. Frankie had thought about that last night as well. What role would he play in the attack? What would he be expected to do? He'd really missed Winston last night—if he'd been there, they could have talked about it. Winston would have said something weird but sort of true at the same time, something that would have eased the pressure, even if just a little bit.

Frankie looked at that clay pipe. To hell with the clay pipe! There would never be a good time to ask Joe. He just had to do it. But Joe looked so intense, Frankie found himself backing away. That was when Buck-Buck and Ice Box roared with laughter and hopped up.

Buck-Buck clapped Frankie on the shoulder as they walked by. "Frankie Green, killing machine!"

Joe turned. He took a long pull from the pipe, studying him, then sent smoke twisting up to the sky. "Your brain heavy, nephew. You need a lift." Joe offered up the chalice as if it was the host and Joe a priest. Frankie took a seat, wondered where this smoke might send him. Not anywhere he'd want to go.

"No thanks, Uncle," he said. He needed to stay focused. Plus, he'd never taken a hit from a chalice.

"Me say, take it," Joe said, his face grim, like he had been insulted.

This was important and Frankie wanted to stay focused. But he was already ticking Joe off. He glanced at Aunt Jenny, but she, as usual, was typing on her phone. So he took the pipe.

After the first pull, he felt lighter, his bones as hollow as a bird's. Frankie tried to hand it back, but Joe held up his hand. "Take a next one."

"No, Uncle."

Joe stared Frankie down.

Aunt Jenny looked up. "Leave the boy alone."

"Him have something serious fi say—this will help him."

Without answering, she went back to her phone.

After the second hit, Frankie tried to get out of his head. That was some strong shit.

Joe took the pipe back and offered it to Jenny. "Want a lift?"

She shook her head, annoyed. "You know I don't do that." She turned to Frankie. "What you need, Franklyn?"

He took his time, turned to Joe. "Uncle, I want you to help me get a visa. And a passport." Frankie clung to his strategy despite the ganja cloud in his head. "I want to leave the posse. I can make a lot of money as an engineer in America. A lot! I can send back as much as you want. Whatever you want. Double. Triple. I just want to leave the posse." It could have come out clearer if he hadn't smoked, but at least he'd said it.

Joe seemed surprisingly unsurprised, almost too calm. "So, you feel scared."

"I'm not scared," Frankie said emphatically. "You've seen me on missions—I'm not scared. I just want to leave. I want to study engineering."

"In America?"

"Yes. Daddy is gone. I'll find my way to pay you back and then some, you know I will. So there's no reason—"

Joe's calm flared to fire. "No reason? You took an oath. That is all the reason you need."

But Frankie couldn't back down. "Uncle, this isn't for me. I've studied so hard, my whole life—"

"You're chatting foolishness." Joe brushed ash off his leg, then smiled a smile that held no warmth, only cunning. "Don't let me hear you say this again. This is your final warning, Nephew."

The muscles in Aunt Jenny's jaw, however, were flexing. "Joe," she started, her voice silky, soothing. "It might be time for you to let go of him. He didn't have to be in the posse."

Frankie's breath caught. Maybe—

But Joe flung the pipe to the ground and walked away.

"Uncle!" Frankie scrambled up after him. "Uncle, I can't do this anymore. This is your world. Not mine." He knew he had said the wrong thing, but he couldn't take the words back.

Joe spun like a viper and struck Frankie on the chin. Frankie stumbled, lost his balance, and went down. Dazed, he looked up and he thought for a moment that it was his father, not Joe, standing there, lording over him. How could he ever have thought his uncle was so much cooler than his father? Take away the dreadlocks and the gun and what *was* there?

Forty-Four

he was so angry, so, so angry, that he hardly knew what to do. To keep himself from exploding, he started reconstructing his bike's gears. His chin throbbed, and to add insult to injury, his foot of all things had fallen asleep. He made one last adjustment, then let the screwdriver drop next to the pliers. His bike, upside down, wheels in the air, was almost ready. He aimed the tip of an oil bottle at the chain and squeezed, coaxing out the last drop. He clicked the gears, moved them freely between first and tenth, then spun the back tire. Glints of light hit the spokes.

He stood up to right the bike and nearly toppled over—his damn foot was still asleep. That had happened once before. He'd been working in the bush with Samson, digging up yellow yams. Skin seared from the sun, itching from mosquito bites, bone-tired, Frankie had fallen asleep at the dining table and woke later, foot fast asleep. His father had boiled a small cerasee plant and made him a cup of his bush tea.

"My foot is okay now." Frankie had waved him off.

"Well, it's good for your circulation."

"It's good for circulation?"

"Backache, toothache, bellyache, might even be good for heartache, but you don't know 'bout that yet." He remembered his father laughing.

He remembered how the tea's scent burned his nose, how it tasted even worse than it smelled.

His father had laughed again. "Cerasee is good for you. You should never be afraid of bitter bush. The taste will pass. Just know that it will cure you."

Frankie pressed his hands against his eyes, swallowing the memory. Dad. He gave his foot a shake and accidentally kicked the bike frame, knocking it over. Then he kicked it again, and again. His foot wasn't asleep now, and neither was he.

He charged across the encampment, down toward the ganja field; he'd seen Joe tending to his crop earlier that morning. And there he was, under the baking sun, standing in a middle row of waist-high plants. Cricket and Blow Up were tilting buckets of water onto the shorter plants. Frankie pushed through the greenery. "Uncle."

"One minute, Frankie."

"No, Uncle. I have to talk to you now." He was breathing hard. He would not look away.

Blow Up and Cricket stared, agog.

But Joe merely said, "Soon come" to them and stepped through the plants, not waiting for Frankie.

Frankie followed him through the rows of corn and yams that had been planted alongside the marijuana—they hid the drugs from any long-range surveillance.

Joe suddenly squatted and, unexpectedly, jammed his fingers into the dirt, digging at a weed. "You don't give up."

"Do what you have to, beat me, whatever, but I can't stay." Frankie's stomach muscles instinctively tightened, preparing for a blow.

Weed gone, Joe patted the dirt back into place but stayed in a squat. "Me never want to hit you. No mon, me didn't want that." He reached into his shirt pocket, pulled out a spliff, and lit it. His first pull was long. Like a dragon, two streams of smoke came from his nose. He offered the joint to Frankie.

Frankie shook his head. "I'm good."

Joe took another short pull. "You have any thoughts about what the police sergeant said the other day?"

"No." It still didn't make sense for him to even consider something so crazy.

Joe stood and picked up a machete and a bucket filled with a load of ash. "We're going to hit Taqwan's stash house." He handed the machete to Frankie. "Me need your help to identify which vehicle is the one that's going to the stash house."

"I don't know anything about that," Frankie said, then paused. He knew his uncle well enough to know he was up to something.

Joe grabbed a handful of ash, sprinkling the soil as he went. "Fertilizer," he explained. "Here's how it's going to go: A shipment coming. You and one or two of the other new recruits going to check the airport parking lot to find which car Taqwan's people use to transport di product. You less likely to be recognized, zeen?"

Frankie shook his head. "No. I want out of the posse."

Joe knelt again, stuck one finger in the dirt. Checking the moisture level, Frankie guessed. "If we find out where the stash house is, we're going to knock it off in the next couple of days. And we're going to dead off Taqwan and as many of his men as we can." He brushed the dirt off his finger. "After that, you can go."

Frankie blinked. Had he heard that correctly? "I can go?"

Joe checked the next plant. "Me ask Buck-Buck to talk to some people about getting you a visa and passport—false ones, but they will get you out of the country. You use them once, then destroy them. Babylon always update them things. Me don't have to tell you about technology." Joe reached into his back pocket, took out an envelope, and extended it toward Frankie. Nothing felt real. It felt like one of those great dreams you had, that if you thought too much about it, it would disappear, forever.

Frankie took the envelope gingerly. Joe had changed his mind, but why? No way was he going to ask.

Joe pointed to the envelope. "That's twenty-five hundred US. It's an advance for everything you're about to do. After, yes, you can leave the posse, with all my blessings."

Frankie's eyes burned. His uncle actually did care, in some twisted way. He was so confused, but not too confused to forget to thank him.

"Hear me now. Me going give to you the name of a man in Florida. Me know him long time." Joe scratched through his locks. "Tell everybody in the posse that you're delivering something to him for me. Don't tell them what." He moved to the next plant, sprinkled more ash. "Then you're going to disappear. You will make no more contact with anybody in Jamaica. Don't call, text, nothing. Not me. Not your aunt. No one. You understand?"

Frankie opened his mouth, closed and opened it again. He had to turn his back on everything and everyone he knew? He had to leave Jamaica—forever? *Forever?* "But Uncle—"

Joe pinched out another weed. "You either want to leave the posse or you don't."

This was where he'd been born, what and who he knew.

"Me can't let my people think they can just walk away from the posse, not even my nephew. You know this, Franklyn." Joe stabbed a finger into the air for emphasis. "A posse can't work like that. This is the only way."

Frankie looked down at the envelope, sweat already staining the paper. The envelope contained freedom—but why did there always have to be an effing price? He watched his uncle smoothing an extra pinch of ash around a smaller plant. He was so comfortable with the plants, pulling the weeds, watering them, taking such good care of them. Did he ever rip out a plant and throw it away if it wasn't growing right? Probably not. Plants weren't like people—plants couldn't talk back. He was never going to get a better offer from his uncle. "I understand, Uncle," he said emphatically.

Forty-Five

after dinner, Frankie lay in his shack, trying to get his head around what Joe was giving him and what that took away. And what it all meant for him and Leah. The roof beams above him had been spaced unevenly, probably putting undue stress on all of them. By the slope of the ceiling, Frankie guessed that whoever had built it hadn't used a level—and actually, you didn't even need a level. All they had to do was put a marble on the crossbeam. . . .

His cell phone vibrated. Leah. Want to come over?

He couldn't get there fast enough.

He reached her gate as the sun set, a sole cricket already chirping, warming up for the night's performance. As he rode over, he'd considered telling her that Joe was letting him out of the posse, but he decided he wouldn't until he had his passport and visa in hand: he didn't want to jinx anything. Bouncing happily on his toes, he thought about Penelope. But no, Leah wouldn't have invited him over if Penelope was home. He stuck his hand through the front door grilling and knocked. The door opened. But it wasn't Leah inside, it was Bradford, in uniform, gun in his holster.

Stunned, he couldn't think to say hello.

"Come in!" Bradford sounded way too pleased to see him. Every alarm bell in Frankie's being went off. He should turn. He should run. He'd get a bullet in the back. No, he had to play it cool.

Bradford was motioning him inside. There was nowhere else for Frankie to go. So he stepped past the man into the living room, searching for Leah. What the hell was going on? Bradford was locking the door. *Okayyyyy.* Frankie glanced around, cool, cool, but enough to ascertain that the windows were all grilled and the back door was most likely locked. There was no way out. The house was quiet except for a big wall clock clicking away. Where was Leah?

Bradford sniffed like he had a cold or something. But he didn't look sick. He sniffed again. White powder rimmed his nostrils. Whoa—Bradford might be high. "You strapping?"

Frankie resisted reaching for his gun. "Why you asking?" He tried to modulate his breathing, keep calm. Keep calm.

"Stand there," Bradford ordered, and then patted him down—ribs, waist. He reached under Frankie's shirt and took the gun. He sniffed again, evaluating Frankie's weapon, and then beckoned Frankie to follow him to the living room, where he took a seat at one end of the table, motioned to Frankie to sit opposite. Wait . . . there hadn't been chairs at both ends of the table last time.

And Bradford had scoffed at him when he'd sat at the head of the table last time. Now the sergeant was inviting him to take the very same seat? Ah . . . it made sense now. Sitting opposite afforded Bradford a straight shot. All he had to do was aim and pull the trigger. Keeping his eyes on Bradford, Frankie sat slowly. Then he saw a cell phone on the table. It looked like Leah's. It *was* Leah's. "Leah around?" he asked, casual as could be.

Bradford picked up the phone, looked at it contemplatively. "Leah went to the movies with her friends tonight. She probably thinks she lost her phone." He grinned.

Frankie shifted to the edge of the seat, far enough from the table's edge to fall or run, whatever he could do. "*You* texted me. . . ." He tried to think this through. Bradford had used Leah to get him here. For what?

Bradford leaned forward and started tapping his hand on the table. "Scholarship Boy."

Frankie swallowed the saliva that was welling in his mouth. Bradford was nobody's fool. He knew that . . . now. "So why am I here?"

Bradford stopped tapping and put Frankie's gun on the table, flung one arm over the back of the chair and stared.

Then he exclaimed, "Let's see what you have to say about this." He reached into his shirt, then threw something halfway across the table.

It looked like . . . a black mask . . .

"Pick it up," Bradford ordered.

Frankie reached for it. It was a cloth mask, only a narrow slit for the eyes. Holy shit! Death squad police. He'd heard stories about them. They wore masks like these when they went on murder missions. Bumboclot! Word was that when the police couldn't find a perpetrator, they'd put on those masks, round up four or five "ghetto" teenagers, and kill them all on the spot, figuring that one of them had to be guilty. And if not, oh well— these cops murdered without a warrant or trial, and apparently both political parties secretly approved it all. Skin crawling, Frankie dropped the mask. The mask was Bradford's! And now Frankie knew exactly what the man was telling him.

Bradford's grin grew wider. "So, you know what that is. Good. I'm of the opinion that you feel protected because your uncle and me do business."

Frankie fought the fear sizzling through him. Bradford could off him right now, and no one would ever know. Thoughts ricocheted. If he had told Joe about dating Bradford's daughter, would he have found himself sitting at this table right now, wondering whether Bradford was going to kill him or not?

"My daughter suffers from depression." Bradford, for the first time, looked away. "I know how she is. If I run you off, she'll want to be with you all the more."

What did he mean? By telling him that, what did—oh, *ohh*. Frankie's mouth went dry.

"Come on, Scholarship Boy, figure it out."

Frankie knew he had about ten seconds to figure it out. "Are you telling me to leave her?" He hated that his voice trembled, he hated Bradford for it, for all of it. Bradford was the problem. Bradford, and all the Bradfords out there, were the reason behind the posses. Joe called it—it was all a shitstem. Poltrixters needed votes, and they got them through the posses. Hell, it was even in Leah's art. Didn't Bradford ever *look* at her paintings? Shit.

"You know exactly what I'm telling you. And don't think I'm afraid of your uncle." He stood up. "People disappear all the time in Jamaica, and nobody ever finds out why. You tell Leah or your uncle about *any* of this and you *will* find out why. You get three days. Now, time to go," Bradford said. He pinched his nose. "Show yourself out." He walked away, leaving Frankie's gun on the table.

Forty-Six

frankie watched his clock strike three a.m. He had lain awake in disbelief, in terror, all night, his carousel of mistakes revolving in his head.

Sweat soaked his T-shirt. There was no one to talk to, no one to help him. Not even Winston. Man, he missed Winston. He now fully understood why his father had so hated this world, hated Joe's choices. The bad only led to worse. And now *he* was caught in the worst. He stripped down and hung his shirt out the window to dry, feeling the chill of the night air. Somehow that snapped him from his fears, calming him down. Exhaustion finally got the better of him, and he slept until dawn.

First thing after breakfast, Frankie called Leah, his finger ready to push the end button if Bradford answered.

"Want to hang out after you vote?" she asked first thing, all chipper.

"What?" Was she talking about something at school?

"It's Election Day, dummy. I'm eighteen, and PS, so are you. We should go this morning. The lines might be crazy later."

He'd forgotten that today was the election! He thought about all he'd done to influence the election, and he didn't even know a damn thing about who was running—policies or anything. "Yeah, I don't know." He didn't even have a clue where to go vote in his district.

"Well, if you go, bring a lot of ID. They said at school that they might turn away a bunch of first-time voters because of fraud. Figures, right?"

She had *no* idea. He'd told her about Ray-Ban Boy but not about the reason why the posse had gone to the church. He felt so guilty that he could hardly stay on the phone. "Hey, let me get back to you?"

"Soon, though. I'm not kidding. It's going to be packed later. Hit me back when you're done and we can meet up at school. The studio will be open. See you there, okay?"

"Yeah. Okay."

"Bye."

She was so excited about voting. Frankie put the phone away and picked up the mirror. He looked as whipped as he felt. There was a piece of lint in his hair. He brushed his hair backward like his father had always told him to do. Samson's clippers glinted in a ray of sun. Frankie pressed the button, but it didn't turn on; the batteries were probably dead. He could plug the clippers in and give himself a cut, if there were only some electricity. He thought for a minute. If he grabbed some duct tape, a knife, and a pair of pliers, he could go down the road to the light pole and tap into the electrical feed; he only needed to splice some wires. Which made him realize that he could put in an electric pump for the posse. They could dig deeper and get a sustained supply of water instead of always digging new wells.

But— He caught himself. He was leaving. In one day, he got the best news and the worst. But at least, at least he was leaving the posse. He wouldn't be there long enough to fix anything. He felt a small current of joy. One good thing. At least one. He reached for his good jeans and the white button-down shirt, figuring it was a decent enough look to go vote. How the hell did people even dress for voting? Neither Samson nor his mother had ever voted, at least not that he could recall. As he buttoned his shirt, he thought about how it was now part of the worst events in his life. Ma and Dad's funerals, and in a few hours, breaking up with Leah. Because Bradford wasn't fronting. Not with that mask.

Outside, there wasn't a cloud to be seen, just a blanket of blue. The camp moved in slow motion, quieter than he had ever seen them. It seemed many had had a sleepless night.

Frankie nearly made it to the main road with no one stopping him, needing him to dig more yams or clean breakfast plates— *nearly*, when of course his luck bottomed out.

"Franklyn."

He could have pretended he hadn't heard, but it was Aunt Jenny. She waved him over. "Leave the bike."

Nothing, not one fucking thing, ever went his way. Then he quickly reminded himself—not true. He was getting out of the posse. He walked the bike over.

"You didn't hear me tell you to leave the bike?" Jenny looked upset.

"I figured I should find out what you wanted first."

She grunted, squared her shoulders. "I need you to go with Ice Box and make the delivery to Denetria."

"Me? Why? Can I do that another time?" He wondered if she knew he was leaving the posse.

She answered for him. "Franklyn, you have a responsibility to the posse until the next mission's over."

"So . . . you know?"

She rolled her eyes. "Boy, who you think told Joe to let you out?" Those eyes darkened. "We shouldn't have forced you to join; I'm sorry about that. I cursed out your uncle for doing it, then I went back and forth about it and figured, at least then we could keep an eye on you."

His instinct had been right—he knew it! Aunt Jenny was the brains behind the posse. She might also be the heart and soul. Joe was something else, not quite brains and not exactly muscle. He was more like the front man, the face with the dreadlocks, the Rasta man, the image everybody could get behind, like a politician.

His aunt's face looked complicated. "Joe—he truly thought it was the right thing. Men like him always do. Of course, he was mostly just getting back at Samson." She sighed. "Ultimately, it wasn't about you—it was about your father."

Exactly as Frankie had figured.

"But why? Why are *you* letting me go?"

Jenny didn't miss a beat. "Your heart isn't in it. When that happens, people always make mistakes, bad ones too."

A cold calculation. She was all business. So it wasn't entirely about him for her, either. He looked away, surprised at the hurt he suddenly felt. Still, she had delivered him. He thought about the last words of the "Footprints in the Sand" poem that hung on the wall of Leah's grandmother's house. "When you saw only one set of footprints, it was then that I carried you." Aunt Jenny had carried him and brought him out of the posse.

She made a fist and pumped it, as if telling Frankie to hold on. "I told Denetria we were going to war. She appreciated it and said she was with us two hundred percent. She doesn't like Taqwan at all." She offered a fist bump.

Frankie tapped, and finally smiled. "You're something else, Aunt Jenny."

"Boy, you don't know the half of it." She took his bike out of his hands. "Now, go do your job, and then you can go see your girl."

His eyes went wide, but before he could deny anything, she said, "Yes, my eyes are long too. Longer than your uncle's." She grinned and steered the bike away, the gears clicking.

Frankie thought about telling her what he knew about Bradford, the connection to Leah. Maybe she even knew that already. Probably she did. But did it really matter?

Exhaling, he was oddly proud of Aunt Jenny, the way he

had been of his mother. They were Jamaican women, hips forward.

"Hey, mon, you coming?" Ice Box called from the Toyota.

There was a fat black knapsack on the backseat. Frankie got in.

Forty-Seven

Ice Box parked across from the market. Capleton's "Jah Jah City" was blaring from a nearby store. Higglers swarmed the sidewalks, hawking their wares. A minivan full of beet-red tourists sped past, the driver probably dashing them off to the *safety* of their gated all-inclusive resort.

"You okay?" Ice Box gave Frankie's shoulder a gentle shake. "You're mighty quiet. Got your gun?"

Frankie tapped the handle wedged at his waist. "I'm the killing machine, remember?" He smiled.

"Me almost forget." Ice Box checked out the market. "Let's go."

"I can do it. You don't have to come."

"Too close to Taqwan's turf, Killing Machine." Ice Box got out. Relieved of his weight, the car rose up. Frankie grabbed the knapsack, hiked it over his shoulder, and followed.

The market smelled of fresh straw where a vendor sold hats for tourists. The hum of voices grew as Frankie and Ice Box headed down the first row. A thin, veiny-armed woman selling embroidered shirts glared at Frankie; he wondered if she was a lookout for Denetria. Over his shoulder he saw two tourists talking to a vendor, nothing to worry about. At Denetria's tent, the same teenage girl was once again on her perch by the pile of tees. She gathered up the stack, eyeing Frankie. "Just him," she told Ice Box.

Ice Box cocked his head. "What you say?"

A middle-aged woman and a teenage boy at the next stall over sprang to their feet. Both held subcompact Berettas pointed at the ground. Just past them, a skinny man in a tank top stood in a stall filled with conch shells, also staring, a Glock in his hand.

Controlling his nerves, Frankie turned to Ice Box. "It's okay, I know her." The scowl on Ice Box's face didn't disappear.

"Seriously, I got this," Frankie assured him. Finally Ice Box nodded assent.

The girl opened the folds of the tent and Frankie followed her in, looking left and right uneasily, panic bubbling forward. "Where's Denetria?"

The girl didn't answer, simply piled the tees on one of the black garbage bags, her gun in her hand all the while.

Frankie hooked his thumbs beneath the straps of the backpack. *Play it cool, play it cool.* He felt like a fool. He mustered as tough a voice as he could. "So, what do we do now?"

She continued to ignore him. Sweat ran down Frankie's back—from nerves or humidity, he wasn't sure.

The folds flapped open, and Denetria marched in, a big man behind her. At first Frankie thought it was Ice Box, but no—it was Bradford.

Frankie was sure he was going to die where he stood. Still, he slid his hand toward his gun. He could pull the slide and be shooting in seconds. The girl, however, didn't even need seconds.

The girl raised her nine-millimeter. At the same time, Denetria raised her hands, motioning toward them both. "Calm down."

Frankie's fingertips were on the gun handle.

Bradford, black tee, black cargo pants, missing only his mask, sidled up to Denetria, his jaw muscles flexing. Frankie noticed, oddly, that the pores on Bradford's face were large, the kind heavy drinkers had.

He started noticing other things as he braced for whatever was going to happen next. The girl with the gun was even younger than he had thought, probably only eleven or twelve. Her skin was the kind of smooth kids had. And Denetria's right hand shook at a steady pace, as if she had some sort of affliction. "Where's Jenny?" Denetria asked him, her voice tense.

"She sent me" was all Frankie could manage. Feeling like a coil about to spring, he turned to Bradford.

Denetria glanced at Bradford. The look they shared was one of exasperation.

Frankie forced himself to ask, "What's going on?"

"Jenny should be here," Denetria said. "We just found out

Taqwan is going to attack Joe's camp." She said this as easily as she would quote the price of a T-shirt to a tourist.

Frankie gasped. "When?"

Bradford sniffed. "Today. He probably thinks it's a good time because all the police will be busy covering the politicians and whatnot. *I* even had to work around my commander to get here. No matter, di point is, your posse needs more shottas."

Frankie yanked out his phone and his uncle. *Pick up, Pick up.*

"Nephew."

"Uncle, Taqwan is going to attack the camp."

Bradford took the phone out of Frankie's hand. "Joe. Bradford. Yes, is true." He looked up while he listened. "Hold on, mon! Denetria only found out about two minutes ago. Yes, we expected Jenny." He glanced at Frankie—a sneer. "Yes, sometime this afternoon. Is what you want to do?" Frankie realized Bradford's patois came out with anxiety too.

Frankie began to pace. What if the sergeant was setting them up? He wouldn't, at this point, put it past him. He scanned for clues. Denetria's face was so serene she could have been on vacation. How was she so chill?

"Okay. Me coming with my men," Bradford was saying, clipped, firm. "Heavy. Yeh, mon, two carloads. Later." Bradford closed the phone and tossed it to Frankie.

"God bless," Denetria said to them.

As Frankie turned to leave, Denetria called after him, pointing to the backpack. "Aren't you forgetting something? In case you lose, I don't want to be out of a shipment." She gave a wry smile. "It's a joke. I'm rooting for you."

Frankie swung the backpack off his shoulders, laid it on a garbage bag.

"Hurry up, black boy," Bradford bellowed.

Denetria blinked twice like she was about to say something but didn't. Frankie averted his eyes. This wasn't the time to deal with this racist.

Out of the stall, Ice Box, his face pale, was instantly at Frankie's side. "Is true? Bradford tell me Taqwan coming?"

Frankie held a hand up to block the sun and looked at Bradford, who was already a row away. "I guess."

"Guess? How you mean, you guess?"

"He talked to Joe and everything, but—" Bradford was no longer in sight.

"But what, mon!"

"I just wonder if it's a setup."

"Joe think so?"

"Didn't ask him."

Ice Box wrenched his phone out of his pocket and called. "Buck-Buck . . ."

Forty-Eight

Ice Box threw the Toyota into high gear, nearly sideswiping a woman with a basket of breadfruits balanced on her head, running two red lights.

"Buck-Buck says they don't think Bradford a bait up di thing. Them all getting ready to fight it out," Ice Box updated Frankie. "They not going to run." Pride there.

Frankie nodded. Okay, Bradford wasn't setting them up, but they were still in a world of shit. Bouncing side to side, Frankie realized his seat belt was in his hand. He buckled himself in and started scanning the streets.

As they skidded onto Hope Road, Frankie's phone rang. Aunt Jenny.

"Tell me *exactly* what Denetria said."

"Well, Bradford said—"

"Not Bradford, Denetria."

Frankie spent the next fifteen minutes recounting the last fifteen minutes. The second he was done, Jenny hung up. He'd never felt so tense. Wind whipped his face as he searched for anyone who could be with Taqwan.

The Toyota took the mountain road at sixty miles per hour, pounding over potholes, only slowing to forty on the curves with no guardrails. At one sharp bend, someone stepped out from behind a tree and into the road, twenty-gauge shotgun up and ready.

Frankie reached for his Glock.

"Wait, mon!" Ice Box shouted. "It's Cricket." He slammed the brakes.

Cricket jogged over, a film of sweat over his face.

"Wha gwan?" Ice Box said.

"Joe send me here to look out." He caught his breath. "Is true that Taqwan coming?"

Ice Box nodded, looked up the road ahead. "Your girlfriend stayed?"

"She went down to Troy to look out, but Joe's girl stayed."

"She needs to leave." Ice Box gunned the engine. "Stay strong," he added, then tore off, swinging around the final bend, sending pebbles ricocheting. Frankie slammed hard against the door, then scrambled out of the car the moment it stopped.

Blow Up and Buck-Buck came barreling out of Joe's house, both holding M16s. Machine guns! Taqwan hadn't brought machine guns to the funeral, but he probably would this time.

Holy shit! Before Frankie could even process that—that his uncle had machine guns—he and Aunt Jenny burst out of the front door, Joe announcing, "Cricket says Bradford on his way up, two jeeps of police."

Good. Bradford needed to show up. Cavalry. Crooked cops. Death squad cops. Frankie at that moment didn't care. The posse needed them; his family needed them. He jogged over to his uncle.

Joe nudged him. "Nephew, respect due."

Frankie shrugged. "I just made a phone call."

"Business is business, no matter how simple. And you handled yours."

The roar of engines coming around the bend set Frankie's heart pounding. Bradford's black jeep would pull in at any moment, and sure enough, it appeared, followed by another, kicking up dust. Four men wearing black masks, black tees, and jeans hopped out of the first jeep—one had to be Bradford—and four more scrambled out of the second. They surveyed the camp. One man hand-signaled the others, and they all slapped bulletproof vests into place. Dang—the posse didn't have those!

They seemed more military than police. It was obvious that they'd worked together before. Glad as he was to see them, Frankie was trying not to freak. How many people had *they* killed? Bradford and his men wouldn't have been there if Joe wasn't making them money. A lot of money. This sure wasn't something they taught in his entrepreneurship classes. He was getting a whole other education here. Nothing was done without deals. It wasn't about who had the better plan or better idea; it was all about connections. He had guessed at this before, but now it was bone-chillingly clear.

Four of the men joined Buck-Buck and Blow Up, and they moved quickly to the far end of the camp. Three of the others headed for the opposite end.

As they hustled by him, Frankie caught a whiff of sulfur, as if they'd fired their weapons recently. The fourth man—the one who'd given the hand signals—approached.

"They're using a back road up the mountain to surprise you from the rear." It was Bradford. He went on, "But I left two men on the road with your lookout in case they come up that way."

Frankie scanned Bradford's jeep. A laptop, a radar gun, and some kind of silver box sat inside. He leaned in for a closer look. He knew Bradford had surveillance equipment, but he didn't know he had a Stingray! He'd read about them in a magazine blog; they were like mobile cell phone towers that could intercept phone messages.

"Don't touch that," Bradford barked, noticing. Frankie took a step back.

"How you want to play it?" Joe asked.

"Where are your people and how many are there?" Bradford asked back.

Joe swept his arm from Frankie's shack clear across the other end of camp. "I couldn't get the whole posse here so quick, but we have eighteen men and women all across the back of the mountain. We anticipated the same strategy."

Joe's eyes were long, for sure, Frankie thought. He suddenly felt desperate to know where Big Pelton, Marshal, Greg, and the others were. This shoot-out was going to be bad—he could sense it.

Bradford was telling Joe, Jenny, and Ice Box to come with him. To Frankie, he said, "You stay here to watch the flank, just in case."

Frankie had the bizarre feeling that he was in some action-adventure film from twenty years ago. They were just going to sit and wait for Taqwan's gang to attack? It seemed so . . . third world. Frankie pointed to the Stingray. "Why don't you use that?"

Bradford's eyes flashed. "What do you know 'bout that?"

"Franklyn is a smart boy," Aunt Jenny said, quick. "What you thinkin', Franklyn?"

Frankie cleared his throat, nervous. "It's like, well, the cell phone towers that T-Mobile or Digicel use."

"That little thing?" Ice Box frowned, peering over Frankie's shoulder.

"Yeh, mon. Cell phones are always reaching out for a signal. Stingray frequencies are even more powerful than cell phone towers. It's got GPS, so"—he glanced uneasily at Bradford—"the police, for instance, can use it to monitor when cell phones enter the area. From there, it's just like tracking people on Google Earth."

Bradford was gaping at him. "That's confidential property, right there. And it can't do fuck if no one's here to operate it."

"Confidential?" Joe jeered. "The youth know everything 'bout it. Everything 'pon the Internet now."

Bradford gestured toward the gully. "All those trees, Taqwan's people can hide anywhere. Some might already be down there."

Joe shook his head hard, dreads swaying. "No, mon. My people sweep di area already. Taqwan no come yet."

Bradford looked back and forth between the Stingray and Frankie. "My man who works it took a bullet in the shoulder last night. . . ."

"Franklyn, you know how to work it?"

Now it was Frankie's turn to hesitate. He tried to picture the article he'd read. The writing came back to him—whole paragraphs in their entirety. It was how his brain worked. "Yeah, I can try."

Joe frowned. "Try or do it?"

The vein on the side of Frankie's head throbbed. He'd never operated a Stingray before. But he answered, "I can do it."

Bradford narrowed his eyes. "Okay, when you see new positions appear on the Stingray, assume them to be Taqwan's people." He pointed to Joe and Jenny. "Now, you have their numbers?"

Frankie nodded.

"Good. You effing call and let them know the positions." To Joe and Jenny, he said, "I'll position you two on different sides of the mountain with my men. You let them know where Taqwan's people are coming from. We want coordinated discharge. You copy?"

Joe's nostrils flared. "Yeh, mon, yeh, mon."

"One last thing." Bradford eyed Frankie. "Don't fuck it up."

In the shotgun seat of the jeep, Frankie quickly figured out how to activate the Stingray and, moments later, got it running. It was pretty straightforward, just like the article had said.

With the laptop beside the tracking device, he ran the Stingray signal to Google Earth. Man, it was even easier than downloading Instagram! First the mountaintop appeared on the screen, and then a slew of dots. Frankie immediately recognized that they represented everyone stationed in the gully. A quick count gave him twenty-one. Frankie knew there were more, but some might not have brought phones, or had turned them off. So it had to be twenty-one posse members or police, since Joe had said they'd swept the mountainside for Taqwan's men already.

It was crazy that such a powerful device could be so easy to use. The police had a huge technological advantage. Why didn't they use it more? Or maybe they did, and no one realized it. Frankie still couldn't shake the feeling that this was all a setup. But it couldn't be—Bradford wouldn't have let things progress this far if it was: he would have sprung his ambush already. Frankie told himself he was becoming paranoid, seeing betrayal around every corner. Then again, maybe that was a good thing for a gangster to be?

He was baking sitting in that jeep. Sweat burned his eyes, and he repeatedly wiped it away. He had to keep his focus on the phone, the laptop, and the Stingray—constantly checking the current list of phone numbers, seeing if a new one appeared. A dot that represented Joe was on one side of the mountain with half his posse and four from Bradford's team. Aunt Jenny was a dot on the other side, stationed with Bradford and everybody else. Frankie sat up with a start and checked his phone for battery life. How could he have forgotten? A little more than half. How messed up would it be if he couldn't call Joe or Aunt Jenny? He couldn't screw this up.

Periodically he looked up from the screen to scope out the road, then the bush, in case he or the Stingray had missed something. The quiet was getting to him—he could hear his own pulse in his head. Thoughts of Leah, his father, his mother, Winston, kept trying to push through. *Just focus,* he told himself again and again.

Every minute felt like an hour, and his brain wouldn't stop rehashing details. Bradford had to have a spy in Taqwan's posse to know this attack was coming. Or maybe Denetria had a double agent reporting back to her? Damn, Frankie hoped this wasn't a setup. And damn, he wanted out so bad. Did *this* count as a mission? Focus!

Leaves rustled. He grabbed his Glock and immediately dropped it—it was searing hot from the sun. Gripping it again, he started to wonder if the heat could make it automatically fire. Focus! A chipmunk scampered across the circular driveway. What a fool—freaking out about a rodent. He put the gun back on the seat.

Waiting was a brain fuck.

Then he did a double take. A new cell phone number appeared on the Stingray. A nanosecond later two others blinked on. Frankie's eyes bugged, waiting for the corresponding dots to plot themselves. Finally they began to display. The signals were coming from the main road, down the mountain. He fumbled with the phone, misdialed the first time, then tried again. "Cricket! They're coming up the road!"

"How many?"

"One car, I think." Then two more numbers appeared. That made six. "Two cars, two, I think it's two." Frankie could hear Cricket repeating what he said to the men Bradford had left with him—Bradford knew his shit.

Then five more numbers appeared, and four more on top of that. It was nine new numbers in total. But they were nowhere near where Cricket was stationed. What? Leaning closer, Frankie stared at the map. The new dots plotted out in the gully near Joe's location. Damn! They were attacking from two sides: the road where Cricket was *and* the gully. He had to call Joe. "Cricket, I gotta go."

Every muscle tense, Frankie watched the dots move in unison up the mountainside, toward Joe's position. He wanted to give exact coordinates, so, lips quivering, he punched in, trying to get closer, trying to get a street-level view on the map. But he could only get an overhead angle, about a hundred feet from the ground. Shit! This area was probably too remote a location for street view. He couldn't wait any longer. He tapped in his uncle's number.

"Franklyn?" Joe answered. "What you got?"

"They're coming your way."

"Where?"

It came to him: he knew how to be exact. He put his thumb over the camp, knowing it was about a mile and a half wide.

"Franklyn!"

"Hold on, Uncle." Quickly, using his thumb as a map scale, he figured that Taqwan's people were about two hundred yards away from Joe. Then—*what?*—all the new dots disappeared off the computer screen. Vanished! Was it a glitch? Had he messed up? Face burning, Frankie grabbed the Stingray with both hands and forced himself to stay calm even though he wanted to shake it, throw it out the window. The phone numbers still showed on the Stingray. There was still a chance to figure this out.

"Franklyn! What the hell?"

His mouth went dry. He was failing. "Hold on, Uncle."

They *couldn't* have just disappeared. Had Taqwan's people suddenly turned off their phones? He desperately searched the tracking device. Next to the numbers were the frequencies. Most were 4G, some LTE. And next to the frequencies was the option to redirect. That didn't make sense. He closed his eyes. Think. Think. He had studied systems; they were inner directed. The purpose of this device was to track. Redirect might mean following on another frequency, a lower one, maybe 2G. But if he hit redirect, he might lose all the numbers.

"Franklyn!"

He had to risk it. He clicked redirect. The numbers on the Stingray showed that they were now on a lower frequency. They were all 2G. He looked at the laptop. Still no dots on the overlay.

"Franklyn!"

"One second, Uncle!"

Then points started to pop up on Google Earth again. Five. Then seven. Taqwan's men had moved in—maybe even in firing range! "Uncle, them coming your way, at least seven of them. Looks like they're on the path near the old well."

"Yeh, mon." Joe hung up.

Almost immediately, a barrage of shots echoed in the distance, then went silent. It sounded like they had come from farther down the road. Had those two cars gotten by Cricket and Bradford's men? Frankie clutched his gun just as, from the right, a dozen rounds cracked the silence. Joe and his team should have gotten the first strike. More shots. The firefight was on. Frankie prayed he had read the Stingray correctly.

He felt like a big fat target sitting there in the middle of the empty camp. He slid out of the jeep, ducked behind the open door, checked the brush—nothing. There were popping noises—sounded like handguns—but he couldn't tell how far away. He risked looking back inside at the Stingray. No new dots. Frankie turned to the road—nothing. The staccato *tek tek tek* of machine-gun fire broke out. He couldn't tell from which side of the mountain—their echo reverberated. The volley lasted much longer than the first. He forced himself to breathe.

"See him there!" came a voice. It sounded like Big Pelton's, but Frankie couldn't be sure. He squatted fast, looked through the crawl space under the shacks, scanned the bush. A flash of bright green. He gripped his gun. A teenager wearing a green baseball cap turned backward ran up the slope past a cabin and into the encampment. Frankie recognized him from his father's funeral. He was one of the kids in Taqwan's posse, and he was now creeping along the shacks toward Frankie. The kid suddenly stopped to look back toward the bush when he caught sight of Frankie. He started to lift his handgun, about to shoot.

Without a breath of hesitation, Frankie pulled the trigger of his own gun and kept shooting. The kid crumpled to the ground, screaming once.

His arm started to shake, his vision going watery, his stomach rolling. No! He was not going to let himself think about what he had just done. He waited for a movement or another sound, for reinforcements to come in. He glanced back at the Stingray. Nothing. He listened for car engines. Nothing. So, lowering his gun, Frankie cautiously walked toward the boy. *Tek tek tek.* Machine-gun fire broke out from right behind him. Frankie spun around, too surprised to even lift his weapon. A portly boy, three sweatbands on his arm, collapsed facedown on the ground in front of Joe's shack, a nine-millimeter dropping from his hand. He could have shot Frankie in the back!

As the boy fell, Frankie spied a second person—a masked man in a black tee and jeans, his M16 still aimed in Frankie's direction. Frankie knew immediately who it was. Bradford could shoot Frankie right now. And there was nothing Frankie could do about it.

Branches snapped and they both turned. From the side, Marshal galloped into the camp. "We got Taqwan! And them running away!" He waved to Frankie. "Come, Frankie. You have to come!" Marshal looked crazed.

Bradford lowered his gun, gazed at Frankie for a moment, then jogged back toward the mountainside. Marshal had probably just saved Frankie's life.

Frankie looked one last time at the boy he'd shot, still and silent, then tore after Marshal into the bush, skidding down the mountainside, weaving around trees and bushes.

"How much farther?" he panted.

"Come," Marshal huffed.

They pushed past a thick ficus, and there was Aunt Jenny, on her knees, her gun at her side, hunched over a body lying on the dirt. Blow Up stood next to her, tears streaking his cheeks.

The amber work boots caked with dirt, the long legs, and the splayed dreads. This was why Marshal had come to get him. Frankie stepped forward, as if floating, no sensation in his legs at all.

He laid a hand on Aunt Jenny's shoulder. She was heaving. But Frankie didn't feel that pain. He wasn't holding back tears. His father had always urged him to fight them, but this time there were none to fight. He didn't feel much of anything, in fact. Had he lost so much already that he had nothing left for Joe? He became aware of the quiet. The sound of the bird calls. A breeze shaking the leaves.

Aunt Jenny forced herself up. "Bumboclot!" She wiped her eyes. "We'll come back for him later. Let's make sure we got all of them." She reached down for her gun and strode away, Blow Up beside her, their bodies thrashing through the bush.

Marshal smacked Frankie's shoulder. "C'mon, mon," he muttered, wandering off after Blow Up.

Frankie looked down once more. Joe hadn't believed in an afterlife. But Frankie wanted to believe there was a place— somehow—a place where his uncle's soul might find his father's. Joe didn't believe, but that didn't mean he was right. His father did. And if his father was right, maybe it could happen? Maybe?

Forty-Nine

It was near midnight, and Frankie, bone-tired, stood in the middle of the encampment with the rest of the posse. They'd all survived except for his uncle. Joe was gone, but he stalked around in Frankie's thoughts, maybe everyone else's too.

Mesmerized, he stood listening to the crickets and the beeps of a garbage truck backing into the circular driveway. It had just come back from the Riverton Waste Disposal Site, just outside Kingston. It seemed like it was empty now, but earlier in the evening, Frankie and the others had packed the truck with seventeen of Taqwan's men, along with Taqwan himself. Ice Box and Buck-Buck had awarded themselves the honor of being unofficial pallbearers to the only type of funeral Taqwan would receive.

The truck, one that Joe had commissioned to pick up garbage in Troy and towns all over the mountainside, squealed to a halt next to the two bodies that lay on the ground. They were wrapped head to toe, in white crocus bags. The same type that the posse used to store the ash that fertilized the ganja plants. Frankie thought that was appropriate because his uncle was wrapped in one of those bags. In a lot of ways he was as much a gardener as he was a posse don, maybe more so.

Frankie gazed at the bag next to his uncle's. The kid Frankie shot might be inside, but Frankie didn't want to know for sure. If it was possible, he was going to forget that he had ever pulled the trigger. It was self-defense. It was self-defense.

The three garbagemen said not a word—they just went to work. They got their arms under one of the bags, lifted it, and swung it into the back of the truck.

Frankie, Marshal, Greg, and Big Pelton gathered around the remaining body. Frankie's stomach started churning, churning. He looked over at Aunt Jenny, Buck-Buck, and Ice Box, all standing side by side, several feet away. They all appeared to be gutted. Jenny nodded quickly, seemingly still sure about burning Joe's body along with the rest. Rastas didn't have funerals.

Frankie scanned the bag. Something was wrong. He squatted and lay his hands on where the bag was duct-taped together, where the legs, already rigid from rigor mortis, would be. He slid his hands over what should have been the kneecaps and realized the problem. The body was upside down. "Turn it over," he said. It somehow seemed disrespectful to carry the bag that way.

"No make no difference." Big Pelton's voice was muffled under his shirt. "Rastas no believe in this."

"Turn it over." Frankie felt his temper rising. Big Pelton and the others got their hands under Joe's body and gently turned it, carrying it faceup to the back of the truck, where they lifted it in.

One of the garbagemen slammed the steel gate shut. He latched it, and moments later, the truck rambled off down the dirt road.

Pelton stood nodding, nodding. Cricket and Blow Up, shirts still tied over their noses and mouths, still wearing rubber gloves, began throwing ash and lye on the ground where the bodies had lain.

"Cricket, me hear you shoot up one of Taqwan's cars, mon," Big Pelton said, as proud as if Cricket had run a sprint for the Jamaican team and won.

"Yeh, mon, hear you shoot good today too." Cricket fist-pumped, puffs of ash spilling from his fists.

"Yeh, mon." Big Pelton fist-pumped in response, then turned to Frankie. "You shoot any today?"

Frankie startled. He considered Big Pelton's question. Had he shot any today? "No, mon. Nobody."

"No problem." Big Pelton nodded. "Next time. You did good job with Stingray, mon. Respect due. Likkle later." He strutted off toward his house.

Frankie had no idea what to do next. Had he shot any? Why had he lied? Lying didn't undo it. The kid was still dead. Joe was still dead. Joe was still dead. Frankie found himself in front of the shack that was supposed to be Winston's. He stopped, gazed inside the empty structure. Winston. Winston was dead. He reached his own porch, reached for the door handle.

"Franklyn," Aunt Jenny called. "Stingray, huh? You saved a whole bunch of us today, nearly . . ." A barely perceptible crack chinked her voice.

He thought about who he'd killed and helped to kill. There was no cause for celebration. Nineteen bodies in the garbage truck. If he hadn't used the Stingray, would there have been less? More? More posse, no doubt. But were those lives—

"You all right?" Aunt Jenny brought his thoughts to a halt.

"Crazy day." He shrugged. "But I'm okay. And you?"

"I don't know yet." She looked at him like she hadn't seen him in a while and was impressed by how much he'd grown. "You did good today, Mr. Technology. Listen, I know Joe was getting you that passport and visa. You belong in a university, Franklin. You earned it." She nodded emphatically, as if he'd been arguing differently.

Frankie stared over her head. The outline of the mountains, so majestic, so far away. The mountains never changed. Situations did. Two days ago a visa and passport were the answers to his prayers. Now it was all mired by Bradford and his threat. Could a visa and passport get him far enough away from Leah's father to ever be safe?

Jenny went on, not seeming to notice he hadn't responded. "You will find your way. You will," she assured him.

Frankie gave half a smile. Nothing, nothing had been earned today. But he was glad Aunt Jenny was on his side. "Thank you."

"Franklyn, it's going to take a couple weeks to get the documents." She folded her arms, caught his eye. "And I could use your help in the meantime. Denetria respects you. I think she would adopt you if she could."

He blinked at his aunt. *She* was in charge of the posse now. It was just really registering. Joe had said he could leave the posse after one more errand. He supposed that errand might as well be helping out with Denetria. He didn't have the energy to even argue. "No problem."

"Well, thank you." She bowed her head slightly. "What time is your watch?"

"Five o'clock."

"Better get some shut-eye, then, if you can." She turned to leave.

"Aunt Jenny? I'm sorry about your brother."

"Thank you, Franklyn. I'm sorry about both of them."

Inside, Frankie lit his kerosene lamp, sat on the floor, lowered his head, and breathed long and deep. He saw again the boy in the green baseball cap, running across the encampment. He saw himself taking aim, pulling the trigger. The boy had fallen the same way Ray-Ban Boy had. And he hadn't even shot *that* boy. How could this be his life?

He raised his head, took in Leah's broken steamroller painting. Leah's father would kill him if he didn't break things off with her. With no remorse whatsoever.

Fifty

getting advice on romance from the man who had beaten him within an inch of his life was something Frankie had never imagined possible. But on the long, slow, cautious ride down the mountain into Kingston to Denetria the next day, Frankie was at a complete loss. He'd tried calling Leah three times before finally getting her, and when he did, she was pissed because he'd stood her up yesterday. How could he even begin to tell her about yesterday. His world was so messed up, he had to talk to somebody. So, careful not to mention the parts about the passport, leaving the posse, and who Leah's father happened to be, Frankie told Ice Box about his problem.

Now, sitting shotgun outside the gate in front of Leah's house, Frankie was still listening to the big man, all the while looking left and right, worrying that Bradford might show up. Bradford wouldn't do anything crazy right in front of his house, in this neighborhood, and not with someone like Ice Box around. At least Frankie didn't think so.

"And whatever you do, don't chat about the relationship. It's not no negotiation." Ice Box rubbed the dash as if it were marble. "You start doing that and you going to confuse her. Before you know it, you go from wanting your things back to making a fucking date to go see a romantic comedy."

Frankie tried not to smile. "Thanks, Dr. Ice Box."

He jutted his chin. "Yeh, mon. Me send you bill inna mail. Now, go tek care of business."

Okay. This was it. Out of the car, through the gate, past the carport, no Bradford, no jeep. Up to the veranda. Knock. *Frankie, knock.* He knocked.

Penelope opened the door without a hint of surprise. In fact, she wore the slightest smirky smile. Bradford must have told her to expect him. Frankie wished he could tell her what her son had been up to lately, wipe away that smugness. She pointed haughtily to the hallway. Yep, she'd been expecting him for sure.

"Leah, your . . . the boy from school is here," she called out.

The silence felt like forever. "Send him up."

Penelope did a double take. "Why don't you come down?"

"Send him up, Grandma!"

She frowned but said tersely, "Up the stairs, first door on the left."

Frankie's sneakers squeaked on the tile floor. Outside Leah's room, he heard the sound of paper tearing. He peeked in through the half-open door. She was ripping up sheets of loose-leaf paper and stuffing them into a plastic bag. He stepped inside. It looked like something out of a magazine. All kinds of pillows on the bed. Bed big enough for two or three people! A small couch, lamps, fancy-looking wallpaper, curtains that matched. Whoa. He reminded himself to say, "Hi."

She didn't smile. "You look like crap."

Frankie laughed, leaned against the wall. "Yeah, it's been a little crazy."

"Want to tell me about it?"

"I do, but not right now."

She turned back to her desk, took a handful of torn papers, and stuffed them in the bag. "Nothing good ever comes from a text where your boyfriend says we have to talk." She picked up a notebook, started to open it, then just threw the whole thing in the bag.

"I'm not coming to Florida." There. He'd done it. He'd said it. He'd—

"I figured that." She spun the top of the bag, the beginning of a knot. "Why? You depressed now? Lost all your hope?" She tugged at the bag and finished the knot.

She'd been upset with him before, but never cynical. The cynical felt like a knife.

"You know what, just go." She looked up at him at last. "You said enough. I get it."

So he went. Walking through the hall, a vision of his own face came to him, and he became hyperaware. Hyperaware in the way he got when he saw himself unexpectedly in a mirror—

unprepared to see his true self. Yes, he could *really* see himself now, and it scared the hell out of him. Because he saw that he was afraid of Bradford. Like he'd been afraid of losing his father. Like when he'd been afraid of telling Leah about being in the posse. Each time, the fear made him lose something that was important to him. Bumboclot! No, not this time. He'd gone through too damn much. He was getting a passport. He wanted Leah in his life. No more being afraid.

Frankie pivoted, walked right back into the room. He pulled the bag of papers from her arms and kissed her. She backed off. Her eyes shifted from anger to hope to fear, back to hope. Then, springing forward, she kissed him back. Then she pushed him away.

"Leah, a lot happened with the posse." He stopped to compose himself, lowered his voice. "They're getting me a passport."

She squinted in confusion. "What?"

"I can't explain it all now. But I am coming with you. I'm coming with you." He grabbed her hand. Her eyes were suddenly bright.

She kissed him, hard. She pulled away, and now those same eyes burned with the threat of wrath. "Don't fuck with me."

"I'm not. I swear." He licked his lips. "But here's the thing. You have to make it seem like I broke up with you."

"You're fucking with me—"

"No. Listen, this is really important." He held her gaze. "You have to tell your grandmother and your father—every-fucking-body—that I broke up with you. You have to pretend—only for a month or two, till you leave." He watched her carefully. "You get it?"

She tilted her head. "It's my father."

He avoided her eyes. So she *had* known things about him all along.

"Never mind," Leah said, quick. "Don't answer. I got it. Fuck. I get it."

She leaned forward, put her arms around him, yanking him closer. "You better not be fucking with me."

He felt so happy he could cry. "I'm not, girl. I'm your fucking boyfriend. And don't forget it over there when those American boys try to step to you."

"You better hurry up and get over there, then, gangster boy."

"Look, I have to go," he said, then swallowed and glanced back at the door. "Think you can pretend I broke up with you?"

"You kidding? It's all I've been thinking about since your shitty text."

He kissed her again, wildly, as if for the last time.

She pressed her forehead against his. "It *is* my father, right?" Her eyes were so soft.

Frankie kissed her forehead, pulled away, and nodded. "Whatever you do, don't call or even text me. He'll know. Trust me, he'll know. I'll get messages to you another way. It's just until we leave for Florida." He pleaded with his eyes for her to understand. And she was nodding, nodding.

"I can do it." She held his hand and walked him to the door, kissed him one last time, softly, and then smacked him hard on the ass, shoving him forward.

"Fuck you!" Next, her door slammed. She yelled it again, "Fuck you!"

He smiled. The artist could act. And so could he. Frankie put on a scowl and stormed down the stairs, through the living room, arms swinging. Out of the corner of his eye, he saw Penelope sitting in a recliner, a self-righteous smirk on her lips. He slammed the front door as he left. For good measure, he continued to march across the veranda, swung open the gate, and didn't bother to close it. He got into the black Toyota and slammed that door as well, hard.

Ice Box looked shocked. "Good, mon. You shouldn't confuse her about your intentions."

"No, I made them very clear."

Ice Box started the engine and drove off. "So, Jenny called. She's going to meet us at Denetria's. Something about Taqwan's stash house."

Frankie exhaled. "Bradford going to be there?"

"She never say nothing about him. Why?"

"Nothing. Just wondered where he disappeared to yesterday."

Frankie turned on the radio. The announcer was on location in West Kingston. A man was complaining about the latest results, that the PNP must have stolen the election.

Ice Box slapped Frankie's chest with his meaty hand. "We win!"

Frankie nodded. He knew it was good for the posse, but he also thought about what the man was saying about the election. The shitstem, as Joe had called it. He turned the channel.

Sizzla was dropping a song. He couldn't escape it. He and Ice Box looked at each other at the same time. There was nothing to say. Joe was never going to hear it. Frankie clicked the radio back off.

But then Ice Box said, "Let's listen fi Joe." He turned the radio back on, and they wound through Kingston traffic on the way to the market as Sizzla sang an angry homage to Jamrock, critiquing the evils of Babylon, chanting for the necessity of hope in the face of the impossible.

Fifty-One

turning the final corner toward Denetria's tent, Frankie spotted a lookout standing by a booth. He appeared as solemn and still as the carved wooden masks he was supposed to be selling. The man turned away. But something about his gaze and that of the other lookouts he and Ice Box had passed felt familiar. They had been on full alert when he'd come before. Now, when they saw Frankie, he sensed an ease, born of trust. Outside Denetria's tent, the same young girl, her nine-millimeter probably under her oversize black tee, barely glanced at him either. He was part of it all now, an accepted part of Denetria's crew. He felt a sliver of pride. Yeah, pride, weird. But the other part, the biggest part, wanted to stay the hell out of it. So he'd just bide his time till Aunt Jenny came through with the passport and visa. He vowed to keep to himself as much as he could. He wouldn't get too involved. He'd bag all the ganja she wanted, make a few deliveries if she needed. Then, ciao.

Inside the tent, the first person he saw was Bradford, his uniform crisp. The two locked eyes. He stared long enough to show he wasn't afraid, and looked away before he seemed like he wasn't afraid at all. He hoped he had played the fine line right.

Aunt Jenny was already there, talking to Denetria, and she waved him in. "Well, about time. What happen, you two stop for tea and sponge cake?"

Ice Box threw his hands in the air. "No, mon, we come right away. Traffic is shit here."

Frankie silently thanked Ice Box.

Aunt Jenny wagged a finger at Ice Box. "Don't do no CP time again." She turned to her conversation with Bradford. "But how you know the shipment coming in on that flight?"

"Nice try, but me not going to tell you who me know." Bradford pinched his nose. "All *you* need to know is that this will be the last shipment. It's a big one, and what's left of Taqwan's people will be there to get it."

Frankie thought back to when Bradford had spoken to Joe about hitting Taqwan's stash house. That was what this was about—they wanted to go through with the plan now.

"Okay, you two, make we focus," Denetria said. "It's coming in a week's time. We don't know which of Taqwan's people are still alive, but she should figure they will fight tooth and nail. And most importantly, we need to know which car they'll be in."

It was all coming back to Frankie. Joe had said the cars Taqwan used were bulletproof. Frankie had thought through the problem, focusing on its variables. He had an idea, was pretty sure it would work. He had planned to talk to Joe about it— he thought they'd have time. But time had run out, hadn't it? Frankie opened his mouth, then closed it, realizing what he was about to do. He shouldn't get involved. Couldn't. The passport and visa would be his soon. Just lie low.

Denetria ran her hand through her hair. "If you need backup, I have shottas, ready to use them gun anytime."

"First we need to know the car," Aunt Jenny said.

Frankie sighed heavily. They were talking about another major shoot-out? They were so freakin' lucky to have survived the last one. Shit. His brain started churning. If something happened to Aunt Jenny or any of his friends and he hadn't tried something to help them avoid it, he'd hate himself. And, bumboclot, if Aunt Jenny did get hurt, he probably wouldn't get that damned passport! He knew his idea could work, and they could identify the vehicle with the shipment without gunplay. But, but—damn it, he'd done enough, sacrificed enough—

Bradford stuck his fingers in his belt loops. "Them will most likely take the shipment back to the stash house. There will be more there. Lots more."

It was Aunt Jenny who now showed a rare display of caution. "The stash house is going to be well-armed, especially now," she said. "I don't know if it's worth it."

"We talking big money, you know?" Bradford said. "More than you've ever seen."

Frankie cleared his throat. "I have an idea."

Bradford shook his head dismissively. "Youth, this isn't no argument for you."

"Bradford, even now *you* don't know how fi use no Stingray." Jenny's eyes glittered, looking at Frankie. "Go on, Franklyn."

Bradford ran a hand over the stubble on his cheeks, then waved his hand for Frankie to, yes, go on.

Fifty-Two

a week later, keeping his pace casual, Frankie sauntered past several suitcase-lugging people, past a circle of cab-drivers waiting for the next batch of arrivals, and headed toward the beaten-up white van. Around the back, he knocked on the tinted windows. Buck-Buck pushed open the door to let him in.

"So?" Aunt Jenny called from the driver's seat.

Frankie wiped the sweat from his brow. "We're still looking."

"Me believe it's di BMW," Ice Box said, aiming his chin in the direction of a bullet-gray sedan, sleek as could be.

"No, man, it's di Escalade," Buck-Buck countered. A hulking Cadillac sat three cars ahead of the BMW. "I bet you a thousand J—"

"Look!" Aunt Jenny interrupted. A Denali with tinted

windows slunk by and parked at the other end of the lot.

"Could be dat one too?" Buck-Buck mused.

Aunt Jenny turned to face Frankie. "Where are the others?" Irritation laced her voice.

"Filling up the soccer ball," Frankie said.

"So, you *sure* you sure, if di car is bulletproof, you won't hear any sound when you hit it?" Her voice betrayed how uneasy she was.

He resisted saying something sarcastic. He'd explained it to them all several times now, but this was outside her wheelhouse. She must be crazy nervous. "Yes, Aunt Jenny," he assured her patiently.

"Okay. Go get your ball and check the 'Sclade, BMW, and Denali."

Frankie jumped back out and jogged off through the parking lot. At the airport exit, Cricket and Big Pelton were finally returning from the gas station, the soccer ball perfectly round.

"You get lost?" Frankie said, channeling his aunt's irritation.

"We had to pump it up twice!" Cricket protested. "It have a slow leak. We had to find a patch."

"No matter. We only need it for about two minutes. Okay, so—you see that Escalade, and right behind it, the gray BMW? And that Denali, it's at the other side of the lot?" Frankie tilted his head to the left, not turning around.

The boys scanned the lot. Cricket nodded first. Big Pelton was slow to spot anything. Finally he, too, grunted.

"Okay, let's do it. And remember, look like you're having

fun!" Frankie led the way—though Cricket was more senior in the posse, this was Frankie's plan.

They broke into an easy trot, passing the ball to each other. Cricket kicked it over to the empty Escalade, pretended to lose control, then banged his elbow against the rear window and again against a back panel. Both sounds were loud. He picked up the ball, then dribbled it over to the BMW and pretended to tie his shoelaces.

An old couple dressed country-nice stopped and smiled. "Nice to see young men not on their phones," the man said to his wife.

Cricket kept his head down till they left. But now a tall woman was coming his way. He made as if he were losing his balance and slammed his hand into the fender, hard. The hit resounded. Springing up, he shook his head and passed the ball to Big Pelton.

And Big Pelton—was awful! He could barely dribble the ball. He'd bragged about his soccer skills, but then, everyone did. Frankie should have known better. He thought wistfully of Winston—he looked like a yam, but jeezum, the guy had skills with the ball.

Big Pelton lost control. The ball went rolling too far ahead, toward the Denali. Frankie hopped over a woman's bag and sprinted toward the patch of coconut trees where the Denali was parked. But before either he or Big Pelton could get to the ball, a bulky man with ropy gold chains heaved himself out of the driver's side. He grabbed the ball, volleyed it from foot to foot—total skills—and passed it back to Big Pelton.

Frankie hissed, "Shoot it back." *Please, please don't miss,* he prayed.

Big Pelton wound up and fired a blast toward the passenger-side door of the Denali. The big man extended his long arms and batted away the ball easily. Then he pointed a crooked finger at him. "Bwoy, I am not a goalie. Move away from here!"

Frankie was sure he was going to have heart failure. He took a quick step forward. "What!? You say him can't play! You can't say that 'bout my friend!"

"You crazy or something, bwoy?" the huge man said, clearly confused by Frankie's outburst. He scooped up the ball.

"I can play betta than you!" Frankie insisted, continuing forward. The driver seemed to get bigger as he got closer.

The Denali's passenger-side window slid down to reveal a light-skinned man smoking a cigarette. "What's going on out there?"

"Him say I can't play!" Frankie fronted.

The man blew out smoke and said to his driver, "Why are you troubling the bwoy? We have work to do."

"It wasn't my fault!"

"Get in and stop playing." The tinted window went up.

"Gimme my ball back!" Frankie dug deep for courage, ran up and wrenched the ball out of the man's hands, pretended to fumble it, then threw it against the Denali. It bounced off the side. Nothing. Nothing? Not a sound! The man scooped the ball off the ground with one huge hand and, with a look that could kill, whipped out a knife with the other and rammed it through the ball—*pffff*—deflating it instantly.

"You dead mi' ball, mon!"

"The man crazy to backside!" Cricket added.

"Get the hell out of here, now," the man warned, and all three took off. After circling the entire lot to be extra careful, they returned to the van from the opposite side and jumped in. Frankie scrambled up to his aunt. "It's the Denali," he gasped.

"You sure?"

"There wasn't any sound."

She turned her gaze on Cricket.

"BMW: boom. Escalade: boom. Denali: nada."

She pivoted, seemingly satisfied.

"Me know it was the Denali." Buck-Buck laughed. "Pay up."

"Stop it, you never know," Ice Box scoffed.

"Both of you shut up and watch the lot," Aunt Jenny fumed.

Frankie sat back, suddenly exhausted. The big guy in gold chains was indeed one of Taqwan's men. The Denali was *the* car. He couldn't help but feel, for a moment, pleased. It worked. His idea had *worked*. But he quickly reminded himself that they weren't done. They'd actually barely gotten started. He rubbed the handle of his gun, trying to picture how things might go.

Aunt Jenny leaned forward. "There—"

They all looked.

A bald, thick-necked white man in mirrored sunglasses, pulling a large rolling suitcase, was heading straight toward the Denali. Frankie took several deep breaths and tried, *tried* to calm down. Aunt Jenny had to make the call to Bradford now; his men were stationed in unmarked cars along the road, ready to follow the Denali to the stash house. Aunt Jenny would drive slow, trail far behind, and after getting the word, they would rendezvous with Bradford and his team to attack the stash house together. Frankie took his gun out. One more mission. But even though Bradford's men were good, this wasn't going to be easy. One more mission.

The passenger-side door of the Denali opened and the light-skinned man got out, flicked away his cigarette, and greeted the man with the suitcase.

"Must be him."

Aunt Jenny was tapping the window with the nail of her index finger.

"Jenny?" Buck-Buck put his hand on the dash.

Tap . . . tap . . . tap . . .

Buck-Buck leaned closer to her. "Them leaving, you know."

She took out her phone, called, and waited. "We identified the vehicle. But we're not coming in on the hit. You're going to have to do it yourself." She listened.

This wasn't the plan. Frankie felt as confused as everyone else was, by the looks on their faces. Except Aunt Jenny's. She couldn't look *less* confused.

She cleared her throat. "If you don't give us a split, I don't tell you which car them in." She pursed her lips. "Okay, we can work out the split after. It's a black Denali. Okay."

"What di hell, Jenny?" Stunned, Buck-Buck stared at her.

"We no ready for this." She watched the Denali drive off. "The stash house is going to be rough. Too rough fi us. No . . . Bradford can handle this one." She started the engine and pulled out.

Frankie wondered what Joe would have done about the stash house. He had seen Ray-Ban Boy make the call but had still gone ahead with the attack on the church and almost got them all killed. Aunt Jenny had pulled the plug on the stash house mission. She saw the imminent danger that hitting the stash house presented. She made the unpopular, tough, but smart choice. They would live for another day. Frankie exhaled and put his gun away. Maybe this *was* his last mission. He prayed.

Fifty-Three

ten days after the Monday morning airport hit, Frankie woke up already feeling freakin' exhausted. He'd been bagging yams and ganja, scraping clean knives and forks, and doing watch duty, day and night. While Aunt Jenny had been talking with everyone individually, even the Spanish Town, Kingston, and Stony Mountain crews, motivating them with talk of expansion—roles and payrolls—she had simply assigned Frankie the most boring work that posse life could offer. The days were crawling by so slowly he thought he'd implode. Only spreading ash in the ganja field was remotely interesting, and even that was only because it reminded him of Joe. And that usually led to thoughts of his father, which led to thoughts of Winston. And so the ash spreading felt almost like a way to mourn them all in his own time without other events interfering.

As he came out from the shower, he saw Bradford heading into Aunt Jenny's house. He seemed to be in even grimmer moods after the stash house hit. Maybe because he'd lost two of his men getting the last of Taqwan's drugs? Maybe . . . that had bothered him? Losing his own men? Frankie took his time getting dressed, peeking out the window and listening out for the sound of Bradford's jeep starting up. He deliberately avoided looking at the crab shell—as if somehow Bradford might even *sense* Frankie thinking about his daughter.

The minute Bradford came out, heading for his jeep, Frankie went over to his aunt's house. As the jeep roared to life, someone clasped his arm. He jumped a mile. Buck-Buck. "Jenny wants to talk to you." Frankie's mind raced. "Yeah, I was on my way there." What had Bradford said? He pushed that thought away. Telling his aunt would *not* be how Bradford would handle *that*.

"Yes, come," she called when he knocked.

She sat at a small table, a bunch of papers fanned out. She looked like Frankie's mother when she'd done the monthly bills. "How are things in the vineyard?"

He smiled at Joe's nickname for the ganja field. "Okay."

"Good." She was looking through him. Oh no. Maybe Bradford *had* said something.

He had to ask. "Everything okay with Bradford?"

"Him? He's a pain in my ass, but we working it out." She looked back down at the papers, tapped her nail on the desk.

Relieved, Frankie eyed the papers, ran his hand back over

his hair. Had they made less of a cut because they didn't hit the stash house with Bradford? "Aunt Jenny, at the airport . . . why didn't you . . . why did you call off the mission, really?"

"You with the questions!" She sat up and smiled. "A good one. So, I didn't think it was worth it, didn't from the get-go. The airport was one thing. They couldn't expect a hit there. But they had to be guarding that stash house with everything they had left." She rubbed a finger over a chipped fingernail, frowning. "In the end it came down to having the element of surprise. We had it at the airport. I doubt if we would have had it by the time we got to the stash house."

No moss grew on his aunt Jenny. Joe . . . Joe definitely would have gone through with the stash house hit, and grass would have grown over all their graves days ago.

Jenny eyed him. "Another thing. Me had to show Bradford that me is no joke. Him probably never worked with a woman before, zeen?"

"Ah so di t'ing set!"

"Damn right, that's the way it is, Franklyn." She leaned back and gestured to her night table. "Get that packet for me, no?"

"Open it," she said when he brought it over.

Frankie tore off the flap and reached inside, daring to wonder. His stupid hands were shaking. *Get a grip!* Then he felt the smooth texture of the small book and knew for sure. He had pictured it, hoped for it, and still the sight of his first passport made time stop.

"The visa is inside. Buck-Buck's contact will arrange for the plane ticket too."

He opened the passport, saw the paper, closed it shut again, as if it might evaporate just by looking at it. He stared at his aunt, not knowing what to say.

"Lawd, take that look off your face." She pointed a forefinger. "Now listen, I need you to stay on top of things with Denetria for the next few months. I have to focus on taking over Taqwan's territory."

She went on talking, but Frankie was with his own thoughts, listening to the inner voice that was almost never wrong. It was the sound of his gut, the one that had warned him about joining the posse. The voice was telling him to leave Jamaica *now*. Plus, she had promised one last mission! Next few months? What if something went down while he was dealing with Denetria? A few months could bleed into a long time.

"You listening?"

"I'm listening. And no. I need to go."

She stared through him again. "It's the girl, right?"

Bradford?

"Don't worry, everything's all right. Bradford didn't say anything."

That was a relief, but still . . . "I can't do it, Aunt Jenny." The words sounded like they came out of someone else's mouth, like another version of himself said them. She was family, the last of it, but he couldn't, *couldn't* stay in the posse any longer.

She bit a nail like it was the shell of a nut she was cracking open. "When is she leaving?"

"About a month." He stood up straight. "I can handle the deliveries and things until then."

She picked up a piece of paper and put it back down. "It's all right."

"No, I can do it."

"No, Franklyn, I just wanted to see something."

"What?"

She gathered the papers and stacked them. "To see if you were afraid. If you're going to be with that girl, you can't be afraid of Bradford." Dang! She knew *everything*! Frankie saw her glance at her Glock, then back at him again. "I'll see what I can do about him in time, but for now we need him."

He was pretty sure he knew what she meant. His throat went dry. He felt weak, his reserve dwindling. "I can do it. The things with Denetria, until . . ."

"No, Franklyn, you're going to lie low around the camp and then you're going to leave with your girl. Get that degree, Stingray Boy. That's the way it's going to go."

He wanted to tell her what this meant to him. But how?

"You earned it, boy. Save the soft talk. We have time for that when you're leaving for good." She raised her chin and gestured at the door. "Get Buck-Buck and Ice Box." She wagged her finger. "And don't worry about me. You damn well better know I'm strong like Johnnie Walker." And she smiled a smile that let him know she was happy for him.

At the door, Frankie looked once more at the passport. When he'd gotten the scholarship letter, his father hadn't celebrated it. But Aunt Jenny . . . she was cheering him on, even though she was losing a posse member. But she was not Samson, and Samson was not Aunt Jenny. The thought cascaded in his mind—water bounding down the falls, twisting, turning. Maybe it wasn't so much that his father hadn't understood *him*, but that *he* hadn't truly understood his father. Samson might not have been the ideal father for Frankie, but had Frankie been the ideal son for Samson? He wasn't sure he'd ever know. What he knew was that his father had loved him . . . in his own way.

"So you just going fi stand there all day?"

He grinned, shoved the envelope with the passport into his back pocket. Safer there. He looked back to see Aunt Jenny, a document in hand, reading. "I'll miss you."

She looked up. "Yes, you will, Franklyn." She worked her jaw side to side ever so slightly. "Now get Ice Box and Buck-Buck."

He walked through the encampment—the long wooden table, the curving row of houses. A home, one he'd miss but needed to leave, just like Jamaica itself. There were a lot of problems. Frankie's mother used to say, *The rain is falling but the dirt is tough.*

But still, he hoped he and Leah would come back one day, and help make a difference. Then the sweet mountain breeze caressed his face. He could smell the positivity. All Jamaicans breathed it. *Out of many, one people.*

Acknowledgments

My brilliant and beautiful wife, Maria, for always believing in my crazy dream where I could go from a Madison Avenue ad guy to Boston novelist, and for urging me to work more and more and more on Frankie's character. My children, Oona and Babette: thanks for giving me time and the belief that I could do it—I love you both so much; you're everything. My dad, for teaching me about systems. My amazing editor, Caitlyn Dlouhy—you are simply magical. To Faye Bender—I can't imagine a better and more thoughtful literary agent. To Jenn De Leon: a great novelist, and teacher, who opened so many doors for me. To Victor Levin: a great writer, filmmaker, showrunner, and father, who took the time to open my eyes. To Eve Bridberg, for founding Grub Street, the best writing school anywhere. To

Michelle Hoover: not just a great novelist, but also a teacher who enlightens, identifies problems, and offers brilliant suggestions. To Denis Ellis Bechard: a great novelist and teacher. To Shauna Hall, for the title of this book. To Julia Rold: a great writer, teacher, and excellent friend. To Andrea Meyer—thanks for all your notes over all the years. To my Novel Incubator class at Grub Street, and to my post-Incubator writing group: You all destroy the myth of the solitary writer through your amazing, collective insights that have helped my work become better over the last several years. To Dr. Jose Trevejo and Elmy, for believing and always inspiring; Dr. Richard Balaban, for offering your medical expertise and true belief; and Dr. Alok Kapoor and Dr. Elora Chowdhury, for all your support. To Oral Nurse and Damon Ross: true day-ones. To Lou Koskovolis: a man's man. And Ted and Gina Parrack, my ever-inspiring second family. To Joe Petito and Rob Swadosh: legit big brothers. To Piper Hickman, Carl Desir, and Elodie: a beautiful family that inspires. Fabien and Christine Siegel: entrepreneurial rock stars. Spike Lee, thanks for giving me a shot. To Rossen Ventzislavov: a man of erudition. Linda Cutting—it was great writing with you. To Dr. Greg Snyder and Dr. Adam Keene: thanks for your support. And Sami and Christina, for all your fantastic support. Thanks to Jon and Lisa Gold. To Esther Oluffa Pedersen, for all your help and genius; Bozoma St. John: You are, indeed, badass. To Ole Lund Hansen, Hillary Spann, and Bob Scarpelli: a great teacher. To Michael Brincker, and Tilde Westmark— visionaries. And to Annie Brincker, your steadfast support is so appreciated.